# BETTER TO DIE

# Better to Die

by

Steve Smith

www.penmorepress.com

Better to Die by Steve Smith




This is a work of historical fiction. While based upon historical events, any similarity to any person, circumstance or event is purely coincidental and related to the efforts of the author to portray the characters in historically accurate representations.

ISBN-978-1-950586-73-8(Paperback)
ISBN 978-1-950586-72-1(e-book)

BISAC Subject Headings:
FIC014000FICTION / Historical
FIC032000FICTION / War & Military
FIC031050FICTION / Thrillers / Military
Cover Design by Book Cover Whisperer:
Editor: Chris Wozney

Penmore Press thanks the artist Stuart Brown, Skipper Press Ltd, for permission to use the cover art.

Penmore Press thanks 11 EOD Regiment (who commissioned the painting) for permission to use it for the cover.

Address all correspondence to:

Penmore Press,
920 N Javelina Pl,
Tucson, AZ 85737
USA
or visit our website at:
www.penmorepress.com

'KAPHAR HUNNU BANDHAR MARNU RAMRO.'

It is better to die than live a coward.

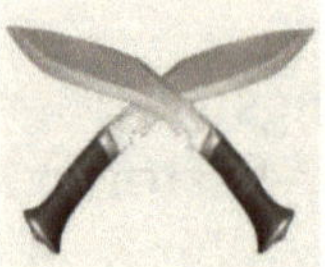

Traditional Gurkha motto

# Dedication

For my father, Alfred Gordon Smith (1924-1983). I think you'd have liked this, Dad.

# Acknowledgements

I would like to offer my heartfelt thanks to Michael James of Penmore Press for taking a chance on this, my first novel, and to Chris Wozney for her eagle-eyed editorial skills. Your combined and unfailing professionalism, humour and support have been tremendous.

I would also like to thank the artist, Stuart Brown, for allowing me to use his excellent painting, *Towards the Bomb*, for the cover design, and 11 EOD Regiment, who commissioned the work, for their permission to use the image.

Although all of the characters in the novel are fictional, many of the events closely mirror real life. I would therefore like to thank the extensive cast of friends, former colleagues, and fellow veterans whose actions—often heroic—contributed to this story.

# Explanatory Note:
# British Army Organisation

*Better to Die* centres on the exploits of the King's Royal Rangers, a fictitious infantry regiment of the British Army. With few exceptions, British Army infantry regiments trace their histories back to the 17th century. Each has its own long history, traditions, battle honours and insignia, and a soldier will generally serve his entire career with the same regiment. A regiment is made up of one or more regular battalions.

A battalion is a unit of 500-800 troops, commanded by a lieutenant colonel. Battalions of the same regiment rarely serve together in the same formation or even the same geographic region.

Each battalion comprises three rifle companies, plus a Fire Support Company and a Headquarters Company. Companies are around 100-150 strong and are commanded by a major.

The rifle companies are made up of three rifle platoons of around 30 soldiers, each commanded by a lieutenant or second lieutenant.

*Border Crossing Point 'Hotel 55', Northern Ireland,*
*5 November 1996*

'They're Sass.'

'Keep yer feckin' voice down!' A hissed response in an Armagh accent, edgy with stress. 'Course they're not Sass. Look at 'em. Those buck eejits couldn't fight their way out of a wet paper bag. And the officer's wearing a tie, for Jesus' sake.'

'Which one's the officer?'

'See that tall lanky fella? The one walking like he's got a twenty-foot pole up his arse, and the face like a long Lurgan spade. Him.'

'Maybe they're in disguise.'

'Then it's a feckin' good disguise. Can y'imagine it? "Right, boys, we're going under cover. Get down to the cookhouse and stuff yer faces for the next six weeks till they're all fat and shiny. And while you're at it, iron yer combats so you look like a bunch of shop window dummies."'

Aidan O'Flynn peered harder at the patrol. For sure, the big man was right. These fellas were acting like they were out on a Sunday dander. Web equipment all over the place, like a mad woman's breakfast. Everyone gawking straight ahead—no one checking the rear or flanks. The lazy bollickses didn't even hold their weapons like SAS. Just out for a bit of the *craic* in so-called Bandit Country. Well, they might just have chosen the wrong day for a visit.

Reassured, Aidan relaxed his grip on his weapon, a Czech-made Kalashnikov assault rifle, and wiggled his fingers to bring some warmth back into them. Only twenty years old, and a townie born and bred, he was way outside his comfort zone in the countryside. As the day wore on, his mild aversion to nature in all its glory had gradually turned to outright loathing.

The four-man IRA team manning the hide had infiltrated overnight. The intent was that they should have the target under constant surveillance well before the attack went in. As the saying goes, 'No plan survives contact with the enemy', but this precaution should at least minimise the risk of any nasty surprises. Following hedgerows, to avoid being lit up by the moon, they had moved stealthily in single file, well spread out, with five metres between each man. Every few minutes they had halted—listening, watching, scanning the horizon. There was always the danger that the op had been compromised and that 'Crown forces' were lying in wait, ready to launch an ambush.

The night had been cold. November in South Armagh always is. But at least it had been dry. It was only after they were in position close to the objective that the rain had started. At first, it had swept across the fields in a dense wall, driven by the bitter wind, swishing off the treetops and flaying the grass in the meadow to their front. The hide was concealed behind a low, grassy bank, amid a clump of ash trees, and the stark autumnal branches had initially provided some feeble protection from the downpour. But, as the day wore on and the torrent subsided, the watchers were subjected to endless dripping, tapping and spattering on unprotected heads and necks.

Morning had passed into afternoon, and Aidan had struggled to control his shivering. He constantly fought the urge to curl up into a ball to preserve his body heat, knowing that the others would be watching him—seeing how he performed on this, his first big op. So he maintained a prone firing position, his hands welded to the clammy, wooden pistol grip and forestock of his weapon. Gradually, the tips of his fingers had turned white, and he was forced to place one hand at a time inside his Barbour jacket to bring the warmth back. He also became aware of a small but steady rivulet, trickling down the bank, weaving a track through the soil, and drenching his jeans. The arrival of the British Army helicopter had at least taken his mind off his growing misery.

Seeking a distraction from the wet and cold, and at the risk of further antagonizing the big man, Aidan spoke again. 'So we're still dead on to go then, boss?' he ventured.

Sean Gallagher didn't answer straight away. His mind was busy weighing up the odds. He didn't like leaving operational matters to chance. He'd come desperate close to being bitten once too often to trust in luck alone. But it would be a big call to cancel the op now. The Provisional IRA had spent months planning this attack down to the last detail. They'd observed their target incessantly—both at close quarters and at long range. They knew every aspect of the routine surrounding the isolated border post: how many troops manned it; where they were deployed and what weapons they had; the schedule for changing over guard positions; and the length of time that each small detachment would spend at the base before being replaced by fresh troops. If the raid succeeded, it would sure smack those Brit bastards. Hard.

And, boy, did Sean want to do that. Because smacking the Brits, whenever and wherever he could, had been his life's whole focus ever since the day his big brother had been blinded by a rubber bullet. Danny had been an innocent bystander—a good Catholic boy of fifteen, with aspirations for the priesthood. He'd been watching some routine aggro in the street outside his home in Newry when the baton round, fired from a British Army riot gun, came crashing through the front room window. The solid lump of rubber, an inch and a half in diameter and weighing a quarter of a pound, had cannoned into the side of his head, smashing both eyeballs as it carved a path across his face, level with the bridge of his nose. Sean was the first into the room. He would never forget the screaming. Never forget and never forgive. That had been twenty years before, and his thirst for vengeance had never left him. But this was no time to let emotions hold sway. Revenge is a dish best served cold.

'Maybe we'd better just be on the safe side, though, eh, Aidy? Get the boys to round up a couple of farmers and have 'em run some dogs out through the undergrowth. We might just as well see if there's anything nasty lying out there. And be feckin' quiet about it!'

'Right you are, big man,' whispered O'Flynn, as he inched his way backwards out of the camouflaged hide from where they'd been observing the patrol.

Border Crossing Point 'Hotel 55', on the Derrynoose Road between Clontibret in the South and Keady in the North, was a tiny outpost. Built in triangular form, it contained two huts —the ops room and the troops' accommodation. Both cabins were reinforced with overhead screens to provide protection from incoming mortar bombs. An observation post, fortified with sandbags and mounted on a small tower, dominated the front left corner of the compound, and a further ground-level sangar was positioned alongside the steel double gates that opened onto the main road. This allowed intimate fire support for the two soldiers outside, involved in checking cars passing across the border.

Under normal circumstances, the post contained thirteen soldiers from A Company, the King's Royal Rangers—a sergeant and three four-man fire teams—along with a policeman from the Royal Ulster Constabulary. But, just thirty minutes before the planned start time for the IRA's attack, A Company's commander, Major Valentine Phillips, had been dropped off by helicopter to pay a surprise visit. Three soldiers from company HQ accompanied him as close-protection escorts. It was his unannounced arrival that had spooked the watchers outside. It had done a fair job of spooking the occupants of Hotel 55 as well.

An hour after turning up at the base, and oblivious to the escalating activity around the perimeter, Major Phillips leaned back in the shabby armchair that graced the small ops room and took a deep swig of coffee from his tin mug. His belt kit and weapon, a 5.56 mm SA-80 rifle, lay discarded on the floor beside him. His unbuttoned combat jacket hung open, revealing body armour worn over a standard issue green pullover. Despite these constricting layers, a pale khaki tie protruded from the crew neck of his jumper. The major considered the wearing of a tie, even in combat dress, to be 'good form'. Northern Ireland might be an operational theatre, but Valentine Phillips was determined to maintain a certain 'style'.

At that moment he was gazing with a bored, petulant expression at a wall-mounted map of the area. A naked bulb hanging from the ceiling cast a weak reflection off the transparent plastic overlay sheet, inscribed with tactical symbols in thick marker-pen. The air was a rank mixture of boot polish, gun oil, sweat, fag smoke and farts. Standing alongside the map, Sergeant Nick Adair was trying to update his company commander on operations at Hotel 55, despite needling interruptions from the major, often completely unrelated to the briefing.

'We're doing well with car searches, sir. Eighty-two in the past ten days. Two of these resulted in arrests. One for trying to smuggle counterfeit cigarettes across the border. The other for a suspected stolen car with false number plates.'

'Why is there no photograph of the brigade commander in the ops room?' interjected the major.

'Er... because company HQ hasn't sent one down, sir.'

Phillips pursed his lips impatiently. 'Well, have you asked for one?'

'It didn't seem like a top priority, sir. The lads have been a bit busy.'

'So what happens if the brigadier turns up on a visit and no one recognises him? How do you think that will go down?'

'Not very well, sir, I guess.'

'Not very well? You guess? I can tell you, Sergeant Adair, it will not go down very well at all. I want it sorted. Today.'

'Sir.'

'And who's that fat knacker on barrier duty outside?'

'Which one, sir?'

'Which one? Are you coming down with lardy arses in Number Two Platoon?'

'No, sir. It's Walters, sir.'

'Walters. Yes, that's the man. When did he last pass his Basic Fitness Test?'

'Don't know, sir.' Nick could feel his responses becoming more truculent as his patience wore thin.

'Well, you bloody well should know! That's the sort of detail that a platoon sergeant needs to carry in his head at all times. It would be embarrassing if the commanding officer asked, and you didn't know. Embarrassing for you, and embarrassing for me.'

'Sir.' Yanked from his focus and annoyed, Nick imagined lifting the major forcibly from the armchair by his jacket and head-butting him so hard that a fountain of blood spurted in an arc from his nose. Or maybe just smashing his combat boot into those infuriatingly arrogant features, sending Phillips' head ricocheting into the seatback. Would it be worth it? Bust to private and six months in the military nick at Colchester? Nah. Maybe not. Nice thought, though.

Either ignorant or indifferent, the major continued, 'Right now, he doesn't look as if he'd stand a chance of running a mile and a half in the time allowed. In fact, he looks like he could barely run at all. On operations, that's a disgrace. If we didn't need every man for this tour, I'd have left him behind on rear party in Tidworth. He shows the battalion in general, and this company in particular, in a bad light. It's totally unacceptable.' The last word was accompanied by a few flecks of spittle spraying from the company commander's plump lips.

'Sir.'

'Well, don't just "sir" me. What are you going to do about it?'

Nick knew the officer commanding A Company well. He'd first encountered Phillips as a 20-year-old second lieutenant—a 'Rupert'—fresh out of Sandhurst. It had been 1986, and the 1st Battalion, The King's Royal Rangers, had been shipped out to Northern Ireland to take their turn supporting the Royal Ulster Constabulary on the urban battlefields of Belfast. The new officer had quickly gained a reputation as a young man full of 'top show'—always the first to be noticed when the commanding officer was on the scene, but skulking in the shadows when the bricks, bottles and petrol bombs started to rain down.

The colonel might not have noticed, but the troops did. By the time Phillips was a captain, he'd already earned the nickname 'The Eternal Flame'. He thought it was a compliment —the rising young star whose career would blaze a trail on its ever-upward path. It wasn't. The Eternal Flame never goes out. And neither did Phillips. At least, not where patrolling out on the ground was concerned. Not if he could help it.

So there had been some bemusement among the troops when Major Phillips had turned up unexpectedly at the remote border post that afternoon. Whatever his motivation, it certainly wouldn't be anything to do with the best interests of his men. If Phillips was going to risk coming out on the ground, it must be something to do with his career. Maybe the colonel had indicated that he'd be paying a visit to the battalion's outstations soon, and the major thought he'd better make sure everything was in order first. Yup, that would do it.

Nick Adair was tough, fit and astute, but such qualities allowed little time for fools. And in Nick's eyes, Phillips was a fool. Unfortunately, the Army's top brass thought otherwise. The regimental hierarchy of the King's Royal Rangers had long viewed Phillips as future 'commanding officer material', slotting him into all the right jobs to ensure his smooth passage to the top. Nick knew this, and it was just one more irritant that was pushing him towards civvy street. Missing his son Jack's first birthday a week earlier because his R&R had been changed at the last minute didn't help. His wife, Sandra, still wasn't speaking to him over that one. Which was a bit of a pisser when you had to queue for half an hour to get on the phone, only to have it slammed down at the other end.

Outside, in the late-afternoon drizzle of the grim November day, the IRA assault group began to manoeuvre into position. Shaking off the weariness of many hours spent huddling against the stinging wind, repeated drenchings and bone gnawing cold, they wormed their way forward. Although dusk was now gathering, the overwatch capability provided by the base's observation tower inhibited any sudden movements. So, with muscles aching from long inactivity, each man inched through the undergrowth—crawling, sliding and slithering, brushing brambles aside and trying to ignore the occasional sharp prick of a thorn. With the earlier squalls having subsided, the scent of damp earth and mouldering leaves wafted upwards. A light mist began to form, clinging to folds in the ground, but not thick enough to guarantee cover from the watchtower.

Senses heightened by nervousness and anticipation, every slight noise became magnified: the bark of an early evening fox marking out its territory half a mile away; the clunk of a car boot closing at the vehicle checkpoint ahead of them; and the seemingly deafening crack of a twig snapping.

From 'H minus 5'—five minutes before the attack was due to start—watchers surrounding the base, in pre-arranged order, began reporting in by short-range radio that the coast was clear of satelliting patrols. At H-Hour, the single-word message was sent to unleash the attack: 'Shamrock'.

Within seconds of the codeword being broadcast, a flatbed truck emerged from a track several hundred yards along the road on the south side of the border. Innocuous in appearance from the outside, internally the vehicle had been prepared for battle. Sandbags lined the driver's cab and had been stacked to form a fortified firing position in the cargo area. In the back, positioned on a tripod and disguised by a tarpaulin, was a 12.7mm Russian DsHK heavy machine gun—a 'Dushka'. Capable of delivering 600 rounds per minute, this fearsome addition transformed the vehicle into a gun truck. When the weapon fired, the shock of the noise alone could paralyse anyone unlucky enough to be caught in its killing zone.

As the vehicle descended the slight hill towards the Border Crossing Point, Lance Corporal Jim Anderson stepped out with his hand raised to bring it to a halt. Ranger 'Walt' Walters stood back to one side, ready to provide covering fire with his SA-80 rifle. Instead of slowing down, the truck seemed to pick up speed as it approached the red and white barrier pole. Walters started to raise his weapon into a firing position but, still unsure quite what was happening, hesitated to shoot. The last thing he needed was the death of an innocent civilian truck driver on his hands.

The lorry drew closer. Now there was no doubt that it was accelerating towards the barrier. Anderson remained in position with his hand raised until the last possible minute before launching himself sideways onto the road. The wagon rammed the blockade at speed, demolishing the barrier pole and juddering to a halt. Walters raised his rifle to his shoulder and loosed off two rounds into the side of the cab. Anderson was still struggling to his feet when the truck's side panels flew open. He just had time to glimpse a hooded figure dressed in green combats bringing the barrel of a Dushka to bear before the rounds smashed into him. The body armour that he wore under his combat jacket offered no protection to the solid 12.7 mm bullets that punched into him at over 800 metres per second, shredding his clothing and tearing massive exit wounds in his back. The impact lifted Anderson off his feet and threw him several yards back across the road. Within seconds a lake of blood was pooling around the shattered body.

Walters saw this and ran. Two large steel gates barred the entrance to the compound, with a smaller pedestrian access door set into the one on the right. Even as he fumbled to get through in haste, two RPG-7 rockets, launched from concealed positions on the far side of the road, exploded against the left-hand gate, tearing holes through the metal.

Outside, the lorry had manoeuvred to allow the Dushka a free field of fire across the entire front of the border post. As Walters dashed towards the ops room, he could hear brickwork and metal being flayed by the incoming rounds. Several punctured the lightweight steel, cover-from-view screening that made up much of the perimeter fence, and he could feel the change in air pressure as they whipped past his head.

In the ops room, the sudden overwhelming racket had interrupted Major Phillips in mid-flow. Grabbing his rifle and hastily shrugging on his body armour, Nick Adair raced towards the entrance, bellowing *'Stand to!'* at the top of his voice. As he flung the door open, he collided with Walters who, in his terror, was desperately seeking any hiding place.

'Walt, with me!' Nick screamed. But Walters barged past him into the ops room. The Dushka stopped firing and Nick spotted two hooded figures charging through the access door in the main gate. A sheet of flame burst from a nozzle in the hands of the lead terrorist. Blazing fire engulfed the rear of the sangar by the front gate, silencing the machine gunner inside.

'Jesus! They've got a flamethrower!' Acting on instinct, Nick shot off five rounds in rapid succession. The torch man stumbled forward and twisted as two rounds slapped into his body, exposing the tanks containing liquid fuel strapped to his back. Nick took aim again and double-tapped into the tanks, but the liquid inside failed to ignite and dribbled harmlessly out through the two puncture holes.

Nick was conscious of the reassuring thump of covering fire from one of the base's General Purpose Machine Guns being laid down by the Ranger occupying the tower sangar. This was abruptly terminated by the impact of another RPG-7 rocket fired from somewhere near the main gates. A third terrorist had now entered the compound, and both of the IRA men still standing were firing Nick's way. With bullets spattering the ground around him, Nick loosed off more shots before retreating to the ops room. The hut door was closed. As he turned to grab the handle, he felt the passing impact of an

AK-47 round ricocheting off the rear ceramic plate of his body armour.

At his first push, the ops room door failed to open. Nick put his shoulder to it and barged, shoving aside a desk that had been jammed up against it from within. The door moved ajar just enough for him to squeeze through as rounds pockmarked the outside of the building.

Inside, he had expected to find Major Phillips and Walters using their combined firepower to transform the open area of the compound into a killing zone. The two occupants had other ideas. In the far corner of the small room, Walters had wedged himself into a wardrobe-sized, lightweight steel locker. He was crouched inside with his arms over his head, while Phillips, pointing his rifle at him with one hand, tried to drag him out with the other.

'Get out, you fat bastard! Move it!' Phillips was screaming, as bullet holes continued to drill through the cabin's thin wooden walls from outside.

Walters' voice had taken on an inhuman keening sound, a wailing cry of 'No, no, no!'

With a final jerk, Phillips ejected Walters, who fell forwards onto the floor, still sobbing and with his hands over his ears. From just outside the door, an AK-47 firing on automatic sprayed 7.62 mm slugs through the woodwork, followed by the leading IRA man's boot crashing into it. With the desk still providing a degree of resistance, the door failed to open fully at the first attempt, giving Nick just enough time to return fire and take out the attacker.

He gave a quick glance over his shoulder to check Phillips' position so that he could co-ordinate his own arc of fire with the major's. But Phillips wasn't there. From the corner of his eye,

Nick glimpsed the company commander crammed into the metal locker and pulling the door closed on himself. As a grenade tumbled into the room, Nick flung himself sideways over Walters, who lay whimpering on the floor. The concussion wave from the explosion swept through the room. Less than a millisecond after the grenade detonated, a steel fragment, no bigger than a child's milk tooth, entered Nick's face just below his right eye, travelling up behind the socket and piercing his brain. He hadn't even heard the explosion that killed him.

# Chapter One


*Twenty-five years later*
*Calvi, Corsica*

It is evening in Calvi, the small city on Corsica's northwest coast that is the island's closest point to mainland France. In the harbour, protected by an extensive breakwater, millionaires' yachts bob at anchor, rubbing shoulders with small pleasure boats and local fishing vessels.

Several jetties extend from the quayside out into the bay, maximising the number of mooring sites, and presenting a forest of masts as the boats muster at the day's end. Back from the water's edge, the promenade is lined with numerous restaurants, cafes, bars and souvenir shops, their brightly coloured awnings becoming redundant as the sun sets. Behind the town, rugged, pine-forested mountains stretch away to the south, turning purple in the fading light and emphasising the fact that Corsica is the most mountainous island in the Mediterranean—the 'mountain in the sea'.

Dominating the skyline is the Citadel, a towering fortress built by the Genoese in the 13th century to protect Corsica from invaders. It sits in brooding majesty above the town, its ochre-coloured ramparts and bastions presenting a magnet for any visiting tourists who have the energy and determination to climb the steep cobbled paths to its entrance. But this is no Disneyesque castle or elaborate mock Hogwarts. Arches are crumbling, wooden doors look like they might fall off their hinges, plaster is peeling off the walls and signs are crudely handmade. One might almost expect a Corsican bandit to step out of the shadows.

Stretching away from the marina, to the east of the town, is a long, sandy beach that traces the crescent-shaped curve of the bay. A stroll of some four miles out of town, keeping the shoreline to the left, brings one to a military barracks. Its entrance is set back from the road, protected by a sliding electric gate. To the right is a guard house that is almost inappropriately pretty, its cream walls set off by a tiled roof of burnt orange and fronted by a hedge-lined veranda. A water tower stands opposite the guard house. Emblazoned on the tank is the regimental badge: an inverted triangle, bearing a winged, serpent-like, oriental dragon. Smack in the middle of the beast's body is a flaming grenade, picked out in gold, on a rectangle painted red and green. Only a compulsive military buff would know that the triangle represents a deployed parachute, the dragon harks back to the unit's early history in Indochina, and red and green are the regimental colours.

The sentry on the gate is wearing parade dress of light khaki, his trousers bloused neatly over black combat boots. The uniform is set off by a broad blue cummerbund, held in place by a green, webbed, combat belt, and green epaulettes trimmed with red fringes. The silver wings of a parachutist glint on his right chest. But it's the hat that is the real giveaway. Such is the renown, or even notoriety, of this particular unit that it is instantly recognisable—*le képi blanc* —the dazzlingly white, flat-topped, circular cap of the French Foreign Legion.

As if further confirmation were necessary, the unit's name is embedded in the wall to the right of the gate, spelt out in gold capital letters: '*2eme Régiment Étrangere des Parachutistes*'—2nd REP—the parachute regiment of the French Foreign Legion. To the left, in even larger gold letters, is the name of the base: Raffalli.

If Calvi's tourists tire of its beautiful sandy beach, its cafes and restaurants, its marina and its historic buildings, the inmates of Camp Raffalli can always be relied upon to add an air of mystery, a hint of danger and, maybe for some, even a night of romance. Tonight, they are out on the town.


'Bollocks to it, Jack! That's all I can say.'

'Bollocks to what, you mad bastard?'

Both speakers necked another long swig of beer straight from the bottle before the one who wasn't Jack spoke again.

'Bollocks to the fact that you're bloody well leaving.'

'Oh for Christ's sake, Josh. Not *that* again. *Ta gueule*—get over it!'

Josh Corrigan was shouting at Jack Adair across the table at full volume, competing with the throbbing music that was making the club's floor vibrate. His face was flushed and sweaty, the disco lights reflecting off the shimmering surface, highlighting the acne scars that peppered his cheeks. Around him sat the rest of the *Mafia Anglais*—ten in all—the hard core of English-speakers within the 2nd REP.

'Come on, Jack. The whole shagging place will just go downhill fast once you're out.'

'Yeah, right! I hardly think so. The REP's been here over fifty years, and I've been here less than five.'

'But it's still not too late. Sign back on, mate. You just *know* you ain't gonna enjoy it out there in the world. This is *living*, mate. *Really* living.'

The group was sprawled around several tables in the corner of the Club Tropique, one of several bars close to the seafront in Calvi. White *képis*, which had earlier been scrubbed to near-luminous perfection in order to satisfy the guard sergeant before leaving camp, now sat on the table amid the debris of bottles of Kronenbourg, packs of Marlboro, Bic lighters and pools of spilled beer. Light khaki dress shirts, meticulously ironed to show fifteen razor-sharp creases, had long since started to wilt in the clammy atmosphere.

The Mafia planned to get drunk. Dead drunk. Not just because Jack was leaving the Legion and tradition demanded it. Not just because it was yet another Friday night in Calvi. Not just because they were all borderline alcoholics, although most came close. But because they were young, and fit, and soldiers. And that's what young, fit soldiers do when they haven't got a war to go to. They get drunk.

'Sorry, mate,' Jack was bawling back at Josh. 'You know I've got plans.'

'Sod the plans. You're already a corporal. You'll make sergeant easy in your next contract. The Legion's your family, man. *Legio Patria Nostra*. Remember? The Legion is our country!'

'Yeah, fine, Josh. But even as a sergeant I'd still get bossed around by twats like Chabot and every other pathetic twenty-something tosser of a second-lieutenant straight out of officer school. It's bad enough now—never mind in ten years' time.'

'So, instead of being bossed around by the tossers and twats, you've decided to become one yourself. I can't believe you wanna be an officer. I was in the British Army before this, mate. They're even worse than the dickheads we've got in charge here. *And* they're a bunch of snobs with their heads up their own arses.'

'Well, I'll just have to make sure I keep my head well away from my arse then, won't I?'

'Yeah, I'll believe that when I see it. Once they take your brain out at Sandhurst, you'll end up just like all the rest. They're all the bloody same.'

Jack shrugged. He'd been hearing the same argument from Josh for months now, and the booze wasn't making it any more persuasive.

'So what mob you going for?'

'Told you already. KRR—King's Royal Rangers.'

'Yeah, I know what you *told* me, mate. But I thought you might've seen sense and changed your mind. I still don't bloody understand it. It's just bollocks. You're an airborne warrior through and through. Why not the Paras? That's what I was in. The Maroon Machine. It's the closest thing the Brits have got to this mob. You'd be bloomin' brilliant. The boys'd love having an ex-Legion para as their boss. Talk about duck to water.'

'Dad was in the Rangers. Got killed in Ireland before I really knew him. Mum never talks about him. She re-married some nerd of a college lecturer—typical save the gay whale type, who hates my guts and despises anything military. That's why I legged it from home and came here. Feel like I still owe the old man, though. Gotta be done.'

'Your choice, mate.'

Jack gazed across the room, through the smoke haze and pulsing lights. A larger group of legionnaires stood near the bar. The 'Chetniks'. Mainly Serbs from the former Yugoslavia. Some, as children, had witnessed at first hand the wars that had ravaged the former Yugoslavia in the 1990s. One or two had even been old enough to fight. More than a few were veterans of Serbia's ultra-violent football firms, like those that supported Belgrade's two main clubs, Red Star and Partizan. Hard bastards to a man. As nails.

At the centre of the group stood Corporal Jannie Draskovic—black eyes set deep into a face that could have been carved out of granite. Implacable, brutal, remorseless. And right now, those eyes were boring straight into Jack.

Jack had been in Draskovic's sights ever since the incident in the hills with Osman the Turk. It had been over a month before, but feuds ran deep with the Chetniks. Everyone knew that. The two corporals had been assigned to assist Sergeant Lacroix with running a course for the latest squad of new recruits to the regiment, coming straight from basic training at Castelnaudary near Toulouse in southern France. The month-long course, known as the *promotion*—or *'promo'*—was intended to convert the new legionnaires into parachutists. It was also a useful means of imprinting them with 2ⁿᵈ REP's very distinct regimental ethos.

Jack knew how desperate the recruits would have been to escape 'Castel's' training regime and get to their new regiment. The journey by ferry across from Marseille to Bastia in Corsica would have seen them out on public display as fully-fledged legionnaires for the first time. Trying to live up to the mystique evoked by their white *képis*. Adopting a touch of swagger. Doing their best to exude the aura of hard-bitten fighting men. Relishing, but not acknowledging, the surreptitious glances they were attracting—some envious, some pitying, but mostly curious. Male tourists with beer bellies, sizing them up, thinking, 'Could I? Would I?' Young women in short holiday skirts, flashing wide smiles, thinking, 'Could I? Would I?'

During the ferry crossing, as tradition demanded, they would have tossed into the waters of the Med the badges of the training unit that they'd just left. But, like all new recruits to the 2ⁿᵈ REP, they quickly learnt that the regiment's sergeants and corporals were no less forgiving than those at Castel. Jack had discovered that within his first hour of arriving at Camp Raffalli, when a Polish corporal's fist had cannoned into his stomach for a minor infraction. His crime had been speaking English at the wrong moment. And as far as the Polish corporal was concerned, *any* moment was the *wrong* moment.

The parachute training for the *promo* was scheduled to last for a month, during which each novice would have to complete six jumps, including one at night, to qualify for his wings. After the arduous routine they'd experienced at Castelnaudary, it sounded like a holiday camp—sitting around in a hangar all day, learning parachute landing falls and swinging from ropes attached to mock harnesses. Except that Sergeant Lacroix had a different view. He was determined that the new arrivals would not become soft during his watch. So, for the first week, they conducted forced marches with full kit over the rugged Corsican countryside. They patrolled, skirmished, set ambushes and practised unarmed combat until they were bruised and bleeding. At the end of each day, standing around a fire under the stars, they sang the Legion's songs and listened as Lacroix regaled them with stories of the REP's past heroic exploits in Algeria, Indochina and Kolwezi.

On their last day in the field, Sergeant Lacroix was required to return to Camp Raffalli to carry out some admin duties. He nominated Jack to drive him, leaving Draskovic in charge. It was already dark when Jack returned alone. As soon as he switched off the vehicle's engine, the sound of Draskovic bawling someone out cut through the night air. This was nothing new. Draskovic wasn't a fan of the Legion's attempts in recent years to eliminate violence as method of punishment. In his eyes, it was the only way to enforce discipline with a bunch of dropouts, hard men, former criminals, and veterans of other wars. But then, he was a borderline psychopath.

'If you'd done this in combat, you'd have been shot, you lazy, useless, piece of shit,' screamed Draskovic. 'Falling asleep on guard duty is one of the easiest ways of getting you, and all your comrades, killed. I don't give a fuck whether you live or die, but if you are dead, you will *fail* in your mission. And the REP *doesn't ever fail!*'

The trainees were gathered in a circle, illuminated by the campfire, which burned some twenty yards away. As Jack walked closer, he could see that they were all transfixed by something about the size of a football in the centre of the ring. This was what Draskovic was shouting at. Then the object moved. It wasn't a ball; it was a head. The body was completely buried under a pile of earth—just like a kids' game on the beach. Except this was no game.

Jack knew instinctively that Draskovic's victim would be Osman the Turk. Osman was the only Muslim in the *promo*, and Draskovic harboured a fanatical hatred for all Muslims. He'd only been eight years old when his Orthodox Christian family had been stopped by a Kosovo Liberation Army checkpoint when returning to their village in Podujevo just after the war. He knew one or two of the Muslim militiamen from his own village by sight. They'd always been friendly enough. He'd even joined in games with their children. But that night he'd sensed the change in atmosphere. He could actually smell his father's fear, as he answered their questions with nervous, stuttering responses. There was something about the look on the men's faces. No trace of a smile. Nothing warm or reassuring about their gestures. Just coldness, as if he and his family had lost their status as human beings.

And they had. The young Jannie realised this when five of them forced his mother from the car and raped her repeatedly like a feral bitch over the bonnet. All the while, one held the muzzle of an AK-47 in his sobbing father's mouth as he looked through the windscreen into his wife's eyes. Mrs Draskovic had lived on for three more years, withdrawn, silent, traumatised, until the ever-present memory eventually overwhelmed her, and she hanged herself in the family barn.

Maybe there were good reasons why Draskovic was a psychopath.

Now the corporal stood over Osman wielding a steel entrenching tool, sizing up the best angle of attack. Continuing to shout obscenities, he swung it, landing a blow just above the Turk's left ear with the reverse side of the spade. Osman let out an agonised shriek, then subsided into barely audible whimpering. Draskovic tossed the entrenching tool to one side and, standing with his legs apart directly in front of Osman's face, undid the zip fly of his combat trousers.

'This is all you're worth. And when I've finished, the rest of the *promo* will each take turns in watering your head. You need a shower to wake you up.' With that, Draskovic extracted his cock and started to piss, the stream of urine falling in an arc on Osman's head. So intent was he on his victim that he remained unaware of Jack's approach.

'Leave him,' Jack barked. 'He's had enough.'

Draskovic half-turned as Jack entered the clearing to his right. 'What the hell has it got to do with you, Adair?'

Jack's *savate* kick smacked into Draskovic's stomach, driving the wind from him and knocking him over backwards, the last drops of urine spattering into the breeze as he fell.

Picking up the shovel, Jack slung it at the nearest Legionnaire. 'You! Legionnaire! Dig Osman out.'

The trainee hesitated for a second, stunned into temporary paralysis by what he'd just witnessed.

'*Now!*' bellowed Jack.

The soldier rushed forward, as did several others, who began scraping away at the earth with their hands. As Osman struggled free, Jack could see Draskovic clambering painfully to his feet. The Serb stood, legs apart, doubled over at the waist, hands resting on his knees. Shoulders heaving as he struggled to regain his breath, he stared across at Jack with a look of pure malice.

'I'll get you, Adair, you English bastard. You are a dead man.'

'You think so? You wanna try it on, then? Come on, I'm up for it.'

Twin beams lit up the clearing as a Peugeot P4 military four-by-four swept into a space between the trees some thirty metres away, spraying up mud and water.

'Looks like you got away with it, Adair,' spat Draskovic. 'That's Lieutenant Chabot come to check up on his boys. Don't think I'm going to forget this. Ever. Just watch your back.'

The Serb drew his hand across his throat in a theatrical slitting motion before turning away to welcome the newly arrived officer as if nothing had happened.

That had been four weeks ago. Jack had sensed a re-match was inevitable. Here it was.

# Chapter Two

Through the fog of alcohol that was starting to cloud his brain, Jack watched in fascination as a beer glass from the other side of the room, describing a perfect parabola, sailed through the air towards him. It smashed into the floor at his feet, glass crystals spraying against his boots.

As Jack's thought processes started to click into place, Josh was already up, ready to engage the fifteen or so Chetniks that were charging across the dance floor. Toby Simmonds, 220 pounds of solid muscle and a former Royal Marine, intercepted the first, smashing a chair straight across the man's mouth.

Josh was screaming at Jack: 'It's you they're after! If they get you, they'll bloody well kill you! Get the fuck out of here through the bog window. We'll see you back at camp.'

Jack had just time to launch his own beer glass at the advancing mob before he felt himself being propelled backwards by his mates through the lavatory door. The door swung shut behind him, blocking out his view of the valiant rear-guard action being fought by the English Mafia. Apart from the steady thump of muffled disco music, the room seemed weirdly silent after the din outside.

Jack crossed to the window set high up on the wall, hauled himself up, squeezed through, and dropped down on the other side. He staggered across the road and sat down on a low wall opposite, allowing the cool night air to clear his head. It seemed only a couple of minutes had passed before he caught sight of another figure in Legion uniform struggling through the same window he had just exited from. It was Josh.

'Here, mate, thought you might need this to get back onto camp.' Josh was holding out a *képi*.

'How did you know it was mine?' asked Jack.

'Because nearly every other bastard has their own mugshot pasted inside. Yours must be the only one with a photo of some other geezer in it, wearing a British Army uniform with a King's Royal Rangers' cap badge. Your old man, right?'

'Yeah, right.'

Josh perched himself on the wall next to Jack.

'That was fun.' With his ears adapting to the quietness outside the club, Josh was still talking at full volume.

'What happened?'

'As soon as he saw you'd gone, Draskovic and his two nasty shadows, Lucovic and that bloody great monster, Kralj, lost interest. I think they disappeared out the front looking for you. Toby Simmonds played a blinder. Took out two of the other fuckers. One's gonna be seeing the dentist first thing in the morning. Then the bar owner started hollering about calling the Military Police, and everyone bomb-burst out of there. Great end to the perfect evening! You're gonna miss all this.'

'Yeah, right!'

With the bar brawl certain to bring the MPs down on Calvi like a swarm of angry hornets, Jack and Josh headed out to the coast road for the four-mile walk back to camp. At least the fresh night air might sober them up enough get past the guard sergeant without incident. Reports of the bust-up downtown would have come straight into the guard room, and he would already be champing at the bit for scalps— whether guilty or innocent.

Sure enough, when they arrived at Camp Raffalli an hour later, all hell had broken loose. The gate guards had been reinforced by regimental police—big men with small brains, and displaying a fine collection of broken noses, cauliflower ears and tattoos. Their intimidating appearance was further enhanced by a couple of Alsatian dogs, straining at their leashes, and snarling and snapping at anyone who came too close.

Four German legionnaires, who'd tumbled drunkenly out of a taxi moments earlier, were being subjected to endless press-ups by the guard sergeant. He was taking great delight in ramming his boot down on random backsides while unleashing a torrent of abuse. The taxi was still parked across the gate, with the driver shouting that he needed more money to pay for cleaning up the vomit in the back. A couple of civil policemen were doing their best to calm him down and move him on, with the resigned air of having witnessed a similar scene many times before.

Amid the pandemonium, Jack and Josh managed to slide in past the guard room with relative ease. They made their way across to the barrack-block and slowly climbed the bare concrete stairs to the first floor. With two sections away on commando training in Perpignan, the accommodation was almost empty.

Walking into the darkened dormitory, Jack could make out the huddled shapes of two legionnaires deeply asleep on their beds. He fumbled for the light switch. As he did so, he noticed some movement at the far end of the room, close to the entrance to the showers. Like wraiths in the mist, three figures rose silently from the beds on which they had been sitting. It was Draskovic, flanked by Lucovic and Kralj, the latter, at six feet five and 240 pounds, looking like some monstrous troll. Jack's hand stopped feeling for the switch and the room remained in semi-darkness.

'Oh look, Josh, that's all we need, a night in with the fucking Marx Brothers,' muttered Jack, now beginning to regret walking back from town. The three Serbs had obviously taken a taxi.

'Yeah, with Drasko being the gobby smart alec, and Kralj being the dumb stupid one.'

'You know what this is about, Adair,' snarled Draskovic. 'No one does such a thing to me and expects to get away with it.'

'So did you bring your friends along to watch, or are they here to get their heads smacked in as well?' Jack inquired, sounding more confident than he felt, weighing up the odds. 'Actually, I don't know why I'm even asking. You couldn't take me on your own, so you've brought your own pet ogre Kralj with you.'

'You insult one of us, you insult all of us. That was the choice you made. Now you face the consequences. Simple as that. Corrigan, it's not your fight. You don't have to stay around for this. But if you do, Kralj will beat you senseless.'

'Not if I can help it!' Silhouetted in the doorway to the shower room, behind the three Serbs, stood Toby Simmonds. As their heads turned to face him, he took three swift steps and launched a flying drop-kick straight into the small of Kralj's back. The giant toppled. Before he could recover, Simmonds was on him, raining punches down against the side of his head.

Lucovic twisted to deliver a kick into Simmonds' rib-cage with the toe of his boot. Simmonds barely felt it, but as Lucovic was drawing his leg back for another kick, Josh Corrigan crashed into him with a rugby tackle at waist height.

Jack closed with Draskovic. Each fell into a semi-crouch, watching for an opening. Jack feinted with a left-handed back-fist to Draskovic's head, following up with a swift jab. Draskovic jerked back sharply, so the fist barely made contact, but Jack felt a stinging sensation near his wrist as his arm snapped back from the punch. In the semi-darkness, he could see a long dark line forming along his forearm, just inches short of his wrist, along with the hot feel of blood leaking out over his hand. He'd been cut. As the Serb moved, Jack caught the quick glint as the lights from the stairwell beyond the dormitory doors reflected off the short, narrow blade of a flick-knife.

'You bastard!' he roared, launching a flurry of kicks. The first, a front-kick with his right foot, sent the blade spinning away across the room. His left followed on with a sharp curving roundhouse kick to the side of Draskovic's head. As the Serb staggered, momentarily stunned, Jack spun through 360 degrees, landing a killer back-kick into his adversary's midriff halfway through the turn.

Draskovic's feet left the ground as he was propelled backwards, landing on his arse. Jack went to spring forward, intending to finish the job off. But as he moved, he felt a hand grip his foot, bringing him down with a crash. Despite Toby Simmonds continuing to punch the side of his head, Kralj had managed to haul himself up onto his knees, just able to reach out and trip Jack before he could start his charge.

Taking Simmonds with him, Kralj hurled himself forward, still on all fours, driving the breath out of Jack's body as he landed on him. Jack tried to crawl from underneath, but Kralj's massive bulk kept him pinned down, spread-eagled. It was Josh Corrigan's toe-cap smacking into Kralj's face that did the trick. Blood sprayed from the big Serb's nose as he threw Simmonds aside and struggled to his feet to take on his latest adversary. He stumbled forward, swinging his fists in powerful arcs, but failing to land the killer blow. As his head turned from side to side, great gobbets of blood flew from his nostrils, spattering floor and furniture alike.

Still winded, but seeing the danger to Josh, Jack managed to stand. Kralj continued forward, punching air, just trying to connect with the one devastating blow that would finish off his prey, but unaware of the two British legionnaires closing with him from behind.

They took him at a rush, seizing his arms and bundling him through the double doors into the stairwell, where they flung him down the first flight. Kralj rolled down the ten steps to the landing, where he lay groaning, blood still bubbling from his nose.

The three Brits looked back into the dormitory. Draskovic and Lucovic were back on their feet, battered and wheezing. Jack switched on the lights. The occupants of the two beds, who, up to that point had done their best to sleep through the ruckus, sat up and began to complain. One threw a boot at Draskovic.

Toby Simmonds advanced towards the Serb corporal. 'Your mate Kralj decided to leave. The fast way. You can either follow him down the stairs, or you can hang around and go out the window. Frankly, I don't care which route you choose. But it's time for you to leave one way or the other. So just fuck off!'

The two Serbs walked to the doorway, Draskovic putting on an arrogant swagger and brushing against Jack as he passed, cobra-black eyes locked on, unwavering. Jack's arm flew up to strike him, but Toby Simmonds held him back.

'Calm down, mate. That's enough damage for one night. You've gotta get out of this place in the morning. What you don't wanna be doing is spending the next month in clink, wearing a shiny steel helmet and waddling round the prison yard like a duck with a rifle held at arm's stretch above your head, 'cos you've been locked up by the MPs for fighting.'

'What do you mean, "in the morning"? It *is* the bloody morning,' murmured Jack, half to himself. 'Anyway, where did you come from?'

'Well, it was bleeding obvious what they was gonna do. That little toe-rag Draskovic only had tonight to get even. When the shindig took off downtown, just after I smacked some twat in the gob with a bar-stool, I spied him and the other two muppets sliding out the door. I knew they wasn't going for a nice quiet cuppa somewhere, so I hightailed it back here to set up me own little reception committee. I thought they was gonna beat me to it, 'cos they grabbed a taxi just ahead of me, but the three of 'em got put through the wringer by the guard sergeant when they rocked up at the front gate. I moseyed up here, but then I was left hanging around the shitter for the best part of an hour waiting for you two to finally pitch up. And, as it happens, it was probably just as well I did. Now, where's the beers?'

Josh was already dragging a crate of Kronenbourg from under the bedsteads. 'I think this'll do nicely,' he said, flipping the top off a bottle and raising it to Jack. 'Another five hours and you'll be out of here. On your way to join the toffee-nosed ranks of the British hoff-icer class. So, you'd better have a few more beers with your real mates before you realise what a massive shagging mistake you've made.'

# Chapter Three

*British Army Careers Information Office, Dover*

Jack pushed open the door leading into the Army Careers Information Office and stepped inside. Two sergeants were manning the desks. Jack recognised the one who had dealt with him just three days earlier when he had made his initial enquiry.

The sergeant recognised Jack too. It was unusual for someone wanting to be an officer simply to walk in off the street. With around ninety per cent of cadets now entering the Royal Military Academy Sandhurst with degrees under their belts, most candidates were dealt with by their nearest universities liaison officer. Many had also spent their undergraduate years as members of the University Officers' Training Corps. They knew the score. Jack was the exception.

He was an exception in other ways too. On his first visit, Jack's standard of dress could hardly have been called 'officer like'. Not for one minute had it occurred to him to wear a jacket and tie. He had come in sporting a faded pair of jeans with holes in the knees and a well-worn, green T-shirt bearing the image of a flaming grenade. They had been five minutes into the conversation before the image on the T-shirt caught the sergeant's eye. He'd seen that badge somewhere before. Where was it? Then the penny dropped.

'Isn't that a French Foreign Legion T-shirt?' he'd asked. 'Did you buy it off the internet?'

'No,' said Jack. 'I've just left. I was in for five years.'

He could sense the palpable change in the sergeant's attitude after that. Jack was certainly the exception in more ways than one.

Now, three days later, he was back. This time for an interview with the retired colonel who dealt with officer candidates in the region. On the sergeant's advice, he was wearing a suit. The sergeant escorted Jack upstairs to the colonel's office, tapped lightly on the door and stuck his head round.

'Your next interview, sir,' he announced, standing aside to let Jack through.

The retired colonel stood up stiffly from behind his desk —the gouty twinges in his knees were giving him particular gyp today. He walked round to greet Jack, appraising him as he went. His eyes alighted on the suit.

It was an unsuitable suit. He took it in with a single sweeping glance. Too tight, too shiny, lapels too narrow, uneven stitching. A perfectly ordinary suit, in its way, of course. One that might be seen at thousands of office desks, weddings and christenings the length and breadth of the country. But hardly 'officer material'. He smiled to himself at his private joke. So what did that say about the man wearing it? Was he also 'not officer material'? Time to find out.

'How d'you do? Colonel James Bartholomew,' he announced briskly, extending his hand as Jack Adair stepped further into the office.

'Pleased to meet you, sir,' Jack responded, unwittingly using a turn of phrase sneered at by the upper classes as a genteel affectation—the 'lower middle classes' trying too hard to sound posh.

For the second time in less than thirty seconds, Colonel Bartholomew inwardly shuddered. First the suit, so unlike the colonel's own, a traditionally tailored tweed number from Saville Row, and now this 'Pleased to meet you'. Pleased to bloody meet you? The colonel didn't have any friends who would ever use that expression. Well, there *was* that major in the Royal Military Police who lived next door on the married quarters patch in Germany a decade ago. But he was hardly a friend. And he *was* RMP, after all. Not exactly a Corps known for being a social elite. As far as Bartholomew was concerned, Jack might as well have said 'All right mate?' Well, he obviously didn't go to a decent school, that's for sure, so that rules out any of the smarter regiments, like the cavalry or the Guards.

'And your name is?'

'Adair, sir. Jack Adair.'

They shook hands. Jack eyed-up the colonel, trying to gauge the man. The cultured accent. The immaculately groomed, swept-back hair, greying, and worn slightly long. A slim, gold Piaget watch on his wrist, matching the crested signet ring and discreetly tasteful cufflinks. But where the bloody hell did he get that suit from? It was like something a mountaineer would have worn to climb the Matterhorn in the 1920s. Talk about vintage; it could only have come from a charity shop. Funny, you'd have thought a classy bloke like that would have a few quid to spare. He felt pleased now that he'd splashed out on a new suit himself. At least that would probably be worth some extra Brownie points. And he'd introduced himself well—firm handshake, looking the colonel straight in the eye, and telling him that he was pleased to meet him. Very officer-like. His mates in 2nd REP would've been impressed. Or would've laughed themselves stupid. He could imagine Josh now, prancing around with his nose in the air, holding his hand out daintily and mimicking him: 'Hellooo... so-o-o pleased to meet you-oo.' Probably better that than 'All right mate?' though.

Colonel Bartholomew indicated one of two large brown leather armchairs that were arranged around a low coffee table. The armchairs were soft and deep, with high armrests. Jack subsided slowly, as if sinking into a deflating bouncy castle.

'So...' opened the colonel, leafing idly through a slim file on his lap, as though trying to work out what on earth Jack was doing sitting in front of him, 'you're interested in a commission in the British Army then?'

'Uh... yes.'

'And it says here that you've got all the qualifications and so on.'

'Yes... three A-levels.'

'But not a university degree.'

'Er, no.'

'And you're no youngster.'

'I'm twenty-six.'

'Most of the chaps who come to us at twenty-six have got degrees. What've you been doing with yourself?'

'I've just finished a five-year contract with the French Foreign Legion. I was in their parachute regiment.' Jack was surprised that the colonel hadn't already picked this up from the background information in front of him. It was obvious that the old soldier hadn't bothered to prepare himself for the interview by reading the file in advance.

'British Army not good enough for you, eh?'

'I thought it would be useful to gain some soldiering experience before I tried to get into Sandhurst.'

'Yeeees...' The colonel drew the word out in a protracted manner as though not at all convinced. 'Some might call it "gaining experience", others might think of it as "gaining bad habits".' He gave a small chuckle, amused at his own wit.

Jack didn't respond. The man was making him feel awkward, inadequate, tongue-tied. Just over a month ago, he'd been a corporal—a section commander—in one of the most renowned fighting forces in the world. He had the stamina of a mountain goat, and the load-carrying capacity of a Nepalese Sherpa. He could parachute, climb, abseil and swim. He was pretty handy with pistol, rifle, machine-gun and, at close quarters, his hands and feet. And this snooty old bloke in a shabby tweed suit, sitting in his big, comfy, leather armchair, had the bloody nerve to dismiss all that as 'bad habits'. Maybe Josh was right. Maybe British Army officers were all snobs with their heads up their own arses.

The colonel continued. 'So... you've had a chance to look through the recruiting literature and what-not. No doubt you've an idea what you'd like to try your hand at. Which bit of the Army do you think you'd be interested in?'

'Well, it would have to be a combat arm. Preferably an infantry regiment,' Jack proffered.

'Mmm... well, the problem is whether an infantry regiment is likely to be interested in *you*. You'll be up against some pretty stiff competition at your age, what with most of your contemporaries being graduates. Had you given any thought to a particular regiment?'

'I thought perhaps the Rangers?'

Jack's answer took Bartholomew off guard, and he almost allowed it to show. But breeding and long experience won through. The involuntary wince that had threatened to cloud the colonel's features transitioned seamlessly into a gracious, but insincere, smile. The young man in front of him had somehow gained the impression that he could elect to join *any* regiment in the British Army as easily as choosing a car or a holiday. He clearly didn't realise that there was a strict hierarchy in such matters. And, on present showing, Jack was somewhere near the bottom of that hierarchy, while the King's Royal Rangers hovered somewhere near the top.

'Do you mean the *King's Royal* Rangers?' the colonel inquired, emphasising the first two words as if to rebuke Jack for his failure to use the regiment's correct title. 'They are, after all, one of Her Majesty's finest infantry regiments, not a football team.'

'Yes, sir. Exactly.'

The colonel drew a deep breath. Of course, there was no such thing as a class structure in the modern British Army. Not officially. Not one that anyone could possibly admit to. But most people knew how the system worked. It was quite simple really. If you'd been to one of the country's top public schools, preferably followed by a decent university, and your parents had a bit of money—preferably 'old money'—any regiment was open to you. If not, it wasn't. Everyone knew that, surely. Except, apparently, this young man Adair, who was either extremely bumptious, or extremely ill-informed.

'Some would say that the King's Royal Rangers—the KRR —are the finest infantry regiment in the British Army. Served alongside them myself, in Northern Ireland. Sound people. Fantastic regiment. In the American War of Independence, they acted as skirmishers and night raiders—you could even say they were the very first commandos. Do you know what their nickname is? "The Soldiers' Regiment". On the first day of the Somme, virtually all of their officers were killed or wounded in the initial wave, so the soldiers took over. Trouble is, nowadays they've got a waiting list as long as your arm. Could take you forever to get in, and it's not as if you've got time on your side. On top of that, there are very strong family connections in the KRR. *Very* strong.'

The colonel paused to let the implications of his last comment sink in. 'Have *you* got any family connections with the KRR?'

Jack saw his chance. 'Well, my father was a sergeant in the King's Royal Rangers, if that's any help?'

It was clearly no help at all. If anything, it was almost certainly a hindrance, given that the colonel now looked as if he had detected a nasty smell under his nose.

'Not quite what I meant, young man. Have you had any relatives who have been *officers* in the regiment?'

'Well, no. But you did say it was known as "The Soldiers' Regiment".'

The colonel let the comment pass without answer. The implication was obvious. The officers of the King's Royal Rangers were an exclusive club and membership of that club was not open to the likes of Jack Adair.

A further long silence followed. From elsewhere in the building came the muffled sounds of conversation, just audible above the noise of heavy traffic passing by outside. The faint clink of china indicated coffee mugs being washed-up somewhere. Occasionally, a distant phone rang. Jack's eyes flitted across the faded photographs that adorned the walls. Most were very similar. Rows of uniformed men facing the camera. The most senior officers seated on a long bench at the front, fists always clenched on the tops of knees—the occasional dog, invariably a Labrador, lolling in the foreground. The remaining troops arrayed in rows behind— shortest at the front, tallest at the rear. All staring expressionlessly straight ahead. In the earlier photos—most of those in black-and-white—the colonel appeared as a youthful subaltern, stuck out on the flanks of the bench. As he increased in years and seniority, and black-and-white gave way to colour, he crept closer to the centre, until eventually, as commanding officer, everyone else was arrayed around *him*.

After a significant pause, the colonel spoke again: 'I could always drop the KRR a note I suppose, to see what they say.' He might as well have added, 'It will be a complete waste of everyone's time, of course,' but Colonel Bartholomew placed a high premium on exquisitely good manners.

'Thank you. I'd appreciate that.' Jack already knew what the regiment's response would be.

The colonel changed tack. 'You could look at a *corps*, rather than a regiment. You know... one of the supporting services. You could build up some very useful qualifications that would serve you very well after you left the Army. They're used to chaps like you coming in late after knocking around the world a bit first. You'd still be able to compete on an equal footing with your peers, instead of being slow off the starting blocks. And there's lots to choose from—logistics, signals, pay and administration, engineering, military police. Maybe not the power *in* the punch, but certainly the power *behind* it.' Another restrained chuckle.

It was obvious that he thought that this was where Jack's best, and possibly only, option lay. 'What do you think?'

What Jack thought was that he'd rather slit his own wrists with a rusty razor blade. Instead, all he could manage was: 'Well, shall we try the letter to the King's Royal Rangers first, to see what they think, and if that doesn't seem to be working, we could look at the various supporting corps after that?'

Two weeks later, Jack received an icily courteous letter telling him that the King's Royal Rangers had already hit their quota for the year and, regrettably, would not be sponsoring any more candidates through the Royal Military Academy Sandhurst for at least six months. Since no potential officer candidate could appear before the Army Officer Selection Board—the assessment process that had to be passed in order to get into Sandhurst—without the sponsorship of a regiment or corps, Jack realised that he would have to look elsewhere... and fast. Consoling himself with the possibility that, if he did well at Sandhurst, he might still be able to attract the selector's eye for an infantry regiment, perhaps even the KRR, Jack submitted to the inevitable and began to sound out the various supporting corps.

Within a month, his name was firmly down for the Royal Logistic Corps. Colonel Bartholomew had moved with surprising speed once he'd detected that Jack had 'seen sense' and was 'fishing in the right pool', and a familiarisation visit to the RLC's headquarters in Hampshire had been rushed through at very short notice. Jack had found his concentration drifting during the briefings on supply and distribution that had formed part of his introduction to the Corps. Having a full mag of ammo and a decent pair of boots was the closest he'd come to logistics before. Anything beyond that had always been somebody else's problem and, frankly, that's the way he preferred it. He tried to reassure himself that this was only a means to an end, and that, hopefully, the KRR might still be within his grasp if he could impress at Sandhurst. Even so, without a university degree and the right family connections, he could not escape the nagging feeling that the chances of gaining a place in an elite regiment might be slim.

# Chapter Four



*Early morning commuter train, Dover to London*

'If you 'ad any manners, you'd stand up and let one of your elders and betters have that seat.'

The speaker was a stubble-faced, obese man in his forties, whose unkempt hair fell in greasy tangles around his ears. A cobweb tattoo stretched across his neck, from just below his right ear-lobe to somewhere under his under his stained grey sweatshirt. More tattoos covered his hands where they emerged from his donkey jacket. His jeans sagged low at the front, giving his belly room to expand over the top. A plastic Adidas sports bag was slung across his shoulder, although he didn't look like someone who played a lot of sport. Darts at most. Maybe.

Standing in the aisle of the crowded railway carriage, he spat out the words with undisguised menace at the studious-looking young teenager in glasses. The boy's mother, sitting opposite him, caught her son's eye and shook her head almost imperceptibly, as if to say, 'Don't do it.'

If she was trying not to draw attention to herself, she failed.

'What's up, luv? Can't he make up his own mind?' sneered the thug.

Nearby passengers, mainly men in suits making their daily journey in to their London offices, studied their newspapers intently, hoping that the situation would just go away. Perhaps the man was right. Perhaps the boy *should* stand up. Never mind the fact that his mother was clearly scared. Never mind the fact that this wasn't really about manners, but about intimidation. Never mind the fact that an underlying hint of menace had been introduced into the carriage. Whatever the rights or wrongs, the situation was toe-curlingly embarrassing. It simply should *not* be happening on the morning commuter train, where, usually, the only display of bad manners centred on some discreet jockeying for position on the station platform to ensure that one didn't go without a seat.

'Well, Harry Potter, you gonna move, or what?' The bully's face twisted into the sort of defiant leer that said, 'Punch me... if you dare.'

Flushed with embarrassment, eyes glistening as he fought to hold back tears, the boy rose and edged out into the aisle. His tormenter barged past into the vacant seat, adjusting his waistband as he sat down to allow his stomach to spill out and settle on his thighs. He looked around with a smug, self-satisfied smile, daring anyone to challenge him. Nobody did. He knew they wouldn't. They never did. These pathetic, office-bound pen-pushers, with their comfortable little lives were too soft to stand up to a *real* man. Wimps, the lot of 'em. Just to rub their noses in the fact that he ruled this carriage, he turned his attention back to his victim.

'If you was a *real* man, you'd have told me to fuck off.'

The boy bit his lip but said nothing. The men-in-suits buried their noses still further into their papers. After all, what else could they possibly be expected to do? The police were always warning against 'having a go' these days. Where would they stand if they got into a fight? What if someone got hurt? More to the point, what if *they* got hurt? In any case, the journey would only last another half-hour or so. Soon they would be at their office desks, the whole situation put behind them and forgotten about. There might be a nagging inward twinge of shame, but, after all, no one else need ever know. This was certainly not a story to tell the wife that evening. She might ask why nobody did anything.

Jack Adair was standing in the aisle next to the boy. For the past five years, he'd been accustomed to sorting out his problems with his fists. But that was the Legion. This was now. And this wasn't his problem.

'It's okay, son, don't worry about it,' he murmured, just loud enough to be heard. The boy looked up, grateful for some support. Jack winked, adding, 'The world's full of goons like that.'

'Did you say something, mate?' challenged the aging yob.

Suppressing the urge to say, 'Yeah, I was just telling the lad here what a dickhead you are,' Jack stared back at him, silent, unblinking, with the dead-eyed, slightly mocking look that suggested he wouldn't be afraid to unleash physical violence. The thug broke eye contact first, allowing Jack to shift his gaze and take in the other passengers.

Sitting next to the bully was a pale, thin man of middle years, wearing a nondescript suit. His most noticeable feature was a large, pointed Adam's apple. His sparse hair was swept across his head in strands in an attempt to hide the bare patches. A middle manager in social services? Maybe a bookkeeper in a small firm? He didn't look as if he could put up much of a fight.

Right alongside the boy's mother, next to the window, was a young man in his early twenties—about the same age as Jack. Blond-haired, slim and fit-looking, albeit with the soft rosy cheeks of someone who had enjoyed a privileged upbringing—probably the product of one of the 'better' public schools. He was gazing fixedly at the distant horizon as if unaware of what had just happened only feet away. Jack instantly marked him down as a coward.

The train slowed to pull in at the next station. The thin, bookish-looking man stood up, struggled into his beige raincoat, and moved towards the aisle. He smiled half apologetically at the boy's mother as he passed.

'There, your lad can have this seat now,' he offered politely, as if that excused his impotence only a few minutes earlier.

The woman returned his smile. He'd wimped out when she'd really needed help, but at least he was kind. Quickly glancing over her shoulder, she gestured to her son with a nod, indicating the now-empty seat. When she looked back, her heart sank to see that the fat chav had meanwhile picked up his sports bag from between his feet and placed it on the adjacent seat. He was now leaning sideways across both seats, using it as a pillow.

The tension in the carriage ratcheted up another notch. Rarely had so many commuters studied their newspapers so intently, while taking in so few printed words. They might as well have been staring at blank pages. Tabloids and broadsheets had become shields.

From his semi-lying position, the man looked directly at the boy and spoke again. 'What's the matter? You too scared to tell me to shift my bag off the seat?' Then he closed his eyes, as if in sleep.

'He may be, but I'm not.'

The bully opened his eyes again. It was the lithe, fit-looking young guy with the crew-cut, wearing the double-breasted dark suit, who'd spoken. The one who'd stared him down a few minutes before. Anticipating trouble, he started to lift his head off the holdall. He was too slow. In a single swift movement, Jack had closed with him and grabbed a handful of the long greasy hair, dragging his head upwards, and tossing the sports bag roughly onto the carriage floor. As a legionnaire, he would have finished the job by smashing his knee into the man's nose, but this time he held back. With the thought flashing through his mind that it might not look good to be arrested and charged with assault while on his way to undertake the British Army's officer selection tests, he contented himself with ramming the guy's head back down onto the vacant seat.

Jack's opponent started struggling to stand up as if to fight back, but quickly saw the younger man's clenched fist, cocked and ready for release.

'Really?' Jack dared. 'Are you sure about that?'

The threat was enough. The thug backed down and resumed his seat, his face a mask of fury. Puce and gasping, he leaned forward to retrieve his holdall, pulling it back across the floor so that it nestled between his feet, while muttering barely audible threats.

Jack heard an elderly, blazer-wearing chap nearby mutter 'Well done!' He was also conscious of one or two tuts of disapproval as people accustomed to a rather safer world displayed their indignation at the unexpected intrusion of violence. The sort of people who could turn a blind eye to injustice, so long as it didn't affect them.

Jack ushered the boy into the now-vacant seat, responding with a cheerful 'No problem' when the woman mouthed a silent 'Thank you'. He then moved along the aisle, attempting to defuse any further ugliness by distancing himself from the immediate scene, while remaining close enough to intervene again should there be any more signs of trouble.

As a degree of calm returned to the carriage, Jack, standing, leaned against a seat-back and took in his surroundings. Most of the newspaper readers seemed entirely unruffled by the incident. He wasn't to know that, behind their flimsy paper shields, hearts were still pounding faster, thoughts were still racing, and whole printed sentences were still not being taken in. But on the surface, all appeared tranquil. His gaze alighted once more on the blond-haired fellow in his twenties by the window.

He was taking in the countryside as it flashed by, seemingly oblivious to what had just happened. Perhaps triggered by some sixth sense, the young man realised that Jack was looking at him. He turned his head and for a fleeting moment their eyes locked. It was no more than a fraction of a second, but it was long enough for Jack to detect that the outwardly languid pose was an act. The guy had been scared. What's more, he knew that Jack knew it. In a blink, blondie averted his eyes and resumed his interest in the passing landscape.

As the train began to slow, pulling into London Saint Pancras, Jack checked his watch. He was well ahead of schedule and still had time in hand before he needed to take his connecting train from Paddington down to Westbury, the small village that, since 1949, had been the home of the Army's Officer Selection Board. Alighting from the train and shouldering his grip, he headed off to satisfy his craving for a hit of the very strongest espresso coffee.

# Chapter Five

*Westbury Station, Wiltshire*

Two hours later, Jack stepped off the train at Westbury. This was his second visit to the Army Officer Selection Board. The first, a few weeks earlier, had been a two-day initial filtering process, designed to sort the wheat from the chaff—identifying and discarding the fantasists, military geeks, mummy's boys, terminally unfit, dull-witted and those that couldn't lead a troop of Boy Scouts. Now it was time for the Board to probe deeper. Time to distinguish the real leaders from those who'd simply managed to put on a passable act up until now.

As he strode across the platform, Jack spotted several young men gathered inside the small waiting room sipping hot drinks from the snack bar. They exuded the unmistakable air of potential British Army officers—suits, tweed jackets, blazers, and hair uniformly trimmed in 'short back and sides' style—more like university undergraduates from the 1950s than aspiring 21st century warriors. Jack ignored them and made his way outside. The prospect of trying to make small talk with a bunch of posh ex-public schoolboys appealed to him about as much as sticking needles in his eyes.

As expected, a coach was parked fifty yards or so from the station entrance, with its doors open. The driver was reading a newspaper. Jack tapped on the door to attract his attention.

'Is this the bus for AOSB?' He knew it was. It couldn't be anything else.

'Yeah mate. This is the one. Portsmouth train's late though. So we're waiting till it turns up. Told the others they might as well go back inside and get themselves a coffee.'

'Oh, right... I'll do the same then.'

Jack walked back into the station and entered the snack bar. Without making eye contact, he crossed to the counter and ordered coffee. Cup in hand, he turned to face the group, two of whom had their backs to him. Their manner, bearing and style of dress could not be more different from the mates he'd left behind in the 2nd REP. Feeling increasingly out of his depth he decided the best option was to introduce himself. He edged onto the outskirts of the tight circle.

'Hi. You guys heading for AOSB?' His words resounded in his ears, coming out sounding thick and brusque—just as they always did when he felt ill at ease.

The nearest individual, a tall young man wearing a charcoal grey, pin-striped suit, turned slowly to face him. The manoeuvre was carried out in the deliberate, unhurried manner that a member of the Royal Family might use if tapped on the shoulder by an autograph hunter. Jack found himself being appraised by a pair of piercing blue eyes set beneath blond hair cut in an Eton flop. For a fraction of a second, there was a glimmer of recognition, but it vanished instantly behind a mask of cold indifference that stopped just short of disdain. It was the blond guy from the train.

'Yah, right, I don't believe we've met. I'm Vyvyan Phillips,' he drawled, making it abundantly clear that, as far as he was concerned, their paths had never crossed before. 'So who are *you*, and what are you down for?' Given the tone of his voice, he might as well have added 'you awful little oik'. In his head, he probably did.

'Down for? Sorry, what do you mean? Down for what?'

'I mean, what *regiment* are you down for?' Phillips explained with smoothly polished condescension.

'I'm Jack Adair, and I'm *down* for the Royal Logistic Corps. How about you?'

Phillips looked at Jack as if he were something unpleasant that had crawled from beneath a stone. 'Oh, I'm down for the King's Royal Rangers,' he announced loftily.

'You're lucky! I was told the KRR had a waiting list as long as your arm,' replied Jack.

'That probably depends on who you are. My brother's Adrian Phillips—the current second-in-command—so nobody actually mentioned a waiting list to me. Of course, the regiment's always known I'd be coming. My father, Valentine Phillips, was commanding officer in the late-90s. He's a general now. So I rather suppose he has a bit of clout. He probably had my name down virtually from the day I was born. If not before. Perhaps your father should have done the same.'

'He was a sergeant. I guess he wouldn't have known much about waiting lists.'

'Mmm, I suppose not,' Phillips responded, as if considering the likely habits and customs of some unfamiliar species. 'And of course, the name wouldn't have helped.'

'What do you mean?' asked Jack, suddenly curious.

'Well, your father just happens to share the same name and rank as one of the regiment's most infamous cowards. Frankly, I should think they'd be very wary about taking any more Adairs on board.'

'I don't follow you.'

'Well, it was a Sergeant Adair who was with my father in Northern Ireland when he won his Military Cross. The IRA attacked a border crossing point with RPGs, a heavy machine gun and a flamethrower. There were only seventeen KRR men and a policeman inside. Four were killed. Place was almost overrun. Seems Pops virtually saved the day. Took out four of the buggers, and held the rest up just long enough for the Quick Reaction Force to be flown in. No thanks to this fellow Adair, though. The story's well known throughout the regiment. I say, he wasn't *your* father, was he?'

'Er, no, but go on,' prompted Jack, a cold feeling starting to come over him. Phillips needed little encouragement. One of his favourite pastimes was bragging about the exploits of his grand military family. He also needed to put this pleb Adair in his place before he had a chance to bring up anything about that awful incident on the train.

'Apparently, this chap Sergeant Adair was briefing my old man in the ops room when the attack happened. As soon as Father heard the shots, he raced outside to see what the commotion was. By that time the IRA were already coming through the perimeter fence, so Pa ran straight into a gun battle at close quarters. After bringing a couple of terrorists down, he tried to take cover back in the ops room, but that bastard Adair had already dragged a table across the door. He almost couldn't get back in, and shots were whacking into the woodwork all around him. Luckily, he managed to force the door open, only to find your namesake gibbering like some terrified imbecile and trying to hide himself inside a metal locker. Father was trying to order him out when a grenade came bouncing into the room. Adair was killed in the explosion, while Pops came out of it pretty unscathed and another Ranger in the room just picked up minor frag wounds. It's all in the citation. Pa thought it was good character-building stuff, so he'd often read it to me and my brother instead of a bedtime story.'

'So Sergeant Adair died then?' asked Jack, already knowing the answer.

'Frankly, it was lucky for him that he did. If he hadn't, Father reckons that he would certainly have been court-martialled for cowardice. So, you can see, even if the KRR had vacancies, having a father with a name like Sergeant Adair—whatever his cap-badge—might not exactly stand you in good stead where the regiment's concerned. What mob was your old man in?'

'Logistic Corps—same as I'm down for,' Jack lied. He felt numb. Although he'd always known that his father had been killed in Northern Ireland, he'd never heard the full story. Whenever he'd questioned his mother about it she'd virtually clammed-up and tried to change the subject as quickly as possible. His stepfather's opposition to anything military had made it even more difficult to discuss the issue. Surely this couldn't be how he died? He had to know more.

'When was this?' Jack inquired flatly, already dreading to hear the final proof.

'Oh that's easy. Fifth of November 1996. Pa always says that it was the biggest firework display he'd ever seen on Guy Fawkes' Night. Why do you ask? I do hope *our* Adair wasn't some sort of relative of yours.'

'Not one I've ever come across.' Jack's face flushed as he Judased his own father.

He suddenly wanted to be anywhere other than Westbury. He needed to sit his mother down and grill her on precisely what she knew. Even though he barely remembered his dad, he'd always put him on a pedestal—Sergeant Nick Adair, the heroic soldier, killed in action fighting for his country, the antithesis of Jack's weirdy-beardy, college lecturer stepfather. Now this. It couldn't be happening. Fuck!

'Oh well, Adair, once you're in the Loggies you'll probably be a great chap to know for getting bits of spare kit and so on. We must keep in touch,' Phillips added unconvincingly. With this patronising dismissal, he turned away, masking his relief at having averted any mention of the incident on the train. He wasn't sure whether Adair had recognised him or not, but flaunting the family war story had been an effective diversionary tactic to ensure the dreadful little man didn't blurt out anything 'inconvenient'. It wouldn't do for people to be thinking that Vyvyan Phillips, son of the gallant Lieutenant General Sir Valentine Phillips, KCB, CBE, MC, lacked guts. No, it wouldn't do at all.

Jack was left with his emotions churning—a confused jumble of anger, indignation, hurt, embarrassment and shame. He wanted to punch somebody. Preferably that arrogant twat Phillips. But in this environment, so carefully mannered, and so far removed from what he'd known for the past five years, even kicking a chair was out of the question.

He found himself staring fixedly at a point somewhere just behind the snack bar's serving counter, fists tightly clenched, jaw clamped shut and his back teeth grinding. To his left, a sturdy-looking individual of average height, wearing glasses—another outcast from the original group of potential officers—was smiling uncertainly at him and holding out his hand in an effort to introduce himself.

'Hi. I'm Mike Lawrence. When I told that prat Phillips I was going for the Intelligence Corps, I got blanked pretty much the same as you. Tell you what, if that's the sort of stuck-up pricks they're recruiting into the Rangers, I'm glad I'm not trying to get into them.'

At last, someone was talking a language Jack understood.

'Yeah, looks like those of us destined to be the power *behind* the punch aren't exactly on a par with those who deliver the punch. But I tell you who I'd like to punch right now.'

'Bloody hell, he certainly managed to wind *you* up, and no mistake,' Mike observed. You haven't *really* got any connection with that sergeant who hid in the locker, have you?'

'Fuck off! Of course not,' Jack retorted—perhaps just a little too emphatically to sound entirely convincing.

# Chapter Six

*Leighton House, Westbury, Wiltshire*

Leighton House, a neo-classical Georgian manor, lay at the centre of a large rural estate on the outskirts of the Wiltshire village of Westbury. Built in 1800, it had passed through several owners before being sold to the War Office on the outbreak of war in 1939. Ten years later it had become the centre for British Army officer selection and had been used for that purpose ever since. In eighty years, the selection methods had changed almost as little as the venue.

For three and a half days, the candidates would be subjected to a battery of tests designed to assess mind, body and spirit. They would write essays, give mini-lectures, participate in debates, undergo interviews, tackle an assault course and attempt to lead small groups over challenging obstacles using a selection of ropes, planks, ladders and oil drums. Throughout, they would be scrutinised by a panel of serving officers, known collectively as the Directing Staff—

the 'DS'. Every perceived triumph or failure would be meticulously noted down.

On arrival, the hopefuls were kitted out with a set of green overalls, a lightweight plastic safety helmet and a coloured bib bearing a number. The colours corresponded to eight-man teams—five in all. In an unconvincing effort to maintain anonymity and avoid favouritism, all of the potential officers would only be addressed by their number during the assessment process. Jack was Red-Six. Maddeningly, Vyvyan Phillips was Red-Four.

The first day had passed comparatively easily, mainly being devoted to online tests. On Day Two the pressure started to escalate as the candidates faced the practical command tasks.

'Oh, for Christ's sake, Number Two, just lift the bloody box above your head, shimmy along the pole and drop down on the other side.' Phillips' voice cut through the fine drizzle like a feudal lord dispensing advice to lowly peasants.

'I don't think it's going to hold my weight,' ventured Red-Two, a gawky, uncoordinated, red-haired lad, who frankly couldn't shimmy along a broad, flat pavement, let alone a wet metal pole with a box above his head.

'Look we haven't got all day, just bloody well get on with it!'

'But what if he...?' Jack started to venture a possible solution, but this was lost in the commotion of Red-Two toppling to his doom in the imaginary river, taking the box with him.

Red Team was on its fourth task—crossing a partially destroyed 'bridge' with vital medical supplies. A scaffolding climbing frame represented the bridge and a sand-filled ammunition box the medical supplies. Various bits of kit—a plank, a pole, an oil drum and two lengths of rope—were on hand to help. They weren't very helpful. Nothing quite bridged the gap, so a precarious cantilever structure had to be cobbled together.

The confusion brought out extremes of character as individuals reacted to the stress in different ways. Some shouted nonstop, whether they were right or wrong. Shrinking violets wilted to the point of invisibility. Good advice fell on deaf ears.

Vyvyan Phillips knew how to play the game. He brazenly courted DS favour. Workable solutions proffered quietly by his less confident teammates were quickly seized upon and promoted as his own. He was always there with the cry for greater urgency, the hearty word of encouragement, or the helping hand—whether needed or not. He was also quick to draw attention to the failures of others with exaggerated displays of exasperation when disaster struck. After all, if others looked bad, it could only help him look good.

Believing that the incident on the train had been successfully pushed under the carpet, Phillips' big mistake was to try the same tactic on Jack Adair. The man was a *sergeant's* son for God's sake. And his performance on the London train with that woman and her ghastly boy had been that of an absolute thug. It was hardly surprising that he was going for the Royal Logistic Corps. It was probably the only cap badge that would have him. The King's Royal Rangers would *always* have a long waiting list where awful little plebs like that were concerned. In fact, for *some* people, the list would always be infinite.

As Jack teetered, perilously close to toppling off a badly cantilevered plank while endeavouring to swing the ammunition box across a gap to one of his teammates, Phillips made his move. 'Come on, Red-Six, get a wiggle on. You'll have to learn how to handle boxes better than that once you're a Loggy. You might as well start now. Or are you going to stick to stacking blankets?'

The incendiary remarks hit their target with unerring accuracy. Jack looked across just in time to see the fine flecks of spittle that accompanied the words 'stick to stacking blankets' spraying from Phillips' mouth. And then he fell.

The plank slid sideways, slipped out of the rope noose that had been holding it steady at one end, and deposited Jack on the ground along with the ammo box. Two of the team laughed. The rest, conscious that the time allocated for the task was evaporating rapidly, and that failure could rebound on them, let out howls of frustration.

'Oh come *on*, Number Six,' yelled the team's DS, a major, derisively from the side-lines. 'Now go back and start again. And *hurry up!*'

Jack glared at Phillips. The desire to sink his knuckles into those plump, pink lips was virtually irresistible. Only one thing held him back. Somewhere, he couldn't remember where, he'd heard that the Board valued 'cool' above all else. You could flunk every obstacle on the AOSB assault course, but Sandhurst would make you physically fit. You could drop every team member into an imaginary minefield on a command task, but Sandhurst would teach you how to work out a plan. What Sandhurst could not do was teach you how to be cool when your natural instinct in the face of chaos was to hit the panic button. Now was the time to be cool. Revenge could come later. As Jack started to regain his position on the obstacle, he had but one thought: 'Right, you supercilious prick, you've got it coming to you.'

That night Jack phoned his mother.

In the four months since he'd left the Legion, he'd only seen her for five days. During that short time, the atmosphere had become increasingly strained. Although she was clearly pleased to have him home, he'd been a virtual stranger to her in the past five years. Apart from a couple of leave periods, spanning no more than a handful of weeks, their only contact had been through infrequent letters and even less frequent phone calls. With his stepfather, there had been almost no contact at all. And there was no doubt that Jack had returned a changed man. Gone was the gangly youth who had taken off for France pretty well as soon as he could. The boy had been replaced by a man of exceptional physical fitness, uncompromising resolve and... a short fuse. It hadn't taken long for Jack to decide that the mix of a hard-nosed former legionnaire, a left-of-centre college lecturer who detested all things military, and a very gentle woman, who would prefer him to settle down in a 'safe' profession, like being a bank clerk, was simply not going to work. Before the first week was over, he'd moved out.

At first he'd tried kipping on the sofas of old school friends—several of whom now had their own properties. In some respects, this had proved as difficult as being at home. He no longer had any touchstone with those who'd been to university, done their degrees, and settled into climbing the greasy career pole as bankers, civil engineers, teachers and solicitors. Eventually, with few other options left, he'd sought out Rick 'Diggsy' Diggle, a former member of *Le Mafia Anglais*, who'd left the 2nd REP the year before. Diggsy had provided him with a floor to sleep on at his flat in Dover and helped fix him up with a job as a delivery van driver while he trained for AOSB.

But now he needed to talk to his mother more than ever before. He needed to know if there was any truth in the story that Phillips had related in the railway station snack-bar.

He was about to click his mobile off when, after five rings, his mother picked up. Quickly skirting round the formalities of how he was, where he was and what he was doing, Jack got down to the issue that had been dominating his every thought for the past 24 hours.

'Mum... how did Dad die?'

'Oh, that's a funny question to ask. You know how he died. He was killed by the IRA in Ireland.'

'Yeah, I know the edited version. Now I want to know how he *really* died. What exactly happened?'

There was a long silence at the other end of the line. Jack could hear his mother's breathing becoming heavier. He had obviously touched a raw nerve and she was battling to control her emotions.

Eventually she replied. 'Why, what have you heard, Jack?'

'I've heard that he was in a base that got attacked. That he hid in a room and barred the door. That he was caught skulking inside a locker. And that a major tried to order him out, but he was still in there when a grenade got lobbed into the room. Mum... I need to know if it's true. Was dad a coward?'

'I don't know what to believe, Jack. There was some nasty talk at the time. I didn't believe it, but they say there were witnesses. So I suppose it must be true. Anyway, your dad never got a military funeral. The regiment seemed to want nothing to do with us. We just had to get on with life and put it all behind us. Look, I've got to go now, your dad's calling.'

'He's not my dad, mum. My dad died over twenty-five years ago.'

The phone went dead.

Jack's mother was late going to bed that night. After her husband had gone up, she sat staring vacantly at the television. She stayed that way for at least an hour, her thoughts wandering to a time long past. Eventually, she could feel, as much as hear, the vibrations from her husband's snores being transmitted through the floor above. Only then did she pull herself wearily from her chair and move across to the bureau tucked away in one corner of the room. She opened a small drawer and slid her flattened hand towards the back. Pushing aside some old letters and bills, her fingers made contact with the purse that she knew to be there. She drew it out. It was small, little more than a child's purse, in red tartan, with a brass clip-fastening running along the top. She popped the clip open, turned the purse upside down, and emptied it onto the surface of the bureau. Only one item fell out. As she picked it up and held it up to the light, a single tear rolled down her cheek. It was a white feather.

She stared at the feather, twisting it by its shaft, and the same old thought came back to her, 'If he was hiding in a steel locker, how come he was the one who died?'

# Chapter Seven

The Red Team candidates filed into the small briefing room and took their seats. The olive drab overalls and helmets of the previous afternoon had been discarded and they were back in suits, albeit still wearing their brightly coloured, numbered bibs to preserve anonymity. The team's DS, an earnest young major from the Royal Engineers, briskly handed out papers face down as if it were a school test.

'Right,' he said. 'You've got an hour to read the problem outlined on the paper in front of you and write down a proposed course of action. There is no right or wrong answer —we just need to see some element of logic in your thinking and the ability to process information quickly against the clock. When you're finished, we'll spend fifteen minutes discussing the pros and cons of the various plans. It'll be your chance to fight your own corner, as well as listening to what the others have got to say. After that, I'll ask each of you in turn to outline the situation, your personal solution, and the whole group's chosen solution. I say again, the *group's chosen solution*—because it may not necessarily be anything like the one that you initially came up with as an individual. Any questions? Right, go.'

Jack started reading through the problem, which covered three pages and included a sketch map and a table of the times and distances between several key points. The improbable story was typical *Boys' Own* stuff: a fictional European country; three Sandhurst cadets on a skiing trip, snowed-in at a hotel; a princess with a sprained ankle; revolution breaking out all around them; rebel forces closing in; and a rescue force held up by snow. Do they stay and fight with a motley collection of hunting guns, or do they make a dash for it with the princess over treacherous roads?

An hour flew past, and Jack was only just putting the finishing touches to his plan when the major called a halt. After a short break to stretch their legs and get their thoughts in order, the candidates were brought back into the room, the chairs placed in a half circle, with the major sitting off to one side, and the discussion began.

The group quickly divided into those who favoured fortifying the hotel and fighting it out, and those who wanted to escape towards the nearest safe border, with the princess, immediately. On the grounds that two hunting rifles and a shotgun provided pretty limited firepower, Jack wanted to make a dash for it. He was just concluding a powerful argument justifying this course of action when Phillips cut him off in mid-sentence.

'I'm sorry,' he drawled, 'but you're talking complete bollocks, Number Six. I don't suppose *you've* been to a ski hotel before in your entire life. You know nothing about the type of terrain that you'd have to contend with. I *know* that sort of ground—I've been skiing in places like that virtually every year since I was born. The *only* option is to stay and fight it out on ground of your own choosing.'

As the hubbub of debate threatened to break out again, with several candidates vying to be heard, Jack spoke. The steely edge to his voice sliced through the rising chatter. Staring directly at Phillips, he spat out his words slowly and deliberately.

'Except that, as we both know, *you* wouldn't have the *nerve* to stay and fight it out.'

Phillips coloured. This bloody sergeant's son was as good as calling him a coward in front of the entire group. And there was nothing he could say about it. If he did, the whole story about the incident on the train might come tumbling out. The little pleb clearly had no breeding, no manners and precious few social skills. Who knew what he might say? Phillips could feel an involuntary bead of sweat breaking out on his brow and start to course its way down the side of his head. The major, whose interest in the discussion had waned, suddenly sat up and took notice, not sure if he'd heard Adair correctly and wondering whether he should cut in.

'What exactly do you mean by that?' Phillips asked, his throat suddenly dry. This was not a confrontation that he wanted to be having in public, but he couldn't just leave Adair's remark hanging.

'Well,' Jack continued in an even tone, 'if you took the risk of fighting it out against overwhelming odds, and the princess was taken hostage, it would give the rebels a massive bargaining chip. I don't think *any* of us would have the nerve to take that chance under those circumstances. It's too big a gamble.'

'Oh... yes... I see what you mean,' Phillips managed to splutter. Adair had given him a way out. But the challenge had definitely been there. He had seen it in the man's eyes. That troublesome young man from the Loggies was desperately in need of a thorough lesson in social etiquette.

At the side of the room, the major relaxed back into his chair. Crisis over.

A five-year contract with the French Foreign Legion hadn't prepared Jack for the formality of a dinner night in a British Army officers' mess. Even though the final night dinner at the Selection Board was only a pale imitation of a lavish function in a regimental mess, it was still a long way from chugging down Kronenbourgs in the *foyer* at Camp Raffalli. Jack knew where he'd rather be.

The candidates gathered for pre-dinner drinks in the anteroom. Many already knew each other through school, university and the Officers' Training Corps. Once again, Jack felt like an outsider. He spotted Mike Lawrence—the guy with his sights set on the Intelligence Corps—and crossed the room to speak to him.

As Mike saw him coming a grin crossed his face. 'Hi Jack. See you've got that twat Phillips in your group. I was glad to avoid that. How's it going?'

'Yeah, okay, thanks. But you're dead right about Phillips. Why just be a bit of a twat when, with a little more effort, you can be a *complete* twat? And he sure is prepared to put the extra effort in.'

'Didn't take much to see that. How's *he* doing?'

'Oh, pretty much as you'd expect for a general's son. Talks down to everybody. Expects the rest of us to obey his every whim. Generally, thinks he's God's gift to the Army. He tried it on with me, but he won't do that again.'

'Why's that? Did you threaten to knock his mouth in?'

'Didn't need to. He's scared enough of me already. Scared that I'm going to tell everyone about a little secret we share.'

'And are you?' asked Mike, trying to sound less curious than he felt.

'Frankly, I don't give a monkey's one way or the other. But *you* might find it amusing.'

Jack started to relate the story of the incident on the train, interrupted every so often by an increasingly incredulous Mike.

'What, you mean you just grabbed him?'

'Yup.'

'And threw his bag on the floor?'

'Yup.'

'And smacked his head back down on the seat?'

'Yup.'

'Bloody hell!'

'Yup. That's pretty much what I started thinking halfway through.'

So what did everyone else do while you were scuffling in a packed railway carriage at rush hour?'

'Well most pretended to read their newspapers. Like, really intently. One or two tutted.'

'I bet they bloody did! And you say our chum Vyvyan just kept looking out of the window the whole time?'

'Yeah. The man's a coward with the spine of a jellyfish.'

'Or maybe just didn't want to get in an unseemly brawl over a seat on a crowded train. Had that occurred to you?'

Jack shrugged. 'It wasn't about the seat. The boy was being bullied, the mother was being hassled, and the fat fucker responsible was challenging anyone in the carriage to do something about it. Someone needed to step in. And it certainly wasn't going to be Vyvyan, 'cos he's a got a yellow streak a mile wide down his back.'

'I heard that, and how dare you?' The blustering voice came from a tall, heavily-built potential officer with a flushed face, tousled dark hair and a bull neck, who was turning to face them from a few feet away. His tailored suit had been cut to accommodate slab-like pecs, and he displayed the ape-armed stance that came with over-developed biceps. His posh accent seemed at odds with his cauliflower ears. The archetypal rugger-bugger. Clearly a man who was used to having his own way.

'You're the chap going for the Loggies, aren't you?' he boomed. 'I'm Graeme Forshaw, and I've known Vyvyan Phillips since we started prep school together. As it happens, he told me earlier this evening about what happened on the way down here. I have to say, his version is somewhat different to yours, and I know which one to believe.' As he spat out each word, Forshaw's naturally florid face reddened further in line with his rising fury.

'Oh really? I suppose in his version he put five bullies to flight using only one hand so as not to have an unfair advantage,' challenged Jack, sizing up his opponent.

'Don't try and be a smart-alec. What he says is that some frail old chap got on struggling with a load of luggage and asked a young lad if he might be prepared to give up his seat.

Apparently you then started throwing your weight about—along with the old boy's luggage—in an attempt to impress the lad's mother, who, I understand, was rather easy on the eye.'

'That's not what happened.'

'Not only do I not believe you, but I'm going to make bloody sure that Vyvyan knows what you're saying behind his back.'

'Why don't you shove it up your arse, mate?' Jack growled.

'My God! Everything Vyvyan says about you is true. You really are the most appalling little pleb!' With that Forshaw strode off to join Phillips on far side of the room.

Almost immediately, Jack was amused to see the meerkat effect take hold as Phillips and his acolytes bobbed up and down, straining their necks to catch a glimpse of him.

'Looks like they've got you in their sights,' Mike observed. 'Does this masterly diplomacy of yours get you into bother often?'

'I've had worse,' Jack muttered quietly, thinking of the thin white scar on his forearm where Draskovic's knife had caught him during the fight in the barrack-block back at Camp Raffalli.

At that moment, the mess manager appeared, rang a small bell for silence, and announced that dinner was served. The candidates filed into the dining room and took their places at table.

# Chapter Eight

The formal dinner held on the third and final night of the Selection Board was steeped in myths, rumours and preposterous fabrications. Traditionally, the DS did not attend the function; so, for the first time in three days, the potential officers were free from their constant scrutiny. Not that they believed this. Speculation was rampant. The elderly barman was rumoured to be the commandant in disguise. The stag's head behind the bar supposedly secreted a CCTV camera, relaying their every move to the DS sitting in another room. The waiters were allegedly handpicked for their detailed knowledge of table etiquette, and would report back on any individual's failings.

Some candidates deliberately limited their alcohol intake in the mistaken belief that every glass was being noted down somewhere. Others approached the dinner in a more cavalier way. For the candidates from established military backgrounds, AOSB was simply a tedious rite of passage—a minor speed bump along the road to joining the chosen family regiment. As far as they were concerned, the whole thing was 'in the bag', and the dinner was an opportunity to let their hair down. After all, the only activity awaiting them the next day was a final race over the obstacle course, with each team competing against the others. As an element of the selection process it probably didn't count for much. As a hangover cure, it was unbeatable.

Jack wasn't taken in by the scaremongering. He reckoned that the DS had probably seen enough of him by now to make their decision. He didn't like the formality of the mess. He didn't like small talk. But he was happy enough to sink a few beers for the first time in a week. Sitting to his left was one of the ten percent of female candidates attending the Board. A slightly plump girl, with dark hair cut in a neat bob, she had the boyish enthusiasm of a hockey team captain and the cut glass tones of an expensive education.

For the first half of the meal she cold-shouldered him, talking animatedly to a serious-looking young man on her other side. Eventually, as the empty plates from the main course were being cleared, she turned her attention to Jack, introduced herself as Pippa Kelly, and began quizzing him expertly. Uncomfortable in situations like this, he immediately felt himself becoming tongue-tied. His responses came out sounding humourless and deadpan, almost truculent. Trying to show an interest that he didn't really feel, he asked her what she currently did for a living.

'Oh, until a week ago I was Norland Nanny,' she said breezily, referring to the college that trained well-bred 'gals' to look after the offspring of wealthy Arabs, A-listers, city bankers, minor royals and any aristocrats who'd managed to keep hold of their family fortunes.

'A what nanny? I don't know what that is,' replied Jack, feeling increasingly out of his depth.

'In that case, you simply haven't been brought up properly.' She issued the snooty put-down and turned away to resume her earlier conversation. Jack was left inwardly fuming, until seconds later she glanced quickly over her shoulder and gave him a fleeting wink. The little minx was playing games!

Deprived of conversation, Jack was left staring idly around the dining room. Further along the table, he could see Phillips, clearly at ease and enjoying himself. And he should be—he had the best seat in the house. Next to him sat possibly the most strikingly beautiful woman Jack had ever seen in his life. Her head was tilted to one side, long shimmering blonde hair falling across one side of her face. Occasionally she would break into vivacious laughter. Even from a distance, Jack was transfixed by her azure eyes that reflected the candlelight with an almost preternatural luminescence.

'That's Gemma Page.' Pippa, the former Norland Nanny, had turned back to speak to him again.

'Who is?' Jack feigned surprise, slightly embarrassed at having been caught out staring at the blonde girl.

'The blonde girl you were ogling. And don't say you weren't. All men do. Some women, too, for that matter. We were at Roedean together. While I took up nannying, she went up to Oxford to read PPE.'

'PPE?' Jack was treading on unknown territory again.

'Oh, *come on,*' urged Pippa, as if mildly berating some backsliding schoolboy. 'Politics, Philosophy and Economics. It's what *all* the big brains do. Then they usually end up in politics. I had her down for a future prime minister, so God knows what made her decide to come here. But she's sporty too, so perhaps that's what's hooked her in.'

While Pippa continued to chatter away, apparently unperturbed by his monosyllabic answers, Jack's thoughts centred wholly on Gemma Page. So, not a dumb blonde, he reflected. Eventually, his reverie was interrupted by the sound of chairs scraping on the floor as the candidates started to leave the table. Jack managed to slide away from his dinner companion and sought out Mike Lawrence for a few more beers.

It was nearing midnight when he decided on bed. He knew that a hangover was already inevitable, but he didn't want it to be too severe with the obstacle course race still ahead.

Although the headquarters and main mess rooms of AOSB were based within Leighton House, the candidates were housed in rather less grand, hutted accommodation in the grounds. Outside, the still night air had taken on a cold nip that heralded frost in the morning. That meant the obstacle course would be slippery, Jack thought. He'd walked about twenty paces along the path towards his hut when he heard a voice call out behind him.

'Hey you! Loggy! Where the hell do you think you're off to so early?'

Jack recognised the voice instantly. He turned. Silhouetted in the lights shining from the main house windows stood Phillips, flanked by two others. One was Graeme Forshaw. The other was a bespectacled, beetle-like youth. Jack remained motionless facing them as they sauntered towards him.

Phillips spoke again. 'I'm sorry you're off to bed so early— I believe we have some unfinished business between us.' He was slurring his words and the alcohol was bolstering his courage.

The distance closed until only about six feet separated Jack from the other three. He quickly weighed up the odds. He already knew that Phillips presented no threat. The man was completely gutless. The general's son might be happy to stick the boot in if the other two took him down, but on his own Phillips wouldn't be able to punch his way out of a paper bag. The 'Beetle' looked pretty harmless too. Forshaw would be a more challenging prospect. He'd obviously experienced a few tussles on the rugby pitch. But rugger had rules. Street fighting had no rules. And Jack had developed a street fighter's instinct for survival.

'I don't know what you're talking about,' Jack responded.

'Oh come on, my Loggy friend, you as much as called me a coward in front of the entire Red Team today. Then I hear you're going around spreading scurrilous gossip about me.'

'Whatever!' Jack deliberately used the whiny intonation of a Californian teen, and started to turn away. He wanted to avoid the confrontation. He wasn't sure that he could win in a three-on-one situation, but he knew that he'd give it a damn good try, and that he'd probably inflict more damage than these guys were expecting in the process. But none of this was likely to enhance his chances of passing the Board. Especially if word got out.

'Adair!' Phillips was shouting now. 'You're not leaving until I get a proper apology, you fucking little pleb.'

Inside Jack's head a switch clicked on. It was the switch marked 'violence'. He stopped and revolved slowly. He no longer cared about the odds, or AOSB, or his future in the Army. Balancing lightly on the balls of his feet, arms hanging loosely by his sides, he stared Phillips straight in the eyes and spoke very deliberately. 'If you're going to do something, do it now. I saw you on the train. You were a coward then, and you're a coward now. Even with your mates to back you up. If you don't think you are, then prove me wrong. One of you, two of you, or all three of you. I don't care. Because I know cowards when I see them. So, unless you have any further business with me, I'd be obliged if you'd leave me alone.'

To his right, Jack glimpsed Forshaw step forward. He knew he had to keep the initiative if he was to stop them mobbing him and taking him down. Instinctively, his right leg flew up fast in a *savate* side kick. As his foot was about to connect, he held back, so that it missed the big man's nose by millimetres. But, rather than return his leg to the ground, Jack retained the pose Bruce Lee-style. The foot hovered threateningly in mid-air at the end of a leg that stretched out ramrod straight, locked in place by well-honed muscles. Forshaw halted, paralysed, gawping at the sole of the shoe that threatened to impact on his nose if he as much as blinked. Phillips and the Beetle froze too.

Stalemate.

Bending his knee, Jack retracted his extended foot, and carefully lowered it to the ground with feline grace.

'You want an apology, Phillips? Here's one. I'm very sorry. I'm very sorry you're a born coward, and I'm very sorry the truth hurts. Now get over it. I'm going to bed.'

Turning again, Jack strode away towards his hut. Behind him, he heard Forshaw exclaim, 'What an awful little man.'

Then another voice, no doubt the Beetle's, asked, 'But why on earth did he have the nerve to accuse *you* of being a coward, Vyvyan?'

# Chapter Nine

*Royal Military Academy Sandhurst*
The new officer cadets had received instructions to arrive at the Royal Military Academy Sandhurst by midday on the Sunday afternoon. Following signs from the main gate, those arriving by car found themselves driving along a narrow, black-tarmac road, with dense woodland pressing in from both sides. On the left, for some 300 yards, a large lake could occasionally be glimpsed through the trees. After about half a mile, a cluster of hideous grey blocks of late-1960s vintage, with the standard flat roofs of municipal buildings of that time, appeared on the right. This was Victory College. Back in 1969, the designers, Messrs Gollins, Ward and Partners, had received the Concrete Society Award for the best concrete structure of the year. The competition could not have been very stiff. And there was only so much you could do with concrete.

One hundred and eighty new cadets were due to arrive that day. Among them was Jack Adair. Soon, the new arrivals would be divided into two companies—Alamein and Amiens —each comprising three platoons of around 30 strong. Jack was disappointed to find that, rather than being housed in the imposing 19th century buildings of New or Old College, which featured heavily in the recruiting brochures, his company, Amiens, would be allocated 'overspill' accommodation in Victory College while New College underwent a makeover.

From the car park, the new cadets, burdened with suitcases, grips and the obligatory ironing boards, followed further signs to 'Reception'. Here they gained their first glimpse of their future instructors—or, at least, the non-commissioned element. Alert-looking men, sergeant-majors and colour sergeants, brandishing pace-sticks and wearing caps with the peaks 'slashed' into a severe angle, cut about briskly. Once the newcomers had had their names ticked-off against a list, they received plastic name badges and were directed to their rooms with instructions to report back to the main parade square by 1300 hours.

Jack made his way up to his room on the first floor. The accommodation was dull and mildly depressing. Going on first impressions, the only improvement over Camp Raffalli was that at least he got a room to himself. The bed was just a mattress laid on top of a long, low, wooden, chest of drawers. There were no springs. A utilitarian vanity unit, containing a small sink, occupied the centre of the wall opposite the bed. Shabby curtains, that looked as if they hadn't been washed for decades, hung limply, framing the limited view that could be gained from a long but narrow window. The smell of boot polish was all-pervading, as if the walls exhaled it.

From 1300 hours, the afternoon passed in a blur as Sandhurst's well-practised conveyor belt kicked into action. The guided tour of the Academy was conducted in platoon squads, marching in quick time. The platoon colour sergeants indicated the buildings, landmarks and other objects of interest in parade ground style, heavily laden with Army humour.

'*Eyes right!* Gentlemen, that large white building is Old College. It was designed by James Wyatt and completed in 1812. In forty-four weeks, *some* of you lucky people will be marching up its front steps, followed by the Academy adjutant on his horse, to the strains of *Auld Lang Syne*, having just received the Queen's Commission. But that is a *very* long way away. And from what I've seen so far, I'd be surprised if *any* of you made it that far. *Eyes front!*'

The induction process was carried out with ruthless efficiency. Within three hours, the cadets found that they had been issued armfuls of equipment and uniforms—some of which fitted—completed numerous administrative forms, been subjected to mandatory haircuts—for which they paid, no matter how short their hair on arrival—and gained a rough appreciation of the layout of the Academy. Also, by the end of this period, most were already marching in step. By 1800 hours, the cadets of the new intake were seated in the Academy's main lecture theatre, the Churchill Hall.

One hundred and seventy-nine new arrivals—one had got cold feet at the last minute and failed to turn up—were about to receive their first exposure to the Academy sergeant major. It was the first breathing space they'd had for several hours, and now was the time to take in the other faces around them. Jack recognised a few from AOSB, but nowhere near as many as he had expected. Mike Lawrence was there, not only in the same company—Amiens Company —but also in No.1 Platoon. He was pleased about that. He was less pleased that Vyvyan Phillips had also made it through, and also shared the same platoon. Obviously AOSB wasn't infallible. Down near the front, sitting with several other female cadets, Jack spotted Pippa Kelly and her stunning blonde friend, Gemma Page. Now *there* was someone he would like to have a lot more contact with. But, for now, the chances of that seemed pretty remote.

*'Room 'shun!'*

From somewhere near the back of the Churchill Hall, a colour sergeant bawled out the command, announcing the arrival of the Academy sergeant major. The cadets stood. Jack could hear the clicking of heavy leather shoes, each studded with thirteen iron hobnails, approaching the stage. Over to the right of the hall, the Academy sergeant major came into view as he climbed the wooden steps onto the stage. He reached the centre, turned to face his audience, and motioned for the cadets to be seated.

Warrant Officer Class One Swift MBE, Grenadier Guards, Academy Sergeant Major of the Royal Military Academy Sandhurst was a big man—in every sense. Academy sergeant majors always are. They are also always drawn from the Brigade of Guards. The Guards ethos underpins everything at Sandhurst. No matter how good a regimental sergeant major might be in any other regiment of the British Army, unless he has risen through the ranks of one of the five regiments of Foot Guards—Grenadier, Coldstream, Scots,

Irish or Welsh—he cannot be selected for the appointment of Academy sergeant major.

WOI Swift stood in the centre of the stage, feet slightly apart, arms held behind his back, the bulled toecaps on his brown shoes glinting in the spotlights. He was wearing an immaculately tailored Service Dress—the khaki parade uniform of the British Army that had changed little since the First World War. Two rows of medal ribbons adorned his left breast. Just above each elbow, picked out in white thread on a dark khaki background, was the Academy sergeant major's unique, large, circular badge of rank, bearing the royal coat-of-arms within a wreath. Tucked under one arm was an additional emblem of authority—a polished mahogany pace stick with brilliantly burnished brass points. He surveyed the room, dominating it. He knew that he had his audience in the palm of his hand.

'Good evening, ladies and gentlemen. My name is Swift... as in "fast". I am the Academy sergeant major, and I am *the most senior* warrant officer class one in the entire British Army.' His voice resonated around the large hall. It was a voice accustomed to command. It was a voice that brooked no argument.

He paused to let this significant piece of information sink in.

'Any of you destined for the Royal Logistic Corps may think that I am wrong about this. You may think that the conductor, Royal Logistic Corps, actually holds this privileged position.'

Jack sat up at the mention of his sponsoring cap badge. During his 'taster' visit to the Corps before attending AOSB, he had heard the proud boast that the ancient and exclusively-RLC appointment of 'conductor' was *the* most senior non-commissioned rank in the entire British Army. Now it looked as if there was some debate about this.

'If any of you ladies or gentlemen are sufficiently misinformed to think that, then you are wrong. Because if you mention "drill" to a conductor, Royal Logistic Corps, his first thought will be a piece of DIY machinery for making holes. You take my point.' Restrained laughter rippled round the room.

'Now, I wouldn't want to ruffle any regimental sensitivities here, so, if any of you wish to challenge me on this point, I am perfectly happy to hear your argument. Not that it will make any difference.'

He paused again, awaiting any note of dissent. None came.

'Right,' he continued. 'It is clear that you all understand my position perfectly. Now, let me talk to you about *your* position. You ladies and gentlemen are officer cadets. That means you hold the equivalent rank of private. You will therefore be subject to all the rigours and privations of military service that apply to other private soldiers.'

Jack detected one or two involuntary looks of apprehension from around the room. *This* hadn't been mentioned in the recruiting brochures!

'In forty-four weeks' time, any of you that are deemed suitable to hold the Queen's Commission will graduate from this Academy and will then be entitled to all the trappings and marks of respect that go with being an officer in Her Majesty's British Army. Until that time, the only acknowledgement that you will have of your current status is that all non-commissioned soldiers within this establishment will call you "Sir" or "Ma'am". Likewise, *you* will refer to *me* as "Sir".'

Another pause.

'The difference is that *you* will mean it.'

'Now, a word to you on dress. Ladies and gentlemen, you may not believe it, but I too own a pair of jeans.' Mr Swift released this information with due gravity, as though revealing some shocking insight into his personal life.

'But *I* only wear them on Sunday mornings when I am washing the car. And, even then, only when nobody else can see me. When I have finished washing the car, I change back into a decent pair of cavalry twill trousers, along with a Vyella shirt in Tattersall check and a country tie, ready to partake off Mrs Swift's mouth-watering Sunday lunch.'

The Academy sergeant major lingered again, as if dreaming wistfully of roast beef and all the trimmings.

'Some of you officer cadets turning up here this afternoon looked as if you were auditioning for the *X Factor*. Well, let me tell you, if you continue to look like that then the only "x" that will apply to you will be "ex" as in "ex-cadets". I would remind you that you are no longer scruffy layabout students. You are aspiring to be commissioned officers in *my* Army. From today, the Queen, heaven help her, is even paying you for that privilege. So I expect you to dress accordingly. This means that when you are off duty, unless you happen to be washing your car, or getting ready for bed in your natty, paisley-patterned, silk pyjamas and polka dot cravats, you will also wear ties. And jackets. Of good taste and befitting your new status. From a decent tailor. Not some off-the-peg, ready-fit tat from George at Asda.'

Jack found himself wondering whether anyone still wore pyjamas these days and, if so, whether they were likely to be of the paisley-patterned silk variety.

'Now, welcome to the Royal Military Academy Sandhurst. You have chosen an honourable career. A career of which you can be proud. For those of you that survive the forthcoming five weeks of initial training, the next time I shall probably see you is when you attend Academy drill parade. In the meantime, good luck. You *will* need it. Colour sergeants, carry on.'

Academy Sergeant Major Swift turned smartly to his right and marched from the stage. The process of breaking the new officer cadets down and rebuilding them the way the Army wanted had begun.

# Chapter Ten

Bulling boots: tedious, time-consuming, repetitive. Take the cloth. Dab it in water. Allow it to dampen—but not too much. Tap the surface of the polish—black *Kiwi*, nothing else will do. *Kiwi Parade Gloss* if you can get it. Just a touch, no more. Then apply. Rubbing gently in inch-wide circles. Round, and round, and round. Until at last the finest shiny film appears. The first inkling of a glossy veneer. Faintly misty, gradually transforming into a dark mirror. After an hour you can see your face in it. But that's not good enough. When you can read a page of a book reflected by dim candlelight at five paces, then it might just pass muster. Gleaming, yet fragile: the glistening layer needing only a touch to mar its looking-glass surface. A careless step likely to send a shimmering flake scuffing off the toe-cap. So fragile that the boots must be carried onto the parade square and only donned at the last minute for fear of causing catastrophic damage to that lustrous finish.

The new intake's first day had not ended with the exit of the Academy sergeant major. There had been yet more introductory speeches, initial interviews for some, a lesson on ironing kit and, as tradition demanded, a demonstration of that arcane practice, bulling boots. The latter would occupy the cadets for many, many hours outside the published curriculum. It was a perfect, yet subtle, sleep deprivation technique.

On the second day Jack encountered the commander of No.1 Platoon, Amiens Company, face-to-face for the first time. Although only thirty years old, Captain Robert McAlease of the Queen's Royal Hussars seemed a product of a different era. He had the open, boyish, 'Let's go, chaps!' kind of face of a perpetual Head Boy. Jack could picture him leading his troops over the top at the Somme—to be cut down seconds later by enemy machine guns. McAlease had a simple view of life, which revolved around three passions: soldiering, outdoor pursuits and Christianity—he'd 'found God' during an Army climbing expedition to Nepal. He also had a wife. She supported him in all of his passions... and came a very close second to them.

In the captain's perfectly packaged world, aspiring officers went to a good school, where they played rugger and became prefects. Then they went on to university—a proper university, mind, none of this former-polytechnic nonsense—joined the Officers' Training Corps and gained a Second Class degree (a First might suggest an overly keen interest in books). After university they didn't just apply to join 'the Army'—that's what the common herd did. 'Proper' officers joined 'a regiment'. That was the tricky bit, getting a decent regiment to take you. But if you could do that, then the Army Officer Selection Board was a mere formality.

Captain McAlease felt most comfortable with others who fitted this neat mould. Unfortunately, the soldiers beneath him were so far removed from it he thought they might as well have come from a different species. The feeling was mutual. They thought he was a tosser.

It was late on the evening of the second day when Jack's turn for an initial interview came around. Captain McAlease had a small office within Victory College Headquarters, a short walk along the internal corridors from the cadets' accommodation. Waiting outside the office was the platoon's colour sergeant, Des Slater of the Grenadier Guards.

Slater spoke first. 'Okay, Mr Adair, come up to attention and let me look at you.' The colour sergeant's eyes flicked over Jack from head to toe, taking in every detail.

He spoke again. 'Not too bad, well done. Now, nothing to be nervous about. I'll open the door and tell the captain that you're here. As soon as he's ready to see you, I'll march you in and halt you in front of his desk. You then salute. Just like you were taught this morning. Think you can do that?'

'Yes, Colour Sergeant. No probs,' said Jack, thinking, 'You just don't know how many times I've done this before. Just have to remember not to give a French Army salute!'

'Good lad. Then let's go.'

Slater knocked on the door and stuck his head round. Seconds later, Jack found himself being marched in with the colour sergeant's words of command ringing in his ears. *'Left, right, left, right! Mark time! Halt! Salute! Stand still!'*

Behind the desk sat an officer wearing a uniform shirt of such a light shade of cream that it was almost white. Three very discreet small pips, denoting his captain's rank, adorned each shoulder. His eyes bored into Jack throughout his performance as if judging a contestant in an ice-skating competition. Jack almost expected him to hold up a scorecard.

'Officer Cadet Adair, sah,' barked the colour sergeant.

'Thank you, Colour Sar'nt. You may leave. Stand at ease, Adair.'

With a further crash of boots, and a whip-crack salute, Slater exited the room.

The captain picked up a large file, flicked to a particular section and began to confirm Jack's details.

'Aged twenty-six?'

'Sir.'

'Not a graduate?'

'No, sir.'

'Spent the last five years in France?'

'Sir.'

'And tell me what that was all about.'

Jack had already decided that he was going to keep quiet about his previous military service until he'd judged the lie of the land. He wanted to start with a blank sheet. So he trotted out the story that he'd previously prepared about travelling and doing odd jobs to get by—like driving and bartending. Although he knew that the details of his Foreign Legion service were held by the British Army, he doubted whether they had filtered down as far as his platoon commander. He was right.

McAlease seemed unimpressed by what he heard. He flicked the folder shut and tossed it carelessly down onto the desk.

'Sounds like you've been a bit rootless to me. So why have you decided to join the Army now? Is this just another short-term project in the life of young Mister Adair, until you get bored with us?'

'No, sir. I'd always intended to have an Army career, sir.'

'Just took you a while to get round to it. Is that a fair comment?'

'Sir.' Jack realised there was no point arguing about it.

'And I see you've been sponsored by the Royal Logistic Corps. Well, your van driving experience should come in useful. I suppose you're the sort of chap who feels that he's better off dealing with stuff rather than people. Still... very important work all the same,' he said unconvincingly. 'Not the sort of job I'd like to do myself. I'd rather close with the Queen's enemies and defeat them in detail. But horses for courses and all that.'

Jack had already made his assessment of McAlease. It came down to one word: tosser!

After Jack had left, Des Slater re-entered the office.

'What do you think, sir?'

'Well, hardly the best of the bunch,' replied the captain. 'Surly, truculent, evenly balanced... in that he has a chip on *both* shoulders.' He paused to chuckle at the old joke, while the colour sergeant remained impassive. 'I suppose AOSB must've seen something in him, but I'm blowed if I can. Hardly likely to be the life and soul of the officers' mess. Still, he's going to the Royal Logistic Corps, so I don't suppose it matters so much. Wouldn't have him in my regiment though, that's for sure. I suggest you keep an eye on him, he may be pretty borderline. Now, let's see the next man.'

'Sah!' Colour Sergeant Slater slammed to attention, saluted, turned to the right and marched from the office. Eleven years in the Grenadier Guards had taught him the value of displaying total, unquestioning loyalty to the chain of command. Sometimes, albeit rarely, it was genuine. More often, it was for display purposes only. His loyalty to Captain McAlease fell into the latter category. As he left the office, he silently mouthed one word: 'Tosser!'

# Chapter Eleven

After the first five weeks' training, the two companies of the Junior Term would 'Pass off the Square'. That is, they would parade before the Academy adjutant to face a test of foot drill and basic Academy knowledge. It was their opportunity to demonstrate that they had been totally absorbed into the military machine. If the Sandhurst method was intended to break individuals down before building them back up again the way the Army wanted them, then Passing off the Square was where the rebuilding process commenced.

For the first five weeks the pace had been relentless. Drill and more drill. Arms swinging high. Boots slamming into the parade ground surface. Physical training till their lungs were close to bursting. From gym to assault course to training area —climbing ropes, vaulting obstacles and running. Always running. But there was a lot to learn as well: lectures and field exercises on weapon handling, first aid, radio procedure, low-level tactics and patrolling. And, every day, at the end of all that, there was bulling. Late into the night. In small groups or alone. Polishing and polishing. Fingers moving in circles. Round and round and round. Dye seeping from wet bulling cloths into the cadets' fingers. When standing at ease, hands clasped behind their backs, the evidence could be seen in the yellow-tinged index fingers. An uninitiated observer might mistake them for nicotine stains. Old soldiers knew better. They reminisced, smiled at the memory and... pitied.

Unless travelling in trucks to the various training areas to practise the essentials of dismounted infantry combat, the cadets were forbidden to leave the Academy. Nor could they invite guests onto the base. Sleep became a rare and precious commodity—there was a very good reason why the main lecture theatre, the Churchill Hall, was known as the 'Concrete Sleeping Bag'. They reached the point where they could fall asleep anywhere: in lectures, in the backs of trucks, on the rifle range... even standing up. The instructors knew the score. They knew that every time a practice night fighting patrol halted for a few minutes on the training area while the patrol commander checked his bearings, somebody would be left behind gently snoring when the time came to move on.

Through all of this, and almost imperceptibly, the cadets were developing their leadership skills. Eventually, they would learn to act as a team. But that was still to come. In the meantime, 'leadership' just meant telling people what to do—usually by shouting the loudest. Most, but not all, would quickly realise that this didn't work so well when twenty-nine others in the platoon were all doing the same.

As Passing off the Square drew near, the new platoons found themselves in fierce competition. None could risk falling short of the mark. For the platoon commanders and platoon colour sergeants, failure would count as a personal humiliation. For the cadets, it would mean another week confined within the perimeter of the Academy without privileges, awaiting a re-test.

With success being so vital, in the week leading up to the test the platoon colour sergeants rehearsed their cadets relentlessly in the required drill. As an extra precaution, the company sergeant major conducted his own dress rehearsal of Amiens Company two days before the event.

Company Sergeant Major Bruce Anderson had joined the Army straight from school at seventeen. With a few minor scrapes with the law under his belt, and barely any educational qualifications, it was the obvious place to go.

The regime was tough. Bullying remained rife, despite the Army's attempts to crack down. As the Army's future infantrymen, aggression and the will to win were highly prized, but such attributes were difficult to turn off when the day's instruction ended. In the rough and tumble of basic training, Bruce Anderson thrived. A big lad, fast with his fists, he'd had an older brother serving with the King's Royal Rangers and, unlike many, had a good idea of what he was letting himself in for. But his brother was already dead. Killed in a gun battle with the IRA, the tragedy had acted as a catalyst to Bruce's ambition. In his mind, the Army was the best way—possibly the only way—of seeking revenge. And Bruce Anderson was very much an eye for an eye kind of guy.

Within a year of his brother's death, Bruce had followed him into the King's Royal Rangers. But, with the Peace Process taking effect in Northern Ireland, he never had his chance to seek his revenge. By then, the British Army was looking elsewhere for its battles—to Bosnia, Kosovo, Sierra Leone, Iraq and Afghanistan—taking Bruce Anderson with it. Although his thirst for vengeance remained unslaked, he continued to flourish, climbing steadily through the ranks to warrant officer class two and a prestigious post as one of the company sergeant majors at Sandhurst. With just over three years left to serve, he had already been notified that further promotion and a return to the King's Royal Rangers for a tour as the regimental sergeant major was next on the cards. Beyond that, he might even gain a captain's commission and, with it, a career through to fifty-five. Life was good

No. 1 Platoon of Amiens Company was drawn up for inspection on New College Square awaiting Sergeant Major Anderson's arrival. The platoon's colour sergeant, Des Slater, would have liked to have marched the cadets about at 'quick time' first, to warm them up and get their brains working, but he couldn't risk the damage that it would do the immaculate, glasslike sheen of their boots. So the cadets waited, at ease, in the cold morning air, as the tips of their fingers first started to sting, then went numb.

From the left of the parade square came the aggressive crunch of iron-studded boots. Eyes swivelled, apprehension rising, as Sergeant Major Anderson came into view, marching directly towards Colour Sergeant Slater at the head of No. 1 Platoon. He slammed to a halt, with a well-practised, short theatrical skid.

Anderson spoke first: 'Good morning, Colour Sergeant.'

'Number One Platoon drawn up awaiting your inspection, Sah!' Slater barked in response.

'Please carry on.'

The pair moved towards the right-hand marker, the sergeant major leading. The inspection did not start well.

Anderson glared at the first man. 'What's that on your beret?'

'Don't know, Company Sergeant Major.'

'It's a hair, you idle layabout, a hair. That thing on your bonce is supposed to be an item of military headgear; not an entry for Crufts Dog Show! Get down and give me twenty press-ups. *Go!*'

He moved along the line. The second cadet, James Lonsdale, blinked nervously from behind circular horn-rimmed glasses. Anderson stared back. And stared harder. He knew Lonsdale. Everybody did. His father had commanded the SAS, so there was great anticipation prior to his arrival at the Academy. Would the son be cut from the same cloth? Apparently not. The tall, thin, bespectacled and somewhat tweedy young man who turned up on day one looked as if he'd taken the wrong turn on the way to theological college and somehow found himself in a military academy. That possibly explained the look of slight bemusement that he habitually wore.

'You in there, Lonsdale?' Anderson demanded, as if struggling to see through the glasses.

'Y-y-yes, Company Sergeant Major,' Lonsdale replied uncertainly.

'Oh good, 'cos I can't see you with all the fucking dust on your lenses. Get down and give me twenty. *Go!*'

Jack Adair was third in line. The sergeant major scrutinised him like a buyer in a slave auction. Starting at the top and moving down, his eyes travelled slowly, taking in every detail, looking for the slightest deviation from perfection. At six feet three inches, Bruce Anderson was the same height as Jack. Their eyes met. For a second, Jack thought he detected just the slightest flicker of recognition in the sergeant major's eyes. But then it was gone.

Having failed to find fault with Jack's turnout, Anderson snapped out a question. 'What is the year of death shown on the Prince Imperial's statue?'

'1879, sir!' Jack barked back. It was an easy one for him. Only two days earlier he'd been thrown out of class for falling asleep, with orders to get to the statue and back in two minutes—with the date. Probably half the rest of the platoon also knew the answer. It was a common punishment for a common offence.

'Correct. Well done.' CSM Anderson started to move on. He had taken half a pace, when he paused and turned back. Once again, he stared into Jack's eyes.

'Name?' he asked.

'Officer Cadet Adair, Company Sergeant Major.'

'Have we met before, Mister Adair?'

'No, Company Sergeant Major.'

'Funny, your face looks familiar.'

With that, Anderson continued with the inspection, but his mind seemed to be elsewhere. Every now and then, he would glance back in Jack's direction. Whatever it was that had thrown him off his stride, the platoon was grateful.

Bruce Anderson had been married once. Like the marriages of so many of his colleagues in the sergeants' mess, it hadn't lasted. He'd returned from exercise one day to find her gone. At first, he thought she might just be out shopping, or perhaps visiting friends. But then it had started to get dark, and there was still no sign of her reappearing. Eventually, he'd started to make a closer inspection around the house. Something wasn't quite right. The first inkling he'd had was when he noticed the absence of several of her precious photographs. The clincher had been when he'd opened her wardrobe door and found it empty.

She'd turned up eventually. By that time, he'd been home for four hours and, out of his mind with worry, had telephoned her parents. They'd put on a good act of sounding surprised, although later he'd discovered that they'd known exactly where she was and what she was up to the whole time.

When she finally appeared, her new man was sitting outside in a car, 'for her protection'. He might have been wiser to worry about his own protection. Bruce Anderson was less upset about the prospect of losing his wife than the fact that some pasty-faced, middle-aged office worker with a pot belly had been shagging her behind his back. Retribution was swift and bloody. Bruce Anderson was very much an eye for an eye kind of guy.

For the past six years since the break-up, he had been an occupant of the sergeants' mess. Over time, he'd developed a well-established and comfortable routine. After work, he would take a three-mile run, followed by a shower, then dinner and two or three pints in the mess bar before bed. But today was different. Something had happened during Amiens Company's rehearsal, and he couldn't quite put his finger on it. It had something to do with that officer cadet, Adair, from No.1 Platoon—he looked familiar, but Anderson was sure that he'd never met him before.

After dinner, he bought a bottle of Famous Grouse whisky from the bar and retired to his room. The television was on, but he wasn't watching it—his mind was too busy travelling down endless different avenues, chasing thoughts that were mere shadows, sifting what little information he had, trying to grasp something that made sense. He'd sunk half of the bottle of whisky before the merest glimmer of an idea started to intrude on his increasingly fuzzy brain. At first he dismissed it. But maybe it wasn't as nonsensical as it first seemed. The more he thought about it....

The sergeant major was a neat man. If he were to own a garden shed, different sizes of nails would be segregated into their own marked tins and kept on a shelf with all of the labels facing the same way. Even after half a bottle of whisky, he knew exactly where to put his hands on what he wanted. At the back of the only wardrobe in the room, on the lowest shelf, was a box that had once housed his wedding album. The album had long since found its way onto a bonfire. Now the box contained other photographs that Bruce Anderson held precious. Sitting on the floor with the box resting on his lap, he lifted the lid and skimmed through the contents. It was easy to find the one he was after. It was larger than the rest—a group photograph in a white cardboard frame showing the individuals' names and ranks in black print along the bottom edge. At the top, along with a regimental crest, was a title engraved in gold. It read: No. 2 Platoon, A Company, 1st Battalion, King's Royal Rangers, Tidworth, August 1996. His brother's platoon.

Anderson's eyes swept quickly across the faces, matching them to the names on the white border. He concentrated on the front rank first. His search took less than ten seconds before he found what he was after. He stared intently at the features gazing blankly out of the picture, tilting the cardboard frame slightly to gain more light. Then he sank back, his head resting against the wall behind him, his eyes fixed on the ceiling, his arms dropping limply to his sides, the photograph still clutched in his right hand.

'Well, fancy that,' he whispered to himself. And as his mind churned over, a plan started to form. Because Bruce Anderson was an eye for an eye kind of guy.

# Chapter Twelve

Amiens Company was going into the field. Again. While the basic building blocks of tactics could be practised on Sandhurst's local training area, Barossa Common—a pleasant patch of Surrey heathland adjoining the Academy—it was necessary to go further afield to find more testing conditions. For Exercise *Second Flush*, the destination would be Stanford Training Area in Norfolk. Here the cadets would spend five days in freezing conditions, being constantly scrutinised, evaluated... and tormented... by the Directing Staff.

Colour Sergeant Slater had pinned the team lists to the platoon notice board, and Vyvyan Phillips was one of the first on the scene. He was quick to vent his feelings.

'Oh my Christ, what a bloody awful group! Two non-teeth arm men and a shagging raghead. That makes three non-swimmers out of four!'

'Oh, you'll be all right, Vyvyan. The cream will always rise to the top,' drawled an unseen voice.

'I don't know—I think I'll have my work cut out. You can take a non-swimmer to water, but you can't make him swim. And I've got three of the buggers.'

Jack could hear the exchange in the corridor outside his room. He'd already seen the list. By chance, he'd been near the platoon notice board just as it was posted. He'd taken a brief look, seen his name, seen Phillips's name above it as team leader, said one word, 'Fuck', and walked away.

It was about five minutes later that he heard Phillips outside in the corridor. That he didn't simply stroll out and rip the general's son a new arsehole at least said something for the modifying effect that Sandhurst was having on his temper. The only redeeming feature was that the team also contained Mike Lawrence. The fourth member was one of the foreign students who made up around ten per cent of the company, Asad bin Hashim—an officer cadet on detachment from the Saudi Arabian National Guard.

A cold winter sun was hanging over the Academy when the three coaches carrying Amiens Company set out for Exercise *Second Flush*. As they travelled further north, the conditions grew progressively bleaker. Just before afternoon faded into dusk, lines of sleet could be seen lashing the surrounding countryside like tracer rounds. By the time the coaches began nudging carefully along country lanes to the designated drop-off points on the training area, the adjacent fields were already covered with a foot of snow.

The plan was simple. The cadets had been organised into teams of four. Every team was allocated its own drop-off point, with several hundred yards between each. The exercise would commence as soon as the cadets left the coaches.

From their starting positions, under cover of darkness, the teams had to infiltrate independently across ten kilometres of 'enemy territory'. Trying to stop them would be Gurkha troops from Sandhurst's own Demonstration Company, who would patrol the area and establish ambush positions along likely approach routes, ably assisted by some of Amiens Company's senior NCOs. By first light, all of the teams would assemble at a pre-arranged rendezvous, ready to launch a dawn attack on an enemy-held bridge.

As No. 1 Platoon's coach disappeared into the distance, its tyres carving further ruts in the snow, the four officer cadets were left by the side of the road making final adjustments to their equipment. After dozing in a warm coach for several hours, all were now feeling the effects of the bitingly cold wind that cut across the landscape. Phillips had a torch out and was carefully perusing the map as he orientated himself to the ground. The other three hoisted their packs onto their shoulders and clustered round him, leaning forward slightly to ease the weight on their shoulders, SA80 rifles cradled in the crooks of their arms.

'Come on,' urged Mike Lawrence. 'The longer we hang around here, the colder we're going to get. We need to start moving or the Gurkhas will come and nab us before we've even left the drop-off point.'

'Okay, okay, calm yourself. Anyway, I need a fag,' Phillips replied.

'Oh for fuck's sake,' muttered Jack, just loud enough to be heard.

'What's the matter, Adair? I suppose your body's a temple?'

'Mike's right. The longer we hang around here, the colder we're going to get. Now let's just get a flipping move on.'

'Don't worry, my little Loggy friend,' said Phillips, stowing the map and lighting up a cigarette. 'You've got an infantryman in charge now. I'll get us through this all right. All I need is for you three to keep up—and that goes especially for you Asda, or whatever your name is.'

'Asad,' muttered the Arab.

'Whatever. I don't want you slowing us down just because you've never seen snow before. Now, let's get going.'

Having thoroughly pissed-off the rest of the group, Phillips took a third long draw on his fag before tossing it aside and leading the way off the road. Behind him, the team shook out into diamond formation as they moved onto the training area. Travelling at a relatively fast pace, the heat soon returned to their bodies and Jack began to enjoy the peacefulness of the snow-covered terrain. Stark black trees standing out against the surrounding white carpet reminded him of night manoeuvres at the French Army's commando training centre high in the Pyrenees. A constant but moderate breeze occasionally lifted small swirls of snow dust like mini-tornadoes.

Every few hundred metres they would stop so that Phillips could check the map, shrouding his upper body with a groundsheet to screen the light from his torch. While he verified their location, the others would drop into all round defence, weapons pointing out into the darkness ready to engage the enemy in an instant.

They'd tabbed for about five kilometres, and were approaching a small wood, when there was a barely audible rustle in the clump of trees immediately ahead. Phillips raised his hand as the signal to halt, and the cadets sank down on one knee, rifles at the ready.

Silence.

They continued to hold the position for another couple of minutes, before Phillips rose to his feet as the signal to press on.

This time they moved more slowly, treading with delicate precision to minimise the noise as snow yielded underfoot. Each deftly placed footfall seeming as loud as a shoebox being crushed. Eyes raking the tree line in front for the slightest sign of movement. Ears straining to detect the faintest whisper. Drawing ever closer to the tree line.

When a machine gun fired it was like a sharp slap in the face. A sudden rasping burst of blank rounds spattered out from the bushes ahead. Asad immediately fell to the ground —maybe deliberately taking cover; more likely through shock. Phillips and Mike Lawrence both froze. Jack loosed off five rounds rapid fire at the tree line, and shouted one word, 'Run!' Four Gurkhas erupted from the undergrowth ahead of them, kicking up snow as they ran and working hard to close the distance.

The team fragmented, swerving left and right, Phillips pairing up with Asad, and Jack with Mike Lawrence.

Jack saw the other two heading back into the open ground, struggling to sprint and hampered by their backpacks. Anticipating that the Gurkhas would chase the more obvious target, he grabbed Mike by the arm and pulled him into the nearest bush. It was a risky move, but running into the open looked suicidally stupid. The only hope was that the Gurkhas would dash straight past. It was a forlorn hope. Within thirty seconds, he could see at least four pairs of feet spread out at even intervals around the bush, weapons pointing in his direction.

Jack and Mike resigned themselves to capture and emerged from the bush. They were quickly disarmed.

'This way. This way. You come,' ordered a Gurkha wearing the two stripes of a corporal on the chest tab of his combat jacket. He gestured with the muzzle of his weapon. With at least two other SA-80s still covering them, they retraced their steps back to the clump of trees where the ambush party had been hiding. Passing through it, they found two more Gurkhas already removing a large camouflage net from a Land Rover that had been carefully concealed behind the tree line.

The corporal indicated that they should take their packs and webbing off, then motioned with his rifle for them to climb into the back of the vehicle. The corporal clambered into the front passenger seat alongside the driver, while the rest of the Gurkhas crammed in alongside Jack and Mike.

The Land Rover set off slowly across the training area, its headlights off, slipping on the snow and ice, and lurching from side to side as it negotiated unseen ruts and potholes. The back of the vehicle had been blacked out with a screen of sack-like Hessian cloth, so Jack and Mike had no idea where they were heading.

The journey across the training area must have taken at least fifteen minutes before the vehicles emerged onto a slush-covered tarmac road. The driver flicked the headlights on, and Jack and Mike were aware of being driven at speed through the darkness. The Gurkhas on either side of them started to nod with tiredness, exacerbated by the mounting heat inside the vehicle. Jack picked up the distinctive smell of khaini, a chewing tobacco mixed with slaked lime, popular with the Gurkhas. Eventually, the Land Rover slowed down and turned sharp left into what appeared to be some sort of training camp. Looking through a small gap past the driver's shoulder, Jack could see a red and white barrier pole being raised by a sentry, illuminated by the lights of a guard room situated in a black wooden hut to the left of the gate.

The driver continued forward for about another fifty metres before swinging the Land Rover into a parking area. As the vehicle came to a halt, those Gurkhas that had been dozing began to stir themselves and scramble out.

The shouting started almost immediately.

'Come on! Let's be having you! Let's see which useless tossers have fallen into the net!'

There was no mistaking the voice. It was Company Sergeant Major Anderson.

# Chapter Thirteen

*West Tofts Camp, Stanford Training Area, Norfolk*
Jack emerged blinking from the back of the Land Rover
and was immediately blinded by a 70,000-candlepower
Dragonlight torch being directed straight into his face from
less than three feet away. As the torch swung away, he could
see Anderson, lips curling with barely suppressed fury, and a
rain of spittle flecking from his mouth as he continued to
hurl abuse.

'Who've we got here? Aah! Mister Adair and Mister
fucking Lawrence. Of all the idle, incompetent, useless young
gentlemen to get caught, it just had to be you two. Well,
"sirs", this is going to be a night to remember, make no
mistake.'

To Anderson's left stood Colour Sergeant Slater, shaking
his head in mock despair. 'You've really let me down, lads,'
he muttered, sounding genuinely aggrieved that two of *his*
platoon should get nabbed.

'Right, leave your weapons and kit here—the Gurkhas will take charge of 'em—and follow me,' Anderson snarled with a hint of menace.

In single file, Jack and Mike followed the sergeant major across the compound of the small training camp and along a narrow path that passed between several wooden huts. A short walk brought them to a basic shower block—a stand-alone brick building with a corrugated iron roof. Inside, the walls were lined with a row of urinals on the left and sinks on the right. A communal shower facility stood at the far end— unscreened by a curtain and with six large shower heads pointing down towards the bare concrete floor. Anderson marched straight towards it, stepped inside and, one by one, swivelled the taps. Six streams of water gushed towards the central drainage hole. There was no steam. The showers were running cold.

Stepping back from the shower area, the sergeant major extracted a small notebook from the breast pocket of his combat jacket and slapped it down on a six-foot bench that stood in the centre of the room. His eyes bored into the two cadets standing before him. The look was venomous, verging on utter hatred.

'Right, gentlemen, I think it's obvious what's gonna happen to you. Colour Sergeant Slater and I are going to take a little stroll outside for two minutes. Just long enough to have a fag. You are to use those minutes to good advantage. By the time we get back, I want to see that notebook filled with information: who your platoon commander is; where you're going; how many of you there are; what your mission is; any special code names or passwords; any timings. In fact, anything and everything about the op you're on. If that notebook's not full of your scribble in minutes few, it's shower time!' Anderson nodded his head in the direction of the cold jets of water streaming from six shower heads.

'Frankly, gentlemen,' Anderson continued, 'I hope you don't write anything down, 'cos it's gonna give me the very greatest pleasure to see you two useless muppets getting an early bath. Don't say you haven't been warned. Come on, Colour, let's go for a gasper, and leave these two numpties to their writing.'

The pair strutted out of the shower room, locking its green wooden door behind them.

Mike Lawrence looked mournfully at Jack, as if the bottom had just dropped out of his world. 'What the heck do we do now?'

'I don't know about you, but I'm going out of that!'

Mike followed Jack's gaze. High up in one corner of the shower room was a small window. Covered in rust and cobwebs, it looked like it hadn't been opened in years. Chances were, it wouldn't open now. Chances were, even if it did, it would be too narrow to squeeze through. But it was worth a shot.

Jack dragged the wooden bench across the room until it was beneath the window. Mike watched him dubiously.

'But we can't do that. It's not in the rules. They'll bloody well kill us.'

'Look, we've got less than two minutes. Sticking us under a cold shower when it's snowing like buggery outside isn't in the rules either. So if they're gonna break the rules, so am I. We haven't got time to argue about it. Either you're coming with me, or I'm going on my own. But I'm going. Now!'

'Okay... I'm with you,' said Mike with only the slightest trace of hesitation.

Jack jumped up on the bench and tried to release the catch on the window. There was no give in it at all. Layers of paint and rust had built up over the years to form a rigid seal.

'Quick, give me something hard,' Jack demanded urgently.

'I didn't know you cared,' Mike grinned.

'We haven't got time to fuck about. Give me something I can knock this with. A torch, a clasp knife... anything.'

Mike fumbled inside his combat jacket, produced a metal-cased Maglite torch, and passed it up. Jack immediately started hammering with it against the stubborn window catch. It flew up at the third smack and the cold night air drifted in. Jack heaved himself up into the opening, gave a quick check left and right, and started to wriggle through. With his upper body clear, he bent forwards at the waist, let go and dropped head first into the cushion of snow outside.

'Right, come on, you need to get a move on,' he whispered sharply.

Seconds later, Mike's head appeared. His shoulders slid through without too much trouble. There was momentary panic when it looked like his hips were about to jam, but a quick tug on his arms by Jack had him tumbling forwards into the snow.

Jack jumped up to flip the window shut behind them, then looked around for some immediate cover. A rubbish skip standing between two of the huts about twenty yards away offered the answer. Grabbing the front of Mike's combat jacket, he rushed him across the gap between the huts.

'Quick, into the skip, and let's just hope they don't spot our tracks in the snow.'

As they ducked down amongst the rubbish—piles of cardboard boxes, scraps of wood and discarded floor tiles—pandemonium broke out inside the shower block. The shouting travelled a long way in the still night air.

'The little bastards have fucking disappeared! Where the fuck have they got to?'

Anderson and Slater could be heard racing back out of the building into the compound.

'Mr Adair and Mr fucking Lawrence, you two are bloody well dead when we get you. *Get out here now!'* roared Anderson.

Colour Sergeant Slater joined in the rant. 'This is now a disciplinary matter. This is nothing to do with the exercise. You show yourselves now or you won't know what hit you when we get back.'

Giving a resigned shrug, Mike started to move. 'We'd better do what they say,' he whispered.

'You can, if you like, but you could at least give me the chance to get clear before you give the game away,' Jack hissed back.

Mike sank back down into the skip.

Outside, the uproar continued. And so did the threats. After ten minutes, being shot at dawn sounded like the most merciful option the officer cadets could expect. While Anderson hollered, Slater cajoled. Mr Nasty and Mr Nice. Several times their boots could be heard crunching through the snow near the skip. Jack and Mike stiffened and held their breaths, but no one looked in.

After a while, the camp returned to silence.

'So, what now, Houdini?' ventured Mike.

Jack shifted awkwardly in the skip and thought for a few seconds, assessing their options. Although they could make a run for it, without their weapons they'd be of no use to the platoon, and without their kit, in freezing conditions, they'd actually be a danger to themselves. No, if they were going to pull this off successfully, they had to be an asset, not a burden, when they finally tracked down the platoon.

'We need to get our kit and weapons back. We can't go anywhere without them. We can't survive, and we can't fight. So without them we might as well give up. They must've put them in one of the buildings. Let's go and have a look.'

Leading the way, Jack crept cautiously towards the nearest hut. The entrance was through a wooden door at one end. Gingerly, he reached forward and, with all the care of a professional housebreaker, pressed down on the lever-handle. As the latch clicked free, he eased the door ajar—just enough to slip inside.

Jack's eyes adjusted to the pitch blackness inside. Shapes started to form. His foot nudged against something heavy but soft. He peered down. Despite the gloom, he could just make out the shape of a large Bergen rucksack with a rifle resting against it. And another, also propping up a weapon. He leaned forward, hands performing a finger-tip search of the immediate floor area. They made contact with what seemed like a jumble of web equipment—belts, water bottles, magazine pouches—two complete belt kits. He'd found their gear! All of it.

A slight rustle indicated movement further inside the hut. Jack stared, not sure what he was seeing. He picked out a tiny reflection as clouds parted momentarily to let in a sliver of moonlight through the partially open door behind him. Then the reflection blinked. It was an eye, and it was looking at him. A head, shrouded by a sleeping bag, started to lift off a camp cot positioned near the door. It was a Gurkha. And not just one. As Jack's eyes adapted better to the dark, he could make out virtually a platoon's worth of troops bedded down inside, their camp cots arranged in two neat rows running the length of the hut.

Jack grinned at the waking soldier and gave a thumbs-up sign. The Gurkha returned the smile and settled back down into his sleeping bag. As far as he was concerned, Jack's was just another white face.

With immense care, Jack leaned forward and extracted the two Bergens, the rifles and the webbing from the hut, passing them gingerly back to Mike in the doorway behind him. Then, with equal care, he stepped out himself and silently closed the door.

'Okay,' whispered Mike, 'what next? We've escaped and we've got our kit. But we have absolutely no idea where we are, we're probably friggin' miles from the rest of the company, and Anderson and Slater want to cut our balls off and roast them slowly over a barbecue while we watch.'

'It'll be fine,' Jack hissed back, with more confidence than he felt. 'Everything we've done so far has been text-book. You know the drill. Easiest time to escape is just after capture. Well, that's just what we've done. And we've even re-armed ourselves. We're on a roll. Nothing's gonna stop us now! We just need to go to ground long enough for them to think we've left the camp, find out where the fuck we are, then link up with the rest of the company. Easy!'

As Jack set off across the compound looking for another bolt-hole, Mike rolled his eyes in the darkness—but followed all the same.

The vehicle park where they'd been ordered out of the Land Rover was only a short distance away. Several vehicles were lined up, now covered with a fine dusting of snow. Jack started trying the rear doors. The first two were locked, but the handle of the third depressed at his touch, and the door swung open. They clambered inside.

Minutes later, furious bellowing exploded from the direction of the Gurkhas' sleeping accommodation.

'They've got their shagging kit!' bawled Anderson, registering at least a five on the Richter Scale.

'You *are* kidding me?' Slater shouted back, disbelievingly, as he jogged across to look for himself. 'You sure you're looking in the right hut?'

Huddled under a groundsheet in the back of the Land Rover, Jack started to think he might have bitten off more than he could chew. Even so, there was nothing to be gained by giving up now. The only way he could salvage the situation was to see it through. And that meant finding and re-joining Amiens Company before being intercepted by the DS. But, for the meantime, as the enraged voices receded into the distance, he closed his eyes and drifted into sleep.

# Chapter Fourteen

At 5 a.m. Lance Corporal Saunders opened the door of one of the wooden huts and gasped as the icy air hit his exposed chest. Wearing just combat trousers and flip-flops, with a towel slung around his neck, and carrying a wash bag, he began to pick his way unsteadily across the snow to the shower block. After the first ten paces, he was already regretting his decision not to pull on a T-shirt.

A driver by trade, Saunders was nearing the end of his three-year posting with the Academy's dedicated transport squadron. This was the third time he'd manned a vehicle on Exercise *Second Flush*. That's probably why the troop staff sergeant had stuck him down to drive Amiens Company's officer commanding, Major Breeze—or 'Stiffy' as he was known to the troops. It was always safer to give the OC a driver who knew every inch of the training area. After all, it wouldn't do for Stiffy to get lost. No... it wouldn't do at all. Especially as shit has a habit of rolling downhill.

Saunders didn't mind. The OC was an early riser. That was a pain in the arse. But he was pretty relaxed in the vehicle. Could even be quite funny. And, who knew, a good word from Stiffy, in the right place at the right time, might well be worth a few extra points when it came to the next Promotions Board.

He had just lathered up his face and started to shave when he heard a noise behind him. Looking into the mirror, he was surprised to see two soldiers walking into the washroom. They were dressed for the field, in combat kit, with cam-cream on their faces, wearing helmets, and carrying SA-80 rifles and Bergens. The Sandhurst cadets were out on the training area, and Saunders knew that they weren't supposed to be anywhere near the camp. So, who were these buggers?

'Excuse me, mate,' said the taller one. 'Can you tell us which camp we're in? We're kinda lost.' It was a deadpan accent. Hard to place. Not boarding school snooty like most of the cadets. He had a map in his hand, which he now held out.

Saunders didn't bother taking the map. Something just wasn't right here. 'Yeah right—that's bollocks, chum!' he challenged. 'No one... I mean like no one... wanders around a training camp in uniform, carrying weapons, and doesn't know what bastard camp they're in. So what's going on, lads? And if you don't spill in double quick time, I'm straight off down the guard room. So, what's it gonna be?'

Jack weighed up the odds of getting the Lance Corporal on side. Looked like he didn't have a choice. 'We're with Amiens Company, okay?'

'Amiens? Then what the hell are you doing here? You're bloody miles off course.'

Jack did his best to look hopeless. 'We were part of a team that got ambushed last night. We got nabbed by the DS and brought here. Trouble is, they drove us around for half an hour in the back of a blacked-out Land Rover, so we haven't a bloody Scooby where we've ended up.'

'So what's the score now then? Is this some kind of initiative test? I suppose they gave you all your kit back and told you to hop it back to the exercise. Yeah?' Saunders ventured.

'No.'

'No?'

'No. Sarn't Major Anderson and Colour Sarn't Slater locked us in the shower room and told us they'd be back to interrogate us. Much as we were looking forward to that little treat, our social diaries were simply too busy, so we had to make our excuses and leave.'

'What? And they just let you go?'

'No, we legged it out the window.'

'Fuck me! They'll be bloody furious.'

'They are. Now, we've got a map, and we know where we're supposed to be going. We just need to know where we're starting from. Can you help?'

Saunders beamed. 'Oh yes, gentlemen. It will be my *absolute* pleasure. Allow me!'

About half an hour later, still grinning to himself, Lance Corporal Saunders was standing at the head of the queue for early breakfast in the cookhouse. As the chefs brought the food out onto the hotplates, two individuals barged in front of him. It was Anderson and Slater, and they weren't smiling.

The sergeant major turned and looked Saunders up and down.

'What you fucking looking at, Saunders? You fancy me or something?'

'No, sir.'

'I don't fucking believe you. Get down and give me twenty push-ups.'

'What for, Sergeant Major?'

'Don't you "what for?" me. Just get down and do 'em. And I'll tell you what for. Because you are having a fucking easy time on this exercise just driving around the company commander, while everyone else is working their shagging balls off. That's what for.'

The chef standing behind the hot plate with serving ladle in hand laughed. He also thought Saunders had landed an easy number. More to the point, he didn't want to get on the wrong side of Anderson.

Saunders assumed the position and started pushing them out.

'And to make matters worse,' Anderson continued, 'two of the "young gentlemen" that we picked up last night have somehow escaped, and are now swanning around the training area, in the snow, doing their own shagging thing, when they're supposed to be taking part in an all singing, all dancing, company attack on a bridge this morning. So, if you happen to see either of 'em in your travels, you can give 'em my compliments to get their useless arses in gear and rejoin the fucking exercise.'

'Yes, Sergeant Major,' replied Saunders, standing back up. His face no longer wore a grin; it was a blank mask. But he was still grinning in his head, as the thought crossed his mind that he could so *very* easily have helped the sergeant major out. And he would have done. Shame about the press-ups.

# Chapter Fifteen



*Stanford Training Area, Norfolk*

Swishing at the snow with his blackthorn cane, Captain McAlease stomped along angrily behind his platoon as it moved in double-file down a forestry block track. He was spitting feathers. Out of the entire company, only two cadets had been captured during the night infiltration. And those cadets came from No. 1 Platoon. His platoon! Of course, it *would* be Officer Cadets Adair and Lawrence. Typical. Trust it to be two of the chaps going to non-teeth arm units. Why were they never as good as the others? A serious man, he had not reacted well to the ribbing that he had received courtesy of his fellow platoon commanders within Amiens Company. Although he had cracked the obligatory smile, and appeared to take the jests in good part, inwardly he was seething.

McAlease had yet to speak to Sergeant Major Anderson and Colour Sergeant Slater to get the full picture. But he'd been at the company RV in the early hours of the morning when Phillips' team had turned up two short. The story sounded simple enough. The team had bumped a section of Gurkhas lying in ambush. Phillips had explained that, while he and bin Hashim had put down covering fire and withdrawn in good order, Adair and Lawrence had simply run off into the dark.

'You mean they panicked and just ran away?' he'd asked.

'I can't say that, sir,' Phillips had replied *Good man,* thought the captain. *Clearly not the sort to drop his brother officers in it!* But the implication was clear. Not just totally lacking in leadership skills, but cowards as well. They hadn't even bothered to engage the enemy before legging it. It was about time those two young men were taught a lesson.

He supposed that they would be returned to the company sometime during the morning—probably too late to take part in the attack. Well, they had missed breakfast—which would jolly well serve them right—and they should stand by for any dirty tasks that happened to be flying about.

Unknown to the captain, the two absent cadets were actually closer than he thought. Having escaped from the camp over an hour before, they had set off at a smart pace of alternate jogging and marching. Initially, they had made a conscious effort to avoid any military transport crossing the training area. But, as the snow-covered terrain became more open, this grew increasingly difficult. It was while they were crossing a half-kilometre exposed stretch that lay between two tree lines that a Land Rover had appeared careering along at high speed behind them. In their green and brown mottled camouflage, they stuck out like sore thumbs against the snow. Running would have looked highly suspicious, so they decided to trust to luck that the vehicle did not contain

Anderson and Slater, and hope against hope that it was from any military unit other than Sandhurst.

Their hope was short-lived. Within a minute, the Land Rover was pulling up alongside them. It was the company commander, Major Breeze. He leaned out of the passenger-side window and addressed them in a calm, mellow tone. 'Ah... so we have Cadets Adair and Lawrence. And how are we today, gentlemen? You seem to be a tad late for breakfast.'

'Yes, sir,' replied Jack, saluting. 'We got picked up last night by a section of Gurkhas. Then we were driven to a training camp for interrogation. But we managed to escape. Now we aim to link up with the rest of the company in time for the attack on the bridge. Sir.'

'Ye-e-s,' purred the Major. 'Lance Corporal Saunders here did tell me that you'd caused a bit of a stir amongst the senior NCO community. I do hope for your sakes that tempers have cooled somewhat before you next run into the company sergeant major and Colour Sergeant Slater. The word on the streets is that they're both in a state of high dudgeon.'

With that, Major Breeze signalled to his driver to move off. As the Land Rover started to pull away, almost as an afterthought, he shouted back at them: 'Well done on the escape, by the way. It's the best bit of initiative I've seen demonstrated by any cadets in the two years that I've been here. Good work... and good luck. You might need it.'

At least Stiffy was on side!

Fifteen minutes later, Jack and Mike were approaching the company RV, located deep within one of the forestry blocks. Chances were, they were too late. Chances were, the company had already set off for the attack on the bridge. But, just for once, chance was on their side. Rounding a bend in the track, they virtually bumped into Amiens Company advancing towards them in double-file, with the standard, tactical, five metres spacing between each man.

At the head was James Lonsdale, the cadet nominated to command No. 1 Platoon for the first phase of the exercise. Glasses pushed askew by the over-large combat helmet pressing down on them, he hardly looked the image of a 21st century warrior-leader, but a beaming smile cracked his camouflage cream from ear to ear when he spotted Jack and Mike heading towards him.

'Hello, ch-chaps. Someone said you'd been nabbed, and that you were probably doing time in clink by now. What happened, did they let you out for the attack?'

'No. We escaped,' commented Jack laconically.

'You're j-joking! I didn't know the rules let you do that sort of thing.'

'No, I didn't think they did either.'

'Bloody hell! You'd b-better slot in behind me then. McAlease is striding along at the back frothing at the mouth like s-some rabid dog, all because of you two, so you m-might want to avoid him for a while.'

The attack on the bridge went as well as could be expected. Which wasn't very well at all. As the cadets lumbered through the snow towards the objective, they bunched together, crossed each other's lines of fire, failed to cover each other while moving, dropped ammunition, and fell over—accompanied all the while by a stream of enthusiastic but ineffectual shouting, as the thrusters tried to *sound* as if they knew what they were doing, even if they didn't *know*. If live rounds had been flying around, at least a third of the company would have been taken out by friendly fire.

Some of the DS reacted mockingly; others—especially those who'd witnessed casualties in combat—watched in grimly silent consternation; but most bellowed as if seized by Tourette's. Jack winced as he heard the ever-polite James Lonsdale attempt to bark out orders: 'Julian, w-would you mind t-taking the machine gun up to the t-top of that embankment, please?' met with the instant response from a nearby colour sergeant: 'It's not fucking "Julian", it's not fucking "would you mind", it's not a fucking "machine gun", and it's not fucking "please"! It's "Edwards, get that fucking gun up there *now*!" Understood? Sir?'

'Yes, of c-course, Colour Sergeant!'

Luckily for the attackers, the Gurkhas of the Demonstration Company were well drilled in their script. As the first sections of cadets staggered, lungs bursting, onto the objective, some of the enemy obligingly died in place while the rest bugged out, making a fighting withdrawal to the nearest tree line. Within twenty minutes of the attack starting, the bridge was in the hands of Amiens Company, and the task of digging defensive positions commenced.

Jack and Mike had managed to scrape a couple of feet beneath the icy hard surface by the time Captain McAlease arrived on the scene. His face wore a look of thunder as he bore down on them.

'I hear you two were captured,' he sneered accusingly. 'You were the only two to be captured out of all three platoons. You should be thoroughly ashamed of yourselves. Phillips tells me you virtually gave yourselves up as soon as the Gurkhas opened fire. You're a complete disgrace. Both of you. I take it you missed breakfast?'

'Yes, sir.'

'Well, it bloody well serves you right. This is a serious black mark on your Sandhurst records.'

With that, he stomped off, anger visibly pulsing through every vein. If he heard the hiss of a single, barely-audible word, 'Tosser', being exhaled behind him as he marched away, he showed no sign of it.

Jack and Mike turned their attention back to trying to carve a semblance of a trench out of the granite-hard earth, hoping that they had seen the last of McAlease for the rest of the morning. It was Jack who was the first to spot the captain heading back towards them some thirty minutes later. 'It's that God-bothering tosser again. What the hell can he want this time?' he sighed.

'Perhaps he's come to hear us confess our sins for getting caught,' snorted Mike derisively. 'Perhaps only then will we be allowed back into McAlease's own private flock. For we have strayed, and we must repent. We are the black sheep of his family. Baa-aah.'

As McAlease drew closer, the cadets could see that he was carrying a loaf of bread, a carton of butter and a pot of jam. He stopped at the lip of the trench. 'Major Breeze has just told me a bit more about your little adventure last night. It seems you two displayed quite a bit of initiative. I know you've missed breakfast, but I thought this might help quell the pangs of hunger. Well done, the pair of you. Oh... and by the way... I'd steer pretty clear of Company Sergeant Major Anderson and Colour Sergeant Slater for the next day or so.'

With that, he was off, spreading the benefit of his military wisdom and Christian goodwill to the rest of No.1 Platoon.

'He's still a tosser, though,' muttered Jack.

# Chapter Sixteen

*Chatham, Kent*

Ivan had been a hero once. He had the medal to prove it. Now, he was a drunk. Not just someone who liked to get drunk quite often. Not just someone who went on an occasional mega-binge. But a dedicated, out-and-out, full-blown alcoholic. If he failed to keep his levels topped-up, he suffered. The sickness, the trembling, the sweating and the craving invaded his body and refused to leave until appeased by yet more fluid ounces of the hard stuff. Preferably at eighty proof or higher.

At first he drank to take the edge off the fear that one day his big lie would be found out. He needed to blot out the past, because the past contained the truth. And Ivan couldn't face the truth. Too much of his life relied on the maintenance of a falsehood. If the facts ever surfaced, he stood to lose everything. The irony was that his drinking had become so corrosive, so self-destructive and so embarrassing that he was losing everything anyway.

The first loss had been his driving licence following a late-night stop on the hard shoulder of a rain-swept motorway, the flashing lights from the police car illuminating his positive breath test. Then his friends had gone. He had barely noticed as they started to drift away, their growing reluctance to spend time with him hidden behind a façade of polite excuses. Initially, as his behaviour became increasingly unpredictable, the married couples had begun to exclude him from their social circle. Then his single friends followed suit, as traits that had once been funny became awkward and embarrassing.

Next to go was his health. Even when he was at his fittest during his time in the Army, Ivan had always been one of the stouter members of the regiment. Without the brake imposed by military discipline, unrestrained alcohol abuse accelerated his descent into outright obesity. And with the colossal weight gain came other problems: black depressions, tremors, blackouts, alcoholic gastritis and hallucinations.

Ivan found that some of these conditions were controllable; it just needed more alcohol to make them go away. Except that more alcohol required more money. More money than Ivan could earn. So he fell back on credit cards to bridge the gap. Even when he found himself having to switch from one card to another to pay off the spiralling debt, Ivan figured that something would come up. It did. He lost his job.

That was when Michelle decided that she'd had enough. They'd been at school together. He had carried a flame for her as she flitted from one boyfriend to the next, hiding his jealousy and dreaming of a chance that would never come his way. Until one day it did. Five years out of school, Ivan was suddenly a big man as the newspapers carried pictures of the local hero being decorated with the Military Cross. Michelle was on the rebound when Ivan had bumped into her in a nightclub in the town centre. He was just what she needed at that time: a strong, decent man with a heart of gold. And brave too. Within a year they were married, Ivan resplendent in his Number One Dress, the silver medal gleaming brilliantly on his chest in the early spring sunshine. They had been together ever since.

But now she had gone. She had stuck with him through all the agitation, lying, lethargy and temper tantrums, but the loss of his job, and with it, the imminent and inevitable loss of their home—a dull but serviceable, 1970s, end-of-terrace—had pushed her over the edge. With their only daughter, Anna, away at university, she took her chance and, after nearly twenty years of marriage, headed back to mum and dad.

Ivan was distraught. He wanted to explain, but that would require telling her his secret—and it was the shame of that secret that had driven him to drink in the first place. It was a vicious circle: to get her back, he would have to tell her the truth, but if he told her the truth, he would lose her.

Slumped at the bare wooden table in the kitchen, Ivan reached out for his only remaining friend. But the glass was empty. As was the bottle. It was nine o'clock in the evening, and there was no more whisky in the house. Worse still, there was no more alcohol of any description—not even the sticky bottle of cherry brandy, a relic of Christmases past, that Ivan had found under the sink and promptly guzzled. He guessed that Michelle had hidden it there to keep him away from it. She hadn't reckoned on an alcoholic's determination. She should have poured it down the drain.

Ivan hauled himself from the plastic chair and stumbled around the kitchen searching every cupboard. There had to be some booze somewhere, some secret stash that he'd overlooked, some cunningly disguised container that he'd filled when he was still trying to hide his habit from Michelle —an old bottle of mineral water perhaps, or the vinegar bottle tucked away at the back of the pantry. Nothing.

Searching upstairs, he tried his bedside table and under the bed, to no avail. Fumbling through the wardrobe, his hopes rose when his hand closed around a hip flask tucked away in the pocket of an ancient waterproof jacket. It was empty. He'd been there before.

Returning downstairs, he moved to the garage. In the past, it had offered an endless variety of devious hiding places—old meths bottles, screen wash containers, assorted jam jars and tins of cleaning fluid—but they'd all been plundered before and now stood dry.

Desperation was starting to set in. As Ivan hunted he could feel the agitation rising, along with the tremor in his hands. He groped clumsily in his pockets. Three one-pound coins and a fifty pence piece. Not enough for a good slug of the hard stuff. It would only get him a few cans of gnat's piss lager. That might have to do, unless he could scratch together some more coins from elsewhere in the house.

He staggered back into the kitchen, cursing as he tripped over the overflowing pedal bin by the side door. On the work surface was a tall German beer stein, heavily patterned in garish reds, blues and yellows, a reminder of happier days in the sergeants' mess in Osnabruck. He thumbed down on the lever that opened the aluminium lid and tipped the stein upside down. The contents spilled out over the work surface and onto the floor: some drawing pins and paper clips, a comb, several supermarket receipts, a chain store loyalty card, three pens and... a two-pound coin. The coin hit the floor and span in a wide arc on its edge before disappearing under the fridge.

Ivan was immediately on his knees, scrabbling with his hands among the dead spiders and dust under the fridge to retrieve it, his breathing coming in heavy gasps as he struggled with the unexpected physical exertion. He couldn't quite reach. A yellow fly swat, sticky with dead insects, rested against the side of the fridge, and a couple of sweeps with that managed to flick the coin back out into the open. Now he had five pounds fifty. Enough at least for a half-bottle of cheap blended whisky.

Ivan headed for the door and out into the humdrum, terrace-lined streets of Chatham. The rest of the country might be facing house price chaos and waves of property developers on the make, but Chatham seemed blissfully unaware. Having avoided the invasion of artisan coffee shops and bakeries, ordinary houses remained vaguely affordable. Just. But in some areas 'affordable' meant 'deprived'. The closure of the dockyard—the biggest employer in the area—in 1984 had marked the start of an inexorable decline.

From his front door, an inebriated stumble of less than one hundred yards took Ivan across the boundary from humdrum to rundown. It didn't need a visible line on the ground to mark the separation. The signs were obvious: the rusting fridge-freezer in the overgrown front garden; the car up on bricks with no tyres, leaking oil; and the house in the middle of a terrace that burnt out two years ago, but which remained a blackened shell.

The nearest off-licence was just around the corner, sitting among a row of dilapidated shop fronts that included a Pakistani-owned newsagent's and general store, a kebab shop, a launderette and a nail bar. Two other premises were boarded up. The night air was chill, and Ivan began to wish that he'd stopped to put on a coat. As he rounded the corner, he could see several teenagers picked out in the amber glow of the streetlights, a couple of bikes leaning up against a shop window. He put his head down, determined to ignore them, and made straight for the familiar entrance. A few yards from the door he looked up briefly. Two girls were leaning against the wooden lower ledge of the off-licence window. They were almost identical: shiny tracksuits, white trainers, big hoop earrings, heavy on bling, dyed blonde hair pulled back into tight ponytails.

Ivan accidentally made eye contact. One spoke: 'What you staring at, you old git? You fancy me or sumfin?'

Ivan looked away and went to enter the shop door. A tall black kid in dark clothes, baseball cap and hoodie top hiding his features, slid in front of him and blocked his path. 'Hey man, she talking to you.'

Ivan was aware of two other hooded figures closing in on each side. One of the girls shouted out again. 'Fuckin' do the old git, Jamal. He looks like a fuckin' paedo to me.'

The first Ivan knew of the punch was when his eye exploded in a shock of pain. As he was pushed to the ground, he could feel the numbness setting in as the skin stretched taut over the swelling. Then the kicking started. Two blows, aimed for his balls, landed on his stomach before he managed to curl up into a ball to protect himself as best he could. The youths carried on kicking his legs and the back of his head. He could hear himself crying out, sobbing for them to leave him alone: 'No, no, no!' He knew that they were going to rob him.

And then he pissed himself.

As the urine soaked through his trousers and pooled onto the paving stones, the attack stopped. The teenagers backed off, shouting out their derision. 'Oh, man, he's only gone and pissed hisself, the disgusting old bastard.' The girls joined in, laughing with high-pitched squeals.

A police car moved slowly along the street. Ivan began to stand up and dust himself off, feeling the last trickles of urine run down the inside of his trouser legs. Two of the teenage boys mounted bikes and sped off into the darkness down a side alley. The others peeled themselves away from the shop front and sauntered after them, looking warily over their shoulders in case the coppers chose to stop.

Ivan reeled unsteadily into the off licence. Saleem the shop owner knew him well. He also knew that he was an alcoholic. But that had never stopped him serving Ivan more booze. After all, business was business.

Saleem had seen the incident outside through his shop window. He hadn't had time to intervene. Even if he had, the likelihood is that he would have remained inside. Business wasn't so good that he could afford to keep replacing his plate glass windows every time he upset the local yobs. Saleem looked up as Ivan entered. He involuntarily wrinkled his nose as the smell of urine washed over him. He forced himself to smile politely. 'You should go to A&E to get that eye seen to,' he said.

'Yeah, thanks. I will,' replied Ivan, with no intention of doing so. He couldn't tell exactly what the damage was, but his vision was becoming restricted as the swelling flesh started to close over his eye. The sharp pain had stopped as soon as the numbness set in, to be replaced by a dull, throbbing ache. He tried to pretend that nothing was wrong as he selected and paid for his small bottle of whisky.

Ivan completed his purchase and left. Clasping his precious bottle to his chest, he tottered back home, peering nervously around him in case the youths reappeared. No one would think that he had been a hero once. He had the medal to prove it. But now he was just a drunk.

# Chapter Seventeen



*Royal Military Academy Sandhurst*

It was a week since Amiens Company had returned from Exercise *Second Flush* and the cadets of No. 1 Platoon were being put through a two-hour 'beasting'—the imposition of sustained arduous exercises—courtesy of the Physical Training staff. Along with the other two platoons in the company, they were rotating through three activities.

The first event had comprised a series of gym-based physical tests to check individual progress. Personal bests in push-ups, sit-ups, dips, heaves and rope-climbs had been recorded with disproportionate gravity by sleekly muscled PT instructors bearing clipboards. These were iron men, who prided themselves on their ability to pump out vein-bursting repetitions with machine-like efficiency. Men with a seemingly unquenchable desire always to see 'the last man'.

'I want to see the last man to do ten push-ups. Go!'

'I want to see the last man to touch the far wall and get back. Go!'

'I want to see the last man to run five times around my beautiful body. Go!'

Never the first man; always the last. And the command invariably ending in the shrill yelp, 'Go!'

These gym-based demigods had little time for those cadets with reed-thin arms, weak stomachs or a fragile grip. Unfortunately, at least half the company exhibited one or more of these traits.

From the gym, the platoon had formed up in three ranks and jogged towards the lake, where the start-line had been set up for a one-mile timed run. As the squad drew closer Jack noticed Captain McAlease and Colour Sergeant Slater standing to one side. McAlease was wearing combat trousers, boots and a yellow rugby top. He was stamping his feet and swinging his arms around his body to keep warm in the chill morning air. His dog, Buster, a brown and white spaniel, was cavorting at his feet.

The platoon came to a halt. Although the PTI was champing at the bit to get his hands on the latest arrivals, he briefly stood aside for Captain McAlease, who wished to deliver a short sermon.

'Right, One Platoon, I'm very keen to see how your physical training's been progressing. During Exercise *Second Flush* it was obvious that a few of you were having trouble keeping up. Well, let me tell you, the Army has no place for leaders who can't keep up. Now, you have eight minutes to complete this course of one mile. All of you should be able to do it much faster than that. Frankly, anyone who can't do it in less than six and a half minutes should question whether they have any business remaining here. Just to make sure there's no slacking, I shall run myself. Note that I am wearing boots, not trainers. Anyone who falls behind me should be ashamed of themselves and should look towards their motivation for wanting to remain at Sandhurst. Okay, PTI, carry on.'

In the background, the PTI sneezed loudly. It was an odd-sounding sneeze, muffled by his hands. Several of the cadets thought they might have detected the word 'Tosser!' No... couldn't be. But no time to dwell on that now. The little terrier in the blue tracksuit top was already issuing the commands that would get the platoon drawn up behind the start-line.

For Jack, this was going to be a piece of cake, but he was concerned about Mike Lawrence, who struggled with PT. As the whistle peeped, the hares sprang away from the start. Within the first twenty seconds, the group had split into three: a handful of sprinters breaking away from the main pack; the main body, settling down into a steady jog; and the small number of slow movers at the back—generally those carrying a little more weight than the rest.

Mike started well up with the main pack, but within the first hundred yards was already dropping back. Jack jogged alongside him, torn between the urge to tear away with the front runners and the need to encourage his friend.

Captain McAlease had lined up behind the row of runners at the start line so that he could see how every individual in his platoon performed. Soon, his hectoring voice could be heard shouting encouragement.

'Watkins, you fat slacker, keep up!'

'Mr Dennis, but some effort into it!'

'They won't want you in the infantry if this is the best you can do, Mr Taylor!'

As he passed Jack and Mike the helpful advice continued.

'Come on, Mr Adair and Mr Lawrence, get a move on. Just as well you two aren't down for the teeth arms,' he shouted in the chivvying style of a prep school housemaster.

Jack might have taken any other jibe in his stride. But this one hit home. The smug bastard needed to be taught a lesson. Keeping his voice low, he muttered to Mike: 'Right, I'm gonna show that useless tosser. I'm relying on you to do your best without me. Don't let me down.'

'Go for it,' gasped Mike, redoubling his efforts to keep up.

With that, Jack increased his own pace and fell in alongside McAlease, whose heavy breathing and lack of shouting indicated that he was close to full stretch.

'Fine day for it, sir.'

'Ah... Mr Adair... finally decided to join the rest of us did you?' There was a short pause while he took another couple of deep gasps. 'I want to see best effort from you, young man, so you'd best save your breath and concentrate on your running.' With that, McAlease increased his pace.

Jack lengthened his own stride, easily keeping pace with the older man. Then he threw down the challenge: 'You might want to do the same yourself, sir. Sounds like you're having a bit of trouble there.'

'Watch your tone, Adair,' snapped McAlease, and attempted to pull into the lead.

Jack fell back, moved effortlessly across behind McAlease, then popped up on his other side.

'Wouldn't want to be beaten by a Loggy, would you, sir?' The challenge was obvious.

McAlease's face set hard, his lips forming a thin line. His pride had been pricked and his irritation was obvious. With

500 yards to go, both men stepped up the pace to just below an outright sprint. McAlease had long since given up trying to hurry the others along. His eyes were fixed on the finish line as he ploughed through the other runners. One or two of the faster cadets had already crossed the line and turned to take an interest in the progress of their colleagues. They could see the race developing between Adair and McAlease, and the odd shout started to go up.

'Come on, Adair!'

'Well done, Captain McAlease, sir!' from one shameless crawler.

Jack had been holding some back in reserve. McAlease was clearly at his limit; nothing left to give. He made the false assumption that Adair was the same. He could not have been more wrong. Jack picked his moment to move just fifty yards from the line. His breathing still well under control, he turned to McAlease and said, 'Perhaps I should consider one of the teeth arms after all. What do you think, sir?'

With that, he switched gear and pulled easily into the lead. To the enthusiastic whoops of the other cadets, he crossed the line ten paces ahead of the platoon commander. Jack took a few strides, swinging his arms outwards and throwing his head back to swallow large gulps of air. Then he paused and bent over at the waist, hands on his hips, the sweat dripping from his forehead onto the tarmac between his feet. A pair of combat boots came into his field of view, standing immediately in front of him. McAlease was standing there, hand outstretched in forced congratulation.

'Well done, Mr Adair,' muttered McAlease. His fury was barely suppressed, but his principles demanded that he congratulate the winner.

'Thank you, sir. There must be more to us Loggies than meets the eye.'

Captain McAlease snorted and turned his attention to the stragglers who were still crossing the finish line.

Within minutes, the PTI was shouting for the cadets to fall back into three ranks for the jog back to the gym for the third event: milling.

# Chapter Eighteen

The PTI started shouting the moment the cadets streamed through the doors of the gym.

'Right, Number One Platoon, get yourselves sorted out sitting on the benches that make up the hollow square over there. I want roughly equal numbers down each side, facing inwards.'

The cadets already knew what they were in for. While No. 1 Platoon had been struggling through the physical tests, they'd been able to see the blood of No. 2 Platoon being liberally splashed about on the far side of the gym. They shuffled into position, sitting shoulder-to-shoulder. The aura of apprehension was inescapable. Three PTIs were running the session. The most senior, a staff sergeant, stepped into the centre of the square that would become a makeshift boxing ring.

'Okay, gentlemen. This is your introduction to milling. It originated with the commando units of World War Two and is still used as part of the selection process for the Airborne Forces, with which I am proud to have served.'

Twenty-nine eyes took in the blue and white parachute wings stitched to the upper right sleeve of his PTI's dark blue tracksuit top.

'It also used to feature in virtually all recruit training establishments, including the Royal Military Academy Sandhurst, until the powers that be got so worried about health and safety that they went all soft and fluffy about it. Well, gentlemen, owing to a special request by your company commander, for you, it's back. All that was needed was a qualified PTI to run the session, and, gentlemen, there are probably few PTIs better qualified to do that than me. So be grateful.'

The PTI's look was one of pure delight. The cadets looked anything but grateful.

'The only difference between the milling we do now and the milling we once did is that nowadays you young gentlemen get to wear headguards, gumshields and seventeen-ounce gloves that are so fucking big it'll be like hitting each other with a pair of well-padded cushions. In my view, this is yet another sign that the Army is going soft. But that is a matter for those well above my pay grade. The aim is to give sixty seconds' worth of one hundred per cent effort, aggression and bottle. It is designed to demonstrate that in a firefight with a determined enemy, you will have the will to win, rather than cowering in the dirt while his bullets chew you up. There are no rules. Do not bother with any fancy boxing or other ninja technique that you might have learnt elsewhere. I do not want to see you poncing about with blocking, ducking or defending in any way. It's not about scoring points with body blows—it's only head shots that count. Likewise, it is not just about doing more damage to the other guy than he does to you. That's because if he has given total effort, and you haven't, *you... will... still... lose!*'

He spat out the last four words in slow succession for emphasis.

'You will also know you have lost if you open your eyes to see the other bloke's dainty size tens stepping on your face. Now, pair yourselves off in roughly equal height and weight, and we'll have the first pair in the ring. As there are twenty-nine of you, one of you is going to have to fight twice, so, unless one of your platoon staff wants to volunteer, you'd better give some thought to who that's going to be.'

'That's all right, Staff. I'll fight.' CSM Anderson peeled himself away from the wall against which he had been leaning and strolled over to the ring. 'In fact, I'll go first, just so the young gentlemen can see what we require of them. Come on, Mr Adair. You and me.'

Jack, sitting with his back to the door, had not seen the sergeant major enter the gym.

'B-bloody hell!' breathed James Lonsdale, next to him.

'No worries, mate,' Jack murmured, rising from the bench into the position of attention, and answering Anderson's implicit threat with an unwavering 'Yes, Company Sergeant Major!'

Two PTIs stationed at diagonally opposite corners of the makeshift ring handed out the gloves, gumshields and headguards and quickly helped the two fighters into them. While the laces were being pulled tight on his gloves, Jack quizzed the PTI sergeant assigned to his corner.

'Can you just remind me of the rules again?'

'I thought the staff sergeant made that quite clear, sir. The only rule is for you to get in there, mix it, and show one hundred per cent aggression for a full minute without backing down or turning away. No fancy ducking or diving. Just get in there and whack him. Oh, and you'd better watch out. I know the sergeant major. He gets the red mist.'

Gloves and headguards fastened, the two fighters came to attention on opposite sides of the hollow square, looking outwards, then, on command, simultaneously executed a smart 'about turn' through 180 degrees as they turned to face each other. The PTI peeped his whistle and jumped back from the centre of the ring as the opponents flew at each other across the intervening space.

The first fifteen seconds must have seen as many as twenty flailing blows traded by each side. Neither gave ground. Jack felt a hard right connect with his left eye with such force that he could taste the pins and needles in his mouth. The stinging across the left side of his forehead told him that his eyebrow had been opened. He shook his head to clear his vision, obscured by the inevitable stream of blood. As he did so, another flying fist caught him across the right cheek. He replied with three fast right-handed jabs, one of which connected hard with Anderson's nose, drawing blood. The pace was relentless, with fatigue setting in before the halfway point had been reached.

Distracted by the damage to his nose, Anderson stepped back one pace for a fraction of a second, preparing himself for a renewed assault. Jack saw his chance. The couple of feet of space between them gave him the opportunity he needed. As the sergeant major moved forward to launch a fresh attack, Jack retreated a further pace to widen the gap. With lightning speed, he raised his knee and snapped out his lower leg in a whip-fast front-kick. The toe of his training shoe flew straight into the point of Anderson's jaw. The effect was instant and devastating. The sergeant major stopped in mid-attack, completely pole-axed by the surprise blow. He careered over to his right, falling heavily onto his side.

Determined not to be beaten, he struggled to get up, but he moved like a mortally wounded beast. He pushed at the floor with his hands, but the effort proved too much, and he sank back down onto the floor again. Inside his skull, his brain seemed to carry on spinning like a carousel ride.

Jack stepped back, aware that the gym had gone silent. The cadets from No. 3 Platoon on the far side, who'd been carrying out the indoor tests, had stopped dead in their tracks and were staring across at the sergeant major. There was a shocked pause of about ten seconds while everyone took in what had happened. Then the PTI staff sergeant sprang into action. Beckoning to two his two assistants, he quickly had the sergeant major helped to his feet and escorted to the changing room. Spatters of blood from Anderson's nose marked the route. Trying to move on quickly from the incident, the staff sergeant turned back to the cadets.

'Right, now let's have the next two. And you, Bruce fucking Lee,' he said, glaring at Jack, 'I don't know what the bloody hell you thought you were doing, but you'd better get your gloves off, sit down and shut up. I'll have a word with you afterwards.'

'But... you said there were no rules,' Jack started to protest.

'Sir, I just advised you to shut up. I'd be obliged if you'd obey my last instruction. And while you're at it, you can stop dripping blood all over *my* gymnasium floor.'

# Chapter Nineteen

'Adair, you're an absolute disgrace, and you should not be an officer cadet at this Academy.'

'Sir.'

'You are supposed to act like a gentleman, but time and time again, it appears that you have more in common with the gutter.'

'Sir.'

'And standing there like some private soldier, staring into the middle distance and simply repeating "sir" is not going to get you off the hook. What the hell did you think you were playing at this afternoon?'

Captain McAlease was not merely angry; he was white with fury.

'Well, answer me.'

'Sir, I checked on the rules. I was told that there were none, other than to show aggression and not back down. I showed aggression and did not back down.'

'Adair, you are missing the point entirely.' McAlease was now speaking each word clearly and precisely, as if addressing a five-year-old child. 'At what point did the PT staff say that you could kick your opponent? And in the head, of all things. What possessed you to kick Sergeant Major Anderson in the head?'

'It seemed the logical thing to do at the time. I believe Sergeant Major Anderson is pursuing a vendetta against me for making him look a fool on Exercise *Second Flush*. That's why he wanted to fight me. He wanted to put me on the ground. I finished it first. Using controlled aggression. Sir.'

'Adair, your conduct today was a disgrace. You are an ill-mannered, cocky, unofficerlike thug. There is no place for you in this Academy. Very soon, you will realise this yourself and remove yourself from it. Should that realisation not come to you first, I am sure that others, higher in the chain of command than me, will figure this out for themselves. Either way, mark my words, your remaining time here is strictly limited. I may not be able to effect your removal yet, but I fully anticipate that you will *not* be commissioned from Sandhurst. In the meantime, you should be aware that Sergeant Major Anderson has been taken to the medical centre, where he's under observation for possible concussion. It would be in your best interests to get across there and apologise to him. Now get out!'

'Sir!'

Jack saluted rigidly and turned smartly to the right, smashing his booted right foot down into the office floor as he completed the perfect drill manoeuvre.

As he left the office, he could feel his face burning. He knew damned well that Anderson had it in for him and had counted on the opportunity to beat him to a pulp in front of the other cadets—and all within the rules of the game. The fact that the rules had turned against the sergeant major was hardly Jack's fault. Fucking McAlease! This was a cap badge issue. We can't have the tame Loggy acting like a real fighting man, can we? Jolly nice people to know for 'getting bits of kit', but let's not have them showing aggression and a refusal to back down. That's for the teeth arms. What a tosser!

Sergeant Major Anderson was sitting up in bed reading a copy of the *Sun* when Jack was shown into the small overnight ward at the Academy medical centre. He was the only occupant. He looked up briefly to see who had come in, then returned to his newspaper. Jack walked forward and stood next to the bed.

Without looking up, Anderson broke the silence. 'What the fuck do you want?'

'Captain McAlease suggested that it would be in my best interests to come across and apologise for kicking you in the head during the milling. So here I am.'

'Good. So you've apologised. Now fuck off.'

Jack shrugged and made to leave. He'd taken a few steps back towards the door when he halted and turned to confront the sergeant major again. Anderson remained engrossed in his paper.

'What's your problem, Sergeant Major?' Jack asked, an exasperated tone creeping into his voice.

Anderson looked up for the first time. Lowering his newspaper, he stared across the room at Jack. His eyes showed one emotion: pure, undiluted loathing.

'You're my problem, Mr Adair. Okay? Got it?'

'No. I don't "get it". What the hell have I done to piss you off? Fine, I can see why you're angry about us escaping on the exercise, but why me any more than Mr Lawrence? It's almost like you've got some personal vendetta against me or something.'

'Yeah, you could say that. A personal vendetta. Yeah, that's a good way of putting it. Okay, you wanna know what's going on? I'll tell you. You ever heard of Lance Corporal Jim Anderson of the King's Royal Rangers?'

'No. Why? Should I?'

'Yes. You bloody well should. Because that man was my brother. He was also a hero. Unlike your father. Sergeant Nick Adair, if I'm not mistaken? Who was a disgusting coward. Your father was in charge of Hotel 55 when it got taken out by the IRA. While my brother was dying on the front gate, your old man was hiding in a steel locker. And, yes, I know he died before he could pay the penalty for his cowardice, but that doesn't bring my brother back. And now you're here. Another Adair trying to be a soldier. But I bet under the skin you're just as big a coward as your dad was. And there isn't room in *my* Army for cowards. So I want you out. And if you won't get out of your own free will, then I'll either drive you out or I'll break you. There. Clear now? So, if you don't mind, I'm trying to read the paper. So I'd be awfully grateful if you'd just fuck off. Sir.'

'Okay. Got it. You won't drive me out. And you certainly won't break me. Give it your best shot, Sergeant Major. But I'm here to stay. So just go screw yourself.' Jack turned on his heel, red-faced, and stormed from the room, angrily brushing past the duty nurse outside.

# Chapter Twenty

Entering his room in Victory College, Jack took a kick at the waste bin, sending it flying across the room. He crossed to the window and stared out at the line of dark pine trees fifty yards away, silhouetted starkly against the moonlit sky. He wanted to be back in the Legion. This time it wasn't just the idle whim that he'd felt in moments of despondency several times before. This was a burning desire to be back with the old gang, downing Kronenbourgs in the *foyer* with real mates like Josh Corrigan, Toby Simmonds and the rest of *Le Mafia Anglais*. He was sick to the back teeth of Sandhurst. Josh's personal assessment of British Army officers was coming back to haunt him: 'a bunch of snobs with their heads up their own arses'. Thanks, Josh. Right as usual.

Gradually, he collected his thoughts. He'd made his choice. He wanted his commission. He needed to get through Sandhurst, and no one was going to stop him. So what if his father had been a coward? He wasn't his father. He'd show those bastards—Anderson, McAlease, Phillips, and anyone else who stood in his way—Jack Adair was here to stay. As his anger subsided, he became aware of the ache in his jaw where he'd been grinding his teeth, and the fingernail imprints in his palms from his clenched fists. He needed a drink. And he also needed to get away from the Academy for a few hours.

His mind still buzzing with subdued rage, Jack began to change into the obligatory walking out dress of jacket and tie. From his wardrobe he selected the cadet-issue, double-breasted blazer bearing shiny Sandhurst buttons, and the Academy tie in dark blue with red and gold diagonal stripes. Combined with his short haircut, there could be no doubt that he was a Sandhurst cadet. With any luck, maybe some drunken yob would have a pop at him. He was in the mood to give someone a smack. He set off downtown, truculent and bristling for a fight.

All of the pubs within three miles of the Academy were out of bounds to cadets. But that suited Jack's mood. If anything, he was almost willing himself to be caught, with his Sandhurst blazer standing out like a beacon. Crossing the road from the Academy gates, he headed straight for the Cambridge Hotel just a few hundred yards away at the top of the High Street. As old as the town itself, this once-grand edifice was long past its glory days. 'Faded elegance' would be a polite description. Run-down chav-magnet might be more realistic. The presence of bouncers on the door indicated the likely clientele. It was the usual pairing of doormen: the tall, monosyllabic, shaven-headed, heavy-browed, tattooed one, and the short, monosyllabic, shaven-headed, heavy-browed, tattooed one.

As Jack drew closer, the bouncers broke off their monosyllabic conversation and eyed him suspiciously from under their heavy brows.

The short one took a pace forward. 'Outta bounds to Sandhurst cadets, mate. You know that.'

'Their rules or yours?' Jack challenged.

'You wanna risk it, chum, that's up to you. Don't blame me.'

'Thanks for the tip.' With that, Jack wandered inside. If anyone was going to find him breaking the rules, this would be the place—less than one hundred yards from the Academy gates.

For two hours, he sat alone at the bar, nursing successive pints of lager, his fixed scowl not inviting company. The pub was relatively quiet and, even wearing his Sandhurst blazer, nobody seemed to take more than a passing interest in him. But at least the alcohol did its trick in dulling his senses.

It was nearing eleven o'clock by the time Jack eased himself off his bar stool and commenced the walk back to Victory College. He had only covered a short distance towards the Academy gates when he saw a car crawling down the street ahead of him. It was about a hundred feet away when it stopped. A figure stepped out from the dark shadow of a shop doorway. Even from that distance, Jack could tell that it was another Sandhurst cadet—short haircut, regulation jacket and tie.

The young man gave a cursory glance up and down the street, then leaned into the car to shake hands with those inside. When he drew back from the vehicle, he was holding a black holdall. Bidding some swift farewells to the car's two occupants, he made his way up the street towards the Academy. There was no acknowledgement that he'd seen Jack during his swift scan of the street.

Jack increased his pace to see if it was someone he knew. As he drew closer, he recognised Asad. He quickly gained on the Arab, who strolled along slowly, apparently deep in thought.

'Hi, Asad.' Jack could have sworn that Asad jumped as he spoke. 'Sorry, hope I didn't make you jump.'

'Oh, hello, Jack. You did rather. I wasn't expecting to see anyone from the Academy out here. My relatives in London have just had a friend deliver to me some foodstuffs that will remind me of home. You have tried *halva* perhaps? It is an Arabic sweet made out of ground roasted sesame seeds and honey.'

'Yes, not bad in limited quantities, but a bit too sweet for my taste.'

'Well, we Muslims must have some form of indulgence. After all, we are forbidden from taking alcohol,' Asad laughed.

'Yeah, that must be tough.'

'If you do not take it, you do not miss it. And when we come to the West, we can see the damage that it does. Especially the damage that it does to your women.'

'Perhaps, but all societies have their flaws.'

'Indeed. Only God is perfect.'

After crossing the A30 main road that ran past the Academy grounds, separating the camp from the town, they passed through Sandhurst's impressive front gate. A blue-uniformed security guard checked their passes. They still had a further half-mile or so to walk, much of it beside the lake, before reaching Victory College.

After a few minutes, Asad resumed the conversation. 'You made Sergeant Major Anderson look like a fool today.'

'Do you think so? I thought I was only entering into the spirit of the thing.'

'It is obvious to me that he has a personal grudge against you,' continued Asad. 'He wanted to finish you off in that ring. But you surprised him. I think you need even more to watch out for him now. He will be keen to get you.'

'He can try,' Jack responded, thinking about his conversation with Anderson only a few hours earlier.

'He holds a very powerful position.'

'He thinks he does, but I've seen his sort before.'

'Yes. I think you have served as a soldier before, Jack. Have you not?'

'I have a little previous experience. Not very much.'

'I think you are teasing me now, Jack. I have seen you on exercise. You know how to carry your kit and your weapon as if it were second nature. But I accept that you may not wish to talk about it.'

'And do you have previous military experience, Asad?'

'Like you, Jack. A little. Not very much. Enough for this experience not to come as quite the shock that it obviously has to some others.'

They walked on in silence to Victory College, sitting like a dark, gloomy bunker beneath the bright lights of New College that dominated the horizon.

At the entrance, they parted to go to their separate rooms.

'Goodnight, Jack. I enjoyed our conversation. But you should watch the sergeant major. He has even more reason to seek revenge on you now. We Arabs know about revenge. It is our way. Even if it is a disagreement between great-grandparents, the successive generations will still hate each other. And Anderson is clearly a vengeful man. Goodnight again, Jack.'

As Jack headed for his room, his thoughts flitted back to the look the sergeant major had given him in the hospital. It was the same look he'd seen on Draskovic's face just before the first beer glass came sailing across the bar at the *Club Tropique*. It was the look of an eye for an eye kind of guy.

# Chapter Twenty-One

*Chatham, Kent*

When Ivan lifted his face from the table, he could feel the sheet of paper sticking to it. He moved his right hand to brush it away, with all the precision of someone wearing sixteen-ounce boxing gloves. The sheet dropped to the table, skimmed across the surface and glided onto the floor, where it settled amid a snowfall of other discarded sheets and screwed-up paper balls. The tabletop was covered with paper too, providing an impromptu cloth for the empty bottles and glasses that stood on it. Ivan had been writing. Scribbling, more like. Trying in his whisky-fuelled state to express the dark thoughts that crowded his head. So that someone would know the truth. Finally.

Sometimes he had repeated himself. Pages and pages, with only two or three lines in a clumsy, big-handed, childish scrawl. All saying the same thing: 'It wasn't me—it was him', and 'Coward'. Sometimes there were pictures. Crude, angry drawings sketched with such force that the pencil had sliced through to the table beneath. Sometimes the words and pictures were crossed out, over and over again—so many times that the white paper only appeared in glimpses through the relentless graphite scribbles.

Ivan had no idea of the time, or how long he'd been sitting at the kitchen table. But then again, he didn't care. Because soon it was all going to stop. All of the lying, the fear, the self-loathing, the failure—they were all going to stop. Finally.

He pulled himself to his feet. God, his head hurt. Like fuck. On the work surface six feet away, he could see a bottle that still contained some of the precious fluid that would ease his pain, in more ways than one. He took a couple of stumbling steps and made a grab for it. Lifting the bottle, he broke the sticky seal of stale, spilt liquor that bonded it to the work surface. He held it to his lips and gulped. Better! Much better!

The warmth flushed through his chest, and his body responded to the elixir it demanded. He needed to get moving with his plan. Before he changed his mind. The truth might be about to come out into the open, but he didn't intend to be around to face it when it did.

From the kitchen he moved slowly into the hallway, his shoulder barging off the doorframe as he passed through it. Sinking down onto his knees, he prised open the door of the cupboard under the stairs. It didn't take him long to lay his hands on what he was after—the extension hose for the vacuum cleaner. He sank back onto the floor, holding up the hose like a prize.

'Hello, my beauty,' he slurred with a smile. 'Are you going to help me on my little journey?'

He paused again—long enough for his head to start nodding. As his chin fell forward onto his chest, he jerked awake with a start. The hose was still in his hand. He looked at it curiously for a second as if wondering what it was doing there. Then he remembered his plan. Today was the day. But first, he needed to get properly dressed.

After returning briefly to the kitchen for another fortifying gulp of whisky, he made his way unsteadily upstairs. He had already taken out his uniform the night before—before the whisky haze had set in again. It was suspended from the bedroom door, still pristinely wrapped in cellophane from its last trip to the dry cleaner's five years ago.

Ivan reached out for the coat hanger and missed. His hand slid off the cellophane shroud, dislodging the hanger hook from the door frame and sending the garments tumbling to the floor. He swore, scooped up the uniform, and carried it through into his bedroom. It took him seconds to rip off the flimsy transparent covering.

The uniform lay revealed on the bed. It was Number Two Dress—the British Army's standard parade dress. Made of smooth, khaki, woollen cloth, it bore regimental insignia on the lapels and four black buttons down the front. Displayed on the right arm, just above the elbow, in black with yellow edging, were the three stripes and crown of a colour sergeant. Above the left breast pocket was a single row of five coloured ribbons, representing the campaign medals for Northern Ireland and Bosnia, the commemorative medal for the Queen's Golden Jubilee, the Long Service and Good Conduct Medal, and... the Military Cross for gallantry.

From his wardrobe, Ivan extracted a khaki shirt and tie and an immaculate pair of black boots, bulled to mirrored perfection. It took him a while to get dressed. Several times he lurched, bouncing off the full-length mirror on the wardrobe door, and occasionally falling back onto the bed. All the time, he was talking to himself—a constant mumbled undertone: 'You show 'em, Ivan. You fuckin' show 'em. See what they think then. Bastards. Fuck 'em all.'

When he was finally dressed, Ivan looked at himself admiringly in the mirror. Okay, so he couldn't get the jacket done up, and the zip-fly of his trousers was half undone to accommodate a waistline that had ballooned astronomically over the past five years. But the effect wasn't half bad. He looked like a soldier again. Sort of.

From the top left hand drawer of a dresser, he withdrew an envelope-shaped package made of green felt. Inside were his five medals—court-mounted in a rigid group and suspended from a single fixing pin. Ivan took them out and struggled to pin them into position on his jacket. It had been so much easier to do when he was still serving—when his hands didn't shake all the time.

With the medals in place, he came to attention in front of the mirror, and looked himself up and down one last time. Then he saluted. 'May I have your permission to carry on, sir, please?' he barked. With that, he turned smartly to the right, as if being dismissed from parade, and headed for the stairs to commence the final phase of his mission.

That final phase would take place in the garage. It would involve a car engine, a vacuum cleaner extension hose, and a lungful of carbon monoxide gas.

*'Ivan! What the hell do you think you're doing?'*

Ivan was slumped forward with his head resting on the steering wheel. He could feel the vibrations from the engine being transmitted into his forehead. The entire car stank of petrol fumes. He wanted to gag. With enormous effort, he forced his eyes to open into small slits. As the eyelids parted, his pupils were hit by the sunlight streaming through the open garage door, making him flinch. He knew that he'd shut the door behind him before he'd got into the car for what was intended to be his final journey—a journey to nowhere. Now it was open. And he was still alive.

As his eyes focused, he could see a figure silhouetted in the doorway. It was Michelle. She was still screaming at him. But now she was running. Running straight at the car. She ripped the door open and grabbed Ivan by the shoulder, propelling him sideways out of the driver's seat and onto the garage floor. He hit his head against the wall on the way down, but it would be hours before he would feel it.

Michelle reached in and switched off the engine. Then she slammed the door shut so that she could get to Ivan, who was now lying in a crumpled heap behind it. She started pulling at his ankles, desperately trying to drag him clear of the smoke-filled garage. And that was when he passed out.

# Chapter Twenty-Two

*Royal Military Academy Sandhurst*

Sovereign's Parade. For the Senior Term, the culmination of forty-four weeks' training, passing out in front of the Queen or her representative—on this occasion, Prince Charles. For the Intermediate and Junior Terms, a fleeting glimpse of the light at the end of the tunnel. The event is the embodiment of the Sandhurst spirit, and the face that outsiders are most likely to recognise. Over 600 cadets on parade, boots gleaming and bayonets fixed, resplendent in their dark blue, Number One Dress uniforms, the high jacket collars bearing white gorget patches, and the trousers trimmed with red stripes. As a graduation ceremony, it is unsurpassed. But for Jack and the other cadets of Amiens Company, passing out of the Academy was still two terms away. This time, theirs would be a supporting role only.

As part of the Junior Division, they would be the last on parade, swinging into view to the refrain of the old-time music hall song, 'Here we are again, happy as can be'—the most cheerful tune of the day being reserved for those with least to be cheerful about. The irony was not lost on them.

From mid-morning the guests began to arrive—a long, straggling herd of bright dresses, extravagant hats and sombre suits, making their way towards the recently erected viewing stands that lined one side of the parade square. Dotted among them meandered a handful of officers in full regimental regalia, medals glinting—some of them proud fathers whose offspring were following the family tradition.

Across the far side of the square facing the stands stood the imposing cream-coloured sprawl of Old College, its Grand Entrance fronted by six massive Doric pillars. The culmination of the parade would see the newly commissioned officers of the Senior Division slow-march up the steps between these pillars, followed by the Academy adjutant on his charger. Being able to ride went with the adjutant's job. Performing this circus trick three times a year in front of hundreds of spectators was an added extra. But it was expected. Eighty years of tradition demanded it. And no adjutant had failed yet.

Some five hundred yards away from Old College, Amiens Company was forming up on New College square. As usual, the cadets had walked across from Victory College in just their socks, carrying the immaculate boots that glistened after many hours of devoted attention. They had each then checked every aspect of their appearance in the full-length mirrors, discreetly positioned in alcoves by the front of the building, before taking their designated places in the ranks. Seemingly endless rehearsals over recent weeks meant that it should all run like clockwork. Except that, within No.1 Platoon, there was a problem. Asad had not appeared.

He had certainly been present with the others earlier in the morning, when they'd taken a swift one-mile run, followed by a hearty breakfast—Colour Sergeant Slater's favoured preparation for avoiding fainting on parade. His car was still on the square outside the Victory College. Somebody recalled having seen him earlier at the row of sinks in the ablutions area, putting the final gloss on his boots with water and a wodge of cotton wool. He hadn't told anybody that he was going sick. But now he was missing from parade.

On discovering the news, Colour Sergeant Slater did his best to retain an air of icy calm. This lasted for about ten seconds. Then the bellowing started. 'Mr Dennis! Get yourself over to the medical centre at the double. See if he's there. You've got ten minutes. *Sprint man!* Mr Taylor! Go to Victory College. Check the public rooms. See if he's dozed off over a newspaper or something. *Move it!* Mr Adair! You can do his room. Check the ablutions area at the same time. *Go!* The rest of you keep your eyes open and let me know the minute he gets here. I am gonna fucking kill him!'

Jack set off at a jog towards Victory College, the high collar of his blues jacket chafing against his neck. He was cursing Asad with every stride as the polish on his boots cracked and started to flake off. It took him three minutes to cover the distance, by which time beads of sweat were already coursing down his face.

He slammed into the double doors at the entrance and, without pausing, hit the wooden staircase at a run heading for the first floor. First stop was the ablutions area, which was nearer to the staircase than Asad's room. Jack kicked the door open, shouting. 'Asad, are you in here? You're late. Slater's going bloody berserk. Where are you?'

He rammed each of the cubicle doors with his open palm. All of them crashed back on their hinges. The washroom was empty.

Then Jack was running along the long straight corridor, yelling as he ran. 'Come on, Asad. You're late. Get out here. Fast!'

Nothing stirred at the far end of the corridor. Panting, Jack reached Asad's room. He knocked with his right hand while simultaneously grabbing and pushing with his left. As the door swung open, he heard movement inside.

He caught a glimpse of Asad standing just to the right of the door. He was dressed in his blues trousers with their distinctive red stripe, but he had yet to put on his tunic. In his hand, he was holding a pistol. Jack's brain only had time to register 'suicide vest' before the pistol crashed down on his head, knocking him cold.

Asad cocked the pistol, bent over Jack and pressed the cold muzzle into the soft tissue behind his right ear. Then he paused. Jack hadn't stirred—he was obviously out for the count. Perhaps he didn't need to die today. After all, Jack had been one of the very few cadets to have shown him any sort of friendship. No, today, Jack could live. Others would die.

Out on New College square, Colour Sergeant Slater was seething. Fifteen minutes had passed, and the Junior Division were about to step off. Out of the three cadets that he had sent off to track down Asad, only two had returned. Now Asad was still missing, and Adair along with him. He heard the click of hobnailed boots close by. It was Company Sergeant Major Anderson. That was all he needed.

'Everything all right, Colour?' inquired the sergeant major.

Slater's momentary hesitation was almost imperceptible. Almost. It was *his* platoon. Whatever happened in it was down to him. That included having two cadets missing from parade. It took him a fraction of a second to consider attempting the obvious lie. But he immediately discounted it. Anderson had a nose that could sniff out trouble like a bloodhound, and Slater could see it already starting to twitch.

'I take that's a no then, Colour?' Anderson had spotted Slater's momentary flicker of hesitation and was onto it in a flash.

'No, sir. Er... I mean, yes, sir.'

'And?'

'It's bin Hashim and Adair, sir. Not on parade.'

'You mean to tell me that Amiens Company is precisely five minutes and thirty seconds from marching onto Old College square for Sovereign's Parade, and you have two cadets AWOL?'

'Yes, sir.'

'Right, whether they fucking turn up or don't fucking turn up, I want your boots in front of my desk, in my office, immediately after this parade. Got it, Colour?'

'Got it, sir,' Slater replied glumly.

With a despairing shake of the head Sergeant Major Anderson turned on his heel and headed back across the square. Just for a second the merest hint of a smile alighted on his face. Anyone who noticed it might almost have thought it was a look of satisfaction. They'd have been wrong. It was a look of triumph.

Meanwhile, Slater began to vent his fury on No. 1 Platoon.

'Gentlemen, you have let me down. Worse still, you have made me look a total muppet in front of the company sergeant major. Nobody, I mean *nobody*, does that. Contrary to popular belief, I am not here to wipe your sad, useless arses every minute of the sodding day. One of you should have spotted Asad missing bloody hours ago when we could have done something about it. Right, you can forget about going on leave tomorrow. You'll be back here at first light, marching up and down in quick time to my command until I'm convinced Number One Platoon can get its shagging act together. Got it?'

'Yes, Colour Sergeant!'

'And if any of you swinging dicks have got a problem with that, you can blame your mates Mr bin Hashim and Mr Adair, both of whom will be in front of the company commander as soon as we get this parade over and done with. Got it?'

*'Yes, Colour Sergeant!'*

Quickly rearranging the ranks to cover the gap left by the two missing cadets, Colour Sergeant Slater prepared to march the platoon towards Old College parade square.

# Chapter Twenty-Three

When Jack came to, it took him a moment to take in where he was. All he knew was that his head hurt like crazy. He felt his temple, from where most of the throbbing seemed to come. His hand passed over a massive bruise that still appeared to be swelling. A few feet away on the floor were his hat and rifle. They looked as if they had been carelessly tossed aside. What were they doing on the floor? What was *he* doing on the floor?

Gradually his senses returned. His eyes focused on the detail of the room. He knew it wasn't his, although it looked very similar. The sink and bed had changed sides. It was as if someone had created a mirror image of his own room.

He struggled to his knees. He was in his dress blues. What the hell was he doing lying on the floor of somebody else's room in his best parade uniform? His eye line was now level with the bedside shelf. On it was a single photo frame. Jack reached out for it clumsily, almost knocking it off the table at his first attempt. He grabbed the frame and flipped it round to face him. An Arab family stared out of the picture. In the middle of the group, looking like the much-adored favourite son, was Asad bin Hashim.

And then he knew exactly where he was. And as he realised, he started to run.

*Wage war on all the idolaters as they are waging war on all of you, and know that Allah is with those who keep their duty unto him.* Asad was mumbling the verses from the Koran as he flew down the stairs of Victory College. In the distance, he could hear the band playing. It wasn't supposed to have been like this. Nothing was going according to plan. When he'd rehearsed it over and over again in his head, it had all seemed so simple. Having put on the suicide vest, he would tape the wire leading to the initiation switch to his bare right arm, to prevent it become dislodged beneath his tunic sleeve. Then he would simply slip his jacket over the top, before spending time in prayer to purify himself for the task ahead. In due course, he would join the ranks of his fellow cadets, from where he would launch his attack on the heir to the throne during the march past. *For those that make war against God and His apostle and spread disorder in the land shall be slain and crucified.*

The fact that it was all going wrong was entirely his fault. He had made the fundamental mistake of only rehearsing the procedure in his head. Although he'd examined the suicide vest in detail, looking for any flaws—a loose wire or a weak connection—he had not tried it on under his blues jacket. Why hadn't he thought of this? He *knew* that the tunic was a tight fit. Somehow he'd imagined that he would be able to fit the vest underneath it without it showing. How stupid! *Oh*

*Allah, grant me sincerity, correctness, acceptance, steadfastness and a good ending.*

Instead of preparing himself in good time, saying his last prayers, and walking out to join No.1 Platoon on parade, he'd found himself making frantic last-minute adjustments to the vest to force it to fit under his clothes. With sweat pouring from his forehead and his hands shaking wildly, he had carefully pulled the detonators from two of the slabs of plastic explosive. Then he'd discarded those two slabs, reducing the vest's overall bulk. This still left four other slabs, each laced with over fifty ball bearings to achieve the required fragmentation effect. At a range of less than two metres, he reasoned, the difference between four and six slabs would be negligible. Prince Charles would still be shredded by the explosion. *For garments of fire have been prepared for the unbelievers.*

As the time for the parade had drawn near, the corridor outside his room had come alive with the sound of exuberant voices mingled with the clomping of boots. Somebody's fist had thumped against his door on the way past, startling him: 'Come on, Asad. We're on!' But nobody had tried the handle. As the noise had faded into the distance and silence fell, his sense of panic had increased. He'd had to hurry to make the final adjustments, knowing that his absence from the squad would soon be noticed. *But it is better to sit alone than in company with the bad.*

By the time he'd strapped the vest on, the entire floor had been quiet for ten minutes. He only had to tape down the wire leading to the initiation switch, when he'd heard running footsteps pounding down the corridor, and a lone voice bellowing. It was Jack Adair. Of course they would send out search parties! He'd just had time to grab the Glock 17 pistol that lay at the bottom of the black holdall sitting on his bed, when Jack had cannoned into the door. *Fight in the cause of Allah those who fight you.*

Having seen Jack in action during the milling, Asad knew that he only had one chance to put him down. Instinctively he smashed the butt end of the pistol into Jack's right temple, felling him instantly, like a sheep in an abattoir. It had taken him two more minutes to fix the wire, button up his tunic, and clip on his white belt, before sprinting from the room. He would probably be too late to join the march past, but if he moved with stealth and speed, he could still launch a devastating attack. *For they have drawn on themselves wrath upon wrath. And humiliating is the punishment of those who reject Faith.*

Jack had no idea how long he'd been unconscious. As he dashed through the doors of Victory College and out onto the small front courtyard he half expected to see a pall of smoke rising from the direction of Old College square. Instead, he was greeted by the sound of the band playing. He still had time to stop Asad. He just didn't know how much.

The distance between Victory College and Old College was about a quarter of a mile. It was a straight run across the immaculately tended sports pitches, with just one obstacle in the way—the Wishstream—a small river that skirted two sides of the Victory College. Around two feet deep, and lined on either side by sloping concrete banks, it might as well have been a miniature moat. But, although it barred his route, Jack didn't have the time to divert around it to the nearest bridge a couple of hundred yards away.

He hit the edge of the Wishstream at a run and leapt into the water. It washed over his knees, causing him to fall forward and completely immersing him. He stood up spluttering and drove on for the far bank about fifteen feet away. By the time he reached the angled concrete side, he was struggling to maintain his pace. He slammed his boot into the incline, felt it slip and plunged back down full length into the water. He struggled up again and threw himself forward, scrabbling to grasp the top edge of the man-made bank and pull himself up. And then he was out and running, oblivious to his waterlogged boots and saturated uniform. In the distance he could see the parade commencing. He knew that he only had minutes to stop Asad getting through to the saluting base. He had to get there first.

Asad had crossed the Wishstream just minutes before Jack but had discounted the sprint across the sports field. Prince Charles's presence would necessitate a substantial security cordon—no matter how discreet—and he couldn't afford to blunder into it. Now was the time for stealth. If he kept to the tree-lined riverbank, he could work his way round to the woods bordering Sandhurst's lake. That would give him a covered approach to within a couple of hundred yards of the spectator stands and the saluting base. If he smartened himself up, he might be able to march confidently across the last bit of open ground without being challenged. And if he was, he would just have to count on speed to get through to his target without being intercepted. *Be quick in the race for forgiveness from your Lord, for a garden, whose width is that of the heavens and of the earth, is prepared for the righteous.*

On Old College square, the Academy's entire complement of six companies had marched into position, and the waiting had commenced. The long line of cadets arrayed in 'Review Order' facing the long line of spectators in the stands. Family and friends trying to pick out their loved ones in the identically uniformed ranks. Cadets trying to pick out the prettiest girls in the crowd—anything to take their minds off the bead of sweat coursing down the forehead, the itchy nose, the slightly dislodged cap, or the increasing weight of the rifle. Colour sergeants at the rear, eyes constantly scanning for signs of idleness or 'bobbing' in the ranks.

Waiting.

Waiting for the limousine carrying the Prince to glide into view and pull up smoothly by the statue of Queen Victoria, some 250 yards from the parade square. Waiting for one of the most famous men in the world to alight and, accompanied by a small entourage and two baton-carrying cadets, to walk down the unerringly straight road that led to the saluting base.

Jack scanned the open sports field ahead of him. There was no sign of Asad. Then he thought he detected a flicker of movement in the trees further to his left. Had he imagined it? He stared harder. There it was again. No doubt now. It was Asad, creeping stealthily through the undergrowth near the lake, moving slowly but inexorably towards his target. Jack stepped back into the tree line himself in an effort to remain unseen. If he could circle round behind the Arab, he might be able to stop him in his tracks before he was detected.

The smooth purr of a car engine drew his attention back to Victoria's statue. Even from that distance, he could pick out the distinctive figure of Prince Charles alighting from a Bentley, the Academy commandant fluttering around him like an over-attentive mother hen. A small posse of military assistants, equerries and other hangers-on, bunching loosely together, followed in their wake.

He quickly shot a look back in Asad's direction. The Arab had moved forward slightly but didn't look ready to make his dash for the target. He must have decided to wait until the Prince was on the saluting dais and everyone's concentration was on the parade.

Jack had to move fast. Crouching low, he made short dashes through the tree line, pausing every few yards or so to check his quarry. Asad, now kneeling, continued staring straight ahead, obviously weighing up his options and oblivious to the approaching threat. As Jack drew closer, he moved well beyond the range of Asad's peripheral vision, until he was virtually directly behind him. Only another ten yards or so to go.

Then the twig snapped.

In an instant Asad swung round and was staring right at him. The Arab stood, twisting to face Jack, and bringing the Glock up into a straight-armed firing position in a single smooth movement.

'I gave you a chance, Adair. Shame you have wasted it.'

Less than 300 yards away everything had gone silent on the parade square as the Prince and his entourage drew closer to the viewing stands.

'You can't shoot me now,' Jack growled contemptuously. 'As soon as they hear the shots they'll put a ring of steel round the Prince and you won't get anywhere near him.'

'Jack, you rehearsed this parade many, many times. You know it well. In two minutes, Charles gets to the saluting base. Then, the entire Academy presents arms for the royal salute, and the band plays the National Anthem. That is when you die. Will any notice the single pop of this pistol from three hundred yards? Drink in the view and take your last breath, *kuffar.*'

'Okay, what's going on, gentlemen?'

The voice came from the road alongside the tree line. In the intensity of the moment, neither Jack nor Asad had noticed the approach of two uniformed police constables from the Royal Protection Squad. Both were carrying Heckler and Koch MP5s, which they were already unshouldering. As Asad momentarily looked sideways, Jack took his chance, hurling himself into a charge. Hearing the rustle of foliage as Jack pounded forward, Asad turned and loosed off two unaimed shots in rapid succession from the Glock. The bullets flew wide. In desperation he tried to correct his aim and fired again. But then Jack was on him, driving his entire bodyweight into the Arab's midriff and bowling him over. The pistol flew away into the undergrowth.

Asad pushed off from the ground with all his strength, trying to send Jack flying backwards, but only succeeded in dislodging him so that he slid over to one side. With a superhuman effort, Jack launched himself again, but his adversary used the moment of freedom to lash out with a kick that caught him in the face. Struggling to his feet, the

Arab turned to start his sprint, but was tripped by Jack making a desperate grab at his ankle. As he fell, Jack pounced once more, landing heavily on Asad's back. A length of white electrical flex dangling from Asad's tunic sleeve caught his eye. It was the firing switch for the bomb. He lunged for it but missed. The Arab realised what Jack was doing and fumbled to seize control of the switch himself. He would rather join the martyrs, and take this *kuffar* with him, than surrender. Jack could see the wire whipping around but couldn't get to it. Instead, he concentrated all of his efforts on restraining the Arab's hands.

So intent was he on preventing Asad gaining the switching mechanism for the device that he'd completely forgotten about the armed police only yards away, now with their weapons shouldered in the firing position.

*'Stop. Armed police. Stay where you are!'*

By now, Jack had Asad's arms pinned to the floor, but he knew that he dare not release his grip.

'He's a suicide bomber, he's got a bomb!' screamed Jack.

'Get clear, get clear, I'm going to shoot!' one of the police shouted back.

From the parade square, the first bars of the National Anthem struck up as Sandhurst presented arms for the royal salute to the heir to the throne.

Jack made an instant decision. He would have to trust to the copper's good aim, or they would both go up. With all his remaining strength, he flung Asad's wrists away from him and rolled clear, throwing his own hands over his head as he did so. Immediately, he could hear two shots crack out.

Asad's body jerked as the rounds hit it. Disabled, but moving, he was still fumbling for the initiation switch, his actions clumsy, like those of a drunk, and slowing by the second. Jack took his chance. Reaching round to his right hip, he groped frantically for the bayonet that hung from his white ceremonial belt. His first thought was to try to cut the wire, but Asad could grab it at any second. Naked, brute survival instinct kicked in. Bringing his right arm over in an arc from his hip, Jack plunged the bayonet up to its hilt in Asad's throat. A fountain of blood from the severed jugular sprayed into the air, drenching Jack's head and shoulders, and drawing a splattered line across the leaf-strewn grass.

Asad's body went into spasm as the life ebbed from it. Jack collapsed forward, his head resting on the Arab's chest. He felt the Asad's lungs heave their last couple of gasps before becoming still. Dead still.

# Chapter Twenty-Four



*Headquarters, Royal Military Academy Sandhurst*

Major General Johnny Moncrieff, Commandant of the Royal Military Academy Sandhurst, sat back in his chair at the head of the conference table, rested his elbows on the armrests and steepled his fingers. 'Thank God for Adair, that's all I can say.'

There were ten others in the room: the key members of the Academy Headquarters staff, along with Major Breeze and Captain McAlease from Amiens Company. Some of those present nodded solemnly in agreement with the general. Nobody spoke. The enormity of the events of the last twenty-four hours had had a numbing effect. The lapse of security that had allowed a suicide bomber to get so close to the heir to the throne at one of the world's most prestigious military academies was scandalous.

Behind the scenes, in a flurry of embarrassment, the British Security Service—MI5—was hastily conducting its own internal witch hunt to explain its failure to identify Asad bin Hashim as a member of al Qaeda. It was like a game of pass the parcel—when the music stopped, somebody would be carrying the can. General Moncrieff sincerely hoped that it wouldn't be him. After all, he told himself, the Academy just accepts what it's sent—it's not as if it undertakes the background vetting of cadets. But still he felt uneasy. Ministers under pressure had a habit of shovelling shit downhill.

Coming out of his reverie, the general once again broke the sombre blanket of silence that had settled on the room. 'Well, gentlemen, in the words of the Duke of Wellington, it was a damn near run thing. Now we need to deal with the aftermath. The official line is to play the whole thing down. This was an unfortunate incident in which one of our overseas students took his own life with a firearm because he feared that his performance wasn't up to scratch and he couldn't face the shame back in his home country. Officer Cadet Adair stumbled across him with the loaded gun, tried to talk him out of it, but bin Hashim fired at Adair before turning the weapon on himself. Now, let me make this clear. There was *no* suicide vest. There was *no* al Qaeda involvement. And there was certainly *no* bayonet. We're also avoiding any reference to the Glock handgun. The assumption should be that this was carried out with a standard service SA80 rifle. Just to emphasise the point, there is now a strict D-Notice on this. That means, no talking to the press. At all. Everyone got that?'

The general's piercing gaze swept round the room, making eye contact with every single individual in it— searching for any sign of uncertainty. Any weakness.

He continued, 'Added to which, this... um... "incident" now has an operational name: Op *Cormorant*. It's classified Top Secret. So, anyone breathing a word outside will find themselves in contravention of the Official Secrets Act. Is that also understood?'

'Sir,' came the murmured response.

'The Academy adjutant will ask you all to sign in to the classified compartment in due course. In the meantime, we need to do something with Adair that meets the expectations of all concerned. We now have an unexpected hero in our midst. But one whose heroism cannot be publicly trumpeted. The Prime Minister wants the heat taken off his Defence Secretary. MI5 wants to avoid any embarrassment. The Chief of the General Staff wants the Army shown in the best possible light. And, against all of this, we must balance Adair's own interests. Which, I'm afraid, for the time being, fall very much in last place. What's he like?' Who's his company commander?'

Major Breeze cleared his throat. All eyes turned to him.

'Yes, Tony?'

'Frankly, sir, he's a bit of a mixed bag. His record shows that he completed a full five-year engagement with the French Foreign Legion's Parachute Regiment before joining the British Army. He's sponsored by the Royal Logistic Corps but, not surprisingly, has done very well on field exercises. He's pretty aggressive. This can be to his advantage, but he's also pretty hot-headed, and there's no love lost between him and his company sergeant major.'

'Why on earth did he go to the Loggies after being a Foreign Legion para?' quizzed General Moncrieff, who had spent much of his career with the SAS and had little time for the people who brought up the fuel, ammunition, spare parts and rations.

'His age, sir. He's twenty-six, and not a graduate. The teeth arms didn't want to sponsor someone without a degree who was already getting on a bit in comparison with his peers. He can also come across as being a bit truculent.'

The general rolled his eyes. 'And I suppose he didn't go to the right school either, eh? Well, he shouldn't have any trouble getting into any regiment of his choice now. I'm sure they'll all be sniffing around once the rumours get out,' the Commandant observed, with just a touch of cynicism. 'I wouldn't want to make any predictions, but certain very senior people might look quizzically at us if he doesn't get the Sword of Honour as best cadet of his intake. And that's a feather in the cap for any regiment that signs him up. On top of that, he's bound to pick up a gong for gallantry. Perhaps not one of the top tier awards—we don't want to stoke up the media circus—but certainly some sort of worthwhile trinket.'

As the commandant paused to let his words sink in, one or two of those present considered how their own careers might have soared if they'd joined their regiments straight from Sandhurst with the twin advantages of the Sword of Honour *and* a gallantry award.

'What's his platoon commander got to say about him?' The general surveyed the room looking for a likely candidate. His eyes alighted on Captain McAlease, who was already visibly struggling to form his words from his place at the far end of the table.

'To be honest, sir, until the incident yesterday, the man's been a walking disaster. In terms of personality, he's defiant of authority and displays a surly, uncooperative manner.

Undoubtedly, he has a certain degree of self-confidence, but it comes with an aggressive streak and a chip on his shoulder a mile wide. He has very few friends, and he's completely alienated both his company sergeant major *and* his platoon colour sergeant.'

'Not quite your cup of tea then, Robert?' the general suggested, almost mockingly. 'Wouldn't have anything to do with his performance on Exercise *Second Flush* would it?'

'Oh! You know about that then, sir.'

'Yes. Perhaps your commandant's not quite so out of touch as you might like to think.' The general resisted the urge to add, 'you tosser'.

Captain McAlease, missing the subtle warning in the commandant's tone, continued. 'In that case, General, you'll be aware that he was one of only two cadets captured during the infiltration phase of the exercise. He led the other cadet in an escape attempt that admittedly showed a fair degree of initiative, but it was typical of his unthinking selfishness. Such a caper in weather conditions below freezing could have caused an enormous amount of disruption and anxiety. Another hour and a full hue and cry would have been launched, bringing the whole exercise to a halt.'

'Okay, so that's strike one against him. And what else has he done to blot his copybook? The milling, perhaps? Was that strike two?'

'Oh! You know about that too, sir.'

The general said nothing, but continued to hold the captain in his level, unwavering gaze.

'Sir, he was paired with Company Sergeant Major Anderson during a milling exercise in the gym. He was issued with boxing gloves but broke the rules by kicking the sergeant major in the head and knocking him out. I had to speak to him afterwards about lack of officer-like qualities, but I'm still not sure he even grasped that he'd done anything wrong.'

The general mulled this information over before speaking again. 'Well, you obviously don't like him. But then, leaders aren't there to be liked. And from everything I've heard, he sounds like a leader to me. A leader with a maverick spirit perhaps, but a leader, nonetheless. And that's what we're trying to produce here. Not people who like to follow the rule books slavishly.'

The commandant looked pointedly at Captain McAlease, who reddened at the implied rebuke.

'Now, assuming that we don't plan to throw him out anytime soon,' the General again stared at Captain McAlease, 'I want him very carefully handled. He is *not* to give any press interviews. He is *not* to appear on any television shows. And he is *not* to let this whole business go to his head. Are we all quite clear?'

'Yes, sir,' chorused the room.

'Oh, and Captain McAlease.'

'Sir?'

'You'd better let him know that several of the regimental representatives from the combat arms might now be quite interested in talking to him. He could well stand a chance of getting into the regiment of his choice after all.'

# Chapter Twenty-Five

Even as General Moncricff was speaking, the phone was ringing at the regimental headquarters of the King's Royal Rangers. Based in Shrewsbury, well away from the 1st and 2nd Battalions, in Tidworth and Colchester respectively, the headquarters had no operational role. Instead, it acted as the custodian of the regimental spirit, confining itself to regimental custom and tradition, dress, ceremonial, welfare matters and recruiting. At the centre of the headquarters sat the regimental colonel. Now in his mid-fifties, Colonel Dick Millen was an officer of the old school. A man of austere tastes, with thirty-three years' service under his belt, he was feared by every subordinate in the regiment. Even one or two senior officers treated him with a degree of wariness.

As a younger officer, Dick Millen had gained a reputation for being 'difficult'. Although rigidly courteous, the man lacked warmth. His manner was always stern, always terse. It was not an approach that endeared him to his men. It might also have been the final deciding factor when his superiors concluded that, in terms of further promotion, Dick Millen had reached his ceiling.

He answered the phone in his customary brusque style. 'Millen.'

'Aah, Dick, how lovely to hear your voice,' Lieutenant General Sir Valentine Phillips purred down the line, dripping insincerity with every word.

It wasn't lovely for either of them. Having passed out of Sandhurst at the same time as Valentine Phillips, Dick Millen resented the fact such a self-seeking, unprincipled arse-licker should have overtaken him in the promotion stakes. No one had been more surprised than Millen when Phillips had won the Military Cross for leading the heroic defence of Hotel 55. Even all these years later, he still thought there was something fishy about that. No proof, just gut instinct, but something about it smelt. Of fish. For his part, Phillips looked down with disdain upon a man who, in his lofty opinion, failed to display the effortless charm and style that one would expect from an officer of the King's Royal Rangers. The awkward, but mannered, posturing between the pair disguised more than three decades of mutual loathing.

'Good to hear you too, sir. What can I do for you?' Colonel Millen preferred to use 'sir', rather than the more congenial 'General'. The formality suited his nature. It also reminded him that he should respect Valentine Phillips for the rank he held—even if he didn't respect him as a man.

'Dick, I'm sure you're already onto it,' drawled the general, 'but there's a whisper of a rumour coming out of Sandhurst that an officer cadet saved Prince Charles's life during yesterday's Sovereign's Parade. Are you up to speed on this yet?'

'No, sir, I've no idea what you're talking about.'

'Oh.' The general managed to sound slightly peeved, as if implying that regimental headquarters was behind the power curve as usual.

Without waiting for a response, he carried on. 'Well, it's like this. One of the overseas cadets was killed yesterday, in the woods down near the lake, while the parade was actually in progress. They're trying to pass it off as a straightforward suicide with an SA80. But I've heard on the QT that there's more to it. Seems that said student was fully kitted-out with a suicide vest but was intercepted by one of the British officer cadets, who took him out with... get this... a bayonet. A chap called Adair. As it happens, Adair's in the same Sandhurst platoon as my youngest, Vyvyan. I spoke to my boy last night. I'll be honest with you, Vyvyan can't stand the man. Says he's a bit of a yob. Tells me that Adair actually tried for the KRR, but we turned him down, so he's currently sponsored by the Logistic Corps. I'm sure you can see what a waste it would be for a chap like that to go to the Loggies. Sandbags would be daft not to give him the Sword of Honour for saving Charles's life, and he's bound to get a gallantry gong to boot. Just the sort of image we need to attract some really topflight candidates. After all, it's not as if we'd have to hang on to him forever. If he's no good, we can give him the heave-ho after a three-year, short service commission. But by that time, he might have been just the shot-in-the-arm we need to boost our recruiting.'

Colonel Millen heaved an inward sigh. 'Okay, leave it with me, sir. I'll do some digging around and get back to you as soon as I can.'

'Jolly good, Dick. Knew I could count on you. Don't hang around, though. As soon as this slips out there'll be a queue a mile long after him.'

It took Colonel Millen fifteen minutes or so to find the thin file relating to Officer Cadet Jack Adair. He called the general back.

'Hello, sir, Dick Millen again. I think I've found the file on the man you're after. If it's the same chap, he came to us about six months ago looking for sponsorship through AOSB.'

'So what happened?'

'Looks like we gave him pretty short shrift. There's a letter on file from a retired cavalry officer responsible for officer recruiting in the Dover area. It's hardly a ringing endorsement. If anything, it damns with faint praise. So we palmed Adair off with some nonsense about not having any vacancies. I guess our chances of nabbing him will therefore depend on how pissed-off he is with us for turning him down the first time.'

Valentine Phillips winced as the words 'pissed-off' travelled down the line. 'Dick, I'm counting on you. If anyone can get him for us, I know you can. It's important. Not for me, not for you, but for the regiment. Go to it. Okay?'

'Sir.' Colonel Millen heard the click of the handset ringing off at the other end. He replaced his own receiver and sat looking down at the phone on his desk.

'Twat,' he said, as if addressing General Phillips in person.

True to his ascetic outlook, Dick Millen's work ethic was both meticulous and unshakeable. Like his hero, the Duke of Wellington, he believed in doing the work *of* the day *in* the day. He expected this of his staff too, which did not make him the easiest boss to work for. It also made for very late office hours. It was not unusual for Colonel Millen's subordinates to bring two berets in to work. As long as an officer's beret was visible in the office, that officer just *had* to be in the headquarters somewhere—one could not leave the building in uniform without headgear. The second beret facilitated the chance for a brief escape, even if only to nip home to bathe the kids before bedtime or to grab a quick bite to eat before heading back to work.

That afternoon, after his conversation with General Phillips, Dick Millen just could not settle. He had always harboured strong suspicions that events at Hotel 55 were not as they seemed, and the call, with the mention of Sergeant Nick Adair, had brought his doubts flooding back. He tried to push them away and focus on the business of the day, but he could not shake that brainworm niggling away inside his head. Eventually, exasperated with himself, he realised that if he didn't address it, none of the day's work would get done. That would mean doing the work *of* the day the *next* day. And that would never do.

He reached inside the top drawer of his desk for the key to the filing cabinet in the corner of the room—the filing cabinet that held the regiment's most sensitive archives. In amongst the details of disciplinary matters, sackings for incompetence, letters of censure, and investigations into fatalities, lay the bulging file on the battle of Hotel 55. He knew it well. Every time the 'niggle' took him, he would be drawn to it. Not that he could prove anything, but certain details just did not add up.

For starters, he could not understand why Sergeant Nick Adair, formerly one of the regiment's top soldiers, would suddenly become its number one coward—albeit a dead one. Adair had been in action before, and had always led from the front. Turning chicken and hiding in a steel locker during an attack was entirely out-of-character.

By contrast, the only two witnesses to his death were hardly known for their bravery. As a platoon commander in Northern Ireland, Valentine Phillips had earned himself a reputation for trying to find any excuse *not* to go out on patrol—even nicknamed 'the Eternal Flame' by the lads because he never went out. Walters was a fat knacker, who struggled to pass his fitness test, and would never have made it past lance corporal were it not for Hotel 55. As it was, he ended up as a colour sergeant, strutting about with a Military Cross on his chest. No, nothing added up.

Millen took out the file and returned to his desk. It was the Coroner's report into Adair's death that interested him most, because that held the photographs taken by a Royal Military Police investigator shortly after the battle. He extracted the brown cardboard folder containing the photographs and began to flick through. There were twenty pictures in all. Some focused on specific damage within the operations room at Hotel 55. These generally bore small, stick-on, coloured arrows, highlighting particular impact points. Others were more general shots, trying to take in the whole room from different angles.

Millen scrutinised one of the wide-view photographs of the room, taken from the doorway. Much of the blast seemed to have gone upwards and outwards from the floor, blowing out a substantial portion of the right-hand wall. The opposite wall, on the left, showed less damage. This is where the lightweight steel, wardrobe-sized locker stood. Certainly, there seemed to be some small fragmentation holes in the locker door, but they were curiously high up, given that Adair was believed to have been crouching down when he was killed. Also, in addition to the fatal wound, caused by the grenade fragment that entered his brain, Adair had suffered at least sixteen other non-fatal wounds, principally down his right arm and right leg. But where were the corresponding holes in the door?

When this had been raised at the Coroner's inquest, Valentine Phillips had suggested that the door may have swung open at the last minute. This *might* explain the lack of holes in the door consistent with Sergeant Adair's injuries, as he would have been completely exposed to the blast. But, if that had happened, surely some fragments would have hit and pierced the *inside* of the door if it were open? Instead, close-up photographs of the few impact holes showed which way the metal around them had deformed and splayed. The evidence suggested that the fragments had punched through the door from the *outside*. They could only have done this if the door had been closed when the grenade detonated. Except—and this came right back to the original point—if it had been closed, there should be more holes. None of it made sense.

Added to that, why did Adair, protected by the locker, suffer such catastrophic injuries, compared to Phillips and Walters, who were supposedly both in the open? Somehow, all of this had been glossed over at the inquest. Millen suspected that the matching testimony of two 'heroes', along with the fact that the Coroner was dealing with three other deaths in the same incident, had blinded everyone to the obvious—that something about Hotel 55 smelt. Of fish.

# Chapter Twenty-Six

*Medway Maritime Hospital, Kent*

'Luckily, gassing oneself in a car is becoming increasingly difficult now that catalytic converters remove about ninety-nine per cent of the carbon monoxide. Even so, if someone is in an enclosed space with a car engine idling for a sufficiently long period, unconsciousness and even death are the likely outcomes. You see, carbon monoxide combines with haemoglobin to form carboxyhaemoglobin in the blood. As a result, oxygen is unable to bind with the haemoglobin, so the oxygen-carrying capacity of the blood is reduced. This in turn leads to hypoxia, affecting those organ systems of the body that are most reliant on oxygen—principally the central nervous system and the heart. Have you any idea how long he'd been in the garage?'

Michelle, who had become increasingly baffled by the medical jargon, was taken by surprise by the sudden question. The doctor, a thin-faced man with bifocals and dark hair parted with ruthless precision just above his left ear, was staring at her with a piercing intensity, awaiting her answer.

'Erm... I don't know. I'd only just turned up, and he wasn't in the house. Then I heard the car engine running in the garage. So I thought, that's funny. What's he doing with the car? So I went to have a look, and there he was.'

'And you say he was in the driving seat, with a hose coming from the exhaust?'

'Yes, doctor. It looked as if he was trying to kill himself.'

'And have you any idea why he would want to do that?'

'Um... yes... er... no... I don't really know. We'd separated, you see. He was drinking a lot. An awful lot. It was ruining us. He'd lost his job and his driving licence. Then he couldn't pay the mortgage, so we were going to lose the house. Nothing I said seemed to change him... to make him realise what he was doing. Even when I'd shout and bawl. It was like nothing could get through to him. He was dragging us both down. So in the end, I left him.'

'And you turned up back at the house today and just stumbled across him?'

'Yeah. I decided to give him one more chance. We've been together since we weren't much more than kids. Even went to the same school. My dad said he'd help us out with the mortgage if I really wanted to give it one last go. But Ivan was going to have to get himself sorted out. Proper like. Once and for all. So I came home to talk it over with him. To see if there was anything still there.'

The tears that had formed in the corners of Michelle's eyes started to flow down her cheeks. The doctor proffered a tissue and motioned that it was fine to stop speaking. She took it, but waved a hand, indicating that she wished to carry on.

'When I got into the house, I could see that he'd been drinking out of control. When I was living there, he'd try and do it in secret so that I didn't nag him all the time. At least that held him back a bit. But the minute I walked in today, the stink of booze hit me. There were empty bottles everywhere. And writing.'

'Writing? What do you mean?'

'He'd been writing stuff. On bits of paper. Scribbles and scrawls most of it. Just like a kid's. Saying he never did it. Over and over again. And pictures of soldiers. Dead ones, lying in pools of blood. And lots of times he'd written "coward" in big letters all over the paper.'

'Michelle, it sounds as if your husband has some significant underlying problem. Whether he was really trying to kill himself today, or whether it was just a cry for help, it seems to me that the alcoholism is a reaction to something that he's buried deep inside. Do you think there's any significance in the drawings of soldiers? Was he in the Army at any stage, for example?'

'Yeah, he was in for twenty-two years. Won the Military Cross. I don't think that would be the problem though. He was always happiest when he was still in the Army. It was when he came out that the problems started.'

'Well, you never know. Sometimes these things are so deeply hidden that it takes quite a while to drag them out and deal with them. I'm no psychologist, but I am going to recommend a course of counseling once he gets over the physical effects of the carbon monoxide. I just hope that he takes up my recommendation and sticks with it.'

'Yes. I hope so too, doctor. But I don't think it will have been anything to do with the Army. Ivan was always a hero, you see. He even has the medal to prove it.'

# Chapter Twenty-Seven

*Royal Military Academy Sandhurst*

In the old days, they would have aspired to be field marshals. But that was in the days of a bigger Army. Nowadays, being a member of the Royal Family was the qualification for that hallowed rank. For *real* officers, the ceiling stopped at general. But they were still the inner circle, those three- and four-star officers who had passed effortlessly through each promotion, rarely lingering long at each. Several traits were common amongst them: charisma, bravery, intelligence and impeccable connections. It was rare for any individual to possess all four; most could only count two or three. But a fifth factor unified them all: opportunity. They had all, at some stage, been in just the right place at just the right time. Enough to propel them through each of the concentric outer layers towards the centre of power, as if wearing rocket packs, bypassing others less blessed along the way.

And now Jack Adair was getting his own booster pack. Because he had been in just the right place at just the right time. And because, when tested, he had been brave.

The approach from the KRR had been only days in coming: a note through the internal mail asking if Jack might 'pop across' to meet the regiment's representative at Sandhurst, a major commanding one of the other training companies. An invitation to supper followed. The Royal Logistic Corps made a valiant play to retain Jack's interest, but he already had his sights set on a different goal. Towards the end of his intermediate term, he was one of ten candidates summoned to a formal interview with the Rangers' Regimental Selection Board. It was a surprisingly relaxed affair. There was enormous interest in his former service with the Legion. No longer was it seen as an experience likely to develop 'bad habits'. Indeed, the Board seemed to hang on his every word. His lack of a degree wasn't even mentioned. Nor was he asked about his family connections with the regiment. The latter was the one area where Jack thought he might still have a problem, and he'd thoroughly rehearsed his responses. But the question never came. And Jack certainly wasn't going to raise it. As he entered his third and final term, he knew his place with the KRR was secure. The icing on the cake came with his own graduation at Sovereign's Parade, when, as predicted, he marched forward proudly from the ranks to receive the Sword of Honour, all the time thinking, 'Stuff you, Josh Corrigan. Look at me now!'

And that was the day that Lieutenant General Sir Valentine Phillips, KCB, CBE, MC, finally realised the truth.

With his own son, Vyvyan, passing out on the same day, General Phillips had been one of the first people to be introduced to Jack Adair after the parade. The graduating cadets had been assembled for pre-lunch drinks in the historic Indian Army Room, close to the Grand Entrance through which they had slow-marched only a short while before. Despite his son's undisguised abhorrence for the latest Sword of Honour winner, the general was triumphant that his regiment had landed such a prize catch. He made a beeline for Jack as soon as he stepped into the room.

The conversation had been cheerful but brief. The general had too many people to see to linger over one young pup. Nearly four decades of military service had provided him with a large set of admirers and sycophants, and he was keen to bask in the warm glow of their deference. With a great display of well-wishing for Jack's immediate future, Valentine Phillips had moved on, 'working the room' as he always did. Like an ageing rock star, his very essence fed on the adoration of those around him.

It was past midnight when the general's nightmare returned. He was in the small wooden hut again. At first, most of the light had been coming from a single electric bulb dangling naked from the ceiling. But then more and more daylight had started to intrude. Shafts of light streaming through holes in the wall. Bullet holes. And every second more of them appeared, so that the beams of daylight criss-crossed the room like lasers. He wanted to put his hands over his head and make it go away. He had to hide. But there was nowhere to go.

Then he saw the wardrobe-sized, green-painted, steel locker standing in the corner of the room. That would do. He would be safe there. Except that somebody was already in it. A fat soldier in combat dress was squeezing himself inside and trying to close the door. He couldn't be allowed to do that. He was using Valentine's hiding place. He had to be pulled out. Quickly. Because the holes were still being punched in the walls all around him. Getting closer each time.

He felt himself race across the room and grab the soldier's arm. He started pulling, but the arm was like elastic. The more he pulled, the further it stretched—until it had stretched almost all of the way across the room. And the soldier was still in the locker, getting fatter by the second, expanding so that he completely filled the void. He heard himself shouting orders, screaming at the coward to get out, holding his rifle to the man's head. Until finally the fat soldier moved. He exploded out of the locker with a pop like a cork coming out of a champagne bottle, and louder than the whip-crack of bullets smashing through the walls.

Valentine dived inside the small compartment. It would be safe there. He knew it would be safe because he could see his teddy on the floor—the one that he had taken with him on his first day at boarding school. He cuddled the teddy to his chest and started to pull the door closed. If he didn't cry, perhaps Matron would give him a sweetie for being so brave. As he reached for the door, he looked up, locking eyes with somebody else in the room. Somebody that he hadn't known was there. It was another soldier. But this one had a ghastly grey face, like that of a corpse, with blue lips and dark purple lines under the eyes... Officer Cadet Jack Adair's eyes.

Valentine Phillips sat bolt upright in bed. Although he was bathed in sweat, he was shivering with the cold... and fear. The room was pitch-black. At that moment, he no longer felt like a general. He just felt like a very scared little boy. He looked around for the bullet holes in the walls.

Gradually, the realisation came to him that he was safe in his own bedroom, with his wife, Sara, sleeping soundly beside him. As his eyes adjusted to the darkness, he could just make out a glimpse of faint moonlight through the crack in the curtains, just enough for him to pick out some of the furniture in the room and gain his bearings.

As his eyes focused, so did his mind. He'd had the dream again. He knew it, even though the precise details were fading fast. This time, there had been something about an elastic arm. That hadn't happened before. It didn't surprise him. There was always an odd element to the dream—something extra to unnerve him.

Then he thought about the corpse-like soldier's eyes. They had looked so familiar. He struggled to remember the details. Yes, that's right, they were the eyes of the officer cadet that he had met for the first time today—the Sword of Honour winner who was coming to the King's Royal Rangers. Yet he was sure that he'd seen those eyes before. What was the boy's name again? Adair?

And then the truth hit him.


Colonel Dick Millen had barely settled into his office at regimental headquarters in Shrewsbury when the phone rang shortly after 8.30 am. It was Lieutenant General Sir Valentine Phillips. He did not waste time with preamble.

'Dick, I went to the Sovereign's Parade at Sandhurst yesterday.'

'Yes, sir, your son was passing out, wasn't he?'

'Yes, never mind that. Are you aware who this chap Adair is?'

'I'm sorry, sir, which particular "chap Adair" are we talking about?'

'The bloody Sword of Honour winner, of course.'

'Is this the same "bloody Sword of Honour winner" that you were so keen for me to entice into the regiment six months ago, sir?'

'Yes, of course that's who I mean. Please stop being so obtuse.'

Colonel Millen gritted his teeth to keep his emotions in check before responding. 'I take it from your tone, sir, that he's no longer flavour of the month. What's he done to upset you?'

'It's not him. It's his bloody father. Do you have any idea who his father is?'

'No, sir. Nor do I care. I thought we recruited people based on their ability these days—not on who their father was.'

'Er... yes, yes, quite. That's certainly the modern view. But are you aware that on this occasion we seem to have recruited into the regiment the son of one of its most infamous cowards, Sergeant Nick Adair? And I should know what the man was like. I was there!'

'Like father, like son, eh, sir? Is that what you mean?'

'That's exactly what I mean. It simply cannot be allowed to happen. I don't care what the boy's done; we cannot possibly have him in the regiment.'

'I think it's a bit late for that, don't you, sir?'

'What do you mean? Of course it's not too late. He's barely out of Sandhurst. He still has to get through the Platoon Commanders' Battle Course with the School of

Infantry before he joins one of the battalions proper. Surely we can do something in the meantime?'

'And how do you propose we do that, sir? First, before he even joins the Army, we tell him we have no vacancies. Then, after he saves the heir to the throne's life, we suddenly start wooing him like some lovestruck suitor. Then we find out who his father was, and we decide that it was all a mistake after all. Can you imagine what the press would make of that if it got out? I don't think we'd have a leg to stand on. I'm sorry, sir, Jack Adair's coming to the regiment, and there's nothing that you, or I, or anyone else can do about it.'

Colonel Millen just managed to catch the snort of disgust at the other end of the line before the phone was slammed down. He replaced his own receiver and sat gazing at it for a moment or two.

'Twat!' he said, before turning his attention to more pressing matters.

# Chapter Twenty-Eight

*Infantry Battle School, Brecon, Wales*

Following their graduation from Sandhurst, newly-commissioned infantry officers report to the Infantry Battle School, to complete the three-month Platoon Commanders' Battle Course. Although cynically labelled 'the fourth term at Sandhurst', it's better than that. It takes the raw product shaped by the Academy to the next level. The students learn the full array of techniques required to bring cold death to the Queen's enemies, honing their expertise in infantry weapon systems and endlessly practising battle drills in attack and defence up to company level. By the end of the course, the young officers should be capable of providing effective leadership to soldiers doing extraordinary things in difficult and dangerous circumstances. The operative word is 'should'.

The Infantry Battle School is located in Brecon, Wales. There's a good reason for this. Brecon may be one of the most picturesque parts of the country, with its dramatic landscapes and spectacular views, but it is also one of the most testing. Field conditions are severe. The terrain is punishing—steep slopes vie with evil-smelling bogs covered in ankle twisting clumps of grass—often worsened by torrential downpours and sub-zero temperatures. As the jet stream rolls in off the Irish Sea, the cold, moisture-laden, sea air transforms into fog and driving rain as it hits the mountains. But such an unforgiving environment tests strength of character and the ability to lead under pressure. It is a perfect backdrop for assessment.

Nevertheless, on the face of it, there were compensations. After the rudimentary accommodation of Sandhurst, the officers' mess at Brecon offered modern, purpose-built rooms with en suite facilities and even heated towel rails. But there was a catch. The story went that if an officer left his dog in his room at Brecon, it would die of starvation before he saw it again, such was the frequency and duration of field exercises. Nobody brought their dog.

For the first time, the young officers were now encountering soldiers at close quarters. In the field, NCOs from a specially-assigned infantry company filled the roles of section commanders and fire team leaders. The students either acted as platoon commanders and sergeants, or made up the numbers as buckshee riflemen. It gave the new second lieutenants the chance to see how *real* NCOs actually operate. For the soldiers, it confirmed their view that most officers were snobs with their heads up their own arses. Most, but not all. Jack Adair was an exception.

Jack rarely received mail. Even after his return to the UK, his contact with his mother and stepfather remained as sparse as it had throughout his five years in the Legion. Occasionally, a gaudy postcard turned up from the remaining members of *Le Mafia Anglais* when they found themselves off on some new foreign jaunt. But his former mates weren't exactly the letter writing kind—unless it was graphically lewd correspondence with some besotted French girl who'd spent her summer holiday in Corsica. He was therefore surprised to find two letters awaiting him in his pigeon-hole in the foyer of the officers' mess at Brecon.

The envelopes couldn't be more different. One was plain, flimsy and purely functional—the type that comes from a supermarket 'value' line. Jack's name and address were scribbled in an almost indecipherable scrawl. He knew immediately that it came from Mike Lawrence, now undergoing his own specialist young officer training with the Intelligence Corps. The other was far more impressive. Immaculately crisp, smooth and cream-coloured, it bore the Royal Coat-of-Arms engraved on its stick-down flap, underneath which, in discreet red capitals, were the words 'Buckingham Palace'.

The letter from the Palace was not unexpected. Shortly after leaving Sandhurst, Jack's name had featured on the New Year's Honours List for the award of the Queen's Gallantry Medal. It was less than he deserved. British gallantry medals fall into one of three levels, according to the percentage chance of getting killed. To qualify for a Level 1 award—the Victoria Cross or George Cross—the likelihood of getting killed should be at least ninety per cent. Unsurprisingly, the rate of posthumous awards is high.

The QGM counts as a Level 3, where the prospect of death is 'only' reckoned at twenty per cent. Jack knew he deserved better. A handgun *and* a suicide vest? That had to be more than fifty per cent at least! But he'd also been clearly briefed on why the incident was being played down. Getting the Sword of Honour sweetened the deal. There could be no doubt that it also smoothed his passage into the King's Royal Rangers. Not a bad trade for his silence about what had really happened.

He quickly scanned the letter from the Palace. It was an invitation, written of course in the commanding, formal style of the Royal Court:

> Sir,
>
> The Queen will hold an investiture at Buckingham Palace, at which your attendance is requested...

There was no question that he could attend. The military chain of command had been required by the Palace to ascertain Jack's availability long before the invitation was issued. It would never do for the Queen to suffer the indignity of a refusal. Good form dictates that one *always* accepts the Queen's invitations, and the military is a stickler for good form.

Of more immediate interest was the letter from Mike. Unless dragged out of himself, Jack could easily slip into the role of lone wolf. At Sandhurst, it had been Mike's friendship that had prevented this happening—a friendship that had been sealed by their triumphant escape during Exercise *Second Flush*. Now, it seemed that Mike was determined to keep the friendship alive, which was just as well, because, left to his own devices, Jack would probably have allowed it to wither on the vine.

Jack ripped the envelope open. No letter this time, just a white card with the silhouette of a dinner-jacketed James Bond seen through the grooved barrel of a gun. All of the printing on the card was in black, with one exception: the cypress green beret of the Intelligence Corps photoshopped onto James Bond's head. It was an invitation from Mike Lawrence to a '007 party' at the Defence College of Intelligence on the forthcoming Saturday. Maybe the Army's latest batch of new spooks were already getting bored with their studies. Just as well they weren't at the Infantry Battle School, Jack reflected. Brecon didn't leave much time to get bored. Weekends were generally spent recovering from the last field exercise, or preparing for the next one. Often both. But, on this occasion, he was lucky. The Monday after the party was scheduled to be classroom-based, so he could just about fit in the dash to the Int Corps' centre in Bedfordshire and back.

That evening, Jack decided to call his mother to invite her to his investiture at the Palace. The fact that he would have to invite his stepfather as well was an unfortunate, but probably unavoidable, irritant. He thumbed in the numbers and listened to the call tone, hoping that it would be his mother who picked up.

'Hello.' It was the brusque voice of his stepfather, John Robbins.

'Hi. It's Jack,' Jack said, feeling the animosity instinctively starting to rise.

'I expect you want to talk to your mother then,' came the terse response.

'Uh, yeah. Please.'

Jack waited. He could hear a rustling sound at the other end, along with snatches of whispered conversation, as if someone was holding their hand over the phone. Eventually his mother came on the line.

'Hello, Jack?'

'Hi, Mum.'

'I haven't heard from you in three weeks,' she said accusingly.

'Yeah. I know. Sorry, I've been a bit busy.'

'We've all got busy lives to lead, Jack.'

'Yeah, I know. I'll try to do better,' Jack muttered awkwardly, rolling his eyes at the customary rebuke, before continuing. 'Look, Mum, I've had the invitation from Buckingham Palace. They want me to go along so that they can pin the gong on me. You remember? I'm supposed to be getting the Queen's Gallantry Medal? It says I can bring three guests, and I'd like you and John to be there.'

There was a pause at the other end. Jack could hear his mother's breathing, the hesitation and unease unmistakable.

'When is it?' she asked flatly, almost as if it were an unnecessary burden.

Jack gave the date, matching his tone to his mum's joyless response, while thinking that the odd glimmer of excitement or pride might not have gone amiss. There was another long pause. Jack could sense that the matter was being discussed. He shifted position impatiently and began to study the backs of his hands, still cracked and raw from extended exposure to the elements on the most recent field exercise. As the seconds ticked by, his irritation grew. What was there to think about? This was important. Shouldn't this just be an automatic 'yes'?

His mother came back on the line. 'It's very nice of you to invite us, but I'm sorry that we can't make it that day.'

'Can't or won't? Look, Mum, this isn't a family trip to McDonald's that we're talking about here. This is a once-in-a-lifetime occasion. How could you not be there to see your own son getting the Queen's Gallantry Medal? If nothing else, it's an excuse for a new hat.'

'I know it's very important to you, Jack. But I'm not sure I could stand it. The Army took your dad away from me, and I didn't get any bits of tin off them then. In fact, nobody wanted to come near us after your dad was killed. Now they've nearly taken you, and you haven't even been in for a year. If you'd been killed, I'm not sure a bit of tin on a ribbon would have been any consolation. I know I sound bitter, but you haven't been through what I have. I hate the Army. So does John. On top of that, you know he's anti-monarchy. It would be totally against his principles to be at the Palace. He's just said he thinks they should divide it up into flats and hand it over to the homeless.'

'Yeah, that figures. He always was a complete dick.'

'Oh, come on, he's been very good to you. That's no way to speak about him. If you carry on like that I'll have to put the phone down.'

'Don't bother. I'll do it for you.' Jack's thumb pressed the button and the line went dead.

# Chapter Twenty-Nine

*Officers' Mess, Defence College of Intelligence,*
*Chicksands, Bedfordshire*

Just like Jack, Mike Lawrence was now going through his own specialist young officer training—at the Defence College of Intelligence, at Chicksands in Bedfordshire. There the similarity ended. While Jack was spending his days humping large loads over arduous terrain and blasting through hundreds of rounds of ammunition—both live and blank—Mike was finding himself largely classroom-based and learning the intricacies of his trade: problem solving, recognizing pattern setting, and providing prediction and insight. In short, being schooled in everything that contributes to the Intelligence Corps' core skill of turning raw information into useful intelligence, or, as the rest of the Army would see it, gluing maps together, colouring in maps, drawing lines on maps and putting stickers on maps.

There was another significant difference. Although the barracks housing the Infantry Battle School had been modernized, it was purely—almost brutally—functional. By contrast, the centerpiece of Chicksands Camp was a 12th Century Gilbertine Priory, set in Grade 1 listed parkland. After the dissolution of the monasteries in the sixteenth century, the Priory had passed into private hands, where it had remained for nearly 400 years, before being sold to the War Department just prior to the Second World War. Ever since then it had been associated with intelligence operations, including a spell intercepting coded German signals before they were passed on to Bletchley Park—Station X—for decryption. It was also said to be haunted by the ghost of a nun who had been walled up as punishment for becoming pregnant by a monk.

Brutally functional versus interestingly quirky—the bases might almost have been designed to reflect their occupants.

Against his normal nature, Jack actually found himself looking forward to the party being thrown by the Intelligence Corps' latest batch of young officers. Since entering the British Army thirteen months before, his life had been one long round of training, of constantly trying to justify his place, of trying to outdo his peers. At first, his concern had been that he wouldn't be bright enough to keep up with all those graduates who'd been swotting away at university while he'd been experiencing the rough and tumble of the Legion. He needn't have worried. He soon worked out that most degrees were simply attendance certificates: if you turned up for three years, you got a degree. Jack's higher education had simply been at a different sort of institution. One where soldiering skills were paramount. And, as an aspiring infantry officer, that was no bad education to have.

His worries over his academic qualifications had quickly vanished—only to be replaced by the compulsive drive to exorcise the shadow cast by his father's reputation within the KRR. The craving had been so strong that it had virtually eradicated any form of relaxation or enjoyment from his life. His only satisfaction came from winning—an approach that did not always endear him to his fellow officers. Mike Lawrence's invitation finally offered the prospect of being able to let his hair down.

By the time Jack and Mike started to make their way down from Mike's room in the officers' mess, they'd already sunk half a bottle of whisky between them. Eventually, the pulsating music thumping up from the ground floor had reminded them that they had a party to go to.

A party popper exploded next to his ear as Jack walked through the door. He took in the scene while Mike went in search of drinks. Quite a few dinner jackets—lots of James Bonds. Too easy. No effort there—everyone who went through Sandhurst had to buy a dinner jacket. A couple of psychedelic Austin Powers types. A few girls. Not enough. Several Pussy Galores in black leather trousers and tight polo-necked tops. Some guys he knew from Sandhurst, who shouted 'Hi' above the music.

Jack felt like an idiot. He always did in fancy dress. As a form of obstinate protest, he'd come as a Frenchman—blue and white striped tee-shirt, red neckerchief, jeans and a black beret at a jaunty angle. One of the passing James Bonds quipped, 'I say, didn't you know it was supposed to be a spies' party?' To which his deadpan response had been, 'Sorry, my spy kit's in the wash.' Sensing that this wasn't someone to be messed with, the 007 clone had moved on quickly.

Then Jack spotted Gemma Page. He should have realised she'd be there. He knew she was going to the Int Corps, but he hadn't connected that with the fact that she would obviously be on the same Young Officers' course as Mike Lawrence. Standing close to an impressive fireplace on the far side of the room, she was surrounded by three guys who, if they were ten years younger, would have been bouncing footballs on their heads or doing wheelies on their bikes in a desperate bid to impress. He was still staring at her when he felt a nudge at his elbow.

'Hi! Still eyeing up the blondes then? Remember me? We were at AOSB together. You sat next to me at the dinner. Didn't realise what a rising star you were going to be then. Gallantry decoration *and* the Sword of Honour! Not a bad clutch for your first year in the Army. How are you going to beat that next year?' Pippa Kelly had retained her brisk, jolly-hockey-sticks manner, but forty-four weeks at Sandhurst had slimmed her down into a more streamlined version of the slightly plump Norland Nanny that Jack had met at Westbury.

Jack felt embarrassed—both at being caught yet again gawping at Gemma Page and at being so openly flattered. 'What brings you here?' he asked, his discomfiture lending an unnecessarily gruff tone to his voice.

Pippa remained unfazed. 'Oh, Gemma invited me. I don't know if you remember, but Gemma and I were at school together.'

'So, what are you doing now?'

'I'm with the RLC. I think even the mighty Jack Adair considered them at one stage. Didn't you?'

'Yeah, I did, but that doesn't sound like the sort of job for a former Roedean girl. I thought girls like you might be looking for a job prancing around Hyde Park on a horse with the King's Troop Royal Horse Artillery.'

'So you remember that I went to Roedean. I'm impressed. I thought you only had eyes for Gemma that night. And, yes, you might suppose I'd want to be a donkey walloper, but I was never a great one for horses—dishonourably discharged from the Pony Club at an early age—and big guns don't really fire my rockets, if you'll forgive the pun. I didn't fancy building bridges and roads, so the Engineers were out of the question. And I certainly didn't see my head under the bonnet of a vehicle, so that rather scotched the REME. All that grease and grime would have played havoc with my nails. So the RLC it was. What's your connection with this place?'

'Mike Lawrence. The guy with the glasses over there. He did AOSB and Sandhurst at the same time as us. He's a good mate of mine.'

'Yes, I know. I was rather hoping to get to meet him. I'll tell you what. Why don't we do a deal. If you introduce me to Mike, what about me doing the same for you and Gemma?'

'Oh, come on. That would be just too embarrassing. What on earth would I say to her?'

'I wouldn't worry about that. You're a genuine, bona fide, all-singing, all-dancing hero. I'm sure she'll find enough to talk to *you* about. Look, don't start thinking about it. You'll just end up tongue-tied with her. Guys do all the time. Look at those idiots prancing around trying to outdo each other in front of her now. Complete no-hopers. Come on, we're going in. Whether you like it or not.'

Grabbing Jack by the arm, Pippa made her way through the crowd. 'Gemma, do you remember Jack from Sandhurst?'

Gemma turned gracefully to face the new arrivals and extended her hand. She was dressed in a beige trench-coat gathered-in with a loosely-knotted belt, and, like Jack, wore a black French beret perched at a jaunty angle—a Second World War resistance fighter. 'Hello, Jack. I see we're both in French mode tonight. Of course I remember you from Sandhurst. I don't think anyone who was there at that particular Sovereign's Parade is ever likely to forget you, are they? While we were all marching about in front of the crowds like so many toy soldiers, you were doing your best to stop some poor overseas cadet from killing himself.'

As Gemma spoke, Jack became conscious that everything within his field of view had narrowed. It was as if he was looking at her through a small screen. Everything outside that screen took on a fuzzy unreality. The other men surrounding Gemma, Pippa Kelly, indeed the whole party, had simply ceased to exist. His entire focus was on the beautiful woman in front of him—the sheen of her blonde hair, the deep blue of her eyes, the perfect Cupid's bow shape of her lips, the...

'... can you?'

'I'm sorry?' Jack was suddenly jerked back to reality.

'I said, I bet you can't wait to get to your regiment, can you?'

'Oh, er, yes. Of course,' he stammered, embarrassed at having been caught out so obviously gawping at her.

A hand suddenly slapped him on the back, rescuing the situation. It was Mike Lawrence. 'Trust you to make a beeline for our top student. You want to watch out, Jack. This girl's got more brains than you and me put together. She'll soon be running rings round your pathetic attempts at conversation.'

Gemma managed to deflect the compliment by introducing Pippa, who was still standing on the edge of the group.

'I can't believe we were all on the same AOSB, but didn't even bump into you girls until after nearly a year at Sandbags,' said Mike.

'That's not true,' said Pippa. 'Jack and I actually sat together at the final night dinner at AOSB. He told me that he didn't know what a Norland Nanny was, so of course I immediately knew that he hadn't been properly brought up.'

'I don't care whether he was properly brought up or not, I bet you had more fun with Jack sitting next to you at that dinner than I did,' countered Gemma. 'I've never met such an arrogant plonker in all my life as the guy I was sitting next to. He was just so completely up himself. What's his name? Vyvyan Phillips. You know, the general's son. What a.... Oh my God, I'm so sorry, Jack,' she exclaimed as the realisation hit her. 'He's in your regiment, isn't he? Do please forgive me.'

Jack laughed, surprised at her directness, and suddenly finding himself relaxing in her company, 'I think your first assessment was probably correct. He's certainly no friend of mine. But I do remember seeing you at that dinner. I thought you were absolutely entranced by him.' As he said it, Jack mentally kicked himself for blurting out that he'd been taking such a close interest in her.

'Oh noooooo! I simply have very well developed social skills,' she retorted, pretending not to notice Jack's gaffe, but secretly flattered by it.

'Come on, let's all dance,' yelled Pippa, grabbing Mike Lawrence by the arm, and leading him onto the small space that had been transformed into a dance floor.

Jack looked hesitantly at Gemma.

'What's the matter?' she asked. 'Don't you want to?'

'Er... yeah... of course. It's just that I don't.'

'Well, you do now.' And with that she propelled him onto the floor.

When Jack woke up in a sleeping bag on the floor of Mike's room, his first thought was, 'Where's my rifle?' It took him a second or two to realise that he wasn't lying in some freezing, muddy field on yet another exercise. As he moved, he heard a groan coming from the bed on the other side of the room. 'Oh, Jesus Christ, my bloody head,' grumbled Mike.

Jack tried to sit up, felt his own head start thumping, and immediately lay down again. As he did, he started to recall the night before, and despite the whisky-induced, sledgehammer headache, smiled to himself. 'That was one bloody brilliant night, mate. Thanks for the invite.'

'My pleasure. Looks like you were quite a hit with the Intelligence Corps' most beautiful asset.'

'Do you think so? I thought I might have been behaving like a bit of a knob.'

'Yeah... well, of course I'm used to you being like that anyway. Luckily she's not. So I think you might have got away with it.'

'Cheeky bastard!'

'You're welcome. But I'll tell you what. If you want to see her again, you'd better get in pretty damn quick. Almost every man she meets wants to snap her up, so I wouldn't hang around if I were you. Especially as she actually looked interested for a change. Which, frankly, I find bloody difficult to digest. But I guess there's no accounting for taste. Ouch!' Mike yelped as Jack's flying shoe bounced off his forehead.

When Jack left for Brecon later that afternoon, the smile was still on his face.

# Chapter Thirty



*Buckingham Palace*

'When you speak to the Queen for the first time, you should address her as "Your Majesty". After that, you may revert to "Ma'am". Please note how I pronounce it. It is "Mam" as in "jam", not "Marm" as in "harm". Having said that, many people find the whole business of meeting Her Majesty in person a tad daunting. She understands this, and is quite prepared to make allowances. So, if you happen to be standing in front of her, and you suddenly find that you can't quite get your tongue around "Your Majesty", then "Ma'am" will do perfectly well.'

The speaker was the Queen's Equerry, a young major from the Grenadier Guards. He was dressed in a flawless uniform frock coat of dark blue Melton cloth, embellished with six double rows of black lace, sewn so that the pointed ends dangled loose down its front. His enthusiastic manner was that of a head boy of a major public school, which, fifteen years before, is exactly what he'd been. His audience comprised the 120 recipients of honours and awards who were to be presented to the Queen at the investiture that morning. It was just after 10.15 am, and they were gathered in an anteroom inside Buckingham Palace, close to the State Ballroom where the ceremony would take place in less than an hour's time. The Equerry's job was to make sure that they got it right.

The major continued his briefing. 'Before the ceremony starts, you will have been positioned, in precise order, in a queue, just outside the side-door to the State Ballroom. The Queen will take up her position on a dais at the head of the room. She will be accompanied by two Gurkha orderlies, five Yeomen of the Guard, and the Lord Chamberlain. The Lord Chamberlain will call each of you forward in turn. He will do this by announcing the category of the award, then your name, and a quick one-liner explaining why you have been so honoured. This will be your signal to enter the room. You will walk across, past the rows of guests seated to your right, until you are level with the dais. Then you will turn to your left to face the Queen. Men will bow; ladies will curtsey. Please, please, *please* ensure that you remember to do this *before* you step forward to receive the award. The Queen will then present you with your insignia or device and, after she has done this, she will exchange a few words with you. And I mean a *few*. Please do not treat this as an opportunity to hold a full-blown conversation with her as if she has just popped round for tea. Remember, she has over one hundred people to get through.'

The major paused as a chuckle ran round the room.

'You will not have to worry about knowing when to break away. When the Queen has finished talking to you, she will shake your hand. As she does so, she will give a gentle push which will propel you away from her. This is your signal to leave. At this point, you should once again bow or curtsey, turn to your right, and continue your journey across the room, leaving by the door *opposite* the one from which you entered. This will lead you out into the Inner Quadrangle, where the official photographers will be waiting for you, and you will be joined by your nearest and dearest in due course.'

A sardonic smile flitted across Jack's face. His 'nearest and dearest' would not be there to meet him in the Inner Quadrangle. A couple of follow-up telephone conversations on the subject with his mother had confirmed that beyond all doubt. Both had ended as badly as the first. It irked him that she would not be there to see him reclaim the family honour.

However, as the expression goes, every cloud has a silver lining. In this case, the silver lining was the fact that the decision by Jack's mother and stepfather not to attend meant that he still had three free tickets at his disposal. And what better way to impress a girl than to take her on a date to Buckingham Palace?

When he'd called Gemma three days after the party to ask her, his mouth had been dry with nervousness. It was not a familiar feeling. The relief when she'd accepted had been so great that he'd immediately gone to the officers' mess bar and bought a bottle of champagne to share with all-comers. To top it off, Mike Lawrence and Pippa Kelly had agreed to come along as well.

Having dumped their overnight bags at the Victory Services Club—an inexpensive but comfortable hotel for servicemen and ex-servicemen near Marble Arch—the party had travelled together to the Palace by taxi. On entering,

Gemma, Mike and Pippa had been directed immediately to the State Ballroom to take up their seats facing the dais on which the Queen would stand. Jack, meanwhile, was ushered off for the rehearsal. He was in a room with a varied cast of characters: three actors, a newsreader, some minor celebrities whose fame had long expired, a couple of sportsmen, numerous local town 'worthies' and charity organisers, many civil servants and a handful of servicemen. Most of the men were in morning coats, a few in lounge suits, and the military personnel in uniform. One distinctive old boy stood out because he looked like he was dressed as a Highland ghillie from the 19th century—right down to the *skean dhu* dagger tucked into his knee-length woollen socks and a pair of sandals that wouldn't have looked out of place in a Viking re-enactment society.

Jack was resplendent in the No.1 Dress uniform of the King's Royal Rangers: a high-collared tunic in rifle green, with red braid trimming and black buttons, and black trousers trimmed with a two-inch wide band of black braid down the outside seam. A black, patent leather cross-belt, decked out with solid silver trappings, crossed his chest diagonally from his left shoulder to underneath his right arm. The overall effect was subtle but immaculate. When his turn came to cross the floor of the State Ballroom, there was only one woman in the room that he was out to impress. And it wasn't the Queen.

The award recipients were waiting in the Picture Gallery, one of the Palace's nineteen state rooms, situated adjacent to the State Ballroom in the West Wing. At nearly fifty metres long, it had been designed by John Nash in the 1820s to house the Royal Family's magnificent art collection. It still served this purpose, and over seventy classical paintings, mounted in substantial gilt frames, lined the walls. They included famous works by Holbein, Rembrandt, Rubens, Titian, Vermeer, Canaletto and van Dyck. The walls themselves were covered in heavily patterned, salmon pink silk—the royal equivalent of wallpaper. The room would have been dark and oppressive were it not for a glass skylight ceiling that allowed through just enough softly filtered natural light. To Jack, the whole place looked antiquated, overdone and slightly eccentric—not unlike Royal Family itself, he mused.

He had been positioned right at the back of the queue, along with two other officers in uniform, both captains: one from the Scots Guards and the other from the Royal Signals. Jack noticed the parachute wings on the guardsman's upper right sleeve. Not the standard wings as worn by conventional Airborne Forces, but the feathered pattern based on an ancient Egyptian design—the sole preserve of the SAS.

The Guards officer spoke. It was the upper class, languid drawl usually guaranteed to put Jack's back up, but without the customary haughtiness. Maybe a couple of years in Special Forces had knocked any arrogance out of him. SAS senior NCOs were good at doing that to bumptious young Ruperts.

'I don't know what you've been up to, old man, and I'm not going to embarrass you by asking, but it must have been something pretty special. They always put people like us at the back. They reckon that the press will have had their fill of the celebrities and politicians by the time we get through the other side, so we'll attract less attention.'

'People like us,' thought Jack. Only just out of Sandhurst, and an SAS captain was treating him like one of the gang. Suddenly, he felt ten feet tall.

The queue shortened rapidly. Jack watched the backs of those ahead of him vanishing through the door, like parachutists exiting a plane. The Signals officer disappeared. Then the Scots Guards captain. And then he was at the door, with his name being announced. Through the opening, he could see the diminutive figure of the Queen waiting on the dais. His heartbeat quickened. Unexpectedly nervous, he suddenly felt that leaping out of a plane was exactly where he would rather be.

'So, you going to get the recording of your big day, then?' Mike was slurring his words. Jack opened one eye and shook his head. They were in the back of a black cab with Gemma and Pippa heading back to the Victory Services Club. It was nearing 11 pm and it had been a long day.

The ceremony and photographs had been over by one o'clock, and the foursome had returned briefly to the hotel to get changed. Then they'd hit the town big-style. Lunch in the Grill Room at the Dorchester, surrounded by a riot of tartan and enormous paintings of long-dead Highland lairds, had been followed by a trip into Covent Garden, where they'd tossed coins down at the street performers from the balcony of the Punch and Judy pub. Later in the afternoon, they'd headed across the Strand for afternoon tea at the Savoy. Emerging as the autumn evening dusk had started to fall, they'd strolled through the streets, taking in the sights and stopping for the occasional drink, until they'd finally ended up at a Chinese restaurant in Soho, before commencing the journey back to the hotel.

Jack was stretched out on the rear seat, Gemma leaning against him, her blonde hair trailing across her face. As the day had worn on, they'd grown increasingly close. He'd noticed how, after leaving the Palace, she'd very deliberately walked alongside him, their arms frequently brushing. Later, in the midst of exuberant conversation, her fingers had often skipped lightly across the back of his hand when she was emphasising a point. Each time she did this, a small thrill shot up his arm. At first he'd assumed that she was completely unaware of the effect she was having—that he was just being hyper-sensitive to her touch. But then she'd taken his arm as they strolled together through Soho. At that moment he knew this wasn't just a one-way thing—a flight of fancy that existed only in his own mind. This stunningly beautiful woman might actually be interested in him. Now the big question facing him was how not to screw this up.

They piled out of the taxi at the Victory Services Club and made their way into the brightly lit entrance hall.

'Anyone for a night cap?' asked Mike, trying to wring the last moments of enjoyment out of the day.

Jack smiled to himself. His mind flicked back to just over a year ago, to his last night at Camp Raffalli; the night he'd found Draskovic and his two Serb buddies lying in wait in the barrack room. Just before Toby Simmonds had waded into them with a flying drop-kick. Only a year away, but another world. It was a world the likes of which the other three had never known, and, even though they were all now in the Army, probably never would.

'You boys do what you like, but actually I'm ready for bed,' yawned Pippa.

'Me too,' added Gemma. 'I guess we'll see you in the morning then.'

Jack put his arm round Mike's shoulders. 'Mike, you look done in to me. I think you're just trying to keep the day going for my sake. You know what? I think that's really kind, but I'm probably just as whacked as you. I'm gonna call it a night as well.'

'Yeah, you're right. It's been one heck of a say,' said Mike, looking almost relieved at the prospect of hitting the sack. 'I'm ready for some flying practice myself.'

'Flying practice?' queried Pippa.

'Yeah, you know—climb to three feet and level out.'

Jack had only been in his room for about ten minutes when he thought he heard a knock. Still dressed, he was lying at full stretch on the bed, bathed in contentment after the day's events. He'd left the room in darkness, but the walls reflected the orange glow of the streetlights outside. He listened, lying absolutely still.

Silence.

Then another two quick taps on the door, lightly and in rapid succession.

He reached over and switched on the bedside light, then crossed to the door and opened it. Gemma was standing outside in the corridor looking apologetic.

'I'm so sorry. I didn't know if you were asleep already. I *really* want a cup of tea, but they haven't left me any milk. Have you got any spare?'

'I can do better than that,' replied Jack, his thoughts suddenly doing cartwheels, 'I can make you a brew myself.'

'Oh, no, that's all right. I didn't mean to cause you any trouble. That's fine. I can wait till breakfast.'

'It's no trouble. I was only lying on my bed thinking about the day. I probably wouldn't get to sleep for hours. Some company would be good.'

'Well, only if you're sure.' She stepped into the tiny room and sat down on the bed.

Jack moved across to the kettle and switched it on. 'How do you take it?'

'Tea, no sugar, and, obviously, milk, please.'

'Thank you for coming today. It was quite a trip for someone who hardly knows me. Not even my own mother was prepared to make it.'

'Jack, you're not serious. What do you mean your own mother wasn't even prepared to make it? You are joking, aren't you?'

'Not at all. I asked her. She said no. Simple as that.'

'I can't believe it's *that* simple.'

'No, you're right. It's not simple at all. It's a long story, but it's a bit late at night for long stories. You only came in for a cup of tea.'

'Actually, that's not strictly true. I came in because I really enjoyed your company today, and I wanted to see you again before I went to bed.'

'Now it's you that's joking.'

'No. I mean it. I like you. I think I like you quite a lot.' An embarrassed look crossed her face. 'Oh bugger. Now I've said it, and you'll think I'm the biggest idiot on the planet. I bet you get girls coming onto you all the time—especially after the Sovereign's Parade thing. Now you'll think I'm just another one of those gallantry groupies. Look, forget the tea. Just give me the milk I asked for. I'm obviously so pissed that I'm letting my lips run away with me. Time for bed, I think.'

Jack leaned across, brushed a strand of hair away from her eyes and kissed her gently on the lips. Then he drew back slightly. 'There, now we've both got runaway lips.'

'Yes, but at least you don't let yours say stupid things.'

'No. I just let them *do* stupid things. Like this.' He drew her closer and kissed her again. Longer this time, but still gently.

She pulled away, looking flushed. 'Do you think that's stupid then?'

'Only when I risk getting my face slapped.'

'Why? Do you get your face slapped often?'

'No. But I'd hate to get it slapped by you. Because that would mean that I'd really cocked up. And I don't want to cock it up where you're concerned.'

'The only way you're going to cock this up, if you'll pardon the expression, Mr Adair, is by not kissing me again.' Wrapping her arms tightly round his neck, Gemma drew him to her.

# Chapter Thirty-One

*Chatham, Kent*

Ivan was writing again. But his writing was no longer fuelled by alcohol. This time he had a clear head. It had taken him months to reach this point—a point that had seemed unattainable only a short while before. His fight-back had started on the day that he'd almost died. It was as if being on nodding terms with death had underscored the value of life. On that day, Michelle had realised that her husband wasn't just drinking for personal gratification. Perhaps more significantly, so had he. The desperate urge to obliterate the thoughts that constantly pressed in on him was what drove the habit. Perhaps now was the time to confront those thoughts, because only death was likely to make them go away completely. And Ivan had learnt that he wasn't ready for death yet.

Whether his suicide bid had been a cry for help or not, help is what he got. Before long, he'd found himself sitting down in front of a counsellor. Initially, it had been uncomfortable. For the first two sessions, the counsellor barely spoke. The result was that there were long silences. Ivan had waited for the counsellor to break them. But he hadn't. He'd seemed almost oblivious to them. Ivan reckoned that if he himself hadn't spoken for the full hour of each session, the counsellor would have been quite content to let him.

He'd expected probing questions—to be led to recovery by someone who knew better than he did how his own mind worked. He'd seen psychotherapists on TV. They always asked the same things: 'What was your relationship like with your father?' 'Do you think your mother loved you?' 'Do you feel that the world has a grudge against you?' But not this man. Silence. So disconcerting that Ivan felt compelled to break it himself. So he started to talk.

It was only by the third session that Ivan realized quite how much he had talked. About things that he never thought he would tell anyone else. His deepest fears and worries. The embarrassment of being the fattest kid in the school playground. The anxiety that Michelle would one day wake up to the type of man she lived with and walk out on him. And finally, the biggest secret of all. The one that had haunted him every day for over twenty years. The one that was both the foundation of his success, and the seed of his self-destruction.

He spilled it all out on a plate. Finally, the counsellor had something to work with. He had the full story from beginning to end. Perhaps now he would start talking himself and tell Ivan what to do to make it all better. But he didn't. True, the silences were less prolonged. The counsellor interjected every now and then—just the odd question—just enough to provide a little nudge on the tiller and steer Ivan's rambling thoughts. But he didn't provide any solutions. Because the only way this was going to work would be when Ivan realised the solutions for himself.

There had been no single blinding flash of enlightenment. The answers had come piecemeal—individual tiny fragments building up the jigsaw. It had taken all of Ivan's inner strength to openly explore the feelings of shame and guilt that had dogged him for years. But his openness hadn't been therapeutic—at least, not to start with. There was no sense of liberation or healing. Rather, each session left him feeling as if his very essence had been drained from him. Until, at last, the tiniest glimmer of what he could do to put things right flickered into his consciousness. And that was when he started to write.

At first he wrote to Michelle. He knew that he couldn't just sit her down and tell her everything. He wouldn't be able to find the right words. He might back down. He might even break down. No. Writing gave him the chance to frame his words with careful precision. It also meant that once Michelle had the letter in her hands there was no going back. She would see him exposed for the man he really was—warts and all. Except Ivan's warts were more like aggressive tumours, eating him up from the inside.

Michelle had taken the letter and sat by the fireplace to read it, illuminated by just one small table-lamp. Ivan sat opposite her, leaning forward, eagerly watching for the slightest nuances in her facial expression. He had never been so scared in his entire life... well, maybe just once. He had no idea what to anticipate: cold anger, rage, insults, accusations, recriminations. He fully expected her to storm from the house and abandon him once again. But when he saw a solitary tear start to etch a glistening stain down the side of her face, he knew that everything would be all right.

Michelle had taken him in her arms. She'd held him close as they sobbed together.

'Why didn't you tell me?' she asked through her tears.

'I couldn't,' was the simple response. That night they went to bed and made love with a passion that Ivan thought had long since vanished from their marriage.

It was in the morning, as they lay bathed in the afterglow of the night before, that Michelle had uttered the half-question, half-instruction, 'You know what you must do now?'

And that was when he started to write his second letter.

# Chapter Thirty-Two

*Lucknow Barracks, Tidworth Camp, Wiltshire*
During the First World War, Aldershot was the largest military garrison in the country. Ever since, the town has made the proud boast that it is the 'Home of the British Army'—although some might claim that this is nothing to boast about, especially when a couple of rival cap badges clash outside the chip shop just off the High Street on a Friday night.

In terms of troop numbers, Aldershot has long been eclipsed by the mass concentration of units clustered around Salisbury Plain. Many of these are garrisoned in Tidworth Camp, among them the 1st Battalion, the King's Royal Rangers. The names of the barracks in the sprawling camp evoke memories of battles in India and Afghanistan—Aliwal, Assaye, Bhurtpore, Jellallabad and Mooltan. The KRR occupied Lucknow.

Jack Adair looked at his watch. He had inherited a very low boredom threshold from his father, and now that threshold was being tested to the limit. He was sitting in the adjutant's office within battalion headquarters. As senior captain, the adjutant acted as the commanding officer's personal staff officer; everything going to the top man passed through his office, and that included new subalterns. Seated alongside Jack was Vyvyan Phillips. This was their first morning in the battalion and they were waiting to present themselves formally to the CO. It had already been a long wait.

The adjutant, Captain Dan Makepeace, had been called through into the CO's office some twenty minutes before. Occasionally, from the other side of the connecting door, snatches of mumbled conversation could be heard, the words too indistinct to catch.

Feeling like he was in a dentist's waiting room, Jack stood up and crossed to the window. From the first floor of battalion headquarters he had a panoramic view of the parade square. In the distance, but out of sight, he could hear hectoring shouts. As he watched, a runner in PT kit came sprinting around the corner of a distant barrack block. He was followed by another. Then another. Gradually more came into sight, until about thirty soldiers—an entire platoon —were strung out along the road that skirted the far side of the parade ground. Jack quickly noted that the runners fell into three distinct groups. The hares at the front simply flew along with effortless long strides, their arms pumping. In the middle came a bunch of steady plodders, who looked as if they could keep up the same rhythmic pace for mile after mile. Then there were the tail-enders, making the most effort for the least gain. Several of these were barely running at all, and a couple seemed on the verge of collapse. Switching his gaze back to the front of the squad, Jack could see that the lead men were now only about fifty yards from the finish line. As they drew closer, a small PTI with a stopwatch started yapping at them like a demented terrier.

Jack heard the CO's door open and turned to see Captain Makepeace step through.

'The commanding officer will see you now, Vyvyan,' said Dan, retaining his hold on the door.

Second Lieutenant Phillips stood up, smoothed down his Service Dress trousers, adjusted his peaked cap, and marched stiffly into the CO's office. Dan shut the door behind him and grinned across at Jack. 'Won't be long now,' he offered by way of comfort, before immersing himself in his in-tray.

Three strides took Phillips to the centre of the office. He came to attention and saluted. The CO, seated behind a massive oak desk—a trophy from the Crimea—continued working, not looking up. Phillips couldn't see his face, just the tightly curled black hair that had earned him the nickname 'Black Max' Macklin.

Lieutenant Colonel Macklin came to the bottom of the document that he was proof-reading and signed it with a flourish, stabbing down with his fountain pen to dot the 'i' in his surname. Then he looked up and acknowledged the young officer for the first time. A smile creased his features as he stood to shake hands.

'Ah, Vyvyan! Yet another member of the illustrious Phillips family to join the regiment. Welcome. How's your father?'

'Thank you, sir. My father's very well, sir.'

'Good, good. I haven't seen him for ages. Must be over a year. Although we spoke on the phone only last week.'

'He sends his very best regards, sir,' lied Phillips.

'Thank you. Look, Vyvyan, I won't beat about the bush. I've known you for years as you've grown up within the regimental family. In fact, it might embarrass you to know that I still remember you crawling around the floor of the mess during families' curry lunches on a Sunday when I was a young second lieutenant and you were a lively little ankle biter. I've seen you at pretty well every stage from prep school to university. I don't know if you recall, but I even baby-sat you on a couple of occasions when I was your father's adjutant—although I don't think it was a particularly pleasant experience for either of us. What I'm driving at is that I probably don't need to find out all about you and your background in the same way that I have to for most of the other young officers joining us—like Jack Adair, for example. That means that I can lay my cards on the table from the outset.'

Phillips looked at the CO quizzically. He wasn't sure what 'laying cards on the table from the outset' meant, but it didn't sound good.

The CO continued. 'You see, it seems the regiment has over-recruited this year. You'll be aware that the KRR took four subalterns from the last Sandhurst intake—two for each battalion—and you and Adair have ended up with us in the First. The problem we have is that there is only one platoon currently available in this battalion, and that's Number Two Platoon in A Company. I have to give it to the best man, and despite your long family history with the regiment, I'm afraid the best man, on paper at least, is Jack Adair. After all, he's not just Sandhurst's most recent Sword of Honour winner, he holds the Queen's Gallantry Medal as well. Without a shadow of a doubt, it's an impressive CV.'

The CO's comments stung Phillips like a whiplash. A hot flush coloured his cheeks. The thought of that bloody sergeant's son pipping him to the only available platoon in the battalion was quite outrageous. *Wait till my father hears about it. Who the hell does Macklin think he is?*

'And what am I supposed to do in the meantime, sir?' he croaked, his throat suddenly feeling as dry as parchment.

'Ah, well, I'm sure you won't be disappointed. As you know, the battalion's scheduled for a tour on the Turkish border in three months' time. The ops officer, Henry Marchant, will be under enormous pressure. It would be a tremendous help to him, and also a huge boost to your own military education, to help him out as the assistant ops officer in the lead-up to the tour and the subsequent deployment. In fact, in many ways, once we're in theatre, you'll undoubtedly find that you're filling an absolutely pivotal role.'

'So when would I get my platoon, sir?'

'Well, in the normal course of things, we stand to have a vacancy about nine months from now. So you'd finish the Turkey tour as assistant ops officer, then step straight into your platoon as soon as we get back to UK. Of course, and I hate to say this, but as you know the casualty rates from so-called Islamic State's actions have been on the rise in theatre at the moment. The Grenadiers lost a subaltern only last week. I wouldn't be surprised if a platoon came your way rather sooner than that. But let's not think about that option for the time being. In the meantime, I'd like you to get alongside Captain Marchant and really concentrate on making the best possible go of the assistant ops officer's role.'

'Have you discussed this with my father, sir?'

'No, Vyvyan, I haven't. Funnily enough, that's because I command the First Battalion, and your father, despite being a general, doesn't. Why do you ask?'

'Well, he *is* currently the KRR's most senior serving officer, and I don't think he'll be very pleased, sir.'

'And what precisely is that supposed to mean, Vyvyan? I hope you're not implying that if I want *my* career to prosper, I'd better look after the general's son? That couldn't be what you meant. Could it?'

'Oh no, sir,' protested Phillips, despite that being exactly what he'd meant. 'It's not just the fact that *I* won't be getting a platoon. It's the thought of *Jack Adair* getting one when I don't. I mean, given the history of the regiment....'

'Ah, you mean because Jack Adair just happens to be the son of a sergeant in the regiment who died in rather inglorious circumstances. Is that it, Vyvyan?'

'You already know about that, sir?'

'Yes, of course I know. In fact it was on that very subject that General Phillips telephoned me last week. And I'll tell you the same thing that I told your father. Jack Adair has gained his commission in this regiment in a perfectly fair and above-board manner. The fact that he turns out to be the son of Sergeant Nick Adair has absolutely no bearing whatsoever. Do I make myself clear?'

'Yes, sir.'

'Good. Then that's all I have for you for the time being. As I said, in the long run, this will probably be very beneficial for your all-round officer education. Now, go and report to the ops officer and he'll get you settled in. I'll look forward to seeing you in the mess in due course. Oh, and please ask the adjutant to send Jack Adair in. Thank you, Vyvyan.'

'Sir!' Vyvyan Phillips raised his hand in salute, turned to his right and marched from the CO's office, his face, and his indignation, still burning.

As Phillips exited the room, Lieutenant Colonel Macklin sat back in his chair and exhaled long and hard. He was certain he'd done the right thing. On paper, Adair beat Phillips hands down. No amount of whining that 'Daddy won't like it' was going to change his mind. But the Phillips family wielded a tremendous amount of influence within the regiment. He hoped that he hadn't just signed the death warrant for his own career. Suddenly he felt very clammy.

Thirty minutes later, Jack emerged from his own initial interview in the CO's office to find his platoon sergeant, Sergeant Joe Pegg, waiting for him. Pegg was a London east-ender with close-cropped ginger hair and a mischievous grin —the complete stereotype of a British senior NCO, straight out of *Commando Comics*. If this was a film about a Second World War POW camp, Pegg would be the one cadging cigarettes off the 'goons'.

'All right, sir? Platoon's all lined up in A Company lines awaiting your inspection. I'm sure you'll wanna be saying a few words to the boys. New platoon commanders always do. Must be something they teach you at Sandhurst. But we should just stick our heads round the RSM's door on the way. Pay our compliments, like, sir. You wouldn't wanna get on the wrong side of him. He don't take no prisoners. And that includes young officers, if you don't mind me saying, sir. You might know him, sir. He was a company sergeant major at Sandhurst before he came back to the battalion a couple of months ago.'

A cold feeling hit Jack in the pit of his stomach. He didn't need Sergeant Pegg to tell him that the RSM was the kind of man who didn't take prisoners. He already knew it. And in this case, the grudge had been festering for over twenty-five years.

They walked out of the adjutant's office and into the central corridor that ran through battalion headquarters. The RSM's office was the next on the right. Sergeant Pegg knocked on the door, introduced Jack, and held the door open for the new second lieutenant to walk in. And there behind the desk, like a tarantula sitting at the centre of its domain, sat Regimental Sergeant Major Bruce Anderson.

Anderson looked up. A smile that veered dangerously close towards being a self-satisfied leer flitted across his face. 'Ah, Mr Adair. All dressed up for your first day in the battalion, I see. You just cannot begin to comprehend how very pleased I am to see you. Come on in, sir, please.' His tone stayed just short of open disrespect. But only just.

He looked past Jack at the sergeant hovering in the doorway. 'Shut the door please, Sergeant Pegg. Mr Adair and I know each other of old. We'd like a few words in private, thank you.'

The door closed behind Jack.

Anderson rose, moved out from behind his desk, and prowled across the room, exuding menace with each step, until he was toecap-to-toecap with Jack. For half a minute he simply stared into Jack's eyes. Unblinking. Waiting for Jack to look away. Jack held his gaze. Finally, Anderson spoke.

'I've been waiting for this day for months now. Oh, yes. It is particularly gratifying to have you here in the regiment, Mr Adair. *Particularly* gratifying. It means that we have the opportunity to settle up our outstanding debts. And you owe me. Big time.'

'Get a life, Anderson. I didn't kill your brother. Neither did my dad. Whatever my dad did or didn't do, your brother would have died anyway.'

'Except my brother behaved like a hero that day. And your old man behaved like a coward. And I hate cowards.'

'But you know I'm no coward. You can see the ribbon on my chest. Proof positive.'

'Don't kid yourself, Mr Adair. It's in your genes. You may try to fight it, but it's there. Just waiting to get out. It's just lucky that I'm here to make sure it never does. Because, as I told you before, there's no room in *my* Army for cowards. I warned you that I would either drive you out or break you. Well, I haven't succeeded in the former, so you've left me with only one choice. I'm just gonna have to break you.'

'You can try, but I'll tell you now, you won't stand a chance.'

'Oh I will. Believe me, I will. That's all, Mr Adair. You can go now.'

'Fuck you, Anderson.' Jack ripped the door open and strode from the office, his face a white mask of fury.

Sergeant Pegg was waiting outside. 'Everything all right, sir?'

'Yes. Everything's absolutely bloody marvelous. Now just take me over to see the boys.'

'I only asked, sir.'

'Yes, of course you did. I'm sorry. I just had something on my mind. Let's go and meet the guys, shall we?' Jack cracked a smile and Sergeant Pegg instantly relaxed, although the thought flashed through his mind that he wouldn't like to get on the wrong side of Jack Adair.

# Chapter Thirty-Three

Jack leaned back in the wooden chair in the office that he shared with Sergeant Pegg and placed his feet up on the desk. He'd completed his first inspection of No. 2 Platoon and had tried to say a few words of introduction without sounding like a typical Rupert, straight out of the 'factory', with his head up his own arse. *Thanks for that, Josh!*

He hadn't needed to try very hard. The troops could sense that Jack was different from the norm: no uncertainty, no first-day nerves, no weak jokes. Everything about him suggested that this was a man who knew the business of soldiering. He carried himself with an easy confidence, his gaze level, alert and slightly challenging. Despite a wry sense of humour and a quiet tone, the troops instinctively knew that he was not a man to cross. His reputation had preceded him. Sword of Honour winner at Sandhurst, Queen's Gallantry Medal... someone even said he was an ex-Legion para—now that just *had* to be a load of barrack-block bollocks. But there was no doubt about the single medal ribbon on his chest—the QGM. Maybe the rest was true too.

'Whaddya think of 'em then, sir?' asked Sergeant Pegg.

'Pretty mixed bunch, aren't they?' replied Jack, who was still wondering quite *what* to think of the random selection of individuals that he'd met that morning.

'Bloody good in the field though, sir. No other platoon like 'em in the entire battalion. Two Platoon's the best by far.'

'I'll take your word for it.'

Of the thirty-two soldiers that appeared on the platoon roll, only twenty-four had been rounded-up for Jack's scrutiny that day. Compassionate leave, training courses, sickness and camp duties had accounted for the missing eight. As Sergeant Pegg set about busying himself at his desk with some routine administrative tasks, Jack began to mull over the various names and faces that he'd been introduced to so far.

Ranger Galloway was a sallow-faced Liverpudlian, who looked a decade older than his thirty-one years, and was still a private soldier after twelve years' service. He stood out because of his inability to remain completely upright while standing to attention—he seemed to be leaning off to one side. Jack had challenged him, thinking the man was taking the piss, only to be embarrassed when told that Galloway had suffered ninety per cent burns in a gas-cylinder explosion as a baby. Just his face, hands and feet were left unscarred. Incredibly, he'd been fit enough to pass the Army medical, but every few years his skin grafts began to tighten. The effect was to pull his head and neck over to one side until surgeons could make the appropriate incisions to loosen-up his skin again. With typical, dark, squaddie humour, the lads had nicknamed him Frankie, after Frankenstein's monster. And with typical dark squaddie humour, Galloway revelled in it. Within the platoon, he was infamous for a chat-up line that went:

'Have you ever slept with a lizard?'

'No. Why?'

''Cos under me clothes, I look like one.'

Bizarrely, it succeeded more often than it failed. Perhaps that was an indication of the sort of girls that Galloway went for. Or perhaps how drunk they were.

Ranger 'Tank' Taylor was another one who stuck out in Jack's mind. Only 19 years old, he was married to Marcia, a thirty-seven year old woman with five kids. Of these, just one —the youngest—was his. It didn't take a genius to work out why Taylor was in this position. A chubby individual with limited self-confidence, he would have found it hard to chat-up a girl of his own age. For Marcia's part, after two previous broken marriages, stability with a man who had a regular wage coming in, and who didn't knock her around whenever he got drunk, was as good as it got. The arrangement suited them both, and Sergeant Pegg reckoned that they were amongst the most happily married couples in the battalion. Jack wondered what this said about the others.

Ranger Ryan Pollard's situation was at the opposite end of the scale. Like Tank Taylor, he was only nineteen, but his wife was twenty-one years younger than Marcia, being just sixteen. They already had a child between them—hers, not his—the product of a drunken shag behind a nightclub in her hometown of Swindon. A stunningly attractive girl, she would normally have been way out of Pollard's league. But when she'd confided all to him in desperation while he was home on leave, he'd offered to take her on. It was a trade-off. He got a beautiful young wife, but one who came complete with an unborn baby. She got a husband with a steady job and a father for her child. Not that his parents knew this; they doted on the boy they thought to be their first grandson.

In all, the platoon seemed to house more than its fair share of rogues, wide-boys, oddballs and misfits. Hardly a squad of elite shock troops. Shock*ing* more like. But together they were a team. And Jack already loved them.

'You're gonna have to speak up for Galloway, sir.'

It was three days later, and Jack and Sergeant Pegg were in the platoon office, chewing the fat over a mid-morning mug of coffee.

'What do you mean, Sergeant Pegg?' asked Jack.

'He's up in front of the CO next week. Charge of conduct prejudicial to good order and military discipline. Could get banged-up for 28 days.'

'Why? What's he done?'

'Nicked a urinal, sir. From The Rifles' barracks. Caused a right stink. In more ways than one. Needs an officer to go along and say what a good bloke he is. Now you're his platoon commander, looks like you drew the short straw, sir.'

'But I barely know him.'

'That don't matter, sir. Just needs to have an officer there speaking up for him.'

'Why? Sounds like he's got it coming to him.'

'You don't understand, sir. Galloway's always in trouble. Always has been—ever since Pontius was a pilot. But he don't mean no harm. And when he's in the field, he's one of the best. Just he don't settle down very well to life in barracks.

Trouble is, the Army's his life. He don't know nothing else. His mum's an alcoholic and his younger bruv got stabbed to death in a gang fight last year. The Army's the only thing he's got. But he's never got promoted past Ranger in twelve years. If he gets another jailing, they're almost certain to boot him out SNLR.'

'SNLR?'

'Services No Longer Required, sir. It's like being made redundant. Out on his earhole. You gotta do it, sir. For Galloway. And for the boys. They're all counting on you, sir.'

Jack accepted the inevitable, and for the next week spent his time quizzing Galloway and burying his nose in Queen's Regulations and the Manual of Military Law.


'87352731, Ranger Galloway, D. I., you are charged under the Army Act 1955, Section 69, with conduct prejudicial to good order and military discipline in that you, at Normandy Barracks, Aldershot, did steal a urinal from the Junior Ranks' Club of Fourth Battalion, The Rifles.'

The atmosphere in the CO's office was rather less welcoming than it had been on Jack's initial visit just a few days before. Galloway stood at attention before the massive oak desk as the CO read the charge out to him. Dan Makepeace, the adjutant, had taken up position, standing just behind the CO's right shoulder, ready to assist with any of the complicated paperwork generated by the disciplinary process. Jack stood to one side, waiting to be called on to testify to Galloway's good character. Or, at least, to make Galloway's bad character sound better than it was.

Having read out the charge, the CO turned to the evidence. The main case against Galloway consisted of a written statement taken from a Lance Corporal in The Rifles. Lieutenant Colonel Macklin adopted his gravest manner as he flicked through the paperwork on his desk.

'Ranger Galloway, I have here a statement from Lance Corporal Golightly of the Fourth Battalion, The Rifles. He states that he was sitting alone at a table in the Junior Ranks' Club in Normandy Barracks, Aldershot, on the evening in question, when he was approached by an extremely drunken soldier that he didn't recognise, but who introduced himself as "Frankie". I believe that is your nickname, Galloway, yes?'

'Sir.'

'And that you were present at Normandy Barracks on that particular day, having travelled there to play a game of football for the battalion against the Rifles?'

'Sir.'

The CO continued. 'Corporal Golightly goes on to say that "Frankie" asked him whether he wanted to buy a urinal. When Golightly asked why, the other soldier is alleged to have replied, "Because I've got one outside." Further investigation revealed that a urinal had indeed been ripped from the wall of the lavatory in the Junior Ranks' Club of Normandy Barracks and was now sitting outside the front entrance. Do you understand the evidence against you, Galloway?'

'Sir.'

'Well, what have you got to say for yourself?'

'I don't really know what to say, sir. I don't remember any of that, like. But it does sound like the sort of thing I'd do when I'm that drunk. So shall we just agree that I did it, sir?'

'Yes, Galloway, I think we better had,' said the colonel in a steely tone.

Jack noticed the menacing edge that had crept into the CO's voice—as if only a superhuman act of restraint was holding him back from inflicting serious violence on the soldier standing in front of him.

The CO turned to the adjutant. 'Do we have a character statement from his platoon commander?'

Dan Makepeace motioned for Jack to step forward.

For the next two minutes, Jack gave a performance worthy of a Queen's Counsel defending a murder suspect at the Old Bailey. Anyone who did not know Galloway would have marvelled at the man's unparalleled military professionalism, whilst shedding a tear for his appalling domestic and family circumstances. Even the hardest of hearts would have melted.

When Jack had finished, an oppressive silence descended once more. He snuck a look at the colonel. The CO was holding his head in his hands, with his elbows planted firmly on the desk in front of him. The peak of his cap masked his eyes. For a moment, he saw Colonel Macklin's shoulders twitch. Surely the CO wasn't shedding a tear over Galloway's appalling family circumstances? Surely his character statement on Galloway's behalf hadn't melted this hardest of hearts? No, it hadn't. In fact, he got the distinct impression that the colonel might be trying to stop himself laughing.

Eventually the CO looked up. Any trace of amusement, if indeed it had ever been there, had vanished. The look of iron severity had returned. And then Colonel Macklin started to tell Galloway precisely what he thought about him. It was not kind, and it was not pretty.

Outside the CO's office, Dan Makepeace slapped Jack on the back. 'That was absolutely bloody marvellous. It was like watching something out of a John Grisham novel. I've never seen a performance like it from a new subaltern.'

'Thanks,' muttered Jack, still unsure whether Dan was taking the piss.

'No, I mean it. By rights, Galloway should have gone down for twenty-eight days. Instead, the CO simply admonished him and told him to assist one of the assault pioneers in putting the urinal back. You did exactly the right thing. The CO's got a soft spot for Galloway—used to be his company commander when he was a major. He knew that if the old rogue went down for anything serious it was probably the end of his career. And if he's booted out, he's got nothing in the world. At all. So, I think the boss is secretly very pleased with the way you handled it. Well done.'

Jack's reputation had already been sky-high when he took over No. 2 Platoon. His triumph in securing what amounted to a trivial punishment for Galloway sealed it. It showed that the new boss would stand up for his boys through thick and thin. And that meant that they would walk through fire for him. Enemy fire.

# Chapter Thirty-Four



*Otterburn Training Area, Northumberland*

Before the battalion came up against enemy fire, it had to get used to controlling friendly fire. Lots of it. By day. By night. At short range. At long range. And the best place to do that was Otterburn, the largest military firing range in the UK. Extending over ninety-three square miles of the southern Cheviot hills, Otterburn offered the facility to fire almost every type of weapon in realistic conditions—not just infantry weapons, but artillery and helicopters too. So the KRR had decamped from Tidworth, lock, stock and barrel for a month. Otterburn had a grim reputation with soldiers: 'Like the Falklands, but colder and wetter.' But it wasn't just the bleak climate and gruelling terrain that presented challenges—over the last ten years, Otterburn had also recorded more than 350 casualties in training.

In recent months, clashes with Syrian-based Islamic State forces infiltrating across the border had become almost daily occurrences for the NATO blocking force now deployed to support their Turkish allies. There could be no doubt that the KRR would see action once on the ground, so the intention was to create the conditions that would simulate real combat as closely as possible. Well, as close as it was possible to get without the added inconvenience of puncture wounds and traumatic amputations. The guys needed to get used to the zip of bullets close to their heads—whether the enemy's or their own. And their own needed to be tightly controlled, because being able to fight their way onto the objective without a blue-on-blue was a basic infantry skill. It was a skill they'd practised time and time again—but that had been with blank rounds. It's easier to cover up slack drills with blanks, because when someone gets it wrong, nobody dies.

By the start of the second week, the training had reached the stage of live-firing platoon attacks. Today's event was tightly scripted to minimise the opportunities for error. The rounds would only be heading one way—into the wooden, man-sized targets pre-positioned by the safety staff. Jack's platoon would attack left-flanking, with two eight-man sections forward and one in reserve. Platoon headquarters would travel in the centre, immediately behind the leading sections. A fire support line of General Purpose Machine Guns—or 'gimpies'—was established 300 metres away, at right angles to the attacking force, on a ridgeline overlooking the enemy position. The gimpies would rip into the target right up until the last safe moment, before stopping and switching to alternative targets just as the close combat troops emerged onto the objective.

As the leading two sections took up their attack formations, fanning out along the start line, Jack moved forward to view the enemy position. His platoon was located at the edge of a wood line, slightly below the enemy's right flank, and about 250 metres from it. Once the fire support group had received Jack's message that he was in position and ready, its machine gunners would open the attack with a hail of automatic fire.

Jack knelt down next to Corporal Wood, his lead left section commander, and peered through the treeline. Pressing the transmit switch on his radio, he sent the predetermined codeword.

'Hello, Two Zero Alpha, this is Two Zero Bravo. Punchbowl. Over.'

'Two Zero Bravo, roger. Out.'

Seconds later, a wave of machine-gun fire erupted from the fire support group on the ridgeline off to Jack's right. Lines of burning tracer sliced across the valley, ripping into the enemy position, flinging up spurts of mud and splintering the wooden targets. Jack shouted, 'Go, go, go!' and the leading two sections jumped to their feet and started skirmishing across the open ground.

The Rangers rushed into the assault. It was classic pairs fire and manoeuvre: first man up—dash five metres—down—start engaging targets; second man up—another five metres —down—provide covering fire. Then repeat. And again. Across the entire platoon frontage. Men pepper-potting forwards. Energy-sapping stuff. Encumbered with body armour, helmets, weapons and ammo. Breaths taken in heaving gulps. Sweat pouring from under helmets, streaming across the eyes to blur the sight picture. Always the temptation to run more than five metres. Wanting to close the distance faster. Taking longer each time to hit the deck to minimise the physically draining ups and downs. But knowing that standing too long would be a death warrant in combat. The feeling of moving in slow motion but needing to maintain momentum. Digging deep for the last reserves of strength. As chests heaved and hands shook, accuracy suffered, and sporadic shots flew wide.

With his platoon headquarters close up behind him, Jack took off, racing forwards five metres and throwing himself into the ground, ready to give covering fire as the soldier to his flank dashed past.

Despite the gruelling effort of skirmishing, it took the lead sections less than three minutes to hit the perimeter flank of the objective. Jack could see the first pair pouring rounds into the targets manning the nearest trench. From the ridge line, the machine guns continued to spray suppressive fire, tracer falling into the centre of the objective, and random burning ricochets spinning off at odd angles. He could already hear the gimpies being given the command to stop firing, prior to switching to targets in depth.

Suddenly, he felt a gobbet of earth fly up from nearby. On the objective, he saw the ground spatter as if hit by a sudden downpour. A tracer bullet lay glowing nearby as its pyrotechnic filling finally burnt out. One of his men was down and bleeding.

From the ridge line, Jack became aware of several panicked voices simultaneously screaming: *'Stop!'* But it was already too late. He was instantly on his feet and running to the centre of the enemy position, frantically waving his arms, and screaming, *'Stop! Stop! Cease fire! Man down! Medic!'* More barked commands could be heard from points across the training area, each echoing the same cry: *'Stop! Cease fire!'*

As the firing ceased from the support group and No. 2 Platoon started to emerge from cover and gather on the objective, wondering what had happened, Jack ran forward to check on the wounded man.

Several of the troops of the lead sections had already beaten him to it and were gathered round the Ranger on the ground. Corporal Wood, the No. 2 Section commander, had taken charge of the scene, and was directing the application of first aid.

On the ground lay Tank Taylor. A bullet wound to the right calf had missed the bone and any major blood vessels. The Rangers from Two Section had already produced all of the available field dressings, compressed within small fabric containers, which were being hurriedly ripped open. One of the men took out a knife, using it to slice through Taylor's trousers so that they could get to the wound more easily and press the dressings down hard to stem the bleeding.

Taylor was still wide awake and talking. 'Fuck me, boys, I hope this don't get me off the tour. I need the rest from the missus and the kids.'

It was a good sign.

Although it seemed like forever, the ambulance that had been situated behind the firing point was quickly on the scene, along with a trained combat med tech. With the arrival of the expert, Jack stood up and took in the scene around him.

As the immediate blood-rush of shock and urgency started to subside, Jack's first thought turned to how this could possibly have happened. Up on the ridge line, he could hear the company sergeant major issuing orders for clearing and checking all weapons. The men of the fire support group were in a line, running through the standard drills, which involved removing magazines and releasing the weapons' working parts under control, whilst supervised by a member of the safety staff.

Then Jack saw him. Standing back from the rest was Second Lieutenant Vyvyan Philips. Fixed to the spot, he was simply staring down the hill at the carnage in the target area. In an instant, Jack made the decision who was to blame for this fiasco. With his mouth set in a grim line, he began striding purposefully towards the hill. Philips was so preoccupied that he did not even notice Jack approaching.

Several of the soldiers who had just finished clearing their weapons looked up at the officer as he stormed past. They could see where he was heading and could guess what was on his mind.

As Jack's open palm cannoned into Philips' chest, he was already shouting.

'Philips, you incompetent bastard, what the fuck happened? You've nearly killed one of my men, you useless arsehole!'

Philips rocked backwards with the impact but didn't try to defend himself.

'I d-don't know. I gave the command to stop, but the number three gun just kept firing.'

Jack didn't want to hear any more. He had already appointed himself judge, jury and executioner, and he was about to unleash all of his violence on Philips. As he took a step forward, the company sergeant major, Joe Foster, inserted himself between the two officers.

'Now then, sir. Let's not get carried away. Not in front of the troops, sir. There's a proper way of doing this, and this ain't it. Come on, back off.'

Jack felt the wind go out of his sails. Like a pot that had just boiled over, all of the hatred that he felt for Philips having rushed to the surface, now spilt over, dissipated and ran down the sides, fizzling out.

He shrugged his arms free from Sergeant Major Foster and, without a further word, walked back down the hill to rejoin his platoon.

Behind him, he could hear the sergeant major detailing off men to take charge of various aspects of the situation. In military terms, this was now a potential crime scene, and had to be treated with the same degree of care as if it had taken place on a city street. The weapons that had been cleared were taken to one side, lined up and covered with a protective tarpaulin. The magazines that had been unloaded were placed alongside the weapons in a pile, still with the same number of rounds in them that there had been when the command to stop firing had been given. Number three gun, which had been left in the same state as when the incident happened, was surrounded with a small cordon of white plastic tape, and a guard placed on it.

That evening, Jack was just about to go through for evening meal in the officers' mess when he was ushered to one side by the mess manager, who had just taken a phone call.

'Commanding officer's compliments, Mr Adair, but he's asked that you should go across to his office right away.'

For the duration of its field firing phase on the Otterburn Ranges, battalion headquarters had taken up residence in a hutted complex in the middle of the training camp. As Jack walked down the main central road towards the temporary HQ, he could see that the CO's light was one of the few still on. In the run-up to the deployment, the boss was obviously burning the midnight oil to ensure that everything went smoothly.

Entering the corridor that ran the length of the building, Jack wasn't surprised to find the adjutant still hard at it as well. It was the unwritten rule: if the CO's at work, so is the 'Adj'—no matter what the time. Dan Makepeace looked up as he heard Jack's boots on the tiled floor just outside his open office door.

'Oh... hi, Jack. Boss'll see you in a couple of minutes. He's just on the phone right now. Take a seat.'

Jack could hear the CO's voice on the other side of the door, the entrance to which was through Dan's office. No one got to see the CO without going through the regiment's senior captain first. It was a useful filter on the way in, and a calming influence for anyone in the shit on the way out.

'Coffee?'

'Is one on offer?'

'I think so. Difficult to tell. I can't really gauge the Old Man's mood.'

Jack declined. The sudden summons was quite unexpected, so he was still unsure whether this was a 'with' or 'without coffee' interview. He suspected the latter. Dan turned his attention back to tapping away at the keys of the laptop on his desk, leaving Jack to flick through the back copies of *Soldier Magazine* and the regimental journal, *The*

*Ranger*, which were arranged on a coffee table for waiting visitors.

Eventually, Jack could tell by the CO's tone that the telephone conversation was drawing to a close, even though the precise words were too indistinct to hear. As the CO put down his handset, a red light that had been illuminated on the adjutant's own set went out.

'I'll see if he's ready for you.'

Dan stood, knocked twice, lightly, and, without waiting for an answer, put his head round the door.

'Jack Adair for you, sir.'

'Ah, Adair, yes, send him in.'

Jack was already standing by the time Dan turned round to give him the nod. He marched in and came to attention in front of the CO's desk—a more utilitarian design than the massive oak monstrosity that graced his office back in Aldershot.

Lieutenant Colonel 'Black Max' Macklin was standing away from his desk, arms folded, surveying the empty, lamplit road outside through the window. He left the junior officer standing at attention for a full minute, before slowly turning to face him.

'Ah... Mr Adair... hmm. I wanted to talk to you about today.'

'Sir?'

'I've just had the hospital on the phone. It seems that Taylor will pull through without any serious long-term consequences. He may even be well enough to join us mid-tour. I've also had the initial reports from the armourer. Apparently, there is nothing about that particular batch of ammunition that has given any cause for concern before, but samples are being taken for testing.'

The CO paused before continuing, obviously weighing his words carefully.

'Even though the armourer hasn't had the chance to conduct a detailed technical breakdown of the weapon concerned, it seems that there's already some suspicion that this was a runaway gun during the last burst of automatic fire. In other words, when the order to stop was given, although the firer took his finger off the trigger, the weapon continued to send rounds down-range. We still haven't got to the bottom of it, but I'm told that the safety sear looks worn, and the gun in question doesn't seem to have been cleaned properly. The gas parts are apparently coked, so there was probably insufficient gas pressure to push the working parts far enough back to reach the sear, where they should have been held in place. In short, an amalgam of two critical errors that proved near-fatal. I should add that the initial evidence also indicates that the command to stop firing was given in good time. We are therefore almost certainly looking at a mechanical failure rather than negligence on the part of one of the safety staff.'

Another pause. This time longer.

'You will see where I am going with this one, Mr Adair. I have had unsettling reports that, in the immediate aftermath of the incident, rather than concerning yourself with the care of your injured man, you took it upon yourself to assault one of your brother officers in full view of a large number of witnesses of all ranks.'

Up until this point, the CO's tone had been perfectly reasonable—at concerned conversational level. Now, Jack could detect a steely edge creeping into it.

'You are not so stupid as not to realise that this is a criminal offence under the Army Act, and liable to trial by court martial. It is the sort of behaviour that could get you kicked out, not just from this regiment, but from the Army altogether.'

'Sir.'

'Do you think I have any room in this battalion for a subaltern who exhibits such rash and uncontrolled behaviour in front of his men?'

Jack assumed that this was a rhetorical question. He remained standing stock-still at attention. He could feel the pulse in his temple beating. The tick of the clock on the wall, which he hadn't even noticed before, suddenly seemed uncomfortably loud. The CO's stare continued to bore through him. It must have been at least a minute before the CO spoke again, although it seemed far longer. His words came slowly, icily, deliberately. Hissed out at a barely audible level but sounding all the more menacing for it.

'I've asked you a question. You might grant me the courtesy of giving me an answer. I shall ask you again. Do you think I have any room in this battalion for a subaltern who exhibits such rash and uncontrolled behaviour in front of his men?'

The question was no longer rhetorical. Jack realised with dawning shock that he might be on the verge of being asked to resign his commission. Suddenly, he felt very cold.

'No, sir.'

*'You're damned right I don't!'* the CO exploded.

For the next five minutes, without deviation, hesitation or repetition, the CO poured forth a stream of invective, detailing in character-crucifying terms all of Jack's faults as he saw them. There were many. By the time he had finished, Jack had no doubt as to precisely what was now required of him. He was immediately to seek out Lieutenant Philips in the officers' mess and apologise. He was to back this apology with a further written expression of deep and sincere regret. He was to be absolutely assiduous in conducting himself as an officer should at every opportunity in future—whether on duty or off. And, above all, there were to be *'no more fuck ups!'*

With a parting comment of, 'Your behaviour today was appalling. *Get out!'* Jack knew that his ordeal was at an end. As he executed a smart about turn, he could see that Dan Makepeace had anticipated his rapid exit and was already holding the door open.

His face smouldering with shame and anger, Jack was left to find his own way out of the building, while the CO summoned his adjutant into the office. As Dan entered, he could see that the 'Old Man' was smiling. Dan felt the tension go out of the air and cracked a grin himself. He could already detect where his boss was coming from.

'Hopefully, that will have taught him a lesson he won't forget in a hurry.'

'Not half, sir,' replied Dan.

'Bloody good officer, but too many rough edges at the moment. Should be all right once we get on ops, so long as he doesn't get himself cashiered for taking part in some street brawl first.'

'Sir.'

'And he's going to have to come to some accommodation with Philips. Can't have bad blood between two brother officers. Keep an eye on the situation, won't you?'

Dan returned to his desk. The Old Man had a point but, he thought, it might take more than 'keeping an eye on the situation' to ensure harmony within the battalion.

# Chapter Thirty-Five



*Lucknow Barracks, Tidworth, Wiltshire*

Jack jogged across the parade square, slamming his feet in and saluting as he came to attention in front of the battalion second-in-command. His shoulders were heaving and slicks of sweat coursed down his cheeks. Behind him, No. 2 Platoon were lying spread out across the tarmac in all-round defence, SA-80s tucked firmly into shoulders, each man scanning his arcs of fire. The boys had performed brilliantly, and he had to work hard to hold back a grin.

'Two Platoon has possession of its objective, sir, and I request your permission to carry on.'

Major Adrian Phillips, the battalion's 2IC, gave a languid wave of his hand that might have doubled as a salute. He was standing to one side of the square, accompanied by the officer commanding A Company, Major Simon Bickerstaff, and the regimental sergeant major, Bruce Anderson.

'Not bad. The skirmishing could have been sharper. And you were slow exiting the helicopter. How many more run-throughs do you plan to do before tomorrow?'

'Probably three or four, sir.'

'Make it five or six.'

'Sir,' Jack replied, a hint of truculence creeping into his voice at the unfair implied criticism.

It may have been the merest hint of defiance, but the 2IC was onto it in a flash. 'Look, Adair, the commanding officer has entrusted *you* with the highlight of the visit tomorrow. By the time the general gets to you, he'll already have sat through endless briefings and displays, and pressed the flesh with sundry soldiers. It's *your* platoon that's going to put the zing back into the day and have him on top form by the time he gets to the officers' mess for lunch. This has *got* to go swimmingly well. In fact, it needs to be downright goddamned perfect. And not just because the general is the KRR's most senior serving officer, but because he just so happens to be my father as well. And I am not having *you* let the battalion down in front on *my* father. Got it?'

'Got it, sir,' Jack's grin had been replaced by a blank, dead-eyed look.

To mark the end of its pre-deployment training, the battalion was to host a visit by Lieutenant General Sir Valentine Phillips, KCB, CBE, MC, accompanied by the regimental colonel, Dick Millen. The senior visitors were due to spend the morning viewing various activities around the barracks. These included briefings on the battalion's missions, tasks and future locations on the Turkish border, and demonstrations of battlefield first aid and IED search drills. At midday, they would take their seats on one side of the parade square for the finale to the morning's events, in which Jack's platoon would stage a mock rescue of international aid workers held captive in a terrorist camp. While a vehicle-mounted, fire support line of gimpies, firing blanks, laid down covering fire, the close assault would go in by helicopter. With the hostages rescued and the enemy despatched, the CO would escort his guests to the officers' mess for a curry lunch.

This was the final dress rehearsal, and it had been close to perfect, but Major Phillips was not one to lavish praise. And he certainly wasn't going to do so where this bloody upstart, Jack Adair, was concerned. The man was the son of one of the regiment's most shameful cowards, for Christ's sake. He should never have been commissioned in the first place, let alone been appointed to take command of the platoon that should, by rights, have gone the 2IC's younger brother, Vyvyan.

Unable to find further fault, the second-in-command started to turn away, then hesitated as an afterthought struck him.

'Oh, just one more thing...'

'Sir?' responded Jack, deadpan.

'It needs a touch more drama. Right now, it's too pedestrian. It looks like something the Army Cadets might lay on for the village summer fete. We need the general to sit up and take notice.'

'Well, I did have an idea. I saw it done once in the Legion, and it worked well there.'

'Yes, Adair, we all know about your previous service in the Foreign bloody Legion. No need to keep reminding us.

And this brilliant idea is what, precisely?' It wasn't quite a sneer, but it came pretty close.

Jack was starting to feel awkward, tongue-tied... and bloody angry, but he pressed on. 'We could sling a dummy out of the door.'

'What the fuck are you talking about? That's going to spice things up is it? Throwing a shagging dummy out of the door? Explain.'

Jack could feel the urge rising to smash his fist into those nauseatingly arrogant features. The fact that RSM Anderson, hovering close behind the 2IC, was now rolling his eyes, as if to say, 'I've heard it all now', didn't help.

Jack continued, his thoughts undoubtedly showing in his tone. 'The dummy's dressed in combats. It gets chucked out when the helicopter starts taking enemy fire. It'd look like one of the door gunners had been taken out by the terrorists. There's a shock factor. Just for a second, the visitors might think it's a real man down.'

'Hmmm.' The 2IC pondered for a second before responding. 'Well. It might work. I haven't got time to see you run through the whole thing again. Give it a go. If it works, add it in. But make sure it looks slick. Let me say again, we cannot afford any fuck-ups on this one. Got it?'

'Yes, sir. Got it. Will you let the CO know about the dummy, sir?'

'Yes, Adair. Yes, yes. I'll let the CO know. Now get back on with the rehearsals before you run out of daylight!'

Major Bickerstaff waited until the party had just moved beyond Jack's hearing when he spoke up. 'Don't you think you were a bit hard on the lad, Adrian? After all, that run-through was damned near perfect.'

'Perfect? Perfect? You call that perfect? Bloody hell, Simon, no wonder your boys in A Company are all over the shop if you thought that was perfect. I tell you, Adair is a nasty, jumped-up, little shit, who is rather too full of himself, and who needs the wind very firmly taken out of his sails. And if you're too soft either to see that, or to do anything about it, then I'm going to have to do it for you. And if the CO gets the faintest whiff that *I'm* having to step in to grip the officers in *your* company, I don't suppose he'll rate your leadership qualities very highly. Your choice.' With that, Major Adrian Philips left the group and strode off towards the officers' mess.

# Chapter Thirty-Six

The visiting senior officers took their seats at the front of the viewing stands as a cold wind swept across the camp. Around them were arrayed the officers, soldiers and families of the battalion. On the parade square, the 'terrorists', appropriately dressed in Arabic robes and headdresses, looked jarringly out of place against the backdrop of an English autumn.

The adjutant, at a microphone, commenced with a running commentary, giving the background story to events thus far, finishing just as the thud of approaching helicopter blades began to intrude.

'Sirs, ladies and gentlemen, if you watch now you see the arrival of the rescue force, which today is represented by Number Two Platoon, A Company, under the command of Second Lieutenant Jack Adair.'

Precisely on cue, as the adjutant finished speaking, four fire support Land Rovers—or WMIKs—swept onto the square, guns blazing. Their tyres threw up a spray of pebbles as they skidded to a halt some seventy-five metres from the objective, where they established a fire support line.

Aboard the helicopter, hovering unseen in a holding position to the rear of the stands, Jack could hear Sergeant Pegg's radio messages from the fire support line on the ground. Using the internal net to the pilot, Jack sent the message for the assault to go in. With a sudden exhilarating lurch, the lead helicopter shot forward, its nose slightly dipped. The second helicopter followed up tightly behind.

The distance from the holding position to the objective took less than a minute. The 'enemy' lifted their heads to see the incoming threat and started to engage from the ground. The choppers pulled up sharp above the parade square, not quite touching the ground. Immediately, the close assault teams were bundling out of the door.

Jack hit the tarmac first, sprinting a few yards and slamming into a prone firing position to start engaging the enemy to his front. He could hear the barrage of firing build up as the rest of his troops joined him. Glancing left and right, he could see everyone had exited the choppers. The downdraft washed over him as the helicopter lifted out of the hot zone, throwing up face-stinging gravel and dust as it turned sharply away from the enemy position. From behind a straggling line of sandbags that marked the outer edge of their camp, the mock terrorists replied with a salvo of blank rounds. Off to one side of the square, the fire support line of vehicle-mounted gimpies continued an unremitting fusillade of automatic fire.

As the helicopters continued their turn, on cue, the uniform-clad dummy flew out of the door. With the combined racket of the gunfire and the hammering of rotor blades, Jack didn't hear the thud as it thumped into the ground. Nor did he hear the momentary gasp from the crowd in the shocked second or two before they twigged that they'd been tricked. All except one. The commanding officer.

Lieutenant Colonel Macklin was marginally short-sighted. He barely needed his glasses. And he certainly wasn't going to wear them in front of the troops. They'd think he'd gone soft. From his grandstand view, all he could see was a soldier plummeting from the chopper as it swung into its turn. As the body hit the ground, he was already out of his seat and racing across the tarmac towards it.

On the square, with his platoon complete around him, Jack jumped to his feet, bellowing, *'Go, go, go!'* In half sections, the line began to skirmish forward, one group moving, the other firing. It was only a short distance to cover across the parade square. Within, twenty yards of the objective, he screamed, *'Charge!'*

Anticipating that the covering fire would now reach a crescendo, Jack was suddenly aware that the salvo of blank rounds chattering from the gimpies had stopped. Even the SA-80s were becoming more sporadic and seemed to be stuttering to a halt. As the gunfire ceased, it was replaced by a lone voice screaming commands from somewhere behind him on the square—screams of, *'Stop! Stop! For God's sake stop! Man down!'*

Looking over his shoulder, Jack could see that only three other soldiers from the sixteen that had exited the helicopters were now standing anywhere near him. The rest had become transfixed, staring back at the spot where the dummy had crashed to earth, and at the commanding officer, who was now standing over it.

In seconds, the full enormity of what had happened struck Jack like a dum-dum bullet between the eyes. The CO didn't know about the dummy. Fuck! The second-in-command obviously hadn't briefed him. A clammy, prickly sensation started at the back of his neck, and he felt momentarily dizzy. Shit! Shit! Fucking shit! He looked across at the dignitaries and the other members of the crowd, most of whom were now standing, staring at the CO.

As the commanding officer bent down and realised his error, Jack could read the lines of fury etched into his face. His expression said only one thing: 'Someone has made me look a complete idiot in front of the battalion's guests, and that someone will pay.'

Black Max Macklin stood up, did his best to adopt a calm and purposeful demeanour, and strode back towards his guests. Without pausing to take his seat, he announced to those within earshot, 'Sorry if we surprised you with our little prank. We just wanted to throw in something a little out of the ordinary. I feel that the stage-managed extraction of the hostages has been rather done to death. Perhaps what is more important is to understand the very real risks that our soldiers have faced in order to achieve this very high standard of performance during their build-up training. Hopefully, these risks faced during training will serve them well in combat. As the expression goes, "Train hard; fight easy." Perhaps you would now like to join us for a spot of lunch in the officers' mess.'

With that, the commanding officer, acting as the beaming, magnanimous host, ushered his guests in the direction of the officers' mess. Jack breathed a sigh of relief that the CO had hidden his gaffe with such a masterly performance. But he guessed that his relief would be short-lived.

Over lunch, a buffet curry, he had the worrying feeling that Colonel Macklin was deliberately cutting him dead. Under normal circumstances, it might have been standard practice for the CO to call Jack across, as lead member of the assaulting platoon during the grand finale, to meet the guests. Pointedly, this did not happen. Indeed, at one stage, Jack inwardly winced when he heard Colonel Dick Millen commenting to the CO, 'Do you know, Max, if I hadn't known you for over twenty years, I'd have sworn that you were taken as much by surprise by that confounded dummy trick as the rest of us were. Bloody good acting!'

Somewhere in Jack's head, a hidden voice went 'Ouch!'

After lunch, Jack went along to the armoury to oversee his platoon's weapon cleaning. The boys were in reserved mode. They could sense that all was not well with their boss, and were doing their best to put a cheerful gloss on things. The call for Jack to attend the CO's office for the second time in a fortnight came immediately after the guests had departed the barracks after lunch.

This time, even Makepeace's usual cheerful demeanour was replaced by the look of a man in mourning. He acknowledged Jack's arrival and stuck his head round the boss's door.

'Second Lieutenant Adair, sir.'

There was a grunt from inside.

Makepeace signalled for Jack to go in, holding the door open for him, and entering behind him. Jack noticed that he was carrying a large writing book with a gold-embossed dark green cover. This looked formal.

Once inside, Jack was surprised to see Major Adrian Philips standing to the rear left of the commanding officer's desk. Captain Makepeace also moved to the rear of the desk, so that now three officers faced him, two standing, and the CO sitting.

Black Max was staring at him with ruthless ferocity, as if he was only just succeeding in controlling some strong inner urge to leap across the desk and tear him apart.

'Adair. Again.'

'Sir.'

'You made me look a fool.'

'I didn't mean to, sir.'

'No. I don't suppose for one minute that you meant to. But you did all the same.'

'I thought you knew what was going to happen, sir.'

'And why would you think that? Do I have a reputation amongst the battalion as a mind-reader? Do my powers as commanding officer now extend to being able to see into the future?'

'No, sir. I thought you had been briefed on what was going to happen.'

'By whom?'

'By the second-in-command, sir. I explained everything to him during the rehearsal. He told me that he would ensure you were fully in the picture.'

It was clear that Jack's words had temporarily taken the wind out of the CO's sails. He looked over his left shoulder at Major Phillips.

'You didn't tell me that, Adrian. Is it true?'

The 2IC didn't hesitate. Staring directly into Jack's eyes, he responded instantly. 'No, sir. If you wish me to call the RSM as a witness, then I'm more than happy to do so. He accompanied me during the rehearsal, and I'm sure he will verify that Mr Adair failed to mention his rather juvenile prank.'

'Well, Adair. You heard the second-in-command. There can be only two interpretations. Either you are lying, or you are mistaken. I sincerely hope that as an officer of this regiment, it is not the former. I am therefore prepared to give you the benefit of the doubt and assume that it is the latter. Unless you wish to argue the toss.'

Jack said nothing.

The CO looked down at his desk as if deep in thought. When he looked up, his eyes bored into Jack like gimlets. He spoke in icily cold measured tones.

'Mister Adair, this is the second time in the space of less than a month that you have appeared in front of me in, shall we say, less than entirely happy circumstances. Last time, I let you off with a warning. This time I must take action. You will go from this office and report to the operations officer. He has already been warned to expect you. From this moment, you will assume the responsibilities of assistant ops officer, taking over from Mister Phillips. You will hold this appointment throughout the battalion's forthcoming operational tour. Second Lieutenant Phillips, meanwhile, will assume command of your platoon. I shall inform him of this development immediately, and you are to ensure that the handover has happened by close of play today.'

'But—'

'You are dismissed.'

The adjutant took over. 'March out, Mister Adair.'

Outside, Jack passed Phillips waiting in the adjutant's office. He had obviously been summoned into 'the presence', in his case to hear the good news.

Before leaving, Jack tried one last appeal to Captain Makepeace. 'He lied, you know.'

Makepeace winced. These were not the words that he wished to hear said about a brother officer of the regiment. A senior one at that.

'That's not how the Old Man sees it. But you can submit a formal redress if you think it's worth it.'

'What do you mean, if I think it's worth it?'

'Well... it's a close-knit regiment, and mud kinda sticks. If you see what I mean.'

'Oh, I think I see what you mean all right.'

Jack came to attention, saluted the adjutant smartly, and left the office.

# Chapter Thirty-Seven



*Argentinian Steakhouse, Bedford*
*—twelve miles from the Defence College of Intelligence*
'He can't do that!' Gemma Page had heard Jack's version
of events and was simmering with outrage.
'He can, and he has. He's the CO.'
'Yes, but you've done all the training with the platoon.
They're *your* blokes. They practically worship you.'
'Hmm.'
'And Vyvyan Phillips, for Christ's sake! The man's a
pompous, arrogant prig. You know what Rousseau said?'
I don't even know who Rousseau is.'
'Was.'
'Sorry. Was.'
'"The greatest braggarts are usually the biggest cowards."'
'Trust you to know something like that.'
It was Saturday evening. Jack Adair and Gemma Page
were sitting in a steak house in Bedford, the nearest big town
to Gemma's Intelligence Corps base. With the pubs yet to
empty out, the place was only half-full—a smattering of

courting couples, a pair of marrieds on an anniversary outing, each lost in their own thoughts, and a group of lads in Tottenham Hotspur shirts, crowning their team's success with beer and rib-eye steaks.

'Well, I reckon Rousseau's got it right in this case. Phillips is all top show. You told me about that incident on the train. I reckon the man's got a yellow streak a mile wide running down his back. I don't see how your CO can be so stupid.'

'He's not being stupid. He thinks that I deliberately made him look a fool in front of the general. If someone did that to me, I'd be bloody angry too.'

'Yes, but he only *thinks* that because Phillips' tosser of a big brother lied to him about what had been agreed.'

'So who's he going to believe? The wet-behind-the-ears, newly commissioned subaltern, who looks like he's been trying to show off, but has only succeeded in embarrassing his CO in the process, or the regimental second-in-command who he's known for over twenty years, backed up by the most senior non-commissioned soldier in the regiment? I think I lose hands down on every count. This time they've got me. Well and truly. And there's sod all I can do about it.'

'But it seems *so* unfair.'

'It *is* unfair. You know what? Maybe I was better off in the Legion. At least I could just get on with soldiering. None of this regimental politics crap and all the snobbery that goes with it. I almost wish I'd never come back.'

'Thanks.'

'Oh, come on... that's not what I meant.'

'I don't know what you meant, Jack. I'm off to the loo. Perhaps you need a few minutes to think what you *do* mean and what you don't.' Gemma stood up smartly from the table and walked towards the back of the room.

Jack let out an exasperated sigh. This was all he needed. Bloody women.

As Gemma moved towards the lavatory, Jack noticed every male eye in the room follow her. The married man on the next table tried to hide his glance. The sharp reprimand from his wife showed that he'd failed. That was one more thing she'd hold against him later when the bedroom lights were switched off and, in the darkness, she started to dissect their evening out. The footie lads were less subtle. Subtlety's hard after a skin full. Jack thought he heard a low wolf whistle and a few comments, all but drowned out by the Roxy Music track playing over the restaurant's sound system. His hackles started to rise.

As Gemma returned to the table, all eyes were on her. By now the music was ending, and there could be no doubt about the comments.

'Look at the fuckin' arse on that!'

Jack was out of seat in an instant, ignoring Gemma's insistent cry of, 'Darling, don't!'

But the Spurs boys had heard, and there was no way they were ignoring it. 'Ooh! *Darling*! Don't!'

Jack stopped by their table, fury oozing from every pore.

'Apologise,' he said, taking them all in, but concentrating on the biggest, a shaven-headed guy in his twenties.

'Apologise for what? Darling,' from the big man.

'Apologise for the comment you just made about my girlfriend.'

'Oh alright, mate. Sorry. Must've got carried away. Won't happen again.'

Jack nodded curtly and turned to rejoin Gemma. As he did, the guy spoke again.

'She has got a fuckin' nice arse though! Darling.'

This time, Jack didn't bother to exchange words. The mounting anger and frustration, accumulated over the past couple of weeks, bubbled, foamed and frothed over. Spinning on his heel, he reached down and deftly scooped up one of the knives lying on the table. Without pausing, he slammed it down hard into the back of the big guy's hand, feeling the blade impact on the wooden surface beneath. One of the others stood. Big mistake. Jack felled him with a head-butt that shattered his nose and sent a fountain of blood gushing onto the floor. The third Spurs fan pushed his chair back from the table, raising his hands, as if to say 'Whoa… enough's enough, mate!' From behind the bar a waiter emerged, nervously trying to calm the situation. Jack reached into his pocket, pulled out a crumpled wad of five ten-pound notes, threw it down on the nearest empty table and turned to pick up Gemma on the way out.

She'd gone.

He rushed to the door, yanked it open, and quickly glanced left and right along the street outside.

She was already out of sight.

Guessing that Gemma would head straight back to her car, Jack chose the right-hand option and hurried down the street. He'd only taken a few steps before his phone beeped. He fumbled for it in the inside pocket of his jacket.

It was a text from Gemma:

> 'That was appalling behaviour. I never want to see you again. Don't follow me back.'

Fuck!

# Chapter Thirty-Eight

*Southern Turkey—5 miles from the Syrian border.*

The two soldiers stand in the cage. They are virtually identical. Camouflaged combats. Shaven heads. They are on opposite sides, about three metres apart, backs to each other, hands gripping the vertical steel bars, looking outwards, staring blankly at the ground. Each wears a metal collar, adorned with inch-long spikes—a man-sized dog collar. A single chain runs down each soldier's back, from the back of the collar descending to the cage floor. Other shackles encircle their bodies, but their arms and legs are free.

Two guards stand motionless outside the cage door. Black beards, black clothes, black boots, black assault rifles, black looks, black hearts—the black colour scheme only broken by sand-coloured ammo vests.

As if on a silent command, one of the guards slings his weapon over his shoulder and turns to unlock the cage. He grabs the first prisoner, jerking him out into the open, and, in one deft, brutal movement, forces him to the ground, onto his hands and knees. The second guard follows suit. Both soldiers are now kneeling, one behind the other. Their chains stretch out behind them as if on leads. Like dogs.

The guards motion for them to move forwards. They scuttle along on all fours, crawling quickly, eager to please, awkwardly raising their bare feet above the barren terrain to stop their toes scraping against the stones and rocks. In a few minutes, scratched toes will be the least of their worries. They are totally compliant, avoiding anything that will enrage their captors.

They don't have far to crawl. A short distance from the cage the guards stop them and jerk them to their feet, placing them alongside each other a few feet apart. Once again they stand silently, neither man looking at the other. They stare straight ahead. Their chain leads lie flat on the desert floor, running out in two straight lines to converge at a central point several metres behind them. Looking closer it's possible to see some sort of off-white cotton material threaded through the chain links. It looks like a rag, but it runs the whole length of each chain.

A command is given and the prisoner on the left speaks. His tone is deadpan, the words overly formal and stilted, as if relaying a memorised script.

'Oh people of Turkey, the humiliation we are in is because of the current Turkish government, and your sons may be in our position one of these days. We have been waiting for the release from our imprisonment for a very long time. But the Turkish government has paid no attention.'

So these guys are Turks.

The second soldier speaks.

'Soldiers of the Turkish state, leave the territories of the Islamic State before you experience the humiliation we have been through.'

Their voices are loud, but curiously devoid of emotion. Maybe there is a lingering hope that publicly voicing their sympathy for Islamic State will save them. They should know better. It only makes them seem weak in their last moments. Easy to say when you're not at gunpoint wearing the chains.

A stern voice rings out in Arabic, quoting from the Koran, passing judgement: 'And if you punish them, punish them with the like of that with which you were afflicted.' Whatever last ditch hopes the prisoners might have harboured, the outcome was always going to be inevitable.

The larger of the two guards reaches into an ammo pouch and extracts a transmitter. He extends the aerial. He stares dispassionately at the prisoners, his face immobile, eyes unblinking. His thumb jabs down on the transmit button. Instantly, a flame flickers on the ground about five metres behind the two Turkish soldiers, at the point where their chains converge. It catches the white rag, which burns as if soaked in petrol. The fire moves fast, splitting in two, with separate flames travelling up each chain, heading towards the backs of the prisoners.

The two Turks stand fast. Don't they know what's happening behind them? Can't they smell the burning? Can't they feel the heat? One leans slightly forward, apparently concentrating on a spot on the ground just feet away. The other holds his head high. Proud. Resolute.

One of the flames travels slightly faster than the other. It reaches the prisoner on the left first—the man leaning forward on his chain. It seems to race the last few inches towards his dog collar. Even when it's virtually touching his neck, he appears oblivious. Perhaps the heat of the desert sun on his back masks its approach. Then it strikes, catching the back of his clothes. They go up in flames.

Screaming, the soldier's arms fly to the exposed flesh at the back of his head, vainly slapping at the flames as they scorch his neck. The blaze quickly gathers momentum. It's obvious that his combats have also been soaked in petrol. He crumples to the ground, kneeling, but upright. Burning. As if accepting his fate and hoping for a quick end.

As the flames hit the second soldier, he also drops to his knees. His survival instinct seems stronger. At first, he tries to protect the back of his head with his hands. Then his training kicks in. He throws himself flat and starts to roll violently from side to side, his movements hampered by the chain that wraps itself around him. He rolls and rolls, desperate to extinguish the fireball that is consuming him.

For a moment, it looks like he might even win the battle. The flames surrounding his upper body have almost fizzled out. But he can't stop the fire raging around his legs, which continue to blaze with a white/orange glow. All of his senses must surely be overwhelmed by the agonising pain. How is he continuing to function?

Somehow he manages to kneel. He slaps ferociously at his legs, until one hand catches fire. He smacks it on the ground, putting out the flame, then continues whacking at the front of his trousers. But the flames simply flow away like water and join again to become fiercer around his back.

He holds his hands over his face and falls forward onto his belly, his back now fully alight. As if accepting his fate, he stretches his arms out in front of him. They burn. He screams. Gut-wrenching. Visceral. Inhuman. Crying for his mother.

His fellow prisoner has accepted the inevitable. All this time, he has remained in the kneeling position, like a human candle, until he eventually keels over. The centre of his own funeral pyre. His head, slightly raised, drops back, mouth open. Even now, his body twitches. Can he still feel pain? Or have all the nerve endings been destroyed? Please let it be so.

Incredibly, the other man is still fighting. Pain searing through every fibre of his body, he has forced himself back up onto his knees in his will to live, but the fire was always going to win. Still kneeling, his head slumps forward and makes contact with the desert. His body is convulsed with spasms. Please let him be dead.

Oh my God! He lifts his head one last time. His tongue creeps out as bubbles form around his lips. His hands shrink to claws as he rocks back and forth, flames now flickering up to ten feet above his blackened body.

And then his eyes open one last time. As one, the audience in the briefing hall utters a gasp of shock, as the final dying moments unfold on film.

The black-clad guard speaks again, his voice sonorous and threatening. His words are in Arabic, but yellow subtitles flow across the bottom of the screen. He stares implacably into the camera, as if directly addressing each individual member of the audience.

'We have taken revenge for the Muslims. If your soldiers do not return, then their fate will be the same. You will become accustomed to this sight. You will witness how they burn at our hands. Then you will put your fingers in your ears so that you don't hear their screaming. If you do not leave the lands of the Islamic State, they will become graveyards for your soldiers. And you will regret having entered therein. What is coming is more devastating and bitter. So wait. We too are waiting for you!'

The last scene shows the guards pouring petrol over the charred bodies. Then the screen goes blank.

As the lights come on, a hubbub of conversation rises—exclamations of shock and disgust. Rising from his seat, Lieutenant Colonel Max Maxwell takes position centre stage and raises his hands for silence. It takes a minute or so for the babble to die down. The entire battalion of 600 soldiers is arrayed before him, seated on wooden benches in the newly erected, corrugated iron briefing hall at the centre of Camp Defender—the British Army's Forward Operating Base on the outskirts of the Turkish city of Gaziantep. It is the first day of in-processing into theatre, and the intention is clearly to dispel any sense of complacency from the very outset.

'That, ladies and gentlemen, is your enemy. Nasty bastards, aren't they? Now, over the next couple of days of theatre in-processing, we're going to tell you all the rules that will stop any of you ever being in the position in which those two Turkish soldiers found themselves. And a lot more besides. So pay attention. Because this is no longer training. This is the real thing. The threat here in southern Turkey is growing every day—as are the casualty numbers. And I am not prepared to allow *that,*' he points at the screen, 'to happen to any of *my* soldiers. Regimental Sergeant Major, carry on!'

Feeling rather less confident than he may have appeared on the surface, Black Max steps down from the stage.

# Chapter Thirty-Nine



*Three miles south of Forward Patrol Base Salamanca*

The key to winning the battle against Islamic State's elements infiltrating into southern Turkey was to dominate the ground. To do this, the KRR had distributed its platoons into a matrix of patrol bases, the intent being to cover the ground between them with vehicle and foot patrols, covert observation posts and speculative ambushes. They would get to know the locals, note their routines, encourage low-level information sharing, and identify any changes to patterns that might indicate enemy activity. That was the intent.

The reality was that the terrorists responded by trying to shut down all movement and bottle up the platoons in their bases. And the easiest way to do that was by the liberal use of improvised explosive devices—IEDs—using victim-operated pressure pads to target the foot patrols, and roadside bombs to inhibit vehicle movement.

As a result, instead of closing with the Queen's enemies and defeating them in detail, the platoons found themselves engaged repeatedly in the tedious and time-consuming task of conducting IED clearance operations. Now, for the third time in as many days, No. 2 Platoon has deployed from its home—Forward Patrol Base Salamanca—to do just that.

Sergeant Jamie d'Angelo blinked away the sweat that ran in rivulets around his eyes and pooled in the bottom of his shades. Squinting through the heat haze, he could just pick out the point man, some 300 metres ahead, swinging his Vallon metal detector in pendulum-like sweeps as he trod cautiously forward. Too fast a swing and the detector might miss an IED lurking just beneath the surface; too slow and the patrol would move at a crawl. A tricky call: the chance of losing your legs versus the frustration of the guys behind.

They were almost there. The suspect device—what looked like a roadside bomb with wires leading out of the back of it —was only about a kilometre away. It had been reported two days before by a civilian truck driver. A patrol had been despatched from Patrol Base Salamanca to check it out and, while staying at a safe distance, had been able to confirm that it certainly looked like an IED. The road was put out of bounds to all military traffic, and a tasking had been put out for 'ATO'—an Ammunition Technical Officer or, in civvy-speak, a 'bomb disposal expert'.

At twenty-seven, Sergeant d'Angelo had been an ATO in theatre for two months. It had taken him two attempts to get through his 'High Threat' course. This wasn't unusual. High Threat was notorious for its dauntingly high failure rate. An eight-week selection course, High Threat took those already qualified in basic bomb disposal and trained them to a whole new level—to a level where they should expect the terrorist would be doing everything in his power to kill the operator. And, in the final week, the operators would be tested.

The format of Test Week had remained virtually unchanged for decades. It had served the Army well in Northern Ireland, Iraq and Afghanistan, and now it was being used for those deploying to the Turkish border with Syria. In the final week of the course, each student was presented with four tasks, each mirroring the type of threat they would face for real 'in theatre'. Only those who passed a minimum of three out of four would be deemed good enough for deployment. On average, only about thirty per cent of each course managed to get through. Sometimes it was none at all. Few got through on their first attempt. Those that passed agreed that doing the job on the ground for real often seemed easier than Test Week. But that was the way it was supposed to be. And that was why so few operators went home in a body bag.

In his two months on deployment, Sergeant d'Angelo had tackled fourteen devices. None were especially complex; about a fifty-fifty split between pressure-pad IEDs, designed to take out anyone who stepped on them, and roadside bombs. Compared to the stories he'd heard in the sergeants' mess from the veterans of 'Afghan', this was a breeze. The thought brought him up sharp. It's when you start to think like that that you die.

The point man came to a halt. Behind him, and some fifty metres ahead of the ATO team, the platoon headquarters group went firm. On the flanks, riflemen took up firing positions, scanning their arcs. Jamie knelt down, taking the opportunity to shift the load on his back, his sweat-sodden combat shirt sticking to his back under his body armour.

Pulling out a pair of mini-binoculars, he scanned the terrain ahead.

He adjusted the focus and tried to zero-in on the point where the IED was supposed to be. Still too far away to pick it out. The picture blurred as a pair of combat trousers crossed his line of sight. They were coming his way. Jamie lowered the binos. It was that platoon commander from the KRR—the guy directing the operation. Dickhead.

'I say, ATO, we need to get a bit of a wiggle on. Look, we're going to move forward and set up the combined incident control point where the track comes in from the left and joins the road about 800 metres ahead.'

Jamie zoomed in on the junction with his binos. He knew he wasn't going to like what he saw. This was going to be a tricky conversation.

'Is that such a good idea, sir?' he hazarded.

Big mistake. Lieutenant Vyvyan Phillips was not an officer who brooked challenges to his authority. 'Look, ATO, you're here to clear the bombs. We're here to do everything else. That includes protecting your sorry arse. So you stick to what you're good at, and we'll do all the rest. Got it?'

'Yes, sir, but—'

'But what, Sergeant?' barked Phillips.

'Well, it's on a junction for a start, so it's an obvious potential booby trap spot. It's around 200 metres back from the device, which is too far. And I'll need to have a separate ICP forward of yours, even closer to the suspect IED. Not a combined one that's too far back.'

'Oh, so you're the world's greatest expert on infantry tactics now are you? The Royal Engineers search adviser says it'll be fine. And if it's okay with RESA, it's okay with me. Now, just get your arse in gear and get with the programme!'

'Sir.'

Lieutenant Phillips turned on his heel and stomped angrily back toward his platoon headquarters group, spread out on the ground about fifty metres away. He felt his face red and burning. It could have been the sun, now high in the sky. Could have been. But it wasn't. It was the mixture of pricked pride and seething fury at having been spoken to like that by that bloody ATO sergeant. Trouble was, there was just the nagging thought that the sergeant might be right. Phillips quickly dismissed the notion and strode on.

As the lieutenant moved out of hearing range, Corporal Dave Cross, Jamie's 'Number Two' on the team, edged over.

'You gonna let him get away with that, boss? The useless bastard'll get us all killed.'

'Yeah, I know. Don't worry. When he's calmed down, I'll explain to him that we need to get much closer to the device because of the range of our kit. That way we can avoid hanging around in his ICP on the junction. But, for now, you just make sure the boys know to stay on cleared surfaces when we move forward. Keep well away from anything that's too dusty or sandy—you don't know what's lurking underneath.'

'Roger that, boss, I'll tell 'em now.' As Corporal Cross moved off to brief the rest of the team. Jamie peered into the heat haze again. Just ahead he could see Sergeant Kev Watson, the Royal Engineers search adviser, also scanning the ground in front of them intently. Jamie walked across to join him. This might be another difficult conversation.

'All right, Kev?'

'Yeah, mate. Spotty dog. How about you?'

'Well, I wasn't so bad 'til I heard you thought that junction with the track up ahead might be a good place for an ICP.'

The RESA sergeant visibly bristled. 'Well, that's where the lieutenant wants to put it, and I told him we could clear it easy enough.'

'Mate, it's on a frigging junction.' Jamie could feel his irritation rising.

'Yeah, it's on a junction. But it's as flat as a pancake. There's nowhere to hide anything, and we can clear it really fast.' The RESA sounded overly confident—maybe he was trying to conceal his own misgivings.

A thought struck Jamie. 'You seem to know it very well....' It was half-question, half-statement.

'I do. We did a job out here three weeks ago. Used it for the ICP then.'

Jamie's temper finally snapped. 'For Christ's sake, Kev. It's on a junction and you're telling me you've had an ICP there before. And the only reason we're here is because some civvy truck driver just happened to tell us, out of the goodness of his heart, where the IED is. Is there nothing in your head screaming alarm bells at you right now? I tell you, that place is gonna be booby-trapped up to fuck!'

'Hey, calm down, mate. Look, you know what a knobhead that lieutenant is. I've already tried to warn him off it. But he's not gonna listen. He's not gonna listen to me, and I didn't see him listening to you just now either. The best we can do is just get on with it. It should be easy to clear. And if we find anything, we just hand it over to you to deal with. Simple.'

'Yeah, simple. Well, I'll tell you what. Me and my team aren't hanging around with you in there. And if anything goes bang, don't say I didn't shagging well warn you.' With that, Jamie turned and headed back to his team.

Two hours later, Jamie found himself looking at the device from his forward ICP just over one hundred metres short of it. It hadn't taken much to talk Phillips round. Having given the lieutenant ten minutes to calm down, Jamie had gone forward to talk to him again. This time he'd laid on the respect with a trowel—so thick it could almost have been a piss-take. Almost—it only just stopped short. Fortunately, Phillips was either too arrogant or too thick to notice. Probably both.

Throwing in lots of tedious technical detail about the kit to explain why his team needed to be closer to the device, Jamie soon hit the upper limit of Lieutenant Phillips' boredom threshold. It was a trick he'd used before with pompous and self-opinionated officers—bore them rigid, sound suitably deferential and, above all, let them think that *they* had made the final decision. Had he known Phillips better, Jamie might have realized that, frankly, it didn't matter what he and his team did, so long as they allowed the platoon commander to stay as far back from the bomb as possible.

With the decision made, the Royal Engineers search team —the 'REST'—had gone to work. First, they'd cleared Lieutenant Phillips' ICP on the junction. Watching from a distance, Jamie had held his breath throughout the entire process, expecting at any moment to see one of the Vallon operators disappear in a cloud of dust, smoke and debris.

But the searchers had emerged unscathed and the platoon headquarters quickly took up position. Jamie's own ICP had been cleared next—a neutral spot of ground some one hundred metres back from the suspect device. This had allowed the young sergeant to get 'eyes on' for the first time. Meanwhile, the REST had gone on to describe a wide 360-degree circle around the roadside bomb, checking for any firing cables coming in from outside the security cordon that could be used to detonate the bomb when Jamie went forward.

Jamie peered intently though his binos. It sure looked like an IED—what appeared to be a piece of kerbstone, dislodged from the side of the road, with some twin-flex just visible coming out of the back. The kerbstone was almost certainly a fake, probably a carefully modelled and painted plastic container, concealing the explosive charge within.

Also watching through binoculars, but another one hundred metres further back from where Jamie now knelt, Lieutenant Vyvyan Phillips surveyed the ground to his front. For the tenth time in as many minutes, he glanced at his watch. This whole task was beginning to drag. Was this really what all that training was for at Sandhurst—to stand about on endless security cordons while some bloody sergeant played prima donna, then waltzed off with all the medals?

Rotating slowly, he swept his binoculars over the defensive positions taken up by the platoon. Six four-man fire teams had pushed out to dominate the ground around the device and at a tactically safe distance from it. This cordon provided a hermetic seal within which ATO could work safely. For a second, Phillips considered walking the ground to ensure the positions were properly sited. But he quickly dismissed the notion. It was all very well moving slowly behind a search team as they cleared the way forward, but wandering randomly across the sandy surface was just asking for trouble. A chap could lose his legs that way! No, this was definitely a job for the platoon sergeant.

Phillips glanced across to where Sergeant Pegg was lying in a firing position, covering his arcs on the left flank.

'Sergeant Pegg!'

Pegg looked over his shoulder to see the lieutenant touching his head with the flat of his hand—the signal for 'on me'. He jumped up and began to jog across the ICP.

Jamie felt the blast before he heard it—the breath of the shockwave against the back of his neck and the slight popping of his ears in response to the change in atmospheric pressure. Then the bang—a muffled roar sweeping across the desert. He spun round in time to see an eruption of dust and debris punching into the air from the centre of the main ICP. Rocks and stones sprayed out from the point of the explosion, lacerating, piercing and bruising those in the path of the onslaught. Black smoke billowed upwards, gathering into a cloud from which more stones showered down like a deadly rainfall. It took maybe ten seconds before the shrapnel stopped falling. Then silence. The acrid smell of explosives drifted across the sand.

Grabbing a Vallon detector, and driven more by instinct than intent, Jamie was up and running—sprinting the distance back to the main ICP. It was carnage.

Like a crumpled bag of washing, blackened and exuding smoke, Sergeant Pegg, or what was left of him, lay in the centre of the ICP. Another soldier stood zombie-like near the body, fumbling ineffectually to extract his field dressing. The platoon radio operator was on his feet, stumbling around in circles, hands over his ears, shaking his head.

'Everyone stand still!' screamed Jamie. '*Stand still!* We don't know if there are any more IEDs.'

The nearest soldier turned to face him. His eyes were wide and staring blankly. Flying gravel had left a pattern of bloody pin-pricks across his face. His mouth opened and shut, but nothing came out. It was Lieutenant Phillips. Spitting mud and sand, and clearly struggling to form coherent words, he finally spoke, 'I only asked him to come over to me...'

Jamie looked past Phillips at the body. Both of Pegg's legs had been ripped off. One above the knee, one below. Not neatly sheared, no precise amputation, but hideously mangled clumps of tissue: each leg a bloody mess of shattered bone, dangling tendons, blood vessels and skin, burnt and filthy with debris. He must surely be dead.

# Chapter Forty



*Main KRR ops room—Camp Defender,*
*Gaziantep, southern Turkey*

The British element of the NATO intervention force had establised Camp Defender, its Forward Operating Base—or FOB—on the outskirts of Gaziantep, a Turkish city of 1.5 million people, just thirty miles from the Syrian border. The FOB acted as the main support hub for the deployed British brigade, providing logistics, a field hospital, repair facilities, and a home for higher headquarters elements.

Back in 2015, when ISIS held half of Syria, Gaziantep had become a major staging post for the so-called Caliphate, with weapons, supplies and international jihadist fighters flowing across into Syria. It was through Gaziantep that three British schoolgirls, Shamima Begum, Kadiza Sultana and Amira Abase, had travelled from Bethnal Green, East London, to become jihadi brides. Theirs was a tragic journey. Within ten days, fifteen-year-old Begum found herself married to a Dutch-born ISIS fighter, who was subsequently captured and imprisoned. She gave birth to three babies, all of whom died of malnutrition and disease and, after becoming a refugee, was stripped of her British citizenship and barred from returning home. Her two friends lost their lives.

Although the combined US and Turkish forces had driven ISIS back in 2019, Gaziantep remained a dangerous place. With a Novotel, Starbucks, Marks and Spencer's, two modern shopping centres full of familiar stores, and upmarket restaurants serving alcohol, it was easy to be lured into a false sense of security. But behind the scenes, Gaziantep was rotting. The war across the border had made it a destination for ISIS sleeper cells, spies, mercenaries, and refugees—four million of whom had crossed over from Syria. The city's sprawling apartments were said to host a thriving trade in people-smuggling and sex slaves—products of war.

Not surprisingly, downtown Gaziantep remained strictly out of bounds to the troops manning the FOB. And, to his disgust and mortification, one of those troops was Jack Adair. As assistant ops officer, based at battalion headquarters, there was no escaping the fact that he was now a 'Fobbit', a safe zone dweller, derided by forward combat troops. Fortunately, no one dared call him that to his face.

'Now we've got everyone on the ground, we really need to pin down precisely who's where. I'm sure that we'll have people tucked away in all sorts of nooks and crannies by this stage. If anything happens, we need to know in an instant who's likely to be affected. We get the locstats in each day. They give us the numbers. But I want to know where every man is at all times. That's your job. If there's a casualty, we don't need any cock-ups over who it was, where and when.'

The speaker was Henry Marchant, the battalion's ops officer, an intense, tautly wired young captain. Jack was already finding his obsessive fussiness beginning to grate. The fact that No. 2 Platoon was somewhere out there in the ulu, ready to take on the Taliban day and night, was hardly conducive to him applying himself whole-heartedly to his new role. Especially when it centred on managing the daily locstats.

'Oh, and another thing,' Henry continued. 'We're already getting complaints about the time it's taking to deploy the new hand-held IED detectors—these so-called Pointers. Get over to the Tech Quartermaster sometime today and make sure it's in hand. Today mind,' he added, in the slightly nannying tone guaranteed to make Jack's hackles rise.

'Yes, Henry.' Jack replied, his tone betraying his lack of enthusiasm. 'Perhaps I'd better get onto it now, before the day starts to get busy,' he said, fixing a temporary escape from the battalion headquarters, which had been established in a small, derelict factory.

Reaching for his helmet, webbing and weapon, Jack exited the ops room, heading towards the QM's.

He'd walked for about two minutes down the main walkway that led between the neat rows of sand-coloured accommodation tents when he saw her. There could be no mistake. Just ahead of him, turning left off the footpath of slatted wooden duckboards, it had to be her. The glimpse of blonde hair just peeking out from under the back of her combat helmet. The way she walked—elegant yet determined. Jack broke into a trot, not knowing whether he wanted to catch up with her or just confirm what he thought

—what he knew—he'd just seen. He reached the intersection of the boardwalks and glanced left. She was just ducking through the zip-up entrance into one of the tents. But there could be no doubt. It was Gemma Page.

Then the Tannoy buzzed into life.

'Listen in. Listen in. This is a message for all personnel. Op *Minimise* is now in force with immediate effect. I say again, Op *Minimise* is now in force with immediate effect. All private internet and telephone use is to cease until further notice. Out.'

'Bugger,' thought Jack. 'Someone's been hit. I hope it's not one of ours.' Immediately putting any thoughts of Gemma to the back of his mind, he turned on his heel and jogged back towards the ops room.

In the five minutes since he'd stepped outside, the atmosphere in the ops room had changed beyond all recognition. Other than occasional radio chatter, the room was in complete silence. Black Max, the CO, had come out of his side office and was leaning forward on the bird table, peering intently at the map, as if willing himself out onto the ground. Henry Marchant was standing off to one side, radio handset to his ear.

He broke off as Jack appeared.

'Oh, there you are, Jack. Thanks for getting back so quickly. You must have heard the Op *Minimise* message. A Company's been hit. Number Two Platoon, I'm afraid. IED strike. One man down. Listed as T1. No further detail—'

An incoming message from the field cut him off.

'Hello, Zero, this is X-ray Two Zero Alpha. I can confirm T1 casualty is zap number 232. I say again. Casualty is zap number 232. Traumatic amputation to both legs and other injuries. Require urgent casevac. ATO and REST in location. Will ensure cleared emergency LZ. Over.'

'Zero, roger out.'

Jack ran his finger down the list of zap numbers. Sergeant Pegg. Fuck!

Sergeant Pegg was dead. But only clinically. His breathing had stopped, and he was in cardiac arrest. Lance Corporal Glyn Jenkins, the platoon medic, knew he had ten minutes to bring Pegg back before the brain cells started to decay. While two Rangers began strapping tourniquets onto the sergeant's shattered legs to stem the flow of blood leaching out onto the sand, Jenkins went to work on his chest, pumping out the compressions at a rate of two per second, until he reached the magic thirty. Then two long breaths, mouth-to-mouth, tilting Pegg's head back to get his airway open. Followed by more compressions—one, two, three....

Pegg's shattered body spasmed as it fought back and struggled for breath. He started to shake as shock took hold. But at least he was now breathing unaided.

'*Yes!*' shouted Jenkins. '*Yes, yes!* Come on, Sarge. Keep breathing. You can do it. Stay with me. Come *on!*'

Further down Pegg's body, Ranger Ryan Pollard was grappling to get a tourniquet in place, his hands slipping in the blood that continued to pump from the appalling injuries. Pegg's legs were pulverised and torn beyond recognition, the gaping wound of the traumatic amputation framed by strips of dirt-encrusted skin and flesh. Pollard swore as his fingers slithered across the tourniquet strap.

Jenkins looked across at him. 'Ryan, for Christ's sake hurry up and get that strap in place before he bleeds out. I'm gonna give him a morphine jab just in case he comes round.'

And that's when the shooting started, as the insurgents lying in concealed positions started to take on the outermost fire teams.

# Chapter Forty-One

*Dear Mrs Adair,*

*It has taken me more than twenty years to pluck up the courage to write this letter, but then I never was a man of much courage. Oh people down the years have thought I was. Even the Queen thought I was once. She pinned a Military Cross on my chest so that everyone could see how brave I was. But I know the truth, and it's the truth that I want to write to you about.*

*The truth is that your late husband, Sergeant Nick Adair, died a hero. When the IRA attacked our Border Crossing Point in Northern Ireland—Hotel 55 —I was so scared I just ran. While I was running away from danger, he chose to run towards it. He killed at least three IRA men that day. If it hadn't been for him, everyone in that base would have been wiped out.*

*People have lied that he tried to hide in a steel locker in the ops room. That's just not true. It was me that was trying to cram myself into the locker. I'd just seen one of my mates chewed up by a machine gun on the front gate. I was scared witless. All I wanted to do was hide.*

*But my company commander, Major Valentine Phillips, saw me get in the locker. He started ordering me out. If I didn't come out, he said he was going to shoot me. I was less scared of him than I was of the IRA men, so I stayed put. When I didn't come out, he grabbed my arm and started dragging me.*

*It didn't take him long to pull me out. When he did, I thought he was going to make me join in the battle. I'll be honest with you, I didn't think I'd be much good because my hands were shaking so much by this time.*

*Anyway, once he'd got me out, I was shocked to see him getting inside the locker himself. He was just pulling the locker door shut when the grenade got thrown into the room. I thought that I'd had it, but your husband threw himself over me. And that's what killed him.*

*I got stunned by the explosion. I wasn't sure what was going on outside, so I just lay there for a minute or two. Shortly after that that I heard the Quick Reaction Force flying in. Then I knew we were safe.*

*Before we saw anyone else, Major Phillips came out of the locker. He was pretty well unscathed. He told me to keep my mouth shut about what had happened. He said that if anyone knew I'd been trying to hide in the locker, he'd have me court-martialled. But if we both said it was your husband who'd been trying to do that, everyone would think we were heroes. So I just went along with it.*

*I know it was the wrong thing to do. It's haunted me all these years. I started drinking heavily when I left the Army. I lost my job because of it, and almost lost my wife and my home. I've been seeing a shrink for six months. I'm much better now, but I know I'll never ever feel right about it until I tell the truth. That's what this letter is all about.*

*I know you'll probably never forgive me. I can't forgive myself. But at least you'll know it was me and Major Phillips that were the cowards that day. Not your husband. He died a very brave man. It's him that deserves the Military Cross, so I've put mine in this envelope. It's yours now. I don't deserve it.*

*If you want to ask me any questions, you can reach me at the address at the top of the letter.*

*Once again, I'm so very, very sorry.*

*Yours sincerely,*
Ivan Walters

It had taken Sandra three weeks to decide what to do with the letter. She'd thought of telling her husband but decided against it. He'd just tell her that it was all in the past and best forgotten about, that her life was with him now, and it didn't matter what 'that warmonger' had done a quarter of a century ago. He'd also probably get pretty narked that someone was still calling her 'Mrs Adair' when she'd been married to him, John Robbins, for the past twenty years. Eventually, she wrote back. Even after all this time, there were questions that she needed to know the answers to. And the only way to get those answers was to speak to Ivan Walters face-to-face.

She recognised him straight away. He wasn't as overweight as she'd expected from his description, but he was still a man of hefty build, wedged in tightly behind a table in the outside seating area at the Costa Coffee at Victoria station. He clocked her too. The mousy-looking woman in her late fifties, dressed in a mid-length black anorak with mock fur around the hood, and black jeans shrouding legs that looked too skinny. Making eye contact, each gave a half-smile of tentative recognition—still time to look away without embarrassment if this was the wrong person. Ivan heaved himself to his feet as Sandra arrived at the table.

'Mrs Adair?' In trying to hide his nervousness, he was coming across as almost too business-like. He could hear himself sounding like an insurance salesman about to start a pre-arranged meeting with a client. He attempted to compensate for his awkwardness with a forced, but unconvincing, smile. It didn't help. His fragile confidence began to evaporate.

'No, Robbins now. But call me Sandra.' She knew her tone was terse, even though she was struggling to be polite. More than twenty-five years of repressed anger threatened to explode at any moment, but first she had to get the information she needed. And that meant keeping her emotions under control.

'Oh yes, of course. Can I get you a drink, Sandra? Coffee maybe?'

'No, thank you,' Sandra replied, still polite, but inwardly thinking, 'No, what I want is your balls on a platter, you cowardly tub of lard... but all in good time.' She settled into the seat facing Ivan. 'I've read your letter. I've read it a lot, in fact. You tell the story very clearly, but there are still some questions I want to ask you. I don't think it will take very long. So do you mind if we get straight on with it?'

'Of course not. Ask away,' said Ivan, still showing a tentative smile, but inwardly bracing himself for a grilling. Sandra tried to ignore the smile; it was just stoking her anger. She couldn't see what there was to smile about. But, holding her emotions in check, she responded. 'First, I want to know, is it true? What you say in the letter, I mean. This isn't some stupid joke you're having at my expense after all these years, is it?'

Ivan dropped the smile and looked Sandra straight in the eyes. 'Sandra, hand on heart, this is absolutely no joke. What I said in the letter is what really happened. I've lived with that lie for twenty-five years, and I'm ashamed of myself. So ashamed that, before I sought professional help, I tried to kill myself. I can assure you, it really is no joke.'

'Then, if you feel so bad now, why did it take you so long to do anything about it? I mean, why now? I've suffered terribly all these years, yet you knew the truth and you said nothing. You could have let me out of this living nightmare at any time, but you chose not to. I don't get it. I need to understand why you would do that. I have one son. Because of you, I could never tell him what happened to his father. Why not? Because what son wants to know that his father died a coward. And now... now, when it's far too late, you tell me that Nick Adair was actually a hero after all. I don't get it. I say again, why would you do that?'

'I can apologise over and over again, and I know it won't make any difference—' started Ivan.

'Do you know, I think you might be right there,' interrupted Sandra.

'—but it's like I said in the letter. At the end of the day, there is no excuse. I was just too scared to do anything different.'

'You were a soldier. How could you be *that* scared, for God's sake? Especially afterwards, once no one was shooting at you. In fact, for years afterwards. How could you live with yourself? What you did was despicable.' Her voice trembled as the anger rose.

'I'm sorry. It was a chain of events that got out of hand. I'd just seen the guy on the front gate with me—his name was Jim Anderson—completely ripped apart by a heavy machine gun from less than ten feet away. Three rounds hit him in the chest. It was like he'd been gouged out. He was lying on his back with his shattered ribcage poking up in the air. In my head I can still see it now. I just panicked. I just wanted to run and hide somewhere.'

'So what about that major who dragged you out of the locker? Are you seriously telling me that he pulled you out so that he could hide in there himself?'

'That's exactly what I'm telling you. But when it was all over, and your husband was lying there dead, he said we were both as guilty as each other, and if we wanted to avoid any trouble, we should just tell the story a different way.'

'What, lie, you mean? What, paint my husband as a coward just so you two could pretend you were fucking heroes?'

'Er, yeah, I guess.' Her swearing came as a jolt. In his head, he'd expected Sandra to accept his apology with good grace, grateful to know the truth after all these years. Suddenly, it occurred to him that he hadn't been the only one suffering for all that time.

'So that's what you did. You both lied. You got a medal, while my husband was despised for ever after as the coward —the sergeant who tried to hide when his mates needed him most. And the major? Did he get a medal, too?'

'Yes, he did. I'm sorry,' he said, beginning to wonder how he could close this down and get out of there as quickly as possible. He'd written the letter. He'd apologised face-to-face. Now he wanted it over.

'And what happened to him afterwards? Where is he now?'

'Look, you're not going to like this, but I swore to tell you the truth, so that's what I'm going to do. After the battle of Hotel 55, he did well. He did very well. He never saw action again, but as far as the Army was concerned, he never needed to prove his bravery ever again either. He got the Military Cross pinned on him. Same as me. Then his career just went stratospheric. He's still in. Lieutenant general now. And a knighthood. Yet nobody knows the truth.'

'And if I wanted to ask him the same questions I've asked you, how could I get in touch with him?' asked Sandra. She'd laid the bait; now she wanted to land the big catch.

'That would be easier than you think. For some bizarre reason, ever since Hotel 55, we've exchanged Christmas cards. Every year, without fail. It's almost as if we're exchanging our guilty secret, and maybe making sure that the other one's not going to say anything to anyone. So I've actually got his home address, here on my phone. You can have it if you like.'

'I'd like that very much.'

Ivan passed his phone across with Valentine Phillips' home address showing in his contacts list. Sandra extracted a cheap ballpoint pen from her handbag, reached across to grab an unused paper napkin from an adjacent table, and quickly scribbled the address down.

She looked up and smiled. But it wasn't a smile of appreciation, or even politeness. She was smiling because she'd got what she wanted.

'That was quicker than I expected,' she said. 'I'll have that coffee now, if it's still on offer. Skinny latte, medium?'

'Coming right up.'

It only took about three minutes for Ivan to queue up, place his order and pay for the coffee. He realised that he'd forgotten to ask Sandra if she took sugar, so he paused to scoop up a handful of sachets from the condiment bar. He stepped out of the main coffee shop and headed back to the table in the outside seating area. It was empty. He did a double-take. Was he at the right table? Yes, there was no doubt about it; his coat was hanging over the back of one of the chairs. But Sandra had gone. Maybe she'd gone to the loo.

Ivan began to settle down with his coffee when he noticed a brown envelope on the table. It was addressed to him. He picked it up and opened it. At first it appeared empty, so he put his fingers inside. There was definitely something there. He grasped it. As he withdrew his hand, he found himself pulling out a white feather.

# Chapter Forty-Two

The 'golden hour' is the sixty-minute period following combat injury when there is the strongest likelihood of preventing death if a casualty can receive surgery or trauma support. By the time the Chinook helicopter carrying Sergeant Pegg was landing at Camp Defender, just over half of that time had already been used up.

It was no one's fault. The flight crews had responded as fast as they could. The casevac message announcing a 'T1' casualty—a soldier suffering life-threatening wounds—had been passed instantly to the flight ops control room. A swift call on the field telephone to the Immediate Reaction Team's standby room had sent the aircrew scurrying across for briefing, slinging on bits of kit as they ran.

Minutes later, out on the flight line a Chinook support helicopter and two Apache gunships were spinning up their rotor blades.

The flight time from Camp Defender to the casualty was less than ten minutes. Flying low and fast they screamed towards the contact, hugging the terrain.

On the ground, confusion reigned. The platoon sergeant was out of action. The platoon commander was still coming out of a zombie-like state after the IED explosion. And an increasing weight of fire was being brought down on the cordon. Two fire teams to the south of the Rangers' position were now engaged in a heavy firefight with as many as ten insurgents spread out to their front.

Initially, there had been just a few sporadic cracks with the typical 'woodpecker' signature of the AK-47 assault rifle, sending rounds whistling overhead, but these were quickly joined by repeated bursts from a couple of PKM light machine-guns and occasional RPG-7 grenades, barrelling towards the Rangers' position, their smoke trails etching dirty white lines through the air.

The troops in contact had to summon up every last ounce of willpower to fight back as the intensity of incoming rounds increased. Gobbets of sand and splintered chips of rock flew up all around them as they shouldered their weapons and let loose a torrent of return fire in a desperate effort to keep the enemies' heads down. Within seconds of the first contact, the firestorm of bullets from the Rangers' SA-80s and light machine-guns rose to crescendo, but the insurgents seemed undeterred. Bullets sliced through the air, smashing into the desert on all sides. The few pieces of foliage scattering the ground were quickly torn to pieces.

On the road, not far from where Sergeant Pegg lay, the search team was working fast to clear a safe landing zone for the incoming Chinook. It would mean moving the casualty but, with one IED already having detonated in the ICP, it was too risky to try to put a chopper down there. Trying to ignore the overshoot of rounds from the firefight taking place only a couple of hundred yards away, the searchers continued their methodical clearance of the LZ.

As the helicopters approached the contact zone, they received a precise, no frills update from the joint terminal attack controller, or 'JTAC'—an RAF Regiment sergeant attached to platoon headquarters. They were approaching a hot LZ, with troops in contact only 100 yards from enemy. Danger close! This would require some very precise shooting from the Apaches to avoid a blue-on-blue. With the clock ticking on Sergeant Pegg's life, the Apaches needed to suppress the opposition as fast as possible. Like ferocious dogs unleashed, their noses dipped as they turned towards their targets. Descending into the attack, the pilots flipped up the trigger guards on their pistol grips, preparing to rain down terror from the sky. The JTAC rapidly transmitted accurate directions to enable them to identify the enemy positions with confidence. Then they went to work.

Resembling two giant hornets, the Apaches swooped. The lead pilot caught several insurgents in his crosshair sights and the remotely controlled gun mounted in the forward chin turret swivelled to obey. He pressed the trigger, raking the desert with a twenty-round burst from the 30 mm canon. The rounds hosed-down the enemy positions, chewing up rocks and foe alike.

In disarray, several of the fighters tried to flee the killing area. Others just hugged the ground in terror. The second Apache pounced, strafing the area with another fusillade. The fire from the enemy positions stuttered and fizzled out.

As the firefight died, the Apaches took up protective positions around the Chinook—one high, one low. The big bird descended, its twin-rotors chugging and throwing up a dust storm of sand and stones. The ramp was open before it hit the deck, the loadmaster beckoning the stretcher bearers to dash forward. Less than a minute after touching the ground, the Chinook was climbing again with its precious cargo aboard.

An oppressive silence hung over battalion HQ. The frenzied activity of just a few hours before had been replaced by an air of despondency. Jack sat with his face cupped in his hands, elbows resting on the 'bird table' that held the operations map. The CO, Black Max, had retired to his side office, off the main ops room, and Henry Marchant had gone for a late meal in the cookhouse, leaving Jack alone with the ops sergeant and a couple of signallers.

Nobody spoke, each man absorbed in his own thoughts about the events of the day. Jack had been at the helicopter landing site with the CO when the Chinook had brought in Sergeant Pegg. The medics had done their best to stabilise him during the flight, but a betting man might have thought twice about backing Pegg's chances of survival. Jack had caught a quick glance of the casualty as he was transferred from the Chinook to a waiting military ambulance for the 300-yard dash to the Field Hospital. Pegg was virtually unrecognisable. His clothing, hands and face were still blackened, bloodied and torn from the explosion. The remnants of his legs were plugged, strapped and swathed with field dressings to staunch the blood flow. But the image that had scarred itself into Jack's mind, and which kept replaying itself over and over, was that of Sergeant Pegg only taking up half of the stretcher.

'You look like you could do with a brew, sir,' One of the signallers interrupted his sullen contemplation.

'Uh? Oh, yeah. That'd be good.'

As Jack shook himself out of his reverie, he heard the clump of boots striding down the corridor towards the ops room. Anticipating the return of Henry Marchant, he was surprised to look up and see an unknown face. The newcomer was a heavy-set officer, in his early-forties. Jack did the usual scan of his uniform to pick up tell-tale identification signs, starting with the head and working down. Bare-headed, so no cap badge. A single rank slide on the chest: lieutenant colonel—the crown and pip edged in dark blue, with the three letters 'RLC', for 'Royal Logistic Corps', beneath. A flash of something in red and yellow on the upper right sleeve—a flaming grenade, signifying an ATO. By the time the officer spoke, Jack already knew who he was. He could only be the commanding officer of the explosive ordnance disposal unit—the 'Bomb Hunters'.

'Evening, young man,' the words came out with a heavy Yorkshire accent. 'I'm Colonel Rick Westoby, Commander Joint Force EOD. Is your boss in?'

Before Jack could answer, Black Max appeared in the door of his office. 'Hi, Rick, good to see you. What brings you here? Fancy a brew?'

The two shook hands.

'Frankly, Max, I'm spitting bloody feathers. I'm sorry about your bloke who lost his legs today, but I've just had a debrief from the Ammo Tech sergeant who was out on the ground, and he reckons it need never have happened. What's more, that young officer who was controlling the clearance op sounds like a total bloody liability. I suppose you know he sited his ICP in precisely the same spot that had been used for a similar op only three weeks before, and on an obvious road junction. What's more, when my man tried to warn him, he got the rough edge of his tongue. I tell you what, if that lieutenant were one o' mine, he'd be on the first plane home.'

'Thanks, Rick. No, I hadn't heard that. Funnily enough, a few bits of the story seem to have been missed out as the report travelled up the chain, although the search team's taking a bit of a bashing for missing the IED in the first sweep.'

'Don't be too hard on 'em, Max,' said Rick. 'They're only young lads. They're under huge pressure, and the insurgents are getting better and better at making devices so the detectors can barely pick 'em up. That's where the new bits of kit should make all the difference, and that's actually what I've come to speak to you about. Have you got somewhere we can talk privately?'

'Of course, come into the office.' Black Max ushered Colonel Westoby through the doorway, turning at the last second to make the universal sign for a cuppa to one of the signallers.

As the commanding officer's door shut, Jack slammed his fist into the bird table. *I fucking knew it!'* he shouted. Standing, he took a kick at one of the folding chairs positioned around the bird table. It sailed across the room and smashed into the far wall.

'Whoa! Steady on, sir,' exclaimed the ops sergeant in alarm.

Before Jack could answer, Henry Marchant stepped into the room. 'Hey, hey, hey! What on earth's going on here?' he inquired, his reasonable tone inflaming Jack all the more.

'Fucking well ask *them*, Henry. Ask *them*. I need some fresh air,' Jack replied, brushing past the captain and storming out.


The wooden duckboards reverberated as Jack stomped towards the cookhouse. He needed to be alone with his thoughts and hoped there'd be a coffee urn on the go. But if there wasn't, he didn't care. He'd just dig out one of the cooks to make one, and he wasn't in the mood to take no for an answer.

He ducked in through the entrance to the marquee-sized tent, part of the so-called Temporary Deployable Accommodation, erected by the multinational contractors making their millions off the back of the conflict. It was close to 11 pm, long after the last meal for the day had ended, and the tent was dimly lit. A six-foot folding table, bearing two urns—one tea, one coffee—stood at right angles to the stainless-steel serving counter. Other than Jack, the cookhouse was empty. He wandered across, picked up a plastic cup, poured himself a brew, and took a seat at a nearby table.

He'd been there for no more than five minutes, lost in his own thoughts and silently fuming, when a female voice brought him up with a start.

'Hello, stranger. Got a seat for a small one?' It was Gemma Page.

'Uh... hey,' Jack managed to stutter out. It had been two months since the incident in the restaurant, and all that Jack had got out of Gemma since then was a wall of silence. He'd tried a couple of tentative texts, but he might as well have thrown confetti at a dartboard. And now here she was, standing just a few feet away and, against the odds... smiling.

'Yes, of course. Please.' He started to stand to pull out a chair, but she'd already beaten him to it.

Gemma sat opposite him, staring down at the table, fingers steepled, as if carefully formulating what to say next. Ten seconds passed, maybe twenty, and then she looked up. Just for a moment Jack almost forgot to breathe as those stunning azure eyes fixed on him.

'I just heard about Sergeant Pegg,' she said. 'I know you really rated him. I'm so sorry. What happened?'

Jack ran back over the events of the day but faltered when he began to talk about the part played by Vyvyan Phillips in the incident. He broke off, his eyes shining and his hands trembling as he felt the pent-up rage threatening to erupt again.

He took a breath and continued, 'And now I'm probably in the shit with Henry Marchant.'

'Henry Marchant?'

'The ops officer. About fifteen minutes ago, just after I'd heard what Phillips had done, I virtually told Henry to go fuck himself and stormed out of the ops room. It's not good, is it?'

'I'm sure he'll understand,' Gemma reassured him, trying hard to sound convincing, despite her own misgivings. 'He'll know you were close to Sergeant Pegg and will be taking it hard. Anyway, I should be renewing my acquaintance with your bosom buddy Vyvyan myself very soon.'

'Really? Why so?' asked Jack, suddenly curious.

'I'm working in the int cell at brigade HQ. My boss has given me a project. He thinks there's a real disconnect between the int we're pushing out at HQ level and the stuff being picked up at the coal face by the platoons and companies. He wants me to get around the forward locations and try to join up the dots. And your chum Vyvyan has been assigned to escort me around A Company's area.'

'Jesus! Good luck with that!' Jack retorted. 'I guess the best that can happen is that he'll just get hopelessly lost.'

'And the worst?'

'That you run into a contact.'

'Thanks. Good to know.'

'So when is this grand tour set to happen?' asked Jack.

'In three days' time. Thursday.'

# Chapter Forty-Three

Jack re-entered the ops room expecting the worst but buoyed up after his encounter with Gemma. Maybe there was a way back there after all. He looked up to see Henry Marchant sitting at the head of the bird table, facing the door.

'Hi, Jack, feeling better?' Henry asked with a quizzical half-smile.

'Yes. Sorry, Henry, I lost it a bit when I heard how Sergeant Pegg got hurt.'

'Look, it's fine. The guys filled me in on the gaps after you left. Pegg was your platoon sergeant. You're bound to feel cut up, especially if you were close. And in the best platoons, the two at the top always are. I should know. The same happened to me in Afghan. That was an IED too. Only my man was killed.'

'Yeah, but I bet it wasn't your cock-up that got him killed.'

'I'd like to think not, but we still don't have the facts about Sergeant Pegg's incident yet. It's all rumour and hearsay. So let's not prejudge it until we know precisely what happened. Anyway, the boss asked to see you as soon as you got back, so you'd better pop your head round the door.'

Fearing the worst, Jack walked across to the CO's office, pulled on his beret, and gave a light tap on the door.

'Come!' called out Black Max from inside.

Jack pushed the door open, stepped in and saluted. 'You wanted to see me, sir.'

'Yes, Jack, come on in and take a seat. I've got a job for you that I think you might like.'

'Taking over Two Platoon from Vyvyan Phillips, sir?' Jack ventured hopefully.

The colonel said nothing, but his eyes spoke for him. They said, 'Nice try, but don't push me, young man.' Jack read the signs and shut up.

'Moving on then, *Mister* Adair,' continued the CO, emphasising Jack's lowly place in the scheme of things, 'you will be aware that I was visited by Commander Joint Force EOD this evening. Well, he didn't just come over to talk to me about today's incident involving Two Platoon. What I am about to discuss with you is top secret. It refers to an operation known as *Boxwood* and is not to be discussed with anyone not read-in to the operation. Roger so far?'

'Roger, sir.'

'You already know that the battalion has just taken delivery of a quantity of Pointers—the latest hand-held IED detectors. These are a step-change in capability. They have a highly sophisticated metal detector, combined with ground penetrating radar. Both elements are programmable. Pointer gives us the very best chance of picking up even the most cleverly-designed, no-metal IEDs. The sort that's catching out our search teams right now.'

The CO continued, 'The trouble is, we know the insurgents are dicking us constantly. The minute they see that we've got a new piece of detection kit, they'll be doing their utmost to find out its exact capabilities. Well, some bright spark in Defence Intelligence has come up with the idea of planting an identical mock-up of a genuine Pointer, except configured so that it only has the capability of our current kit. The plan is that a patrol will go out and "accidentally lose" the mock-up Pointer en route, somewhere near a trail known to be used by the insurgents. Once they've got their hands on it, tried it out and analysed it, it should convince them that we're no better off than we were before. This should at least give us the edge for a few more months until they smell a rat. Jack, I want you to lead that patrol.'

As the CO finished speaking, Jack was already leaning forward in his chair, eager to know more.

'When do you want me to take the patrol out, sir?' was his first question.

'In three days' time. Thursday.'

# Chapter Forty-Four



*Thursday: ten miles south of Gaziantep*

Vyvyan Phillips was having trouble staying awake. The heat from the afternoon sun was proving too much, and the added weight of his helmet and body armour didn't help. The double vehicle convoy, comprising two 'Foxhound' light-protected vehicles, had left the main highway and was now lurching over country roads as it headed towards Two Platoon's location, just north of the town of Geçerli. He felt his eyelids flicker as he fought the urge to doze. A couple of times, his head nodded. On each occasion, his neck jerked back in a guilty reflex response, painfully snapping him back to consciousness. He tried to concentrate on the map spread out across his thighs but looking down only made matters worse.

'You all right, sir?' Vyvyan's driver, Ranger Galloway, had been watching his boss's antics for some time. He could have said nothing, but he thought there might be some light comic

325

relief to be gained out of the situation. And the afternoon sure demanded some of that.

'Oh yes. Quite all right, thanks. And you are asking because?' Vyvyan replied tetchily.

'Just thought you might be nodding there for a minute, sir.'

A couple of large potholes in the road caused the Foxhound to lurch and sway. Vyvyan's map slipped off his legs onto the floor of the vehicle.

'No, not at all. Just trying to get comfortable. Best you concentrate on the road, eh Galloway?'

'Sir.'

Vyvyan retrieved his map. Up ahead he noticed a small village—no more than twenty houses sprawling back from the main thoroughfare. He traced the line of the road on the map with his finger till he found the hamlet, from which he could pinpoint his exact position. Having satisfied himself that they were still on the right track, he sat back in his seat and let his mind wander.

His first thought went to that striking blonde girl in the vehicle behind. What was her name? Oh yes, Gemma. Gemma Page, that was it. He'd met her before—about eighteen months ago, when he was going for selection for Sandhurst. He'd sat next to her at the formal dinner night. Who could forget those eyes? Then later, he'd also seen her at Sandhurst. They were there at the same time, but never really had any contact.

The truth was that, when it came down to it, he was pretty inept around women. Sure, he had a girlfriend, if you could call her that. Harriet. Robust girl. Sturdy thighs. A braying laugh that made her easy to track down at any party.

Great fun in the bedroom, as long as you were used to taking a semi-domesticated mare over some challenging jumps at the gallop, accompanied by a fair amount of hollering during the ride. City power suits during the week; tweeds, tough enough to sandpaper wood, for weekends in the country. It was a bit of an on/off relationship. He quite liked being 'on' her, but she kept going 'off' him. Part of the problem was the Army. She didn't like the fact that he kept disappearing off on exercise every few weeks when she wanted him to be at her beck and call for nights out, and nights in. And she kept harping on about the money. How her chums in the City were making three times Vyvyan's salary as an Army officer. As much as a brigadier at least. But it would take Vyvyan twenty-odd years to get to that rank. With the way the Army was constantly being cut back, chances were he might not even get beyond major in that time.

His thoughts returned to Gemma. Now there was a woman you'd be proud to have on your arm. Bright, dazzlingly attractive, cheerful, obviously very fit... but he'd heard a rumour that she was seeing that bloody peasant Adair. What on earth would a woman like that see in a pleb like him? He'd hoped to have her travelling in his vehicle, but RSM Anderson, her host for the visit around the battalion's locations, had shepherded her to the second Foxhound. Never mind, he might get his chance to impress her later.

They were entering the village now. Crumbling houses of sand coloured stone with red tiled roofs. Lean-to shacks of rusting, corrugated iron. The odd tethered goat. Chickens scratching around in kitchen gardens. A car careering out of the side road at fifty miles an hour straight into their path...

'Jesus Christ! Where did that come from?' Vyvyan threw his hands over his face as Ranger Galloway floored the accelerator and smashed straight into the car amidships. The vehicle crumpled in the middle as it took the direct hit, and slewed round until it was at a diagonal to the main road, half on, half off. Somewhere behind them, coming from the right-hand side of the road, there was a loud explosion, like an anti-tank weapon going off

Then the hail of gunfire. It came from windows, doorways and from over walls. Bullets smashing into the side of the lightly-armoured vehicle, sounding like a drummer beating a discordant rhythm on a galvanised steel dustbin. Out of a gate on the right dashed a man wearing a black combat jacket, camouflaged trousers and a shemagh wrapped around his head. He knelt, shouldering an RPG-7 grenade launcher. Vyvyan just had time to process the image when a burst of GPMG fire from the hatch-mounted weapon behind him punched a mess of bloody holes into the insurgent's torso. The fighter pulled the trigger on the launcher as he was hit, the rocket sailing high and wide. Both top cover sentries were engaging the enemy now from their hatches in the roof of the vehicle, smashing windows, drilling doors and flaying brickwork as they traversed their weapons.

From the vehicle behind came a hurried message over the personal role radio. 'We've been hit. IED strike. Vehicle immobile. Over.'

'What do you wanna do, sir?' screamed Galloway above the racket. 'Are we turning round?'

'No! For God's sake put your foot down and drive. We need to get out of the killing area.'

'Roger that, sir,' and the Foxhound powered forward towards the end of the village.

Two hundred yards beyond the last house, Galloway slammed on the brakes, bringing the Foxhound to a shuddering halt. The two top cover sentries swivelled their gimpies to engage, saturating the road with fire around the stranded rear vehicle behind them, which was leaching smoke from the shattered front right wing where a wheel should have been. A couple of insurgents approached the disabled Foxhound, firing from the hip. The lines of 7.62mm rounds from the Rangers' machine-guns converged, hosing them down, spraying blood and shredding flesh. An RPG grenade flew the length of the road, just passing over Vyvyan's vehicle. The firer remained exposed just too long and the twin gimpies hit him simultaneously. His head exploded and the headless corpse sprawled across the road.

'We need to go back, sir,' screamed Galloway. 'They're stranded back there.'

'No! We're going firm here,' Vyvyan yelled back.

From the hot, cramped rear of the second Foxhound, Gemma had taken a few seconds to compute what was actually happening. Her first irrational thought on hearing the burst of automatic fire was, 'Oh, there must be a shooting range nearby.' Then the roadside bomb, detonating just yards away, shocked her back to reality. An explosively formed projectile—a metal plate deformed instantaneously into a slug capable of penetrating armour—slammed into the front right wheel, sending shards of steel and rubber flying. The vehicle shuddered and stopped. A wave of choking smoke surged into the rear compartment.

Sitting across from her, RSM Anderson was already shouting, 'Is everyone okay? Anyone hit? You guys up front, are you okay?'

A yell came back from the driver, 'Yeah, we're all right, RSM, but the front wheel's been taken out. We ain't going nowhere!'

Then the small arms fire hit. In an instant, all was noise and chaos. Coming from every direction, rounds were smashing along both flanks of the vehicle, denting and gouging the armour. Both top cover sentries ducked down inside as a salvo of PKM fire lashed the Foxhound's roof, missing them by millimetres.

For a moment paralysis gripped all of the occupants of the stricken vehicle. Through the front screen, they could see the lead Foxhound accelerating away towards the edge of the village, before slamming to a stop and returning fire with its twin GPMGs. They watched horror-struck as the terrorist carrying the RPG launcher dashed into the centre of the road and, within seconds, was transformed into a headless corpse.

'Right guys, listen up!' RSM Anderson was the first to break the trance. 'This steel box is about to become a coffin if we stay here any longer. We're gonna have to make a run for it. The other Foxhound's laying down some covering fire, so let's do this thing. You two in the front go first. Then the top cover guys. Right... *go!*'

Looking back down the road, the crew of Vyvyan's vehicle saw the side doors of the damaged Foxhound fly open. Two soldiers rolled out. They crouched for a second behind the open doors, then started their dash to escape the killing zone. Seconds later, both top cover sentries hauled themselves through the top hatches of the stranded vehicle, jumped to the ground, and followed suit. Bullets sliced through the air all around the Rangers, struggling to sprint in their heavy body armour, helmets and chest rigs. More slugs spattered into the road surface at their feet, zinging, whining and ricocheting. The lead runner went down, spinning as he fell. Rounds continued to target the crumpled figure, throwing up dust spurts and causing the body to jerk sporadically. The others raced past, jinking, weaving, lungs bursting, hearts hammering. Another man fell, hit in both legs, his kneecaps exploding as the steel-tipped fragments punched their exit wounds. More shots finished him off, smashing his spine before he hit the ground.

The final two continued their desperate race to the safety of the static Foxhound on the edge of the village, from which a yammering barrage of covering fire was zipping down the street. A third man fell, hit in the neck, a spray of blood spurting from his throat. The last man saw his comrade drop. A burst of PKM bullets flicked up dust at his heels. The firer adjusted his aim, the next burst stitching a line across the road just ahead. Hemmed in, the runner hesitated, then stopped.

The top cover sentries from Vyvyan's Foxhound leaned into their weapons, burning through the ammunition in a frenzy, trying to subdue the enemy long enough for the last man to finish his home run. *'Come on!'* they screamed in unison. But fear had overwhelmed his senses. He turned slowly, raising his hands, and another burst from the PKM took him straight between the eyes.

Vyvyan saw the carnage reflected in his wing mirror and made his call. 'Let's get out of here,' he bawled. Just at that moment, two more soldiers appeared from behind the damaged Foxhound and started to run for their lives....

The sun momentarily dazzled the RSM has he exited the vehicle through the rear doors. With the enemy's fire still concentrating on the runners being cut down in the centre of the village, he and Gemma had a tiny window of opportunity. Out of the corner of his eye, Anderson glimpsed a side road leading off the main drag. It didn't offer much hope, but it might be their only way out of the killing area. He was still weighing up the odds when he felt Gemma grab him roughly by the upper arm, tugging him towards what looked like the only possible route to safety. And it might have been, if a car hadn't roared into position at the first intersection, blocking their path. From both front and rear windows, AK-47 assault rifles pointed directly at the two British soldiers. There was no way out.

'Galloway, put your flaming foot down, and let's get out of here,' roared Vyvyan. At that moment, one of Vyvyan's top cover sentries cut in over the personal role radio. 'Sir, we can't go. I think I just saw the RSM and Ma'am Page dash off down a side street.' Vyvyan hesitated as he wrestled with his conscience. But not for long. 'Whether you saw them or not, they're probably already dead. Just like the others. And if we don't get out of here, we will be too,' he snapped tersely. 'Now, Galloway, floor it.'

# Chapter Forty-Five



*Forward Patrol Base Salamanca*

As the Wildcat helicopter approached Patrol Base Salamanca, it tilted into a banking turn. Adjusting his position to peer out past the door gunner, Jack got a panoramic view of the ground below. Two Platoon's location was a motley collection of tents surrounded by a Hesco-Bastion defensive wall—large, wire-mesh gabions filled with earth and stones. Two elevated wooden sangars, heavily protected with sandbags, occupied diagonally opposite corners within the small outpost. Between them, they dominated most of the open ground that lay between the base and the odd isolated dwellings that dotted the landscape, the closest being about 200 metres away.

The HLS was located outside the perimeter, a short walk —or run—from the front gate. The helicopter dropped height rapidly, and Jack could see the barrel of a GPMG within the nearest sangar swivelling into position, ready to give covering fire should the landing site suddenly turn 'hot'. For the last fifty feet of the descent, the rotor wash set off a choking dust cloud of grit and sand, blotting out any visual references. The pilot flared the machine, allowing the wheels to touch the ground. The co-pilot turned and gave Jack the thumbs-up. It was time to get off the bus.

Jack tugged his seatbelt open and clambered towards the open door, scooping up his Bergen, weapon and the new piece of search equipment, the Pointer, in its protective case. Tossing the Bergen out first, he jumped the few feet to the ground and shielded his eyes as he got his bearings. Squinting through the sandstorm that was blasting his face, Jack could just make out Sergeant O'Rourke, the replacement for Sergeant Pegg, standing on the edge of the HLS. Shouldering his Bergen, Jack jogged across to meet him, the rotor whine subsiding in the background as the pilot cut the engine,

'Hi, Sergeant O'Rourke,' started Jack, but, even as he spoke, he could see that the sergeant wasn't in the mood for pleasantries. Although there was a flicker of a smile of welcome, his jaw remained set firm, his blue eyes flicking across Jack's face as if seeking an urgent answer to an unstated question.

'Hi, sir. Thank Christ you're here. We've got a problem.'

'Okay,' Jack responded, his mind already starting to gear up. 'Best you tell me all about it.'

Sergeant O'Rourke guided Jack hurriedly towards the platoon ops room, explaining the situation as they went. Information was sparse and confused, but it sounded bad. One Foxhound out of a double-mobile had been destroyed. There had been casualties, some of them T4—deceased—but it wasn't clear how many or who they were. The contact had happened in a village about two miles from the patrol base, and they'd received word that the platoon commander, Mr Phillips, was on his way back in now in the undamaged vehicle. Whether he had any casualties on board was still uncertain. Worst case was that everyone in the damaged vehicle had been taken out.

'Jesus,' Jack whistled through his teeth. His first instinct was to get a quick reaction force together and try to launch an immediate hot pursuit and counter-attack. But common sense prevailed. Better to get some int from the ground before dashing blindly into what could turn out to be another ambush. 'How far out is Mr Phillips now? Do we know?'

'The last message was just before I met you on the HLS, sir, about five minutes ago. If they were only a couple of miles away when the contact happened, they should be here any minute.'

Just at that moment, the sound of the metal gates clanking open was followed by the heavy-engined noise of an armoured vehicle entering the compound. Jack hurried outside, followed by Sergeant O'Rourke.

Even at a casual glance, it was clear that the vehicle had been in the thick of some action. Both wing mirrors were shot away, the one on the left dangling upside down from its broken strut. Bullets had pocked, gouged and spattered both flanks. The top cover sentries were up, but there was no trace of banter as they came through the gates. Their faces were bathed in sweat and grime, eyes fixed in the 'thousand-yard stare' so often seen in those emerging from close combat.

As the vehicle came to a halt, the front passenger door swung open and Lieutenant Vyvyan Phillips stepped down.

His face was white, and the corner of his right eye was twitching. He looked blankly at Jack, as if without any trace of recognition.

'Fuck,' he said, his voice little more than a whisper.

Jack took a step closer. 'What happened, Vyvyan?' he asked.

'Fuck,' came the barely audible response, almost as if talking to himself, rather than in answer to Jack's question.

Jack put his face closer. He needed to get as much information out of Vyvyan as he could, and fast. Although his first instinct might have been to slap the platoon commander back to reality, it was obvious that this was going to require special handling.

Putting his hands on Vyvyan's shoulders he looked him square in the eyes and spoke sternly and deliberately. 'Vyvyan, I know it's bad, but we need to know what happened. And we need to know now.'

It was as if Jack had flicked a switch. Bringing his arms up fast, Vyvyan dislodged Jack's hands from his shoulders and pushed him away. 'Get your fucking hands off me, Adair,' he screamed, wild-eyed, his spittle flecking Jack's face. 'We were caught like rats in a trap. They're all dead. All of them, and there's nothing anyone can do about it.'

'Er, that might not be true, sir.' Ranger Galloway had finished parking the Foxhound and now stood nervously to one side of the officers. 'We know that the two top covers and the front cab guys got taken out. After their vehicle took an IED strike, they tried to make a run for it down the village main street. They didn't stand a chance. But we don't know what happened to the RSM and Ma'am Page, the Int Corps officer. They were in the back. One of our top covers saw them trying to get away down a side street, but reckons they got intercepted by a car full of insurgents.'

'*What?*' screamed Jack, as the shocking realisation dawned on him that Gemma had been travelling with the convoy. 'Vyvyan, what the fuck happened to those other two?'

'They're dead, I tell you. Nobody could have got out of there alive.'

Jack stared at him dumbfounded. 'You don't know, do you? You don't fucking well know what happened to them. Why the fuck didn't you do something?'

Vyvyan started to back away, shaking his head. 'There was nothing we could do. It would've been bloody suicide to go back in there.'

Jack turned his head sideways and looked at Galloway. He raised a questioning eyebrow but didn't need to say anything.

Galloway focused on the ground, shaking his head. 'Mr Phillips told us to get out of there, sir. I asked him to go back, but he wouldn't.'

Jack gave Vyvyan a look of disgust and turned away. 'Right, Sergeant O'Rourke, I want one fire team, the helicopter crew, you, Galloway, and the two top covers from the ambush in the ops room in the next two minutes. Go!'

Vyvyan's voice cut in from a few feet behind him. 'You are not taking any of my men back out there, Adair. Understand? That would be utter suicide. This is my platoon, and I say what goes.'

'Yeah, well, we've already seen what happens when you say what goes!'

Vyvyan started to fumble with the catch of his pistol holster. 'I'm telling you, you will not undermine my command. Even if I have to stop you by force.'

The Glock 17 was still only halfway out of the holster by the time Jack had taken three swift strides across the compound and landed a single punch on Vyvyan's jaw that sent him spinning to the ground, out cold. He turned back to face Sergeant O'Rourke and Ranger Galloway, both standing dumbstruck. 'Come on, guys, time's flying, and we've just lost a minute that we can't afford to waste. Let's get moving!'

# Chapter Forty-Six

Gemma Page had been lapsing in and out of consciousness ever since she'd received the blow on the back of the head. She hadn't seen it coming. One minute she'd been running for her life with RSM Anderson down a side street in the village, then the red car had screeched into position ahead of them, blocking off their line of retreat. She was aware of the guys in the car firing their AKs, peppering the intervening ground with 7.62 mm rounds and bringing her and the RSM up sharp. She was vaguely aware of a flurry of movement behind. Then complete blackness.

The first time she came round, she was in the car, squashed on the back seat with the RSM, between two gunmen. The guy next to her leered, revealing front teeth rotting from the local habit of drinking tea through a sugar cube. Leaning towards her, he cupped a hand over her right breast, his eyes fixed on hers. She raised her arm to push him away, but the effort was too much, and she passed out again.

She didn't know how long she'd been in the car. It could have been minutes or hours. She knew it was travelling fast, swaying and lurching over the bumpy country roads, drenching her with nausea, the urge to vomit coming in waves. When the vehicle finally came to a halt, she'd been aware of hands grabbing at her, pulling, tugging, molesting. They tried to force her to walk, but she collapsed again. Then she felt herself being dragged, the toes of her boots drawing lines in the sandy surface behind her.

Cold water thrown from a bucket hit her full in the face, bringing her round once more. Her head was in agony, as if it had been cleaved in half by an axe. She was half-standing, but bent over a table. She tried to move, but couldn't. Her arms were stretched out in front of her, wrists tightly bound, the ropes taut and tied to the table legs on the far side. Her legs were spread wide, secured firmly by the ankles to the nearest pair of table legs. She was naked.

So tightly was Gemma fastened, that her head had been forced down sideways onto the tabletop, and she struggled to bring it up to look around. The sun was full in the sky. At first she thought it was creating a heat haze. Then she realised her vision was still badly blurred after the blow on the head. She blinked a couple of times, the sharp pain caused by each slight movement reminding her of where she'd been hit. Gradually her vision cleared.

She forced herself to take in her surroundings. Although her field of view was limited, she could tell that this was another village, even smaller than the last. Out of the corner of her right eye she could just glimpse a couple of light-grey, stone dwellings with flat roofs and small square windows. Beyond the table, the sunbaked, stony ground, intermittently broken up by coarse, hardy scrub, stretched away to a track, crossing from left to right in the distance.

Gemma became aware that someone was standing several paces in front of the table. She could see combat boots and the lower half of a pair of combat trousers in the British Army's multi-terrain pattern camouflage. With effort, she craned her neck, lifting her chin off the table, to get a better look. It was Regimental Sergeant Major Anderson.

The RSM was standing stock still. It was clear that he'd taken quite a beating. One eye was so swollen that it was virtually closed. A trail of blood, already half dried, coursed down the left side of his face from a gash above his eyebrow. Both ears were swollen, bruised and cut. He was wearing a black leather collar, adorned with inch-long spikes—a man-sized dog collar. A single chain ran down his back, starting from the back of the collar, descending to the ground and stretching out behind him. Threaded through the chain was some sort of off-white cotton material, running its full length. Other shackles encircled his body, but his arms and legs were free. Even from twenty feet away, she could smell the petrol. And that's when she started to shake, uncontrollably, as fear-induced urine trickled down her legs.

Sitting close up behind the aircrew, Jack Adair had a good view out of the large right-hand window of the Wildcat as it swept over the sandy-coloured terrain at close to 180 miles per hour. Across the aisle from him sat Ranger Galloway, his head constantly darting around, trying to spot any signs that might be helpful in tracking down the insurgents. Seated further down the aircraft was a four-man fire-team taken from Two Platoon. Sergeant O'Rourke had

had no difficulty in tracking down volunteers for the task. Within minutes of word getting out, every section commander had formed up in front of him, each with the most persuasive reasons as to why he, more than anyone else, should be leading the team for this mission. The choice had been easy. Corporal Wood was one of the battalion's best junior NCOs, and a dead cert for the next promotion board to sergeant. At only 24 years old, he was also set on having a crack at SAS selection once this tour was behind him.

Jack had added Galloway to the party as well. He knew the ground—maybe not well, but well enough—and his knowledge might just tip the balance when it came to getting the drop on the terrorists.

As soon as the Wildcat was airborne, it had headed low and fast away from the patrol base, hugging the contours of the ground closely. It was only a couple of miles to the village where the contact had happened, and the follow-up needed to take maximum advantage of both speed and surprise. The helicopter skimmed over the small settlement at such low altitude that it was in danger of lifting off some of the roof tiles.

The damaged Foxhound still lay where it had been hit. A small crowd that had gathered round it dispersed in panic as the aircraft zoomed overhead. Even at speed, it was still possible to see the large pools of blood, now drying in the sun, which marked the positions where the Rangers had fallen. The bodies were no longer in sight. No doubt the terrorists had already taken out their hatred on the corpses, bits of which would almost certainly reappear as part of the psychological warfare intended to demoralise the peacekeeping troops.

There was no sign of the ambush party. The crowd seemed to have been made up of old men, women and children, none of whom were carrying weapons—nor of the red car that had been spotted by one of Vyvyan's top cover sentries. Once past the village, the Wildcat power-climbed to a thousand feet in order to get a wide-ranging view of the terrain below.

It had been some thirty minutes since the contact. Given the time it would have taken the terrorists to regroup after the ambush, dispose of the bodies, and move out over the country roads, it was unlikely that they could have travelled more than ten miles. With a strong military presence to the north, the most likely escape route would have been within a wide arc heading south. There was also the strong possibility that they would have gone to ground quickly, anticipating a rapid hot pursuit by the Brits.

Jack was still processing all of this, staring intently at his map, when the pilot, a female staff sergeant, came up over his internal comms headset. 'Sir, we've had some int passed down from brigade HQ. Apparently, sig int has picked up a mass of mobile phone chatter about five clicks south of where we are now. There's mention of two captives. Looks like that might be our best bet.'

'Okay. Sounds good. Let's get going.'

Gemma heard the crunch of boots on gravel coming from her left side. Into view came a tall man, dressed in black combat jacket and trousers, and wearing a chest rig of light-khaki ammo pouches. A black and tan shemagh covered most of his head, with an opening just for the face. Except his face was hidden behind a terrifying silver skull mask.

He came to a halt and turned to face Gemma, his arms folded across his chest. Silent. Gemma felt an involuntary whimper escape her throat.

The man spoke. 'Hello, love. Do you mind not making that awful whining, it's really disconcerting.' His strong Liverpudlian accent shocked Gemma into silence, although her body continued to shake violently.

'You two have presented me with quite a problem,' he continued. 'I'm really not sure what to do with you. You can see what we're gonna do with the big man standing behind me. I know you've seen the video during your in-theatre arrival briefings. How do I know that? Because our people are everywhere, including inside your main base.' He turned to look at the RSM. 'There's not much fat on him, so it might be over quickly.' He faced Gemma again. 'And I've promised my crew that they can have some fun at your expense, which is why we've conveniently removed all your clothes. But it's what order we do it in that's testing my imagination. I mean, would it be more fun for you to see him burn before your very eyes, knowing what's coming next? Or should my men fuck you half to death before we set him alight? It's quite a teaser. But we need to get some formalities out of the way first.'

The insurgent reached down to the side pocket of his combat trousers and drew out a folded piece of paper. He walked across to the RSM and held the paper up before his eyes. 'Now my friend, I want you to read this for the benefit of the camera. I'll be honest with you, it's not gonna save you if you do a good job, but at least I might be tempted to put a bullet into your head to put you out of your misery when the agony becomes too much.'

Up to that point, Anderson had been staring straight ahead, his eyes fixed on some point on the distant horizon. Now, for the first time, he looked his captor in the face. 'Go fuck yourself,' he said.

There was a sudden rush from Gemma's right. Another insurgent, dressed identically to the first, but wearing a black balaclava painted with a white skull, ran at Anderson. He was carrying a three-foot length of scaffolding pipe. Without even pausing, he drew it back and let loose with full force into Anderson's back, precisely over his left kidney. Anderson dropped as if poleaxed. Two more insurgents closed in on him and began hauling him to his feet, accompanying their efforts with a series of kicks, slaps and punches. Gemma tried to look away, but a pair of unseen hands seized her hair from behind, forcing her head up off the table.

'Silver Skull' spoke again. 'Well, at least that's helped make my mind up. Why should he get the pleasure of a live-action porn show before he burns? We might as well just torch him now.' He looked past Gemma at someone standing behind her and issued a command. 'Amir, go and get little Hassan. Tell him I want him to light the fire.'

The Wildcat was skimming the ground at around fifty feet as it closed on the village. Any higher and there was the strong chance that the element of surprise would be lost. They were still half a mile away when the pilot picked up the two parked vehicles on. One of them was a red car.

'Sir, red car dead ahead. I think we've got it,' she alerted Jack over the headset.

Jack turned and gave the thumbs up to the team. 'Get ready to go, boys,' he shouted above the rotor noise. 'Let's hit these bastards hard!'

As the helicopter shot over the first row of buildings, there was almost too much to take in. Below was what looked like a village square, hemmed in by ramshackle stone buildings on three sides. In the centre of the square, a naked woman was bent over a table, to which she was tied. A few paces in front of her stood a soldier in British Army uniform, a chain running from the back of his neck down to the ground and trailing away behind him to some sort of metal box. Next to the soldier was an insurgent, dressed in a black combats, with an AK-47 slung across his shoulder. Behind the naked woman was a half-circle of twenty or so men, all carrying weapons, and wearing a variety of military-style clothing and shemaghs.

The pilot pulled hard over on the stick, banking the aircraft up and to the left, trying to give the door gunner the best possible shot at the group of insurgents, which was already starting to break up in disarray. The gunner pulled the trigger on the gimpy. It began chewing up the belt of 7.62 mm rounds and spitting them out in a tight stream at 722 rounds per minute.

A few of the insurgents had unshouldered their AKs by now, but the return fire was weak, wild and sporadic. A couple of lucky rounds slapped into the Kevlar armour close to the door gunner's head, but the combination of adrenalin rush and sheer noise meant that he didn't even notice.

With the square open on one side, there was plenty of room to put the Wildcat down. Turning the nose into the wind, and trying to ignore the incoming rounds, the pilot concentrated on balancing the machine into a steady hover before touching down. The door gunner continued to hose down the enemy, saturating the square with rounds. Only at the last minute did he cease fire, when the dense brown cloud of dust and grit thrown up by the downwash threatened to obscure his vision to such an extent that there was a danger of hitting the RSM and Gemma.

In the back of the Wildcat, the assault force was ready to go, crouching tight up behind Jack, who was poised in right-hand door, on the opposite side from the door gunner. The wheels hadn't even touched when Jack propelled himself out of the door. Not even checking that the others were behind him, Jack led the dash round the front of the aircraft and into the killing area.

As he passed the nose of the Wildcat and entered the square, Jack was immediately struck by how much the scene had changed in just a matter of seconds. Several corpses were strewn about, limbs at unnatural angles, blood oozing into the earth. The remaining insurgents had run for the cover of the nearest buildings and were trying to return fire, but without much accuracy or effect through all the dust. The continued spraying of the door gunner's gimpy rounds across the front of the buildings was proving successful in winning the firefight.

With the insurgents pushed back to the buildings, the square now only contained the assault force, Gemma Page, RSM Anderson, and, standing just a few feet from the RSM, a young lad, no more than fifteen, dressed all in white, and... holding a transmitter.

As the assault force moved forward, jinking, weaving and firing, using pairs fire and manoeuvre, the boy raised the transmitter above his head, and yelled, 'Allahu Akbar!' Jack raised his weapon. The cross-hairs of his sight locked on the lad's forehead. And just in that instant, he realised the boy's youth. He hesitated. Momentarily. In that same moment, the boy's head exploded, pulped by a single round coming from Jack's right. Jack glanced across to see Galloway grinning and giving him the thumbs-up. 'You can't hesitate, sir,' he bellowed above the noise. 'It was a little fucker like that stabbed my brother.'

Jack looked back... and was shocked to see the first flicker of flame starting to snake its way up the chain. The kid had managed to press the transmitter as he went down! Screaming *'Cover me!'* to Galloway, Jack hurled himself towards the chain. He got to the point where it joined the collar wrapped around the RSM's neck moments ahead of the flame and started tearing at the petrol-soaked cloth in a frenzy, ripping it away.

With enemy fire kicking up constant dust spurts at his feet, Jack drew his bayonet and sliced through the leather collar around the RSM's neck. So intent was he on the task that he didn't see who threw the grenade from one of the nearby buildings. Out of the corner of his eye, he saw it tumble to the ground a few feet away. Shoving Anderson into the dirt, Jack flung himself over the RSM's prostrate body. The concussion wave from the explosion swept over him. Less than a millisecond after the grenade detonated, a steel fragment, no bigger than a child's milk tooth entered Jack's face just below his right eye, travelling up behind the socket. He hadn't even heard the explosion...

# Chapter Forty-Seven

*Somme House, Wiltshire*
*Residence of Lt Gen Sir Valentine Phillips KCB, CBE, MC*

The sound of mail hitting the downstairs hall carpet brought Valentine Phillips round with a start. He went to sit up in bed, but the pain in his head—the product of too many G&Ts, wine and port the night before—prompted him to abandon the attempt and slump back down. He looked across at the bump in the bedclothes taken up by his wife, Sara. Twenty years ago, he might have reached across to stroke her in the hope that he might arouse some interest. But not now. After last night's guest night dinner at the Army Reserve Battalion of the King's Royal Rangers, where he and his wife had been guests of honour, there was no longer any life in the old dog.

He tried lying still for a moment, eyes open, looking at the ceiling. Then the house phone rang—also in the downstairs hall. Any hope he'd had of an undisturbed Friday morning was fast disappearing.

Maybe a coffee would help. Once again, he made to sit up, this time with rather more determination. The house phone was still ringing. Couldn't they tell there was no one in? Well, at least, no one who felt like talking on the phone at this ungodly hour. What time was it, anyway? As he thumped downstairs, he caught sight of the hall clock. It read 11am, meaning he'd only had four hours' sleep.

He got to the phone and put his hand out. As if on cue, it stopped. He couldn't be bothered to look at 'missed calls'. If they wanted him, they could bloody well call again. After all, he was supposed to be on leave today. Scooping up the mail from the mat, he made his way into the kitchen and flicked the kettle on. As it began to froth and bubble, he heard his mobile ringing somewhere in the house. 'Jesus Christ,' he thought. 'If they go on like this, they'll wake Sara.' And that really wouldn't be a good idea. That would set the tone for the whole day, and that tone would be decidedly tetchy.

The general plonked some instant coffee and a single spoon of sugar into a mug and turned his attention to the mail—a couple of items of junk mail and a lavender-coloured envelope with his name and address neatly handwritten on the front. He tossed the junk mail into the bin, fished inside the cutlery drawer for a knife, slit the lavender envelope open and drew out the letter, a single sheet, folded in half. As he did so, he failed to notice a white object fall out and flutter to the kitchen floor. In the background, his mobile had stopped ringing, but now the bloody hall phone was going off again.

He flipped the letter open. It was handwritten, in the same neat hand—probably a woman's, he thought—that had addressed the envelope. Curious now, he began to read.

# Better To Die



Valentine Phillips started to shake as a torrent of sweat drenched his body. Holding the letter out in one hand, he put the other to his head, suddenly feeling faint. Then the bloody hall phone, which had stopped momentarily, started ringing for the third time. 'For Christ's sake!' he hissed under his breath, striding back out into the hall and snatching up the phone.

'Yes, what do you want?' he snapped into the handset.

'Oh, good morning, is that General Valentine Phillips?' asked a voice at the other end, the accent bearing more than a touch of Estuary English.

'This is General *Sir* Valentine Phillips, yes. Who the devil is this?'

'I'm sorry for bothering you, General. I heard you'd had quite a late night, so I wanted to give you a bit of a lie-in, but I've left it as long as I could. My name's Mitchell. I'm defence correspondent for the *Sun* newspaper. It's just that we've been talking to a lady by the name of Sandra Robbins. I don't know if you recognise the name, sir? But it turns out she used to be married to one of the guys who got killed when the Border Crossing Point, Hotel 55, was almost taken out by the IRA back in 1996. He was a sergeant, named Nick Adair. Anyway, she's made some rather shocking claims about your behaviour that day, and says she's got a witness to prove it. A guy called Ivan Walters, who claims he was there with you. We're running a splash on it in the *Sun* tomorrow, General, but we wanted to get your side of the story first. Especially as that's where you won your Military Cross. Would you mind if I came over to see you in the next hour? I'd like to bring a photographer along with me too, if that's all right.'

'No, it isn't bloody all right,' snapped the general. 'I know ex-Colour Sergeant Walters. I also know that since leaving the Army he's become a pathetic, unemployed alcoholic. No doubt he needs the money. So, if you want to put him up against me with his wretched lies, do your damndest. I will, of course, sue for defamation. And I'm sure Sergeant Adair's wife has been nursing her bitterness for well over twenty years as well. Does she need your money, too? Now run along and find your nasty gossip elsewhere, you despicable little man.'

Before Phillips could hang up, the reporter spoke again. 'Look, General, all we want is your side of the story. I'm sure you'll be able to tell us *exactly* what happened at Hotel 55 and set the record straight. I should perhaps just make you aware of one thing. It's not just a case of it being Ivan Walters' word against yours. We've also managed to dig out a copy of the Coroner's report, which, as you know, contains some photographs taken at the time by the Military Police. I'll be honest with you; it raises certain questions that are only answered if Walters' version of events is true.'

'Oh yes?' And what is that supposed to mean, precisely?'

'Well, if you really want to know, we can't work out how Sergeant Nick Adair picked up seventeen wounds from a fragmentation grenade when he was supposedly hiding in a steel locker. The photographs show there were only a handful of penetration holes in the door, and that's not enough to be consistent with his wounds.'

Valentine Phillips gave a loud sigh that was intended to express bored irritation, even though he could feel his hand trembling as it held the receiver. 'Then I suggest you read the Coroner's report in rather more detail. The question arose then, and I explained it to the Coroner's entire satisfaction,' he said.

'I have read it, General. In detail.'

'Then you'll know very well that the strong likelihood is that Adair lost his grip on the door and that it swung open just as the grenade detonated, fully exposing him to the blast,' responded the general tersely.

'Yes. I did see that,' said Mitchell. 'But, unfortunately, that's where I have a bit of a problem with the original story. You see, if the door had swung open, it's the *inside* of the door that would have been hit by some of the stray fragments. But the photos don't show that. If you look closely, you'll see that the way the metal has splayed around the holes indicates that the fragments actually punched their way through the door from the *outside*. Which means the door must still have been closed. And that's not just my opinion. We've had an explosives expert take a detailed look at the evidence, and he's prepared to swear that that's exactly what happened. So, here's the dilemma: if Nick Adair was behind the closed door when he suffered seventeen puncture wounds and lacerations, then the door should have a similar number of holes. But it doesn't. There again, if the door had swung open, leaving him exposed, any fragments would have hit the inside of it, not the outside. But the shape of the holes shows they didn't. None of this makes any sense, unless Ivan Walters' story is true. And just to add to the mystery, most of the blood in the room seems to be on the floor, right in the centre...'

Phillips interrupted him. 'Yes, of course it's mostly in the centre of the room. That's where we dragged Sergeant Adair's body when we tried to administer first aid. Do you really think we'd have left him in the locker when there was a chance that he might still be alive?'

'Yes, General, I get that. But here's another curious thing,' said Mitchell. 'Why are there no blood spatter marks visible inside the locker, and why are there no apparent drag marks on the floor?

'That proves nothing. Other than the wound that killed him, most of the others were pretty superficial.'

'Okay, I hear you. Although I'm still confused as to why the only man in the room to have taken cover in the locker picked up more wounds than you and Walters, when both of you were supposedly exposed in the open. But, that aside, there's one last point that's really starting to bother me. When I told you a couple of minutes ago that we were going to publish a story based on the new revelations of Ivan Walters, your instant reaction was to threaten legal action—that you would sue for defamation. Yet, apart from me telling you about the contradictory evidence concerning Sergeant Adair's wounds, I haven't told you what Walters said about *your* actions that day. Nothing. But you still issued the threat. It strikes me as odd. Unless you're concerned that he might have said something that you wouldn't want anyone else to hear. See what I mean?'

Valentine Phillips had never been a man of courage, but he did know that the best form of defence was attack—or so the old Army maxim went. It was worth a try. 'Listen, Mitchell, I don't think you quite understand who or what you're taking on here. Let me give you some advice. If you publish, I shall set my lawyers on you. Once I do, then you, your editor and your newspaper had better be sure that you all have very deep pockets stuffed with cash, because you will need them. Do I make myself clear?'

There was a long pause. The seconds ticked by. Eventually, Mitchell answered. 'I take it that's a definite "no" to the interview then, General?'

'You can just fuck off!' Phillips slammed the phone down, suddenly feeling as if the world was closing in on him. As if everything he knew, every touchstone in his life, was about to be upended. The shaking was now consuming his whole body, and he could feel sweat trickling down the small of his back. How could this be happening now, more than twenty-five years later? That bloody idiot Walters! The general's mind switched to being stripped of his knighthood... to being asked to hand back his Military Cross... to having to resign his commission in disgrace...

Sara, Lady Valentine Phillips, swore that she'd been jerked out of her sleep by a sudden noise. A loud bang. Somewhere outside. Had it been part of her dream? She couldn't even remember what the dream was now—it was already fading, as dreams so often do. But there was certainly quite a cacophony of bird noises going on in the little copse at the foot of their extensive garden.

She rolled over and reached out for her husband. 'Valentine, be a dear and go and find out what all that bloody racket's about, will you? I'm sure I heard a loud bang outside. Oh, and a mug of coffee would be good, too.' She was surprised when her hand met no resistance against the bedclothes. She pulled back the covers. Her husband's side of the bed was empty.

She lay still for a few more minutes. There were no more strange noises. In fact there were no noises at all. If Valentine was downstairs, he was moving around very quietly. Not like him, especially after the skin-full he'd had last night. He was normally like the proverbial bull who carried his own china shop around with him.

Puzzled now, and slightly irritated, she slid out of bed and threw on her dressing gown that was hanging on the back of the door. As she padded downstairs, she could hear her husband's mobile phone ringing incessantly in the study. She stepped in to turn it off, but it stopped before she could get to it. Then she noticed that the steel cabinet that housed his shotgun was lying open and empty.

Moving slightly faster now, she went into the kitchen. Lying open on the work surface was a sheet of lavender-coloured writing paper. She picked it up and started to read. As she did, she could feel her hands begin to shake. 'Oh dear God.' She whispered. Just then, the hall phone began to ring. She took a pace across the kitchen but stopped as something white lying on the kitchen floor caught her eye. She bent to pick it up. It was a white feather.

At the regimental headquarters of the King's Royal Rangers, in Shrewsbury, Colonel Dick Millen was surprised to find a lavender-coloured envelope delivered into his in-tray along with the rest of the morning mail. Most letters addressed to the regimental colonel would have already been opened by one of the clerks in the orderly room, before they reached his office, but they must have put this one aside as possibly being 'personal'. Whatever it was, it wouldn't be routine. Letters like this often came from anxious, angry or bereaved mums and dads, so he'd better give it priority treatment.

He slit the envelope open. The letter inside was folded in half. As he extracted it, he was puzzled to see a white feather fall out onto his desktop. His interest now seriously piqued, he sat back in his chair and started to read. Some twenty-five years after the event, the letter spelt out in considerable detail a very different version of the events that had happened at Hotel 55 on 5th November 1996. It was the last three sentences that took him by surprise:

*After my husband Nick was killed, I received an envelope, containing a single white feather. No doubt it came from one or more of the officers serving with the regiment at that time. I'm returning it to you now, because I think you're all cowards.*

It was signed by Nick Adair's widow, Sandra Robbins. As he reached the end of the letter, a wry smile started to form on his face. 'Hmmm,' he thought to himself, 'I just knew something about that incident at Hotel 55 smelt. Of fish.'

At that moment, one of the clerks tapped the door and stuck his head round. 'Sorry to bother you, sir, but something must've happened concerning Lieutenant General Phillips. We've had the police and three newspapers on the phone, all in the last five minutes, and they all want to talk to you.'

# Chapter Forty-Eight

*Battalion Headquarters, 1ˢᵗ Battalion KRR,*
*Lucknow Barracks, Tidworth, Wiltshire*

Lieutenant Colonel Max Macklin gave a sigh of relief as he entered his office. He unstrapped his Sam Browne belt, hanging it up carefully, so as to do as little damage to the polish as possible, tossed his hat onto the coat rack in the corner of the room, unbuttoned his khaki, Service Dress jacket, and slumped in his chair. He hated funerals—especially, as was so often the case in the Army, when the deceased was a young man who only days before had been so full of humour and sheer zest for life. This wasn't how he'd anticipated spending one of the days of his mid-tour R&R back in UK; but, whether he hated it or not, it was an important part of the job. As commanding officer he was the battalion's figurehead, and when a young man died in action, and his body was brought back home, the family and friends looked to the figurehead to provide some reassurance and comfort.

There was a knock at the door. Macklin gave an inward sigh. 'Jesus, not already, can't I just have five minutes' peace?' Re-buttoning his jacket, he called out, 'Come.'

Captain Sam Grimes, officer commanding the rear party, while the battalion was still deployed on the Turkish border, entered and braced up. 'Lieutenant Adair to see you, sir.'

'Oh yes, Adair. Crikey, I'd almost forgotten he was down to see me after the funeral. Please show him in.'

A few seconds later, Jack Adair, also decked out in Service Dress, wearing a black mourning band around his upper left sleeve and with a large bandage swathed across half of his face, appeared in the doorway. He marched in, came to a halt and saluted.

Colonel Macklin didn't look up, still apparently busying himself with paperwork on his desk.

One minute passed. Then two. Jack stood immobile, apart from a muscle visibly moving in the side of his head, giving away the fact that he was nervously clenching and unclenching his jaw. Eventually, Colonel Macklin threw his pen down on the table. His eyes met Jack's for the first time. The gaze was steely, and he wasn't smiling.

'How's the war wound?' he asked.

'Fine, sir. They say it'll leave a small scar, but it looks like I got off lightly.'

'We haven't had a chance to talk since you were casevac'd out of theatre,' said the CO.

'No, sir.'

'So we haven't had the opportunity to discuss in detail the circumstances under which you came to be wounded. How you diverted a valuable air asset, without brigade headquarters' authority, to launch an unplanned, half-arsed attack on an enemy position, with an assault force that was outnumbered at least three to one, and which had every prospect of turning into a suicide mission.'

The CO stood and moved around the desk until he was standing alongside Jack, his face only a few inches from the young lieutenant's left ear. Jack braced himself for the coming verbal barrage, his mind already racing ahead to the inevitable court martial and dishonourable discharge from Her Majesty's Service.

It never came.

'Bloody well done,' said the CO, in a voice barely above a whisper. Jack was aware of something moving at waist height. It was a hand. The CO was actually going to shake his hand. Jesus!

'You'd better sit down, Jack.'

The CO continued. 'There are some people who think your actions three weeks back were foolhardy. You stood to lose a valuable helicopter in an unauthorised combat mission. What's more, you could have lost me six more soldiers, the battalion having already sustained four deaths earlier in the day. But you didn't. What you did was to use your initiative, fighting spirit and sheer guts to effect one of the bravest rescues that I've ever come across. And, as such, I'll stand by you no matter what irritated huffing and puffing we hear from those in their comfortable office chairs higher up the chain. In fact, I'm recommending you for a Mention in Despatches. In my view, you deserve more, but, given the circumstances, I think I'd come up against considerable opposition if I tried for anything higher.'

'Sir,' replied Jack, thinking to himself that as long as he wasn't getting the sack, anything else would be a bonus.

Black Max took a deep breath and went on. 'There's also the matter of Vyvyan Phillips. I know that you are now aware of the awful events surrounding his father. Terrible business. Well, while you were being casevac'd, I had to recall Vyvyan to battalion headquarters to inform him of his father's suicide. Before I'd had a chance to break the dreadful news, he launched into a tirade against you, shouting that you'd punched him in front of witnesses, and demanding that you be court-martialled. Luckily for you, that issue rather went onto the backburner once I'd notified him of his father's death. Also, luckily for you, no witnesses have been found to confirm that the incident ever happened. In fact, quite the contrary, there are strong denials that such an event ever took place. But I'm not sure that situation has entirely gone away. I am giving you some serious advice now. You *have* to find a way to work with Vyvyan Phillips, no matter how much you might loathe him personally. The regiment is a family, and you are both part of it.'

'Sir,' answered Jack. 'But the man's a coward.'

Colonel Macklin raised his hands to silence him. 'You're a good officer, Jack. Just as your father was a good sergeant. You would have made him proud. And now you can be proud of him. I'm not going to keep you. I think you might find there's someone else very keen to speak to you who's waiting outside. Now, clear off and get on with the business of getting yourself back to full fitness.

'Sir!' Jack cracked out an immaculate salute, turned smartly to his right and marched from the office.

As Jack stepped through into the outer office, a tall, imposing figure crashed to attention and delivered a salute even more impressive than the one he had given to the CO just a few seconds before. It was Regimental Sergeant Major Anderson. He was stretching out a hand.

'Sir, I'm not sure that my initial welcome to you was in the finest traditions of the regiment. For that, you have my sincere apologies. The regiment needs young officers like you, sir, and I'm mighty pleased to have you aboard. And I know that also goes for every single officer, senior NCO and soldier in the unit. Welcome to the regiment, sir.' The RSM smashed out another salute.

Grinning, Jack walked out of the building into the sunshine. Outside, Gemma Page was waiting behind the wheel of her red VW Golf soft-top. He leaned in and kissed her.

'How did that go?' she asked. "Anything like as bad as you expected?'

'No,' Jack replied. 'Not bad. Really not bad at all.'

# THE END

About the Author

Col. Steve Smith MBE is a former British Army officer who specialized in logistics, intelligence, and high-threat, counter-terrorist, bomb disposal. He served on operations in Northern Ireland, Kosovo and Iraq, and deployed on short-term missions to a number of other hotspots. On leaving the Army as a colonel, Steve became involved in international aid and development. As CEO/board member of several charities, he has overseen programs to reduce armed violence, support refugees, and safeguard children in conflict zones, in Africa and the Middle East.

He was appointed MBE in 1993 for his work in Northern Ireland.

# If You Enjoyed This Book
# Visit

PENMORE PRESS
www.penmorepress.com

All Penmore Press books are available directly through our website.

More books at Penmore Press

# When the Jungle Is Silent

## by

## James Boschert

Set in Borneo during a little known war known as "the Confrontation," this story tells of the British soldiers who fought in one of the densest jungles in the world.

Jason, a young soldier of the Light Infantry who is good with guns, is stationed in Penang, an idyllic island off the coast of Malaysia. He is living aimlessly in paradise until he meets Megan, a bright and intelligent young American from the Peace Corps. Megan challenges his complacent existence and a romance develops, but then the regiment is sent off to Borneo.

After a dismal shipping upriver, the regiment arrives in Kuching, the capital of Sarawak. Jason is moved up to Padawan, close to local populations of Ibans and Dyak headhunters, and right in the path of the Indonesian offensive. Fighting erupts along the border of Sarawak and a small fort is turned into a muddy hell from which Jason is an unlikely survivor.

An SAS Sergeant and his trackers have been drawn to the vicinity by the battle, but who will find Jason first: rescuers or hostiles? Jason is forced to wake up to the cruel harshness of real soldiering while he endeavors stay one step ahead of the Indonesians who are combing the Jungle. And the jungle itself, although neutral, is deadly enough.

PENMORE PRESS
www.penmorepress.com

# SHADOWS

## BY

## CHÉRI VAUSÉ

There is insanity in keeping secrets. So Aiden "Mac" McManus, a young Navy Underwater Demolition Team leader, believes when he is sent by World War II's Supreme Commander, General Eisenhower, to protect two French Résistance spies carrying microfilm of Hitler's *Secret Notebook*. It contains all the formulas and processes for advanced weaponry created by Nazi scientists. But the mission goes horribly wrong.

Twenty-two years later, in a time of social unrest and homegrown terrorism, history repeats itself. Mac is tasked to take on the same evil he faced during the war, leaving his wife Esther and their child behind. But when Esther herself is targeted, their enemies just might find out the hard way that the female of the species can be more deadly than the male.

PENMORE PRESS
www.penmorepress.com

# The Measure of Ella
by
## Toni Bird Jones

The islands frightened her with their uncivilized rawness. They looked like a place where anything could happen, a godforsaken outcrop at the end of the world.

Sea-faring chef Ella Morgan is an honest woman — until her life falls apart. When her dream of owning a restaurant is shattered by the death of her father and loss of her inheritance, she is suddenly alone in the world. Desperate for money, she signs on as crew for a Caribbean drug run, only to find herself fighting for her life in an underworld ruled by violent men.

Set in the Caribbean, The Measure of Ella is a dramatic story of love, murder, high-seas action, and the consequences of pursuing a dream at all costs. Like Patrick O'Brien's novels, including Master and Commander, The Measure of Ella captures the breathtaking and perilous world of blue-water sailing. Like Girl on the Train, it unwinds with gripping suspense from a woman's point of view. With its brave, strong, complex female protagonist at the helm of a high seas adventure, the novel is entirely unique.

PENMORE PRESS
www.penmorepress.com